CW01213320

Chopper Chaplain

OTHER BOOKS BY LAWRENCE WILSON

OLD BUFORD

CRACK OF THE WHIP

Chopper Chaplain

THE HOME OF THE BRAVE

Lawrence Wilson

Copyright © 2019 by Lawrence Wilson.

Library of Congress Control Number: 2019915768
ISBN: Hardcover   978-1-7960-6409-4
                Softcover   978-1-7960-6408-7
                eBook   978-1-7960-6407-0

All rights reserved. No part of this book may be reproduced or transmitted in any form or by any means, electronic or mechanical, including photocopying, recording, or by any information storage and retrieval system, without permission in writing from the copyright owner.

This is a work of fiction. Names, characters, places and incidents either are the product of the author's imagination or are used fictitiously, and any resemblance to any actual persons, living or dead, events, or locales is entirely coincidental.

Any people depicted in stock imagery provided by Getty Images are models, and such images are being used for illustrative purposes only. Certain stock imagery © Getty Images.

Print information available on the last page.

Rev. date: 11/27/2019

To order additional copies of this book, contact:
Xlibris
1-888-795-4274
www.Xlibris.com
Orders@Xlibris.com
803728

CONTENTS

Dedication ix
Author's note..xi
Preface xiii

1	Introduce Loren Whitson – our hero...1
2	Swearing into the Army. Goes to Ft. Meade, Md. 5
3	Arrives at Camp Breckinridge, Ky. 11
4	Loren trains in hand-to-hand combat 17
5	Basic training winds down 27
6	They board the ship for Korea 32
7	Loren prays for the dying. Becomes Chaplain's Ass't................36
8	Assigned to tent outpost. Loren is nicknamed 'Wit'.................41
9	Wit gets a promotion to Corporal. Gets his first kill. 50
10	Kills NK officer and driver. Recovers maps. 58
11	Tent outpost is moved. Falls in love with Nurse Lt. 66
12	Wit saves captured Marines. 72
13	Wit prays for injured Marine. Makes love to Nurse. 79
14	Wit goes on killing rampage after Nurse is killed. 90
15	Wit meets new Nurse. Begins to re-adjust to go home. 94
16	Wit prays for an Atheist. Preaches a sermon........................... 99
17	Wit runs into old friend and ships out to the States. 105
18	Wit feels left out at home. Meets Maggie................................112
19	Wit suffering with stomach. Catches Maggie being porked......118
20	Wit re-enlists. Flies to Ft. Rucker for Chopper training. 127
21	Wit gets in trouble saving a pilot. Goes before a hearing.........134

22	Wit and Rose go to town to rescue drunk guys.	140
23	They start going to more towns to help guy get home.	147
24	Wit graduates and ships out to Germany	152
25	Wit gets his own helicopter. Meets Congresswoman	160
26	Congresswoman describes her story.	166
27	Wit goes to conference in Stuttgart, Germany	176
28	Wit gets a new chopper.	187
29	Wit goes to Munich with Helga, Chaplain's wife	195
30	Wit transports General Shafer. Takes a vacation.	203
31	Colonel Joe dresses down a Lt. Invites Wit to dinner.	217
32	Russ makes a forced landing. Wit saves the day.	224
33	Priscilla recovers from a beating. Wit helps Nurse Mimi	234
34	Wit reveals his plan.	241
35	Vietnam	252
36	Wit trains with the Green Beret	258
37	Wit gets a new nickname 'Jungle Rat'. Roams the jungle	269
38	Building Navy Hospital. Witnesses birth of baby.	276
39	Wit returns to the jungle.	283
40	Jungle Rat increases his killing. VC slaughter a village	290
41	Wit re-acquaints with Dr. Betty. Makes a big mistake	299
42	Wit meets Dr. McElroy and treats her for exhaustion	307
43	Wit helps Dr. Susan recover. Gets an update from Mike	314
44	Wit rescues captive Marines from NV. Collects on IOU	321
45	They test the M-16 rifle. Wit goes to Saigon	330
46	Wit rescues black Nurse from VC. Whiny is killed	340
47	Wit is required to leave 'Nam. Goes to Okinawa.	345
48	Wit addresses Special Forces Unit.	355
49	Wit leaves Okinawa. Terrorizes Commies back in 'Nam	364
50	Wit returns to town to recuperate. Prays for injured friend	373
51	Wit learns about TET and the big offensive	380
52	Lady Marine Lieutenant is injured and rescued by Wit	390
53	Paris Peace Accords. Send Mickey to America	398

54	Final evacuation. Goes to Philippines	407
55	Wit meets Dr. Becky. Flies to Japan	415
56	Wit settles into a routine in Japan. Mimi shows up	425
57	Wit goes to Kuwait during Gulf War.	435
58	Wit rescues sailors. Buys a house on beach in Florida	446
59	Mimi gets cancer and dies and the dog dies.	458
60	Wit explains how he got medals	469
61	Wit's wife receives medals	477
62	Wit writes his will and turns 65.	487
63	Lawyer courts Callie, Wit's housekeeper	496
64	Wit dies and leaves the beach house to Callie.	506

DEDICATION

I dedicate this book to all who have served, and died, bravely and courageously, and those who are serving now and will serve in the future. Also, a special dedication to all those that have served, or are serving, in the Chaplain's Service and the Medical Corp.

GOD BLESS AMERICA

LW

AUTHOR'S NOTE

This is a story of a young man drafted into the Army thinking it was as glamorous as the war movies he watched growing up. He soon found out it was serious business and not what Hollywood tainted it to be to make a good story. He was trained as a combat soldier, and specially trained individually as a killer and, also became a master lover. His career spanned over 40-years in the Chaplain's Service serving in three wars, Korea, Vietnam, and ended in the Gulf War; also including serving in various locations throughout the world administering to the sick in body and mind, all in the name of the Lord. His ingrained kindness and compassion enabled him to be loved and appreciated by all who knew him. Any similarity in names and places are purely coincidental. Few of the incidences are true, but extensive research was done to collect the facts and get the right timelines to actual events to generate an honest story. For the most part, it is fictional and meant to entertain. Hope you enjoy reading it as much as I did in writing it!

Whip Wilson

PREFACE

On June 25th, 1950, the Russian trained communist North Korean Army crossed the 38th parallel (the dividing line) into South Korea with the intention of overtaking and controlling the entire country. Since the North Korean Army was supplied with large Russian tanks and guns, the South Korean Army, or ROK (Republic of Korea), were totally out-manned and out-gunned; the North Koreans met very little resistance. United States President, Harry S. Truman, was determined to stop this advance and decided to send troops and asked NATO to also send troops to assist the South Koreans. The closest troops were the US Army garrisoned in Japan. For the last 5 years after World War 2, these troops were living the good life and became lax in their training and conditioning. They also didn't have the latest in armament. President Truman thought it would be a quick operation and would push the North Koreans north in a matter of a couple months. He referred to it as a 'POLICE ACTION'. It was discovered in short order that they were in a fight for their lives. More troops and Marines were sent, and armament to match that of NK went into production and shipped as quickly as possible. With the magnitude of the death and mayhem, the 'Korean Conflict' suddenly took on all the earmarks of a war. Then the worst of the worst happened. The Chinese, in support of North Korea, sent hordes of troops across the Yalu River. They came in tens of thousands with hardly any equipment but outnumbered the allied forces by 4 to 1 and simply overran the allies. The allies killed them as fast as their guns would fire but, for the most part, the guns burnt up and/or they ran out of ammunition. They soon lost all the ground they had gained.

At the same time, there was an active Selective Service in the United States, or more preferably known as a Military Draft. Every male was required by law to report to his Induction Center, or draft-board, on his 18th birthday, and register for the draft. He would be obligated to complete 8 years of military service. Most likely, if drafted, he would be inducted into the US Army; minimum requirements would be to complete 2 years of active duty with 6 years inactive unless he was desirous to spend his time in one of the reserve units, or re-enlist. Then too, if he was physically impaired in some way, he would be classified 4-F, denied being drafted, and not need to worry about it. If he was lucky enough to go to school or for some reason be deferred, then he might buy some time. Some tried that, but they eventually caught up with the unlucky ones and measured them for a nice shiny uniform. Fact was, it was mostly the poor boys that got drafted. He also had the option of enlisting into one of the other branches of service which could range from 3 years on up of active duty. This is a *fictional* story of such a young man who elected to take his chances with the 2-year draft. If he liked it, he could extend his active duty status. If 2 years was all he wanted of it, he could get out and remain inactive but be on call the final 6 years. Our hero in fact, subsequently, contributed the bulk of his life to the military; a career soldier.

The Police Action later took on the connotation of 'The Forgotten War'. There never was a peace treaty signed. On 27 July 1953 there was a cease-fire agreement signed by all parties involved. With World War 2 getting all the recognition, everyone seemed to forget Korea, thus *The Forgotten War*. Don't know who penned that name but it was fitting. In WW 2 the country was totally into the war effort. The country during the Korean War was in 'business as usual' mode. The economy was booming, and the media didn't splatter the war scenes on the television. It was also thought of as, 'we lost the war'. The military had been scaled down after the big one, therefore handicapping those fighting in Korea.

The label was totally unjustified. Good Gravy! How could we forget 187,530 US casualties, including 33,629 American deaths, and there are still an incomplete number still missing. South Korean military casualties: 1,312,836 including 415,004 dead. Other UN casualties total 16,532 including 3094 dead. The estimate of the communist casualties was 2 million. Finally, about 40 years later, a Korean War Monument was built to honor those that made the great sacrifice. The USA is still the greatest country in the world, and deservingly so, but on this particular occasion, for how it shunned our fellow Americans, we ought to hang our head in shame.

After WW 2, the French remained in Vietnam (a component of Indo-China) and Russian trained Ho Chi Minh was determined to drive them out. He subsequently obtained the advantage, when after the Korean War, the Chinese transported large amounts of more sophisticated and larger-caliber weapons to Minh. With this additional power, it became obvious that the French should pull out or get annihilated, so they pulled out. The dollar signs of the US backers of South Vietnam caused the country to be divided in 1954. North

Vietnamese terrorists started assassinating South Vietnamese officials. US President John F. Kennedy saw this as a threat, so he increased the number of American Military Advisors inside South Vietnam in 1961. The North Vietnamese Army (NVA) enticed the young people of the south, the farmers and villagers, and recruited them as Viet Cong (VC) soldiers to be workers during the day and killers at night. Thus, they added to the melee a low-level guerrilla war in addition to the regular army fought war. This generated the huge problem of not knowing who the enemy was. In 1964 conventional forces from the north emerged ready to take on any enemy infantry unit on the battlefield. US Marines arrived on March 8th, 1965 and the war was on. It was not a conventional war. One Company Commander of a rifle company said he thought he was fighting three different wars: one against terrorism, one against guerrillas, and one against conventional forces.

The Hanoi government never thought the Americans would continue fighting the war because of the anti-war sentiment at home: the anti-war demonstrators, the bad reporting by the press for a number of reasons, and the politicians in Washington trying to dictate the war plan on a day to day basis. One former POW that was in the Hanoi Hilton (prison) related that the people on the street in Hanoi would go undercover at exactly 3:00 pm in the afternoon because they knew the American bombers were due, and then after the bombing, they came back out on the street and continued their business.

The sad fact was the politicians from Washington tried to make the war plan and have it executed their way instead of leaving it to the military leadership in the field. Several Vietnam vets said the politicians lost the war because they couldn't react and execute without the approval of Washington. The saddest fact of the Vietnam War was 58,286 Americans were killed, including 130 Americans that died in captivity. 16,000 South Vietnamese POW died in captivity. 1,100,000 NV combatants died. 2029 Americans are still unaccounted for. So, after all the sacrifice, in 1975, after 10 years of fighting and destroying hundreds of thousands of lives of the military and their families, they saddle up and go home. It is impossible to ascertain what was gained, if anything. It is easy to determine what was lost, the credibility of America on the world stage.

The Persian Gulf War was another example of all wars, trying to attain more power, control, territory, and wealth. Saddam Hussein, Iraq Dictator, amassed 100,000 troops on the border of tiny Republic of Kuwait, and on 2 August 1990 he ordered the invasion to get control of the rich oil fields. 35 countries of the U.N. Security Council, plus the mighty U.S. agreed on 29 November 1990 that was not to be, so began Operation Desert Shield, a buildup of troops and defenses using all the latest in the arsenal of weaponry, and Operation Desert Storm, the combat phase which started on 17 January 1991, pushing the Iraqis back across the border. It only took about 100 days to annihilate the Iraqi military, but they stopped at the border leaving Hussein in power, which many agreed was a mistake. That allowed him 10-12 years to gear up for the next Gulf War, which didn't fare so well for the good guys. Note: (First Gulf War) 147 battle deaths; 145 non-battle deaths; 1 missing in action; 15 women killed; 467 wounded in action.

As has been accurately stated many times, 'WAR IS HELL'.

LW

CHAPTER 1

Loren Whitson was a typical American boy from Southwest Ohio. He grew up during the World War 2 period in a city just north of Cincinnati, Oh, in a large family of 3 Brothers and 3 Sisters. His Father had died early leaving the family to struggle to financially survive. Although he was a good student, he knew college was not in his future because of financial considerations, so he didn't take academic courses in high school but took vocational courses instead. Therefore, he would go into a factory to work after graduation. He wasn't large in stature, only reaching a height of 5 foot 8 inches and 150 pounds. He liked sports and cars and girls like all boys of that age. He paid $30 for his first old clunker of a car which he named 'Jezebel', because naming your first car was common in those days. He and his friends, trying to act grown up and impress the girls, would ride through town in old Jezebel 'cruising chicks' as they called it. They were like a dog chasing a car; they wouldn't know what to do with it if they caught it. They learned quickly after the girls, who were equally trying to act grown up, were eager to accept their offer to ride around town; they offered the boys a few pointers to further their education, if you get the drift.

Loren's Mother was a very inspirational woman and she encouraged all her kids to go to church and live decent productive lives. Their church was struggling until they hired a young Minister whose vision was to get the teenagers involved in a variety of activities and that resulted in attracting more teenagers to attend and take part. The church grew at a rapid rate because of the energy the youth brought in. Loren was encouraged to contribute his part in this growth and was inspired to be baptized into the church in his senior year of high school. Loren was working the night shift at the factory, so he had a little spare time on his hands during the day. The new Minister invited Loren to accompany him to visit sick people and shut-ins; people that couldn't get out and about and were lonely. Loren went on a few occasions and found it to be very rewarding to sit and visit and pray with them; it lifted their spirits.

One morning, after the church service, while everyone was milling around and talking, Loren noticed a gorgeous new girl he had never seen before standing with her Mother and Father. He asked his Sister who that beauty was standing against the far wall. She said, "That's Josie; do you want to meet her?" "Why yes," he quickly responded. Josie was very pretty with an infectious smile, dark hair, and gray eyes. Just the thought of meeting her gave him a tingling sensation up his spine. After a little small talk, he found out she was in the high school class a year behind him and worked the candy counter in one of the Dime Stores, so he set out to learn the time she got off work. He decided to go into the Dime Store for a sack of candy and offer her a ride home, since she didn't have a car, which she accepted graciously, and that began a serious romance; he always considered her his 'first real true love'. They found themselves together at every opportunity; many friends that knew them took for granted that they would marry someday. Her Mother really thought highly of him, and she would contribute the idea of marriage at every opportunity. He brushed off that notion quickly because he knew the military was looming on the horizon and that quelled any such notions, knowing he would likely be called. The law of the land at that time was that every boy would register for the draft on his 18th birthday; he fulfilled his civic duty as required in his senior year of high school.

The Korean War was raging during this time and a lot of the boys were enlisting in the various services. Loren was waiting to get his draft notice and a couple months after taking Josie to her Senior Prom, the notice arrived, 'Your friends and neighbors have selected you to enter military service and you are to report to your Armed Forces Induction Center on so-and-so date at a so-and-so time. Be prepared to spend the day and you will be returned to your induction center.' (Something to that effect). He was excited to get the notice, even though he knew it was about due because he was checking with the draft board every month to see if his name was coming up. This was going to be a new adventure for him, and he could hardly wait. Of course, his Mother didn't share his enthusiasm.

They were bussed to Cincinnati for a series of written tests and a physical. He knew most of the guys on his bus and they all laughed and joked throughout the entire day. He later found out that afterward some of them would go directly to their recruiter and enlist in either the Navy or the Air Force. In a very short time, he was notified he was classified as

1-A and would soon be called to active duty. Josie wanted a commitment from Loren if she was to wait for him. He had seen a lot of the women not be faithful or send 'dear john' letters during the big war and didn't want that in the back of his mind, although most wives and sweethearts were true to their men. Was this 'good thinking'? 'Good decision'? Only time would tell although it was tough leaving Josie. He said goodbye to all the people at the factory where he worked, and they wished him well and the women hugged him. He sold his car to a used car lot and that hurt him more than anything; he loved that old car. He hung out with his friends up to the last minute, and then he proceeded to pack his bag with what the draft notice requested would do him three days. He figured the Army would supply him with whatever he would need for the next two years. His older Brother drove him to the Induction Center early the next morning and he was soon on his way to an adventure far beyond his wildest dream. This time he only recognized a few familiar faces on the bus from the first time they went for their physicals; there were a rash of enlistments in other branches of service. This group was collected from around the entire county, but they had one thing in common; most of them were leaving home for the first time. The local newspaper took a photo of the entire group before they boarded the busses and ran it in the daily edition. The roads were icy and slick and the bus slid all the way.

CHAPTER 2

After arriving at the receiving center in Cincinnati they were sorted into groups in alphabetic order. Loren became acquainted with a guy that would become his closest friend, Bobby L. Williams. Bobby was 6-foot tall with black hair and broad shoulders; he had the Hollywood good looks. He told Loren he was engaged and worked with his future Father-In-Law in construction. The two of them hit it off from the beginning and were comrades in arms until they were later separated in Korea. They were tested again and given repeat physicals and pricked their fingers for a drop of blood to determine their blood type. They then sat down for a one-on-one interview with an officer, with the purpose to place them in an appropriate category and questioned whether they had a problem killing people that were enemies of the United States. Three of the group claimed to be 'conscientious objectors' and they were directed to leave the room through a side door. It was thought they would be excused but when the train left the station that evening, they were on it. The final order of business was to be sworn in and take an oath that the country and the constitution would be defended from all aggressors. They were issued a Serial Number that would identify them for the rest of their lives. If you had a US in front of your number, you were classified as a draftee. If you had an RA in front your number, you were classified as an enlisted man. Loren had a US in front of his 8-digit number. They were now considered members of the armed forces of the United States.

It had been a long day and it was well after dark when they boarded a sleeper train routed to Fort Meade in Maryland. Sleeper train was a misnomer. The way it jerked and jolted all night, sleep proved to be impossible; many of the guys played cards all night. They arrived in Baltimore the next day, with the temperature being 71 degrees, and then boarded busses to take them to Fort Meade. Fort George G. Meade consists of approximately 5400 acres located between Baltimore, Annapolis, and Washington DC. It was named for General Meade whose victory at the battle of Gettysburg turned the tide of the Civil War in favor of the north. It was a training site for soldiers during the First and Second World Wars and a processing center for new recruits during the Korean War. It was formerly used to house almost 1700 German and Italian POWs during World War 2.

It was again late in the evening when they arrived, and they were then herded into rooms where they were threatened if they didn't donate $1 for the Red Cross. After a short introduction, they were paraded down the street carrying their bags to the mess hall, entering and picking up a wet, hot, and steamy tray and a hot plastic cup. They walked down the food line where runny mashed potatoes were slapped on the tray and a scoop of shrimp, in the shell, were piled on the tray next to the potatoes. Then a dipper of red sauce was poured on the shrimp leaving it all in one hell of a mess. Then their cups were filled with coffee. Finding an old wooden table with bench seats, Loren looked at the food and stated, "I can't eat this shit." He sat with two guys from Virginia, who later became two of his very good friends. One said he was a shrimp fisherman and he offered to eat Loren's shrimp. The other guy was 17 years old and was caught stealing gas, so the Judge sentenced him to three years in the Army or three years in jail; of course, he took the Army; Loren choked down the soupy potatoes. From there they were led into a warehouse and were issued bed linens and a blanket and then to an old barracks with double-deck bunks lining both sides of the room. Selecting a bunk and throwing on the bedding, they collapsed for the night.

Morning came too soon, and they were rousted out at 5:00 am and lined up in the middle of the street in front of the barracks. It was pitch black-dark, and now freezing cold with snow flurries, but they were ordered to line up and 'police' the area for trash and pick up cigarette butts. It was almost impossible to see anything, but you had to go through the motions because you were ordered to do so. If you found a butt, then you had to field strip it; that is tear off the paper, release the tobacco into the air and put the paper into your pocket to be discarded later. Loren didn't smoke but that made no difference, the lesson was learned. If you caught a smoker throwing down a butt, get on his ass and let him learn also, or he will have to face the wrath of the gods. After breakfast they were given instructions of how to make up a bunk. There was no such thing as good enough; they had to be perfect. It turned out to be a busy day; they were measured for uniforms and boots but, measurements made no difference because the stuff was thrown at them regardless of the sizes. Loren was unlucky enough to get the old tan rawhide boots with buckles. A lot of the other guys got the shiny black jump boots. It goes without saying, Loren was very unhappy about it; one of the other guys suggested he take them back and tell them they were too big and see if they would exchange them. He did just that and was told his feet would swell. He later tried it again and told them they were too tight. They told him that the boots would stretch; he had to live with them and hated them, mainly because all boots were to be shined. How do you shine rawhide leather? Those that got these dreaded boots were told to put liquid shoe polish on them and burn off the tufts of the leather, put heavy wax on them and try to make them shine; easier said than done. This was just another thing to add to the misery of a disgruntled new Army recruit. The order was then given to put on class 'A' uniforms, and they were marched to the barber shop where a huge line of barbers, mostly foreigners that didn't understand English, removed the hair allowing the clippings to drop down the shirt collar, which created pure torture for the rest of the day; and for that they had to pay $.25. In addition to that misery, Loren's pants were about 4 inches too long, so he rolled them up. Some asshole Sergeant yelled at him to roll them down because he was out of uniform. No excuse was good enough, so he walked on the pant legs the rest of the day. They were instructed to ship all their civilian belongings back home. Bobby L. was made aware of Loren's frustration, when he indicated, "If this is an example of Army life, I'm going to have to declare war against the Army." "It'll get better," Bobby retorted, "you have to understand that there are thousands of dumb shits coming in here every day and that has to try their patience too." The next couple days did get better. Everybody was given work details, some not so pleasant, and Loren lucked out by administering written exams to new arrivals. These exams were to further aim the person toward an assignment more suited to their makeup, or ability; if he so warranted a specialty school. Most however were aimed toward combat training in various military bases throughout the country to prepare them for the inevitable. Korea!

Every day a call went out to muster on the parade ground in front of a huge platform. Up to a 1000-troops gathered around the platform in hopes that their names would be called and told where they were to be assigned. The Sergeant calling out the names has no idea who you are or furthermore doesn't care who you are. One dumb ass yelled out, "Where am I going?" He responded, "You are going to Fort Webb." "Where's that?" the idiot came back all excited. "A half mile up a spider's ass!" the Sarge answered. That brought a loud uproar from everybody. He would call out approximately 100 to 150 assignments each session to ship out to various locations somewhere in the country.

The day came for another joke …. shots. About 200 men are marched to the Infirmary and stand in line; standing in line is an occupation for the Army and requires no training. They filed through one door of the building, got injected, and then proceeded out another door. The line Loren was in had a Medic who was the furthest thing from being a Medic. He didn't inject the needle in the muscle at an angle. He rammed the needle straight in and hit the bone raising a huge welt on Loren's arm and blood ran down, dripping off the finger-tips. Loren yelled out, "Hey! What the hell's going on here?" One of the other Medics yelled back, "Shut up and move on out." Loren's arm burned for about an hour after that and he knew whatever the shot was for didn't take; add another negative about the Army to Loren's list. Not much was going right so far in his short time in the military.

Finally, after eight days of what seemed to be nonsense, a muster was called. This time a different Sergeant called out the names; he was small in stature and very excitable. He called on one recruit and got a stupid answer. He jumped up and down like on a pogo stick. The recruit said, "I'm sorry!" "Don't be sorry, be particular," the Sergeant responded, frustrated. This brought a huge laugh from everybody until he made one guy run to the other side of the parade ground and give 50 pushups, yelling the count loud enough for everybody to hear. Bobby and Loren made a plan that each would stand on the opposite side of the crowd. If, and when, one's name was called the other would answer. "Yo!" and yell back their first name and vise-versa. So finally, "Whitson!" was called. Bobby yelled from the other side of the area, "Yo, Loren." Then when, "Williams," was called, Loren yelled, "Yo, Bobby L.," from the other side. The Sergeant asked, "Where's Williams?" Then Bobby L. yelled, "Over here." The little Sergeant got a bewildered look on his face, was a loss for words for a moment, and then proceeded to call out the rest of the names. "The names I just called out will leave tomorrow for Camp Breckinridge, Kentucky and are to be assigned to the 101st Airborne Division." This pleased Loren because he hoped to get something exciting.

CHAPTER 3

After their joyous vacation in Maryland, they boarded a two-engine prop plane and took a turbulent plane ride that would end in Evansville, Indiana. Puke sacks were issued and about half of them were filled when they finally landed. Evansville is approximately 30 bus miles across the Indiana/Kentucky state line from Camp Breckinridge, Ky. Camp Breckinridge is approximately 36,000 acres located 30 miles from Evansville and approximately 2 miles from Morganfield, Ky. It was the headquarters of the 1st Battalion of the 502nd Airborne Infantry Regiment of the 101st Airborne Division. It was constituted in 1942 and was activated and deactivated 3 times prior to being activated in August 1950, during the Korean War, and then deactivated again in December 1953. Its purpose was to train newly inducted troops as replacements for Korea. Like Fort Meade, it was also previously a POW camp for German and Italian prisoners during WW 2.

After arriving and lining up in the street in front of the barracks, the company commander welcomed them. He said, "You are assigned to 'M' (Mike) company and are to be trained to be replacements for Korea." That sounded like fun, being trained to be cannon fodder. "Your basic training will last 20 weeks but we will not start actually training for two more weeks. In the meantime, you will be kept busy doing various work details, learning to march, military etiquette, keeping your barracks clean, and pertinent orientation. Your Platoon Sergeants will assign your barracks and your bunks, foot lockers and wall lockers. You will be going to chow and then issued bedding. We are going to Mother you and hope you enjoy your stay here." He said all this with a facetious grin, and everybody suspected that the shit was going to hit the fan, so you better brace yourselves for the worst.

The work details were a pain in the ass and generally, the privates assigned to lead them, were only advanced by weeks ahead of those new ones and some of them were on ego trips. One group leader asked for volunteers to dig some trenches and promised them a three-day pass. Loren was aggravated that he didn't get the opportunity, so he could make a quick trip home. Well they dug the trenches and it was all a lie; there were no passes. That irked Loren because he despised anybody that would lie to him or steal from him. This was just another negative notch to add to his list. He was assigned to a work detail that was led by a smart-ass red head from New York. He was to shovel gravel into a dump truck, not a normal dump bed, but one with side extensions which made it quite high to throw the gravel. The New Yorker had only been in service 8 weeks, but he had sadistic tendencies and seemed to take advantage of his power. After a while, Loren began to struggle with each shovel full. His arms began to ache, and he soon had to take a break for a moment because he couldn't get the load over the side. The red head started riding his ass, calling him a 'gold brick', and to quit screwing off. Loren had always been a very gentle person and never had any thought in his mind to harm anyone but, for some reason, he had a strong temptation to wrap that shovel up the side of that guy's head. He came close and then, as luck would have it, a Sergeant came up and asked for volunteers to set up water-cooled machine guns for the infiltration course. They were used to shoot live ammunition over the troop's heads as they crawled under barbed wire through a simulated combat situation. He knew absolutely nothing about water-cooled machine guns, but he was the first to volunteer. It turned out to be a good deal. He worked with non-commissioned officers and they were serious about their project and treated him with civility because people could be killed easily with this training.

Training began in earnest with a lot of PT (physical training), running, marching, and most of all, discipline. They were issued their rifles, a Garand, gas operated, M1, .30 caliber, semi-automatic that was considered the lifeblood of the combat infantrymen. It weighed 9 ¾ pounds and, with the bayonet, it weighed 10 ½ pounds. They started out holding it at arm's length for as long as they could with each arm, and that wasn't very long. The first rifle inspection was held on a Saturday morning after a light rain with the Captain doing the inspecting. When he looked at Loren's rifle, he asked, "I suppose you are going to tell me this dried mud on the butt plate was from this morning?" "Yes sir," he quickly answered. "Well it dried mighty fast. Give this man details for the weekend," the Captain ordered. And they did; he was to cut the grass around the barracks with the bayonet. He got down on his knees and started cutting. The barracks were on block pillars about three feet high and, when Loren cut up close to the pillars, he looked around and seeing no one around, he crawled under the barracks and took a nap.

He learned the importance of caring for that M1, disassembling and reassembling and cleaning it to perfection because if it failed you in combat, it could cost you your life. He treated that rifle like it was a baby. As the training progressed, the M1 became less and less heavy and soon they were flipping it around like a broom handle. All through the course of basic training they received instructions on every light weapon the Army had to offer, except one, the .45 Caliber Grease Gun; it was used extensively in World War 2. They fired rifles, mortars, bazookas, hand grenades, rifle grenades, light air-cooled machine guns, Browning automatic rifle (BAR), .57 recoilless rifles, .45 Cal, semi-automatic hand gun, and one of his favorites, the .30 Cal, M1 Carbine. He qualified as a sharpshooter with the M1 Garand. They fired up to 1000 yards at targets that were almost impossible to see, let alone hit. Loren could handle the physical aspects of the training but his feeling the officers and non-coms were incompetent, convincing him the toughest part of training was going to be mental endurance. All through basic training they were required to run everywhere they went, which was no problem for Loren. He didn't smoke or drink and when they ran, he would pass the smokers gasping for breath. He was less serious about the Army because of the mental aspects and the constant harassing and he decided to declare war against the Army and just do what they asked and nothing more. He made it his motto, 'just play the game'. One morning the Sergeant said, "Whitson you are doing barracks duty today." "What's that, Sarge?" Loren asked. "When the Captain comes in to inspect the barracks, you walk around with him," the Sergeant responded, "and don't mess it up." "You know me, Sarge, I'll give it my usual 100%," Loren replied. "That's what scares me," the Sarge commented.

Loren was putting the final touches on his area; making sure the bunk was perfect; making sure everything in his foot and wall locker were presentable; his shoes displayed and shined. The Captain, and a Sergeant he didn't know, comes in and Loren stands at attention and the Captain asked, "What's your name, soldier?" "Private Loren Whitson, sir," he answered. "Go with me, Private!" the Captain continued. He started at one end and looked at everything as he went; dust on this window-sill; shoes not shined; tore a bunk completely apart that wasn't made properly, burned out light bulb. "Are you writing all this down, Private?" he asked. "I can remember it all," Loren replied. "Well you must have one hell of a memory," the Captain remarked. Later the Platoon Sergeant questioned Loren, "Well, what did the Captain say about the barracks?" "He said a lot of stuff," Loren replied. "Like what?" the Sarge asked, agitated. "I don't remember it all, but he said there was a burned-out light bulb," Loren commented. "Well, did you change it?" the Sarge continued. "No!" Loren answered. "I don't know where the light bulbs are." "Show me the bulb, Whitson," the Sergeant insisted. "It's common sense, Sarge, turn on all the lights and the one that doesn't work is burned out," Loren added. The Sergeant turned on his heel and started walking away and said, "You're hopeless, Whitson." Someone said, "That Sergeant is going to get you one of these days." Loren commented, "Nah, he likes me."

About a week later they were lined up in the street in front of the barracks and the Sergeant was checking them over and he was yelling as he walked down the line, "Ok, ladies, we are going to the Infirmary." When he got in front of Loren, Loren asked, "More shots, Sergeant?" "No!" he replied. "You are going to donate a pint of blood. Are you going to faint, Whitson?" "I don't know, Sarge," Loren added. "I have never given blood before." "Well, you are going to donate it today," the Sarge yelled, "or you are going to sweat it the next three days." After he got further down the line, Loren mumbled to Bobby, "I think I've sweated it the last three days." "I know I have!" Bobby replied. They marched, not ran, which was already unusual, to the Infirmary. They went in and laid on cots and the blood was extracted. The medic said, "We are going to give you a big glass of orange juice and a Hershey bar. A truck outside will take you back to your barracks. Do not do anything strenuous the rest of today; just lay on your bunks and nap." Loren remarked, "Wow, a Hershey bar; I almost forgot what they look like." When they got back to their barracks, there were a lot of disgruntled men pissing and moaning because they were not in agreement with giving the blood, but not Loren. He said, "I told them if I got a day off for one pint, what would you give me for a gallon?" Someone yelled out, "Whitson, you crazy bastard, ain't you serious about nothing?" He answered, "Oh, yeah, I love the Army!" Someone else yelled out, "That's for sure." It felt good just to relax, and soon the entire barracks, which normally was constant noise, was now silent, and they all enjoyed a little nap.

CHAPTER 4

Then one morning they went out in the street for their usual formation, but their old Platoon Sergeant wasn't there. A new Sergeant appeared and introduced himself. He said, "I am your new Platoon Sergeant and I am ordered to make soldiers out of you. I am 21 years old and an Airborne Ranger and I have completed a tour in Korea, and I have seen how untrained troops don't know how to handle themselves in combat and are killed or wounded because of it. I am not going to brow-beat ya, but I am going to work your butts off, and someday you may thank me for it." Loren's first impression of this guy was, "He's a soldier's soldier." He had broad shoulders and narrow at the hips and not an ounce of fat on him anywhere, and he walked with a spring in his step. He had the appearance of Captain Marvel in the comic books. He didn't just say give me 40 pushups, he did them also and counted each one. He didn't just say give me 30 squat-jumps, he did them also. When they double-timed anywhere, he was in front. There were things they soon did that, at one time was considered gruesome, was now becoming routine with less effort. In other words, they were becoming conditioned.

The next chain of events would subsequently change Loren Whitson's life forever. Early one morning they double timed to a large building, marched inside and filing down rows of seats and halted, standing at attention. When the officer in charge commanded, "Seats", they all sat with one loud thud. This was not unusual because that was how they were trained to do it from the very beginning. After the summer temperatures increased to almost unbearable levels, the powers to be decided to go on a summer schedule, that is, to start the days at 3:00 am and cease at 5:00 pm. This was another joke because they found stuff to do up to about 11:00 pm. Therefore, everybody was not only hungry all the time but hot and exhausted. In this event it was somewhat humorous when the officer in charge started his spiel, "I'm Lieutenant Wilson, Division Faculty, General Subjects Section, and today we are going to study and practice hand to hand combat; wake that man up!" The not so humorous part was when everybody stopped for whatever reason, someone would fall asleep almost instantly, and that yard-bird did just that. That brought a big laugh from everybody.

A movie projector had been set up in the middle of the room and a large screen on the platform. They started by showing movies, actual footage of hand to hand combat, Americans against the enemy soldiers, fighting with bayonets. It was to kill or be killed. When that enemy soldier attacked, he was coming to kill with whatever way he could, and in this case, sticking that cold steel into his foes body. Americans were killed as well as the enemy. There were scenes of fighting with both the Germans and the Japanese and in all cases, it was life or death. Chills went up Loren's spine. Just the thought of that blade going into his body and the enemy putting his foot on his chest to pull it back out really got his attention. At the break, he told his friend, Bobby L, "This is some serious shit. I'm going to practice every chance I get and I ain't going to be satisfied until I'll be the best I can be." In the afternoon they went out into a field where simulated figures made of straw stood and spaced at regular intervals. A Sergeant introduced himself as, Sergeant Sands, and let it be known that he was going to introduce and demonstrate the techniques for hand to hand combat. He demonstrated various manipulations with the bayonet attached onto the end of the M1 Garand rifle; the vertical butt stroke, parry left, parry right, etc. He impressed Loren with the seriousness he went about his business. He snarled and growled like an animal and this convinced Loren that he had been there and done that for real. The next several days they practiced, practiced, and practiced using the straw figures as the enemy, knowing the straw wasn't going to fight back. Getting the technique right was tougher than first appeared; doing the exercises were more complicated than watching it being done. If you didn't do it right, Sgt. Sands was on you like stink on shit. Loren didn't mind that though. He knew if he was going to get it right; he had to have someone showing him what he was doing wrong. That M1 that seemed so heavy when basic training began, now went unnoticed. They now had bigger fish to fry, or more accurately, more important fish to fry. Loren became so possessed with it all, he had Bobby and a couple other guys join him at night in the barracks and practice any way they could think of to disarm someone with a knife from the front or the back. They soon became rather efficient at it.

Every Thursday the cooks served C-Rations three meals a day. Loren's famous saying was, "Anybody that had to eat

C-ration corned beef hash for breakfast would eat pure shit!" His favorites were beans and weenies, and the fruit, but they weren't always offered. The entire time he was in the Army there was one thing the cooks made that he really liked, pineapple-upside-down-cake; they had perfected that. On Thursday evenings, when Loren and Bobby could get away, they would go to the PX (Post Exchange) and get baloney sandwiches and donuts and/or a candy bar. It was their opinion that it was a matter of survival. They didn't have a lot to spend, however, because they only made $78 a month, and they had to buy other things like toilet articles.

Every Saturday morning all the units had to assemble on the parade ground and march in formation before the high-ranking officers to pass in review, so the officers could grade each company's performance, and give the one they thought demonstrated the best that day, an award. Loren's company never won. It seemed there was always a screw up that forgot how to march or never knew how in the first place. There was one yard-bird that the Platoon Sergeant ordered to kick a concrete step with his left foot until it got sore, so he would know his left from his right; it seemed he never learned. Having to stand in formation in the extreme heat didn't help. If they stood for an extra-long time, some would become overcome with the heat and pass out. It seemed that if they kept moving it wasn't as crucial. Finally, on graduation day his company won the award, but Loren figured it was to save them from the embarrassment of never winning. If they were lucky, they could have some free time on Saturday afternoons or Sundays. If they were beyond lucky, they could get a weekend pass. One Friday evening, Bobby told Loren he was getting a pass and a bunch of guys were going with a guy from another company, who had a car, and try to go home; he was charging $10 a person. Loren went to the orderly room and asked if he could have a pass and the duty Corporal informed him 'he had KP (Kitchen Police) duty in the Officer's Mess Saturday for lunch'. He also informed him he was to take an exam for OCS (Officer's Candidate School) the following Monday morning. He iterated to Bobby what was planned for him and he remarked, "Can you imagine them wanting me to become a dumb-ass officer? I had taken a test once before and only got 119 when 125 points were required." Bobby sympathized with him, told him not to cause any problems and do just what they asked, and wished him well. Loren went to the Officer's Mess, and low and behold, they had pretty table-cloths on small tables, just like in a nice restaurant, salt and pepper shakers on the tables, and linen napkins with nice silverware. This was the Ritz compared to the big old wood tables, that looked like work benches, they had in their mess hall. He was required to serve them like a waiter, which was different than what he was used too; normally fighting like a pack of dogs just to get his share.

 He did a good job, and afterwards, had the rest of the afternoon off so he decided to go to the PX just to look around. He had eaten some decent food while on KP and wasn't hungry for a change. The PX had everything you could ever want and at a discounted price. He bought for his Mother for 'Mother's Day', a 101st Airborne Division Banner and had it mailed home to her. A juke box was playing a selected song 'KAW-LIGA', sung by Hank Williams. It seemed to be the only song anyone selected because it was the only thing playing every time Loren went there.

 'KAW-LIGA was a wooden Indian standing by the door.

He fell love with an Indian maid over in the antique store
KAW-LIGA just stood there and never let it show --------'
(Kaw-Liga had his problems)

While just moseying around, he spotted Sgt. Sands, the hand to hand combat instructor. He approached the Sergeant and said, "Hi Sarge! I'm Private Whitson, and you've been instructing my company on the bayonet course. I really appreciate your intensity and am convinced it's something we need to be serious about. In fact, I persuaded several other guys in my platoon to practice disarming someone with a knife, whether they come up behind you or attack straight on. To be honest with you, I think we have become pretty good and it has increased my confidence level that I can defend myself. Of course, we don't know how we will react in a real-life situation but it's the best we can do for now." The Sergeant looked him straight in the eyes the entire time he was talking and commented, "I'm glad to have been of service and hope that I have shown you something that may help save your life. I've noticed you on the course and the seriousness you go about your training. Pray to God you never have to use it." Then after a little hesitation, he asked, "Let me ask you this, do you think you could kill a man?" Loren stammered a little and said, "I will never know that until the situation presents itself, but I am sure I won't have a problem, if it is him or me." "If you are really serious," the Sarge followed, "I can give you some private instruction that can make you more of a deadly weapon." That intrigued Loren and he came back with, "I am willing to learn anything that will give me an advantage." The Sarge was silent for a moment and finally said, "What I will teach you is highly sensitive, and you cannot, and I mean cannot, reveal it to anyone. I mean nobody! Are you interested or not?" Then Loren became more curious as to what he was swearing to and said, "I think I need to know a little more about what it is I am going to do that is so secretive that even the Army doesn't know what I'm doing." "I agree," Sands said. "Follow me back to my quarters and I will explain a little more of it to ya. I was the same way when it was first introduced to me back in the big war. Buy whatever it was you came for and we'll go." So, Loren bought some tooth paste and they walked back to Sands' quarters, which was only a short distance away. "Tell me a little something about yourself," Sands requested, as they walked slowly along. "Well there's not much to tell," Loren responded. "I'm just a normal guy that grew up doing normal stuff with one thing in my future, working the rest of my life. I was drafted, and I wanted to see what two years was like before I committed to anymore." They arrived and went into an empty barracks and then into Sands' room which was a normal non-com's living quarters. It was neat and clean and everything in its place. There was a lifelike mannequin standing in the back corner that caught Loren's eye because it seemed to be out of place. "Sit down, and I'll explain what I can in case you want to change your mind. Do you want a beer or something?" "No!" Loren said. "I don't drink and I'm good." He was now more curious than ever, and he was anxious to hear what this guy had to say. "You are probably wondering why I stare into your eyes when you talk," Sands directed. "I try to study the person to see if he is truly qualified to continue this most sensitive issue. I've had several candidates who showed interest, but their hearts and souls weren't into it. I can see you are getting antsy for more information, so let me proceed. I am going to teach you how to kill a person quickly and quietly. Most would probably consider it brutal and sadistic, but it is effective, and it will take practice and training to perfect. I learned it from a veteran of WW 1, and he said he learned it from a veteran of the Civil War. How far back it goes before that I don't know. Are you still interested?" "I am more interested than ever," Loren answered. "Very good," Sands continued. "I could see it in your eyes that you may be the right choice. It is going to require very strong hands. Squeeze my hand as hard as you can." Loren squeezed with his right hand and then with his left hand. Sands squeezed Loren's hands and he winced with the pain. This guy's hands were incredibly strong. He retrieved a little sponge rubber ball from his wall locker and handed it to Loren, "I want you to squeeze this ball continuously with both hands at every opportunity," he continued. "Carry it with you always, and if anyone questions you about it, just tell them you think it will help you with hand to hand combat. Since they realize your sincerity with all your practicing, they will accept your explanation. Another thing, do not cut your fingernails for a couple weeks and I will then show you how to trim them. Are you still interested?" "Yes, I am," Loren responded, with all seriousness, "what about the act itself?" "It might be considered a guerrilla tactic," Sands directed, "because you have to learn to sneak and be as stealth as possible to keep from being detected. It really is more effective at night when the subject is asleep or just sitting inactive. You must become jungle savvy, use face paint, don't carry anything that makes noise or rattles. Don't wear a helmet or cap; tie a rag around your head to absorb any sweat and keep bugs and whatever out of your hair so you won't be distracted. You can carry a side arm and holster but make sure it is held firm against your body. Try to obtain a jungle knife, but until you do, use your bayonet with the scabbard strapped tight against your leg. The idea is for you and everything you carry moves as one, quietly and swiftly as possible, to prevent being detected. Carelessness can cost you your life. Am I making you nervous?" "Not at all," Loren came back. "I am more excited than ever. It sounds adventurous and that's what I've wanted from the beginning." "Ok then! I think you are the right person I've been looking for," Sands said, becoming more relaxed and satisfied. "Step over here to the mannequin and I will demonstrate exactly what you will do. I see you are righthanded, so pull the victim's head back with your left hand, and in one motion with your right hand, rip out his throat. Do it as smoothly and swiftly as possible and he will not be able to utter a sound, or resist. The toughest part will be how well you do an acting job to all those around you. You cannot give the slightest hint to anyone, no matter how close they might be, as to what you are training to do. And later in combat, after you initially kill, then you are to act as innocent as possible. Do you understand? Or not? You cannot reveal in the slightest any part of this. Some will become suspicious and question what you are up to and that is when you must play dumb. I suggest you start practicing immediately and soon it will become a second nature and gets a lot easier. That's all I am going to show you today. I have a hot date with a lady Lieutenant, and I must get ready." He had a guilty look on his face and a slight grin. "How do I get in touch with you for future sessions?" Loren asked. "It may not be easy getting away but, when I do, I won't have a lot of time, especially from my closest friends." He responded, "I am usually here most evenings and Sundays for sure, so you will just have to bang on my door, unless you see me at the PX." As Loren slowly walked back to his barracks, his mind was cluttered with all that was said, and he tried to mull it over one step at a time. The more he thought about it the more pumped he became. He began squeezing the little rubber ball, one hand and then the other.

Bobby L. and the guys were late getting back. They ran into a little problem with the gate guard but with a little explaining, a little begging, and some promises they knew they couldn't keep, he relented and let them in. They got in about an hour before reveille and started the day worn out and half asleep. "Well, Bobby, how was everything in beautiful Ohio?" Loren asked. "It was great," he answered. "I spent all the time I had with my girl-friend, and her Mom fixed me a real good meal. It was like going to Heaven for just a short time. How was your KP duty?" "Oh, it went well," he answered. "I did all they asked and never resisted any orders and kept my mouth shut. You wouldn't believe how fancy that mess hall is compared to our pig pen; tablecloths, silverware, pretty napkins, curtains, and all the trimmings you see in a nice restaurant. The food was top drawer and I got a good meal out of it. I ate until I couldn't eat anymore. For the most part they were all very pleasant and humane, not like we normally see them. Very shortly I go to take the big test and I may become one of them; who knows?" "You mean I may have to salute you?" Bobby said humorously and with a big grin. "I doubt it, "Loren said. "I never passed the last one and I doubt if I got any smarter in the meantime. Besides that, if I do go to OCS, I will have to extend my enlistment; I may not agree to anything like that." He really wanted to tell Bobby about his session with Sgt. Sands but, no, a vow is a vow, and he better get used to the idea of keeping it to himself, forever.

CHAPTER 5

The weeks that followed were filled with a lot of PT, a lot of running, instructions in weaponry, and playing the game, as Loren called it. He got the results of the OCS test and he scored 119 just like the first time, so that issue was dead. He had gotten good scores in science and math and they mentioned he was eligible for Guided Missile Mechanics School and that sounded promising. He was interested in that possibility. In the meantime, he had to plan for the worst, so he met with Sgt. Sands whenever he could sneak out. It was usually evenings when most of the guys went to the movies to avoid work details and he would decline, giving them some lame excuse. Sands filed the fingernails on the right hand like an arrowhead, not long but pointed and sharp, so he could easily dig them into the throat. He made the left hand almost the same, so they wouldn't be questionable. He was getting proficient at tearing the throat out of a mannequin. Sands explained that sometimes if the victim didn't have hair to grab, he may have to reach over his head and put his fingers into his nostrils, putting your knee in his back and snapping his head back, exposing the neck for the right hand, and the kill. It seemed easy enough, but there again, it was not a live body. He became more and more assured of himself and Sands thought he was ready. He explained that the real tough part was the mental. Did he have the killer instinct to go through with it? That was one part that couldn't be taught; it had to be an instinct and rely on his training.

It had now become important for Loren to be alert when there were subjects pertaining to him improving his guerrilla skills. There were instructions on camouflage and concealment; Loren was privately interested in this. It would be beneficial if, and when, he should try to be stealth in his efforts to assassinate an enemy combatant. Face painting was only a small part of camouflage. They learned to conceal themselves with the foliage of the area, stuffing it in their shirt and pants and sticking it to their helmets. They would slowly crawl, hugging the ground as close as they could, to look like the terrain; being particular not to be detected. With this tactic they could creep up to an unsuspecting subject and take him out of action. They learned to camouflage their foxholes and vehicles to keep from being seen on the ground as well as from the air. Small planes would fly over, and the pilots would try to hit them with flour bags to show they were not very well hidden. They had night exercises simulating an ambush in the dark. It could be dangerous if their eyes weren't adjusted to the dark. Moving around in the dark is tricky if you didn't know the area. You could fall into a hole or ditch or run into a fence or even into the side of a building if you weren't alert. The compass is another great and very important tool. It is very easy to get turned around and eventually lost if a person doesn't pay attention to the location of landmarks or buildings in reference to where he is. Getting lost and wandering into an enemy camp doesn't sound like a smart thing to do. Some people have a natural sense of direction but there are some that would get lost in their own back yard. Loren had a fair sense of direction, but he could occasionally get confused as to his location. He knew he had to work on this and get better at it. Loren was paired with a guy on a night exercise and that guy knew exactly where they were and how to get back to the barracks. They were trucked to the exercise area and Loren had no idea where they were. When the exercise was over, instead of being trucked back to the barracks, the guy said, "Follow me and I'll get us back before the rest of them waste a lot of time loading and unloading in those trucks." And he did. Loren was very impressed with this guy's gift. "It gets easier," he said, "when you are observant and pay attention to your surroundings, and you have to practice that." Loren put that valuable advice into his memory bank.

Two weeks to go in basic training and it was time to go to a bivouac area and live in actual conditions of encampment. They learned to pack their back-pack which included a tent half. Each man carried a half a tent and, when it was time to set it up, two guys got together and put their two halves together. They then dug a drainage ditch around the tent, should it rain. The pack weighed about 70 pounds and carrying their rifle, cartridge belt with the canteen and slicker hanging onto it, totaled quite a load to carry in intense heat and they were told the hike was 15 miles; There was a lack of enthusiasm in the company. Trucks full of troops would pass them jeering as they went by. Didn't know who they were, and it really didn't matter because it didn't ease the pain and misery any. They were allowed 10-minute breaks every hour and that helped some. They finally arrived at the camp site but there was no time to rest and take it easy. They had to set up camp immediately if they didn't want to do it in the dark. They went through simulated attacks and setting up defenses being attacked, daytime and nighttime. The idea was to give them the experience of what it is like in real life conditions, except there was no real ammunition being fired. It turned out to be valuable experience as to what and how to respond in real combat.

Loren's company was in great physical condition. The latter part of basic the Airborne Ranger took charge of their training and he had fine-tuned them into a well-conditioned group. Other companies were bivouacking along with Loren's company. They packed up the last day for the long trek back to the barracks area; a company left the area at one-hour intervals and Loren's company was leaving fourth. The Airborne Ranger said, "Those companies ahead of us are going to take 10-minute breaks every hour, but we are not taking any breaks. We are going straight through without stopping. A lot of 'oh shits' were heard throughout the ranks. They did just that. They passed two companies sitting along the road and, when they reached the hill entering the camp, they saw the third company just entering their barracks area. After a good shower and crawling into a clean bunk, nobody moved until reveille the next morning.

Basic training was now essentially over. Everybody was in a better mood and a lot more relaxed. They still had a lot of serious cleaning to do because, after getting back the night before, the barracks were a disaster area. They had all the issued equipment to turn in, including their rifles and bayonets. Now it was time for the most important event, where do they go from here? The practice was that, as each company graduated, they alternated the list of troops that were going to Korea, one company the list started at the top of the alphabet and the next started from the bottom of the alphabet. Since the company that graduated prior to Loren's started with the letter 'A', Loren's company would start with the letter 'Z'; 95% were designated as replacements for Korea. A few were retained for Cadre training; there were a few that were going to OCS; a few to a base in Alaska; and some to Germany. Of course, Loren and his friend Bobby L. were bound for Korea. They were given their orders and the orders stated they were going to Southeast Asia and told they had seven days to report to the Port of Debarkation in San Francisco. One dumb ass remarked that maybe they were not going to Korea since it said SE Asia. "Duh! Where do you think Korea is dumb ass?" Bobby said. The very last thing of importance was getting their final pay. They were warned "BEWARE OF THIEVES". As pitiful as it may sound, a couple had their money stolen by a lowlife(s). There were a lot of shaking of hands and 'see ya later' and getting the hell out of there. Loren and Bobby traveled together back to Ohio.

CHAPTER 6

Loren's Mom laundered all his clothes, mended or altered all that was needed and fed him all his favorite foods. His uniforms didn't need much altering. His weight was exactly the same, no more and no less, as it was when he went in except, he was now in a whole lot better physical condition. He spent time with his friends and went to see Josie, curious to whether she was still waiting for him. She didn't seem too concerned; was no commitment a good decision or good thinking? Seemed like it; she was dating other guys and she didn't seem too excited to see him. Josie's Mother was still in his corner and had his picture on her end table. His friends seemed to be veering toward other interests, one being in an apprenticeship program, one going to school and had joined the Marine Corp Reserve, and one that nobody knew where he was or what he was doing. The girls found jobs or went on to further their education. Everyone had seemed to have changed; their interests and activities were different; the time seemed to pass extremely fast.

Loren met Bobby L. at the airport for the long flight to the west coast; Loren's older Brother transported him to the airport. One other guy from their company, who was a race car driver, was going with them also. Loren told his Brother that the word on the guy's wife was that she was loose, and she might make a play for him. When Loren called home prior to shipping out, his Brother told him she, in fact, invited him home for coffee. Loren said, "That is why I never made any commitments. I didn't need that kind of stuff cluttering up my mind and getting me off the business at hand."

Before shipping out they went through more interviews, took out insurance and designating the beneficiary, and got another series of shots. The Medic knew what he was doing this time. They had orientations and introduced them to what to expect from the people in Korea, a little about their culture, and warned of what to watch out for; after all, it was a dangerous place. As he absorbed this kind of information, he would squeeze the little rubber ball harder and harder. They were allowed more free time and they went off base when they got a chance and looked around. About a week passed and finally they boarded the ship; an old Merchant Marine Ship, The Jeffers. The Army band stood on the dock and played to the tune of 'I wonder who's kissing her now?', as they boarded. They took their gear down to the area they were assigned and then went back up to the top deck and stood at the rail and watched until the process was completed. You could read the faces and tell the ones that had lovers they were leaving and wondering if they would ever see them again, or if they would be there, if, and when, they should return; those that made the big commitment. Was that a good decision? Good thinking?

There were work details on the ship and Loren lucked out by getting in the galley. He learned how to fix scrambled eggs from powdered eggs out of a can. You mix with water, dump into a huge round bottom vat, slosh it up on the sides of the vat, and as they dry, you scrape off the dried eggs from the sides, and that is your scrambled eggs. Some guys had to hand-peel tubs of potatoes for each meal. One day they had potatoes three meals; now that was a lot of peeling. There was an Air Force Unit that was assigned to the hold of the ship and they got seasick and puked all over the place. The ocean wasn't very rough; there were white caps but no storms or huge waves. The last day some Corporal came up and handed Loren a broom and ordered him to sweep the deck. The idiot made the king size mistake. He didn't know that Loren was an expert at getting out of work. He didn't take names and then went off somewhere else; Loren leaned the broom against the bulkhead, snuck up to the top deck and disappeared into the crowd. He had visions of grandeur when he pulled off a coup like that. He said, "That Corporal will make a good officer someday, but not today." After many days bobbing up and down on the ocean, they reached their destination. There were a lot of troops on that ship and it seemed like forever for all the non-coms to gather the ones that were their responsibility, and disembark.

NORTH
KOREA
126°E
128°E
Pyongyang
Korea
Bay
Yellow
Sea
Sea
of
Japan
Korea Strait
Western Channel
Eastern Channel
Demarkation Line
38°N
36°N
34°N
Seoul
Inch'ŏn
Suwŏn
Osan
Ch'unch'ŏn
Hongch'ŏn
Wŏnju
Chonan
Ch'ŏngju
Taejŏn
Chŏnju
Kwangju
Taegu
Pusan
Ulsan
P'ohang
Kangnŭng
Sokcho
Ulchin
Andong
Mokp'o
Yŏsu
Masan
Ch'angwŏn
Chinju
Tsushima
Izuhara
Shimonoseki
Kitakyushu
Ullŭng-do
Huksan-
Chedo
Chin-do
Cheju-haehyŏp
2014

CHAPTER 7

They offloaded in a single file from the ship with their duffel bags on their shoulders and responded when a smart-ass PFC called off their name from his manifest. He yelled out for them to follow him and they hiked for about a mile to the side of a large area where he told them to sit and wait until trucks would come and take them to the front. One guy asked where they were, and the PFC said they were close to Pusan, Korea. The guy then asked where they were going, and the dumb-ass said he didn't know but they would find out when they got there, if they didn't get killed first. That was a hell of a thing to say to a bunch of new guys who were already nervous; they could hear explosions in the distance, and that was unnerving in itself. They sat on their duffel bags and began waiting, as instructed; the PFC then left the area.

It was a very large area; like a tarmac of an airport with long air strips for aircraft. On the other side you could see a large tent with a red cross on top and it was obvious that it was a hospital unit. On the outside of the tent, it wasn't very clear, because of the distance, but it looked like a huge number of stretchers lined up with bodies on them. Trucks, helicopters, ambulances, and anything else that would carry a body were constantly moving in and unloading and immediately moving out again, probably to get another load of casualties or bodies. At one point the transportation ceased and it became quiet, but it allowed Loren's group to hear screaming, crying, and cursing from those lying on the stretchers. Loren got up and said, "I'm going over there." Bobby was surprised at this sudden decision and said, "You can't go over there. The trucks will be here any minute and if you're not here you could be in a heap of trouble." "I don't care!" Loren shouted back as he walked away. "No man should be left to die alone and, if I can ease his mind for just a moment, that's what I am going to do." He walked across the area and approached the bodies and it almost made him sick. There were limbs blown off, a lot of blood, raw flesh, and some badly burned. Some were yelling, "Oh God!" and some yelling, "Mama!" and some just cursing or screaming. A Corporal walked out of the tent and yelled, "Hey Private, what are you doing?" "I'm going to pray with these guys, so they know they are not alone and without God," he answered. "Well, pray for all those that are on the other side of that line because they are not going to make it. On this side of the line we are going to treat them and try to save them. We just don't have the capability to treat them all, so we just have to pick and choose; I'm sorry but that is just the way it is; go ahead and do your thing if you think it will help," he explained. Loren knelt between two stretchers. He looked at the dog tags of one guy and his name was Timothy. Timothy's left arm had been blown off, so Loren took him by the right hand. The other guy's name was John and it looked like he had a serious head wound. He could very weakly lift his eye lids. Loren said, "John if you can hear me take my hand. You guys are in bad shape and I am going to pray with you and ask God to have mercy on you and lead you into Heaven. Is that alright?" They both agreed, and Loren said, "I want you to try to repeat with me the 23rd psalm. Ok?" They motioned to the affirmative, so he began, "The Lord is my shepherd, I shall not want; He maketh me to lie down in green pastures; He leadeth me beside the still water; He restoreth my soul." John tried and weakly muttered for a bit and then Loren felt his hand go limp, and he knew he was gone. Timothy was following a little better, so Loren continued, "He leadeth me in the paths of righteousness for his name's sake. Yea, though I walk through the valley of the shadow of death, I will fear no evil; for thou art with me; thy rod and thy staff they comfort me. Thou preparest a table before me in the presence of mine enemies; Thou anointest my head with oil; my cup runneth over. Surely goodness and mercy shall follow me all the days of my life; and I will dwell in the house of the Lord forever. Amen! Are you still with me, Tim?" He shook his head indicating yes. Loren said, "I am now going to say a prayer to ask God to take you into Heaven and that you are sorry for all your sins." So, he began, "Lord God in Heaven, take the soul of Tim to be by your side in Heaven and forgive him of all his sins and transgressions on earth. Bless his family and loved ones and give them peace and comfort in their loss." Tim had a look of peace as he closed his eyes and he was gone. Loren had to fight back his emotions because he had never done anything like this in his entire life.

The smell of death was all around, and it was nauseating but this was a time to show strength and not weakness. Loren vowed to continue until the trucks came. After what seemed like an hour or so, while he was kneeling and praying, he realized a shadow had engulfed him. He stood up and turned around to see what made the shadow and saw two men standing there watching what he was doing. One was a full-bird Colonel and the other was a Major; he gave them the proper salute. The Colonel asked, "What is it you are doing here Private?" Loren stood tall and spoke direct, "I'm praying and reciting the 23rd psalm with these dying men because no man should be left to die alone. The Corporal said that the men on this side of that line were not going to get treatment and they were doomed to die. They were only going to treat those that had a chance to live. There were not enough facilities and staff to treat them all, so they had to make a choice of who lives. I ask him if I could help them die with dignity. He was gracious enough to allow me and wished me luck." The Major asked, "How many have you prayed with?" "I don't know," Loren replied, "it looks like 10 or 12 maybe." "What outfit are you with?" the Colonel asked. "I'm with that group of replacements across the area. We just got off the ship and are waiting for trucks to pick us up. I heard the screaming and crying and decided to come over and see if I could help out." The Colonel then asked, "Major, didn't you just lose an Assistant? Can you use a man like this?" "I think this man would be perfect," the Major answered. "Would you be interested in being a Chaplain's Assistant?" directing his question to Loren. "Sir, I would be honored to be able to be of assistance to our fighting forces and serving the Lord at the same time," Loren answered, trying not to show his exuberance at the idea. "I'll take it from here, Colonel," the Major replied. "What is your name and serial number, Private, and where did you take your basic training? What ship did you just come in on?" He wrote down all the information as Loren answered his questions. "I'm Major Mike

Malloy, more commonly called Father Mike, and I am one of several Chaplains. Are you Catholic, Whitson?" "No, I am not, Father Mike, I was baptized into the Church of Christ when I was a senior in high school," Loren answered, not knowing if this was going to ruin this great opportunity. "That's not a problem," the Major responded, "in fact, I welcome having a protestant in the group." Then the Major directed, "Whitson, see that Jeep sitting over in front of the hospital tent with the Chaplain's insignia on it? Go get it and drive over to your group and load your gear and come back and pick me up. We need to get to our camp before dark." Loren drove over to get his duffel bag and Bobby was very curious, "What's going on, Loren?" "I'm leaving you boys," he replied. "I'm going to be a Chaplain's Assistant." He got into the Jeep with a big grin on his face, not rubbing it in but to show his joy with the idea. One guy yelled out, "You lucky bastard. You brown nosed your way into that didn't ya?" Loren just brushed that off and started the motor of the Jeep. "I wish you all luck and maybe we'll run into each other again," he yelled as he drove away.

CHAPTER 8

They drove for several hours because the going was slow. They drove past some rice patties in the low ground, where locals were working with their water buffalo, and then they entered some of the poorest terrain imaginable, hills, rocks, burned out villages, bombed buildings, and as they would proceed further, they would pass dead bodies of North Korean soldiers that were the result of recent actions. People were out digging burial trenches and dragging the bodies to the trenches. The results of battles were obvious as they traveled. Loren asked, "How could anybody want to fight over this God forsaken country?" The Major responded, "It's all about politics and control. The north wants to rule over the south and do things their way, which is the Communist way. The Russians are helping the north, so we are helping the south to keep the Communist out. People on both sides die in the process uselessly."

The camp was certainly not a glamorous place. It was a temporary setup of various size tents and guards manning foxholes and trenches with machine guns and mortars around the perimeter of a large cleared area. About 100 yards out from the guard posts was barbed wire strung to slow down any attack from the enemy forces. About 250 feet beyond the wire was a wooded area. The camp was constructed to be moved in a moment's notice, either to escape the Koreans or move up to be closer to the allied forces. Inside was the Chaplain's tent, large enough to hold a prayer service and living quarters for the Chaplain and his staff. There was a hospital tent used to perform as first responders for any casualties and housed two full time Nurses and, at times, a visiting Doctor. Unit Medics worked in coordination with the Nurses. There was a mess tent that fed the normal occupants of the camp and any troops that were on duty there. There were three well qualified cooks that alternated their time, but most of the dirty work was done by troops on KP duty. There were tents to house a certain number of troops assigned to the camp. They had to share the bunks depending who was on duty and who wasn't. Guard duty was just like in the states, two hours on and four hours off. There was a community shower tent with a partition separating the males from the females. Since there were no running water available, large barrels were set up overhead and filled with water. It had holes in the bottom which allowed the water to run out when the showering person pulled a chain unblocking the holes. Conserving the water was a must for obvious reasons. Most of the troops would jump into a river or a creek or a pool whenever they got a chance. The latrine tent was positioned next to the shower tent. Tanks holding the waste would occasionally be changed and contents of the full ones burned. The motor pool tent was on the far edge in the back.

Father Mike sat Loren down for a talk. He first introduced him to Rollie Roland, the Chaplain's Orderly, "Rollie does various tasks, mostly leg work for the Chaplain's office and tries to keep things organized and on schedule. The most important thing in your position as Chaplain's Assistant requires a rank of Corporal, which will give you a little more authority than the ordinary unit soldier, in case you should need to pull rank; so, at your first opportunity, pick up some Corporal stripes and sew them on your uniforms. That will put a little more money in your pocket, too. You have the run of the camp, but your main duty will be to administer to the casualties. If a call comes in that there has been action close by and there are casualties, try to get there and lend assistance, representing the Chaplain's office. You have the use of my Jeep if, and whenever, you should want to run up to the front lines. You will work closely with the medical tent when a casualty comes in; make a beeline over there and do whatever you can to assist. If anything comes up or you have any questions, I am always available, so don't hesitate. I suggest the first thing you do is go over and meet the Nurses. And by the way, the Nurses keep a list of supplies or anything you might need, and they send it in with their truck, which goes regularly to the rear area and the driver will go to the big PX, if you should need anything. You might toss them a couple packs of cigarettes for their trouble, or something they may want, or need."

Loren walked slowly toward the medical tent, being observant and familiarizing himself of everything around him. Arriving at the tent and entering the opening, there were two Nurses, both Lieutenants, sitting at a table. He whipped off a snappy salute and standing at attention spoke sharply, "I'm Private Loren Whitson, the new Chaplain's Assistant, and Father Mike suggested that I come over and introduce myself. He said I was to work closely with the medical tent."

"At ease, Private, sit down and have a cup of coffee with us. We make the best coffee in the Army. Oh, and you don't have to salute us if you are working with us. I'm Evelyn and this is Barbara." Evelyn had brown hair and brown eyes and a few freckles. She had an average build and her teeth shone bright when she smiled, a rather attractive woman. Barbara had muddy blonde hair and gray eyes. She had a trim waste and an overall great build. She had a beautiful, sweet smile. They both looked to be in their low to mid-twenties. Loren relaxed and sat in a chair at the table and Evelyn asked, "How do you like your coffee? Cream? Sugar?" "I don't need sugar. I'm sweet enough," he responded, and that lightened the mood. "Yeah, we can see that!" Barbara answered back, with a slight chuckle. "Where are you from Whitson?" That is the standard inquiry throughout the military when people meet for the first time. "I'm from the beautiful state of Ohio," Loren answered, "how about you ladies?" "Evelyn is from Minnesota," Barbara said, "and there is a Marine Lieutenant that stops in every chance he gets. He went to the same high school as she did, and I think he uses that as an excuse to come in to see her." "That gives us a lot to talk about, people we know, places where we went. He was a couple years ahead of me and we never really knew each other then," Evelyn said apologetically. "Why not?" Loren asked. "That helps break the ice, and who knows, it may lead to something more serious later. Where you from Barbara?" "I'm from Connersville, Indiana," she replied. "I know where that is," Loren said. "My Brother lives in Terra Haute. I dated student Nurses that studied in a big hospital in Cincinnati," Loren said. "Did you get your RN from college or from studying in hospitals?" "We both went to college," Evelyn responded.

Just then a loud voice was heard from outside, "Coming in; got a wounded man here," and two soldiers entered holding the casualty up with support under both arms. "Bring him in and put him on this cot," Barbara instructed. "He has a bullet in each leg and one in the chest," one said. "We'll take it from here," Evelyn replied, "you two can go." Loren stood off to one side, staying out of the way. The way those two Nurses set about their work was masterful. One removed his boots and cartridge belt, which held his side arm, extra clips, slicker, and bayonet, while the other took the patient's vitals. They each grabbed a pair of scissors and started cutting off the pant legs. One grabbed a syringe and injected a shot of morphine to lessen the pain. The patient was moaning and flaying his arms but began to calm down after the morphine started to kick in. They sponged the blood off the legs and applied a local anesthetic at each bullet hole. "We can get the bullets out of the legs but the one in his chest is going to require surgery. I hope he can hang on 'till morning and we can send him to the rear where they have good Doctors," Evelyn explained, as they went about removing the bullets. "We're not set up for that level of treatment." "What are his chances?" Loren asked as he observed the entire proceeding." Barbara looked at him and slowly shook her head indicating not a chance. "He's lost too much blood. Even a transfusion wouldn't help because he is bleeding internally, and it would only delay the inevitable."

The treatment room was divided from other areas by hanging canvases. One area was the so-called lounging area where the folding table, with the coffee pot, sat in the middle of the space and chairs were positioned around the table; then the treatment area; and then the private area where the Nurses slept and took care of their personal needs. The treatment area had four folding, height adjustable cots, a wall locker, a folding cabinet for their supplies, and several floor lamps. A lot of thought was put into the setup. It was obvious it was designed to be mobile, torn down and moved in a moment's notice. The same can be said for the entire camp. Occasionally they were required to move to areas where they were most needed and be closer to the action.

After the Nurses finished wrapping the wounds, they stood and gave a big sigh. "That's pretty much all we can do," Barbara said. Loren then asked, "Do you mind if I can try talking to him?" "Go ahead! I don't know how much he will understand but give it a shot," Evelyn said, and then they both stood back. Loren looked at his dog tags and read his name. "Frank, my name is Loren and I am with the Chaplain's office. Can you hear me?" He shook his head to the affirmative, and then Loren said, "Frank, you are badly injured. Do you believe in God?" Frank moved his lips but was not understandable. Then Loren continued, "I want to talk to you about God while you still have time. I want you to repeat after me the 23rd Psalm. Can you try to do that?" His lips moved again so Loren knew he could still be heard. "The Lord is my shepherd, I shall not want. He maketh me to lie down in green pastures; He leadeth me beside still waters. He restoreth my soul; He leadeth me in the paths of righteousness for His name sake. Can you still hear me, Frank?" He moved his lips to where it was understood he said, "Yes!" "I want to continue, Frank. Can you hang on and follow me?" Loren asked. Again, "Yes!" Loren continued and completed the Psalm. Frank's lips moved at every interval, so Loren knew he understood. "Now, Frank I want to say a prayer. Listen and you can pray along with me if you want to." Loren took Frank by the hand holding it between his and bowing his head, "Dear God in Heaven. Frank may have committed sins in his life but now he has repented and is sorry for his sins. Judge him for what he has done tonight. He has accepted you and is ready to be by your side in Heaven, if you will only bless him and have mercy upon him. He has given his all for mankind and deserves your just reward. Bless his family and loved ones who will grieve when they hear of his passing. Give them the strength in their forthcoming sadness and let them be at peace knowing he has joined you in Heaven. In your precious and gracious Holy Name, I pray, dear God. Amen! and Amen!" Loren had given his all, laid Frank's hand onto his chest, and stood, a little weak kneed. He held onto the edge of the cot as he turned around, and Evelyn took him by the arm to steady him. The two Nurses had stood behind Loren and listened intently to all he had to say. "How long you been doing this sort of thing?" Barbara asked. "Just since I got off the boat," Loren answered. "I guess one day." Then Evelyn said, "I've never heard or seen anything like it. You certainly have a calling." They went back and sat at the table and Evelyn said, "I better make some fresh coffee. Barbara, you better get some sleep. I'll stay up and watch." "No!" Loren said. "You both are droopy eyed; you both need to go and get some rest and I'll stay here and keep an eye on things. If anything happens, I'll call ya." "Well, your Mother would be proud of you tonight," Barbara said. "Holy smoke!" Loren exclaimed. "I need to write my Mom and let her know I got here alright. Do you have some paper and a pencil? I'll just sit right here and write while you two rest." "That's mighty nice of you ...what do they call you?" Evelyn asked. "I don't care what they call me," Loren said, "as long as they call me for supper." "What did you say your name was, Whitson? Do they call you Whit?" "That's it," Barbara added. "You have wit and your name starts with Whit, so from now on we will call you 'Wit'. You have a problem with that?" "No!" Loren said. "And I'll call you ladies Babs and Ev, except when there's an officer around." "Very good," Barbara said. Evelyn laid down some paper and a pencil and an envelope. Then Loren happened to think and said, "I can't give my Mom my address because I don't have one yet. You ladies go on and hit the sack. I'll be right here drinking your best coffee in the Army."

Dear Mom,

Just want to let you know I got here alright. The boat ride wasn't bad. I worked in the galley and learned how to make scrambled eggs from powder out of a can. They weren't bad, but they could have been better if I had some of your good biscuits and gravy to go with them. We docked at Pusan, South Korea and while waiting for trucks to pick us up and take us to the front, the Chaplain, Major Mike Molloy, came upon me praying with some of the badly wounded casualties that were at the nearby hospital tent. He stood and observed for a while and then, with a suggestion from a full-bird Colonel, selected me to be his new Chaplain's Assistant, since his old one rotated back home. The Lord works in mysterious ways, doesn't he? We drove through some of the most desolate and depressing areas I had ever seen. It had been bombed and badly burned and there was very little left. We drove to our outpost, which is more like a tent city. There are no buildings here, only tents. Father Mike told me my primary duty would be to work closely with the hospital tent or I should say, treatment tent. I figure it's all tents because it must be mobile and be ready to move in a moment's notice. There are two Nurses assigned to the treatment tent and they said occasionally a Doctor comes in. Any serious cases are transported to the large hospital tent in the rear area. The two Nurses are both Lieutenants, but they said I didn't have to salute them, if no officers were around. They welcomed me and claimed their coffee is the best in the Army. I'm sitting at their table in their tent and drinking the best coffee while I write this to you. Mail hasn't caught up with me yet and don't get antsy if you don't get a lot. I don't have an address yet, so I can't tell you where to write. There's no post office here. A truck makes a regular run to the rear where they take care of the mail and buy anything we may want. By the way, the Nurses nicknamed me, 'Wit'. I guess it's because I threw out a couple of my witty sayings and because our last name starts with Whit. The best news is I have been promoted to corporal. Father Mike says it goes with the job in case I should have to pull rank. I should be able to send you a little more money now. I'm going to be busy so don't worry if you don't get a lot of mail. I'll send my address in the next letter.

Love ya and tell all hello
Loren (Wit)

CHAPTER 9

About the time Loren finished his letter and addressed the envelope, he was startled by loud horns or bugles blowing. "What the heck?" he exclaimed, not knowing what was happening. One of the Nurses came out and said, "It must be 10:00 o'clock. The North Koreans start blowing horns to keep us awake. I guess they figure if we don't sleep, we'll be too tired to fight the next day." "How long does it last?" Loren asked inquisitively. "Oh, it'll go on for hours. I think they play records over a loud-speaker," she said. "Do you ever get used to it or does it just keep you awake?" he continued. "We have ear plugs, so it doesn't bother us too bad," she answered. "Can you go back to sleep, now?" he asked. "We usually can," she answered. "I'll check on Frank and then I'm going back to bed. When you get extremely tired, you can sleep through anything. We really appreciate you keeping watch and giving us a break." She checked on Frank and thought he was about the same and went back into her quarters. The blaring horns blew till about 2:00 or 3:00 in the morning. Loren was starting to really get irritated. "They won this round," he muttered.

"I'll go out there and get them bastards." He started squeezing his little rubber ball harder and harder, both hands.

The next morning the two Nurses came out yawning and stretching and they found Loren (Wit) had dozed off and his head was resting on his arms on the table. One of them went in and checked on Frank. Wit rose up and asked, "How's he doing?" "He passed during the night," Evelyn said. "We kinda thought he would. The truck will be leaving soon, and they will check in with us before they go. They'll load his body and get our list. Do you have anything to go on the list you think you might want?" "I mainly want to mail my letter and get some Corporal stripes, and I better get a couple Chaplains' pins," he replied. "How can I get them sewed on?" "We have a couple Korean ladies that come outside the fence and pick up our laundry and they can sew anything you want," Babs explained, "just give them something for their trouble, cigarettes or chewing tobacco. You can give them candy bars if you have any." "I better add cigarettes to the list," Wit said, as an afterthought. "Does the driver buy the stuff and I pay him back?" "You might give him some money before he goes," Evelyn said. "He usually buys stuff while he is there and, half the time, he's broke."

"If I may be so bold to ask," Wit questioned. "What will you do with Frank's stuff, like his boots and his cartridge belt?" "We just throw them on the truck," Babs said. "I don't know what the driver does with them; he probably sells 'em. Do you want 'em?" "Let me look at the size of the boots," Wit said, "if they are my size, I could use 'em. My old combat boots are about shot. We had to burn the rawhide tuft off them to get a shine on 'em and my toes are about to break through the tops; and I definitely need that .45 automatic sidearm. I don't have any way to defend myself. Father Mike said there's a carbine in the Jeep, but I think I might need more than that." The boots were his size and in real good shape. Frank must not have been in Korea long enough to mess them up. "Put the stuff under my bunk," Ev said, "and let's go get some breakfast. We need to make a quick stop at the latrine first. It's on the way." "I'll buy!" Wit said jokingly. "Sure, you will," Babs said, as they walked out of the tent toward the mess tent. The ladies introduced Wit to the cook, and they filled their mess kits and sat down at a foldable type table. When the troops came in, they filled their mess kits and left. The normal trays were not used for obvious reasons. They would just add to the stuff that had to be packed when they moved. There was a little lull and the cook came over and sat down with them to get better acquainted. After they ate, Wit said, "Ladies, it's been nice breaking bread with ya, but I need to go try to get a little shut eye; I'll stop in later." He went back and picked up Frank's equipment and went to the Chaplain's tent. Rollie was shining Father Mike's boots and Wit asked, "What ya take to shine my boots?" He had them tied together by their strings and laid them on his bunk. "I'll shine 'em for ya; throw 'em over here," Rollie replied. Wit dropped them at Rollie's feet and threw the cartridge belt under his bunk and said, "I've been up all night over at the medical tent and I need to try to take a little nap. If anything happens and somebody needs me, don't hesitate to wake me. Ok?" "Copy that," Rollie responded. Wit lay down and was out like a light in no time. It had been an awful long day since he arrived at the Pusan docks.

Wit awoke in mid-afternoon with a jerk. He must have been dreaming. He looked around; he found himself to be alone. He sat on the edge of the bunk and was rubbing his eyes when Father Mike came in, and remarked, "I was pleased to hear what you did last night. You have been here a day and have won the respect of everybody in the camp. I'm proud of you." Wit just sat and looked at him in a stupor, not ready to talk. "Father Mike continued, "I've been doing this stuff for over 20 years and I've seen it all. Although what you did was commendable, you can't take to heart every case. You just do what you can, be satisfied that you did your best, and move on. You can't shoulder every hurt of all the cases. It'll get to you in time and drive you crazy. Do you understand what I'm saying?" "Yes sir, I do," Wit spoke up after he figured Father Mike was finished. "Sir, I wrote to my Mother and I couldn't give her my address. Is there anything special about it since we don't have a post office?" "I'll write it down for you," he answered. "I'll give you what it is now, but it may change if we relocate. Just keep reminding me; I don't always think about stuff like that."

Wit shaved and went to the shower tent and took a quick frigid shower. He got dressed and walked out to the perimeter in the direction of where the blaring horns were coming from. He stopped at a trench where two guys were manning a machine gun position, keeping guard. It was aimed out across the open area in the direction of the woods. They had about a half dozen hand grenades laying on the front edge of the trench. One said, "What ya say, Wit?" Boy, it didn't take long for that name to spread around camp. "Which direction are those horns that keep everybody up at night?" he asked. One guard said, "See that grassy knoll on the other side of the woods? It's somewhere beyond that." "How far would you guess that is?" Wit questioned further. "Why? Do you want to go out there?" the other guard said, half-jokingly. Wit stared out in that direction and was thinking out loud, "I'm gonna stick them horns up some Gook's ass." The two guards looked up at him smiling and one said, "Well good luck with that." "Do you have a pair of binoculars?" he queried. One guard said, "Yes," and handed them to Wit. Wit studied the terrain in detail past the barbed wire, through the woods, and up the grassy knoll. He knew it would look different at night, so he better identify anything that he could follow in the dark. He studied until he had a burned picture in his mind. He returned the binoculars and thanked the two guards and went back to see if the two Nurses were ready to eat and if he could join them. They said it had been an uneventful day and they spent their time arranging their supplies to be ready when something did happen; and, of course, they drank their share of the coffee. He spotted a black scarf hanging off a shelf, apparently left by a former casualty. He asked the Nurses if he could have it and they had no problem with him taking it. They had no idea why he wanted it and never bothered to ask.

Wit went about making himself ready to go silence the horns. He put on his face paint, the black scarf around his head, strapped his weapons against his body and made sure there was nothing loose that could make a sound or that could easily snag on a bush or a limb. He checked to make sure he had his compass. He wore his old combat boots rather than his newly acquired ones because he was used to the old ones. He made a mental note to get a pair of tennis shoes. They would be more suitable to move quietly and swiftly, unless it was muddy or cold and snowy. He walked out to the perimeter and was quite an unusual figure for the guards in the trench. He was lucky there was a bright moon that night to make it easier to see for his first mission. "Are there patrols out?" he asked. "Yes, they go out every night and scout around for information," one guard answered. "You're not planning to go out there are ya?" "Where is the opening in the wire?" Wit continued. "Walk toward that largest tree straight ahead," he directed, "and remember it when you come back, if you come back. You can get lost or killed out there if you don't know what you're doing. It's crawling with Gooks." "What is the password?" Wit asked, not to be deterred from his plan. He had trained months for this and felt confident and determined he was able to pull it off. "Uncle Charlie," the guard responded, knowing it was futile to try and talk Wit out of going. "I should be back in an hour or so," Wit commented, and he crouched down as low as he could and moved rapidly toward the wire. He saw where the break was and went through and made a beeline for the large tree. It was easy to see against the skyline. He worked his way through the woods and reached the opening on the other side. He stood in the shadow of a tree and observed for a while to be sure it was safe to continue. Satisfied it was safe, he proceeded up the grassy knoll, and reaching the crest, he paused to scan the area ahead. This was not visible when he first studied the terrain that afternoon. Suddenly he was scared out of his boots when the horns started blaring. He went to his knees and muttered, "What the hell am I doing here? I've never killed anyone in my life, or even thought about it, and here I am going to become an instant assassin." It took a moment to gather and talk himself into proceeding on. "It's now or never," he muttered, took a deep breath and cautiously advanced toward the horns, or whatever they were. Reaching the crest of the rise he lay low and there it was, out of the sight of anyone from the direction of tent city. He saw three Gooks just lounging around. A record player was sitting on a table and the horn blowing was a recording.

There were speakers affixed to the top of a tall tree. Two of the Gooks seemed to be sacked out and the third had moved over to one side to take a dump. He had his pants down and his back was toward Wit. The sound of the horns muffled his sound as he moved swiftly toward the poor guy trying to take a shit. He remembered what Sgt. Sands had said, "Yank the head back and rip out the throat in one quick simultaneous move." He did just exactly that. He thought, "Boy that was easy, and now for the other two." He moved swiftly and quietly as possible to the one nearest him; the horns drowned out any sounds; he was lying on his side. It was a little more awkward getting into the proper position, but he had the throat ripped out and the Gook never uttered a sound. The third guy never moved and was unaware of what was happening. He probably never thought it possible for anyone to sneak up on them, more especially one man. He had that man's throat torn out in short order. He stood up and admired his work; he felt like thumping his chest and give out a Tarzan's yell. Then he went over to the record player, ripped the needle arm off, and stuck it into the mouth and down the throat of one of the victims; he took a large rock and smashed the record player, making it virtually useless. It was now quiet. He dragged the other two Gooks together and wrapped the speaker wire around their necks and tied a square knot, like he learned years ago in the Boy Scouts. He knew there would be other Gooks that would become suspicious and arrive soon, so he had to get out of there and back to camp. He remembered the path he took and moved more swiftly going back. As he crossed the clearing toward the wire, He yelled out in a low tone, "Coming in!" He heard a voice from a guard, "Advance and be recognized!" As he got closer to the guard, the guard said in a low tone,

"Uncle!" Wit responded just above a whisper, "Charlie!" And he proceeded in. "It's nice not to hear those damn horns," One guard said. "Yeah, and now maybe we can get a little sleep tonight," another said. "I doubt we will hear them again, at least here. I sent them a message," Wit responded and started toward his tent. One guard commented, "Damn good job, man! What message?" "Fear! There's a new Sheriff in town!" Wit replied. Wit went back to his tent and removed his garb. He lay down on his bunk and, with no feeling of remorse, slept like a baby.

CHAPTER 10

After a restful night of sleep with no horns blaring, Wit arose early. He spotted his newly acquired boots and Rollie had spit-shined them and had them standing tall where Wit would spot them first thing. "Wow, Rollie, them's beautiful!" he said in an appreciative tone. He was feeling good after his first encounter with enemy soldiers the night before, and he said, "Come on, Rollie, and I'll buy your breakfast." "I think this is C-ration day," Rollie replied. "Oh, no!" Wit exclaimed. "I thought we got away from that stuff when we left basic. Well let's go and see what they are serving; I hope it's not corned-beef-hash." He put on his new shiny boots and strutted out of the tent. "We'll pass by the treatment tent and see if anything happened over there during the night," he added. They met the Nurses coming out and Wit said, "Let's go and see what kind of gourmet food they are serving; I'll buy." As they walked to the mess tent Ev said, "We never had any patients last night and slept like babies, without any blaring horns. I wonder what happened; did the Gooks move into a new area?" Wit never commented and just smiled and thought, "If they only knew."

Entering the mess tent, Wit quickly scanned the food and commented, "We ought to be able to find something in here that we can eat." They sat at a table, proceeded to eat, and the cook came over, "Appreciate the job you did last night, Wit. I don't know how you did it but I'm glad you did. We all slept good and peaceful for a change." The Nurses looked at each other and then at Wit, and Babs questioned, "And just what did you do, Wit?" "He went out last night and took out them Gooks that blow them horns," the cook followed. The Nurses just sat with their eyes wide and their mouths open. "Our Wit went out of the camp last night and killed enemy soldiers?" Ev directed. "That's right," the cook said. The word had spread throughout the camp like a wildfire. Every soldier that came in for his food just stared at Wit. And then the two guards that were in the trench the previous night came in and walked close to Wit's table and commented, "Sleep good last night, Wit?" "Yeah, like my Pappy used to say, 'Sound as a dollar'," he replied. That really put a puzzled look on the Nurses' faces. He was now a man among men, and they respected him for what he had done. Then Wit said, breaking the spell, "Ladies, we need to devise a way we can cook our own breakfast on C-ration day. Is there some way we can get a little cook stove and set it up in your tent, or just outside your tent?" "We can ask the driver if they sell anything like that in the PX," Ev answered. "And," Babs followed, "we'll need some fuel, and we'll need to figure out what we will cook and have the driver bring it the day before C-ration day. And we'll need a skillet or pan of some kind." It seemed like they were in favor of the idea, and then Rollie asked, "If they will allow it, Wit, do you know how to cook?" "Of course," Wit came back, "you won't survive in a large family if you don't learn how to fix your own food." They finished eating and went back to their respective tents.

Wit got out some clean underwear and was preparing to go to the shower tent when Father Mike came in and sat down on the bunk across from Wit's. "I heard what you did last night," he began. "I give you credit. You got guts, but I think you are playing with fire. If I do my job, I am required to file a complete detailed report. The top-brass are going to be asking a lot of questions because this was not a routine operation." "Please do not file a report, Major," Wit begged. "What I did, I did on my own. I was trained for it and I will probably continue to do it again, because it will help the cause. Making a big issue of it will not serve any purpose …. Sir!" "What I understand from the scouting patrol was their throats were torn out," the Major responded. "Where did you say you took your basic training?" "Camp Breckinridge, Kentucky," Wit answered. "Did you ever run into a Sergeant there named 'Sands'? The Major continued. "I knew Sands and that was his trademark. I don't think it is known how many he assassinated, but it was a huge number, and everyone benefitted from each and every one of them." "Yes," Wit answered, "he was my mentor, and as far as I know, I was his only pupil. I put in a lot of time practicing and training to perfect the skill and I had to try it, and I would like to continue. It's like a ball player training for months to play on a team, and the disappointment if he never gets in a game. Once he gets in the game and finds out he is good at it, he can't wait for the next game. So, I ask you, no I beg you, please do not forbid me from doing my part. I'll guarantee it will not interfere with my duties as a Chaplain's Assistant." "Ok, Wit," the Major said, after a moment of thought. The Major stared at Wit for a moment and finally asked, like a priest would do, "Do you feel guilty or have any remorse for what you did?" "No, Father, I feel great. I went out there scared to death. I thought once I was going to wet my pants, but those horns blasting gave me the courage to go through with it. I still almost turned back but, thinking of all the days and nights I trained to do this, I persisted. After I did it and seeing what I had done, I felt like thumping my chest and giving off a Tarzan yell. It gave me such a rush of excitement, I felt like it was something I need to do more of," he explained. The Chaplain looked at him and it ran through his mind, "How could this sweet natured and caring man, who prays with all the love and emotion for his dying comrades go out and brutally assassinate a person like a wild animal and show absolutely no emotion." He quietly sat and shook his head slowly in wonderment and stated, "Your secret is good with me, but if it looks like it's becoming a problem, then we'll be forced to make adjustments."

The next day a patrol brought in a couple North Korean (NK) prisoners. In questioning them, the interrogators learned that a huge numbers of NK troops were moving north after the allied troops whipped the hell out of them. They also revealed there was fear among their troops that the allies had turned loose demons to tear out the throats of their fellow soldiers. The interrogators never put much stock in that because they felt the NKs were a superstitious bunch. It became evident that while the allies were in such a hurry to get to the capital of North Korea, Pyongyang, they were bypassing a lot of the stragglers and these stragglers joined together and made groups of guerrilla teams that ambushed at every opportunity. Some even dressed as civilians and it was impossible to tell the NKs from the South Koreans (ROK). From time to time a wounded soldier or marine would be brought into the medical tent, but the numbers were diminishing. Wit made regular trips out in the country and became an expert of the surrounding territory. The more he went and the more he killed, the more confident and skilled he became. If a patrol came in with an injury due to an ambush and reported an ambush location, Wit made a point to visit that location and annihilate the few troublemakers. There were usually only two or three at the most, but his attacks were effective because of the element of surprise; thus more '*fear*' was generated among the Gooks.

One of the members of a patrol told Wit the exact location of one of the ambushes. Knowing that area, he set out that night to clean it up. Getting to the spot, there were no signs of anyone still there, so he ventured farther out, further than he normally went. Remembering the reports, the larger elements of the NK army were moving north, he ran across old abandoned defenses like entrenchments, pillboxes, and barbed wire, he also became aware that the NK forces had mined the area as they left. As he came across a mine, he would push a stick in the ground to mark it, rip off a strip of his handkerchief and tie it to the stick, so any friendly that came by would be made aware that there was danger there. As he topped a hill, he got a whiff of smoke and began to take a more precautionary look around. He spotted a wisp coming through the top of a small grove of trees that ran along a small creek. He inched his way down for a closer look and spotted a Russian version of an American Jeep parked next to the woods. He inched further and saw two NK soldiers sitting near a small fire and each leaning against his respective tree. They were about 20 feet apart. Getting closer he noticed one was an officer, so the other was probably his driver. They appeared to have dozed off, probably after a long day of searching the area for information. He thought to himself, as he planned his attack, "I can get that officer, but that driver will surely wake up and I may have to fight him." He loosened his knife in its scabbard, leapt on that officer like a cat on a mouse, had his throat torn out, and the officer lay wiggling on the ground holding his torn neck, not having the slightest idea of what just happened. The driver did wake up and, realizing what was happening, jumped to his feet and charged. As luck would have it, he stumbled over a tree root growing above the ground and fell to the ground, a step away from Wit's feet. Realizing his advantage, Wit was on him as soon as he hit the ground and buried his knife into his back twice. He turned him over and stabbed him in the heart. "The Lord sure works in mysterious ways," he muttered to himself, relieved. "Thanks Bobby L. for all the practice we did in the barracks, what now seems like a hundred years ago." He approached the vehicle to search for information and, finding a brief case and looking through it, he found some maps and, what seemed to be valuable documents. He didn't know Korean, so he had no idea what they said. He found a Russian made pair of binoculars in a case that had lettering on it that looked Russian. "I can use this," he thought, "I'll keep it as a souvenir for the fruits of my labor." While working his way back to camp, Wit heard a sound like a moan. He cautiously waited and listened. He heard it again, so he moved silently toward the sound and found a wounded soldier lying in tall grass. He was conscious but unable to walk on his own. "What happened, friend?" Wit asked. "Several of us were captured and, trying to make a break for it, we killed the Gooks holding us, but the other guys were killed, and I was the only one that lived, and now I am trying to go for help. I'm lost and too weak to go on," he explained. "Can you walk if I help you?" Wit asked. "I think so," he replied. Wit gave him a drink from his canteen and they worked their way back to camp and went straight to the treatment tent. The Nurses were still puzzled about Wit going out in the middle of the night into the Gook country. Wit then went directly to see Father Mike and handed him the briefcase. It was late, and the Chaplain was sitting up waiting for him; like a parent waiting for a teenage child that had gone out on their first date. "You're later than usual," he said, taking the brief case from Wit's hand. "What happened? How did you get these?" Wit sat down on his bunk, exhausted, and with his head down looking at the floor. He relayed the entire sequence of events from beginning to end. The Chaplain listened intently, like he was listening to a confession. Loren held the Major in the highest esteem, and it didn't bother him in the least to speak in personal terms. He was more than a boss and Loren considered him his best friend and he certainly was an understanding friend. Thinking Loren had remorse for his deeds, he questioned, "Did it bother you to kill that man in a fight to the death?" the Major asked, trying to get inside Loren. "Not at all," Loren replied, lifting his head and then straightening up. "That was my first hand to hand fight, and I did exactly what I had spent many hours practicing, but I also had a little luck. The Lord surely does work in mysterious ways; like the old saying goes 'dead men tell no tales'. If you are asked where you got this briefcase, just tell them one of the GIs brought them back from a patrol. That will not be a lie. Don't forget to re-emphasize that area is heavily mined." Wit roughly removed his camouflage, lay down on his bunk and was soon off to dreamland. The Major let him sleep in because of the great job he did. What he didn't know was the Major was keeping a written record of all Loren's exploits in case an accounting should come up, but he kept it totally secret, not revealing any part of it to any person.

CHAPTER 11

Following weeks of planning, the upper echelon made the decision the outpost should be moved northward to be closer and more supportive of the fighting forces. The big teardown began, it was likened to a circus tearing down to move to another city. Each item was tagged in accordance to the tent in which it belonged. Tables and chairs were folded and stacked, and small items were packed into foot lockers. A convoy of trucks, with .50 Cal machine guns mounted on top, arrived and each was parked at the tent from which it was to be loaded. Everyone knew exactly what his task was and set about getting it done. The newer troops were assigned to help at specified tents and instructed as to their function. Personnel, associated with the truck with their equipment, rode in the back of that truck. Point men scouted about a mile ahead and then a high-ranking officer led the procession about a 100-yards ahead in his Jeep as the lesser officers followed in their respective Jeeps armed with light machine guns and their gunners. The combat troops hiked with their field packs and weapons alongside the vehicles to provide protection in case of an unexpected attack.

It was mostly cross country traveling with no improved roads so they used the cart trails and tank tracks and animal paths that were going in their direction, and only the trails that were created by the battles that were fought earlier, so the going was slow. They stopped often for the troops to rest. The new outpost was about 30 miles north of the old one. It was well scouted and most ideal because the terrain was almost identical to the old one, which made positioning of the tents, paraphernalia, security, and perimeter less troublesome.

The relocation was the smoothest operation Wit had seen since he'd been a part of the military. The setup went as smoothly as the teardown; Wit had no idea where they were. He helped setup the Chaplain's tent which was quite large. Church services were held in the large area and chairs were provided for all that attended. "Major, where in Korea, are we now?" he asked. They walked over to a large map the Major had just hung and he pointed to their location. He explained, "We are about 60 miles east of Seoul, the capital of South Korea, and about 35 miles west of the east coast of the Sea of Japan, and about 20 miles south of the 38th parallel. The fighting forces have just crossed the 38th parallel pushing the North Koreans, from what I've been told. Mail will continue having difficulty finding us, so I'll need to get new mailing addresses for you and Rollie."

After the Chaplain's tent had been set up to Father Mike's satisfaction, Wit went to the treatment tent to see if the Nurses needed any help and he was hankering for a good cup of coffee. Babs was sitting at the table and Ev came out from their personal area carrying a change of clothes under her arm and her towel, soap, and shampoo. She was on her way to the shower tent. "Sit down, Wit, and rest your bones," Babs directed. Ev walked out and Babs then said, "Ev found out her Marine friend is in the area and she wants to clean up and welcome him with open arms; smelling good." "Is that becoming serious?" Wit asked. "I think so," Babs said. "She won't admit it, but I can tell the way she gets excited, they're saying more than just hello." "How about you, Babs, you have anyone waiting to hold and squeeze ya?" Wit asked with an ornery grin. "Nah, I've never found anybody that really showed any interest in me," she explained. "Oh, I dated in high school some and dated in college some but there was nothing there. After college and getting my Nursing Degree, I went directly into the Army to do my part for Old Glory." "I can't understand that!" Wit replied. "I know a few boys from Indiana and they certainly are always willing to date and party." "What about you, Wit, you got a honey back home?" she asked. "Oh no," he followed, "I had this one girl and we were really close, almost sewed together at the hip, but she wanted a commitment when I left, and I refused. I didn't want to lose focus on what I am supposed to do, get careless and get hurt in the process. When I had a furlough between basic and shipping out, I went to visit her. Her mother loved me and welcomed me like she always did but she was dating other guys and didn't seem to care one way or another if I was shipping out or not; I didn't get worked up over it. And you haven't had anybody hitting on you?" "Nobody wants to hit on me," she responded, staring out the tent opening. "I swear, Babs," he continued, "can I speak freely?" "Of course," she said, looking at him wondering what he was about to say. He began, "I think you are drop dead gorgeous, really well built, have a very sweet personality, very smart, and are damn good at what you do. Any man would be blessed to have a woman like you." She seemed pleased at what he was saying, in fact flattered, and looked directly into his eyes and said, "What about you, Wit? Would you feel blessed to have me?" He seemed a little excited, like she just gave him an opening, and replied, "If I had you, I would treat you like a Queen; I would be honored to walk down any street anywhere with you on my arm and I would love you so completely, you would think you were walking on air." She didn't say anything but just stared affectionately into his eyes. He got up from his chair, walked around the table, put his fingers under her chin and lifted her head, and kissed her long and firmly on those beautiful lips. She didn't resist and all she could say, after a moment was, "Whew!" He walked back around the table, sat down, and said, "Now there is a downside to all this, as beautiful as you are, there are a lot of guys that are going to flirt and hit on you; I am a very jealous individual. Some women feel flattered by a little flirting from other guys and if you responded to that, I would go out of my skull. Josie was very beautiful and like that. Guys would hit on her even when we were together, they would hit on her and she never objected to it." "Well how do you know I would respond like you say?" she asked. "I don't know," he came back. "I'm just saying that, if you ended up with a guy like me, and you did react to that stuff, that could create a lot of serious problems. On the other hand, if you had a couple babies and tacked on a few pounds in the process that would reduce the amount of hitting....... It wouldn't be in the cards for me anyhow because you deserve the best and I don't have anything to offer you; I'm just a factory worker. When I get out, I plan to go to college on the GI bill, and that'll take 4 or 5 years, and I wouldn't be able to support a wife, especially if she should have a child." "Nurses make good money," she offered, "and I could bring in enough money to pay the bills." She was speaking like they were to become an item; she apparently took in all he was saying as a positive and the kiss sealed it. Just then Ev walked in and asked, "What are you all talking about?" Then Wit made a quick come back, like, if you say something in jest, nobody would believe you, "We were just talking about getting married and having babies, buying a farm, and growing sweet taters as long as your arm." "Right!" Ev remarked, and faded into the dressing area. Just then the Marine Lieutenant walked in and Wit jumped to his feet and saluted. "At ease, soldier," the Lieutenant responded, "I'll be in the area the rest of the day." Babs introduced them, and the Marine said, "I've been hearing about you, Wit. They say you represent the Chaplain's office very honorably. That's good! I hope I never need you." "Me too, Lieutenant," he responded, "but you never know in these trying times. I try to do what I can; the best I can." He didn't act like he knew about Wit's off base exploits and that was just fine with Wit. Ev emerged from the dressing area and was looking good. She had her hair fixed a little different and made her a lot more attractive. "Lieutenant Barbara?" Wit injected. "Are you interested in going to get some chow and leave these Minnesotans to talk about old times?" "Yes," she answered, "I'd be honored to walk down the street on your arm." The other two had no idea to what she was referring.

They entered the mess tent and one of the cooks had a radio playing. "Mighty nice music," Wit remarked. "I didn't know a radio would play out here in the boondocks." The cook responded, "Since we moved closer to Seoul, we are now able to get a better reception." A lady broadcaster came on and said, "Why don't you fighting men lay down your arms and stop fighting and go home to your families and visit your corner soda shop?" "That's Seoul City Sue," the cook commented. "She's what they call a Propaganda Broadcaster. Everybody laughs but we enjoy the music." [Note: Seoul City Sue was born Anne Wallis in Lawrence County, Arkansas. She went to Korea as a Southern Methodist Missionary and married a Korean Staffer. She broadcast out of Seoul, the capital of South Korea, and when the North Koreans moved north, she started broadcasting out of Pyongyang, the capital of North Korea. In 1969, she was accused of being a South Korean double-agent and shot. Former propaganda broadcasters from World War 2 were Axis Sally from Germany and Tokyo Rose from Japan.]

Babs and Wit did become an item, but nobody was aware, except Ev. She became suspicious and confronted Babs and Babs finally admitted it was happening. Ev admitted that she and Lt. Chris Clark were getting serious, so when he showed up, Babs would manage to have somewhere to go. And when Wit showed up, a lot of the time, Ev would disappear. She couldn't go out every time because Wit was in, at some point, every day. The fact was they were falling seriously in love.

CHAPTER 12

Wit went to the perimeter to study the new terrain. He stopped at the trench, took out his recently acquired binoculars and started scanning the distance. This was all new territory and he had to get familiar with it. One guard spotted the new eyeglass and asked, "Hey Wit, where did you get those beautiful binoculars?" "Oh, some Gook must have dropped them, and I picked 'em up. I think they are Russian made," he answered. He handed them to the guard and said, "Check 'em out." The guard looked through them, adjusting to different targets and asked, "What ya take for 'em?" "They are not for sale. I just recently got 'em and haven't really tried 'em out. If I decide to sell them, I'll let you know," Wit responded. After he studied the territory, he put them back into the case, and walked back to his tent to try to get in a little nap. He wanted to be rested when he went out later that night.

Wit prepared himself for his night out, including his compass. He had to get acquainted with the area like the old area. He headed straight north thinking that was the obvious direction the NK forces had gone. He had moved cautiously for about an hour seeing no sign of life of any kind. He stopped at the crest of small hill and, with his binoculars he scanned the area in the ravine on the other side. He watched as about 40 or 50 enemy soldiers scrambled up the far hill leaving the area. Looking down at the place where they started from, he spotted a small shack, about 15 feet square, with three remaining soldiers sitting outside around a small camp stove approximately 25 feet from the shack. He inched his way down to get a closer look and then rested in a clump of brush to see if more troops were coming in. He focused his binoculars on the three soldiers and was surprised at what he saw. Those guys wore a soft cap with a big red star on the front of it. "Are they Russians?" he muttered to himself. He concentrated his focus a little better on the faces of the soldiers and muttered, "No, they are Chinese. What are they doing this far south? What is in that shack they are supposedly guarding? I've got to find out what's in that shack. I'll have to kill those three quietly, so the other troops don't hear anything and come back in force." Two lay down on blankets and the third sat against the shack like he was taking first watch. Wit circled around to the rear of the shack and came up the side and peeked around at the guard. The guard had his head down like he was resting, which would be taboo in the US Army; guard duty was serious business. He looked over at the two lying down, seeing that they haven't moved, convinced him they were asleep. He took one giant step around the corner, reaching the guard, had his throat ripped out in a flash, and laying him down to keep him quiet. He crept over and ripped the throat out of one of the other two and was about to grab the second when he raised up facing him with a shocked look on his face. Wit had moved toward him and with the speed of a wild animal, grabbed his head and twisting it simultaneously while grabbing the throat and ripping it out. He hurried over and slowly eased open the door to the shack, not knowing if there might be more Gooks inside. It was dark, and there was a candle burning on one side of the room and he could see there were four figures sitting on the floor tied up and gagged. He pulled out the gags and asked, "Americans?" They answered, "Yes, Marines. Who are you?" "I'm Corporal Whitson and I'm a Chaplain's Assistant," as he cut loose their ties. "Are you all alright? Can you move?" One answered, "We have one who took some shrapnel and he'll need help." There was one huge Marine who mouthed off in a loud voice, "We're being saved by an Army Preacher? What kind of war is this? We're Marines." "Shhh, you-dumb ass," Wit directed, "you want to get us all killed? The place is crawling with Chinese. Go out and search the ones outside and see if they have any documents on 'em; get their weapons and hurry; we got to get out of here." The big Marine must have outweighed Wit by 100 pounds. "We're not taking orders from a little Army guy," he shouted. "Can you guys shut this big idiot's mouth up before he gets us killed?" Wit asked, getting a little pissed off. They searched the Chinese and all they had for weapons were clubs and one Marine said, "They are just kids. They can't be over 14 or 15 years old. How did you kill them? Their throats are missing." "They're soldiers ain't they?" Wit answered. "Then they die like soldiers. I don't care how old they are, they would kill you if they had the chance." Wit took the candle and held it up to get the best look possible at the Marine's injuries. He had learned from the Nurses how to treat minor injuries and stated, "I don't think he has anything life threatening, but he needs treatment as soon as we can get it." "We owe you, Chaplain," one Marine said. "Good!" Wit said. "You can pay me back by not revealing what you have seen here tonight. Swear it!" "We swear it. No one will ever hear it from our lips," one Marine said. "I'm not swearing anything soldier boy. You're trying to make us Marines look bad?" the big guy shouted above a whisper. Wit took charge and directed, "Let's get going; we have to hurry; I'll lead the way; move as quietly and swiftly as possible. You two helping the injured guy, try to keep moving and, if you need a break, let me know and we'll try to find a place with cover. We're about three miles from my base camp and I'll take you there; they have good Nurses on duty." "We're going to an Army camp?" the big man said. "Any of you two know how to quiet this big dumb ass down?" Wit asked, frustrated. "No, he was that way all through boot camp and everybody thought it was funny," one said. "I just hope we get there before he calls attention to where we are," Wit commented. "When they find us gone from that place where you were held, they will be on us like stink on shit." They climbed a small hill with Wit about 50 yards in the lead making sure it was clear before proceeding. When he reached the crest, there was a burnt tree standing there and he broke off a stub of a branch. He was planning to quiet that big mouth Marine, so he waited until they caught up to him and he swung the limb and busted the side of the big ass's head. He staggered, and the blood started running down his face and onto his utilities. He just stood in a daze and Wit told the other three to keep moving that the big ass would catch up; he quietly staggered the rest of the way. When they reached the perimeter, Wit yelled, "Coming in!" The guard responded with, "Advance and be recognized!" They moved in closer and the guard said in a low tone the first word of the password and when Wit responded with the second word; he allowed them to enter. Wit took them directly to the treatment tent and called the Nurses for help. Ev's Marine Lieutenant was there trying to make out with Ev and when he saw the two injured Marines, he asked, "What happened?" Wit directed them to take the Marine with the shrapnel into the treatment room and he told the Nurses, "This man has shrapnel. I think there is only one piece that is large and deep, but the others don't look too bad." The big-mouth Marine PFC sat down and just held his bloodied head. "What happened to him?" the Lieutenant asked. "I busted him up the side of the head with a tree limb to make him shut his big mouth," Wit answered. "What?" Clark shouted. "I'll have you court-martialed for this; you can count on it. Where did you find these men?" One of the other Marines spoke up, "Sir, we were held prisoners by the Chinese and this Chaplain saved us. If it wasn't for him, we would have been heading north to a POW camp somewhere." "Where is your unit Marine?" the officer questioned, trying to act tough. "We were fighting our way toward Seoul and got cutoff somehow and the next thing we knew we were surrounded by Chinese." "And what were you doing out there, Wit?" the Lieutenant continued. "Just happened to be roaming around and finding them? Wit responded. "Is that your job?" the officer persisted. "My job is to assist soldiers wherever they are and look for casualties," Wit answered. It seemed like a light went on in the Nurses' heads and Ev said, "So that's how you quieted the horns when you first arrived; we had no idea." Babs started wiping the blood from the big Marine's head; it wasn't as bad as it seemed with all the blood. "We'll keep you two here for the night and find somewhere for you to stay tomorrow," Ev remarked. "And just remember, Corporal, you are going on report," the Lieutenant insisted, not letting it drop. He was trying to be a bad guy to impress the Nurses and the other Marines. Then Wit responded very mildly and calmly, "And when you do, Lieutenant, make sure you describe how you got your Marines back, so they can fight another day. With your leave, Lieutenant, I am going to sack out." He walked out leaving the officer speechless.

He walked toward the Chaplain's tent and he was proud of himself for not blowing up in front of the officer, especially the Nurses. It was very late and when he entered the tent, he found Rollie and the Major had retired for the night. Rollie, hearing Wit shuffling around, turned over in his bunk. "Rollie, are you awake?" Wit asked. "Yeah, what ya need?" he answered. "I want you to wake up the Major. It's very important," he continued. "Can it wait until morning?" Rollie asked. "I hate to bother the Major at this hour." "Wake him!" Wit said. "I have to talk to him now. Tomorrow may be too late." Rollie went in and awoke the Major and explained what Wit had said and that it wouldn't wait. The Major staggered out, still in a stupor, asked, "What's so all fired important?" "Sorry to bother you, Father, but I have a problem and I must discuss it with you," Wit responded with a sense of urgency in his voice. The Major, aware of Wit's extra-curricular activities, had a feeling it was related and wanted to keep it private, said, "It's a nice night, let's go for a walk and we can talk." Wit described his night in the finest detail, not leaving out anything, and he added, "My biggest concern is that Marine officer digging into my business and maybe killing a good thing." "Don't worry about that shave-tail officer," Father Mike replied, "once he thinks about you saving his fellow Marines, he'll let it slide. He was just trying to impress the Nurses and the other Marines. If he should try to make an issue of it, I'll take care of it." "Do you know him, Major?" Wit asked. "He comes in often to see Lieutenant Evelyn. They got a little something going." "No!" The Major responded. "But if he comes often, I'm sure our paths will cross." "Another thing, Father," "I don't want them to think that I run and tell, especially Babs. I'm not a stool pigeon," he replied. "Babs?" he asked. "Yes, I would kinda like to get something going with her, if I can," he explained. "I know the rank and file are not supposed to fraternize with the officers but, with this world full of turmoil, what's the harm in making a couple people happy?" "Your secret is good with me," he replied, "as far as that Marine goes, I think you can forget about it. I'm proud of you for rescuing those four Marines." He later added the event in his secret historical record he had been keeping on Loren, which is starting to get thick.

CHAPTER 13

The next morning Wit went to see if the Nurses were ready to eat breakfast and he wanted to check on the injured Marines. The Nurses acted slightly different toward him now, knowing what he was doing in his spare time; well, almost knew. The fact was, they were sweeter and more accommodating. They seemed pleased to be seen with him and were getting more men greeting them with pleasant smiles and friendly hellos. The cook even offered to fix him special food if he wanted it. He got the feeling that if the Marine officer wanted to start some shit, he was going to have to deal with the whole US Army in the tent city. The two Marines were moved to one of the troop's tents until they recovered. They were expected to be mobile in a few days. He approached the Marine who had the shrapnel wounds and asked how he was doing, and he thanked Wit repeatedly and expressed his gratitude, "If there is anything, I can ever do for you, don't hesitate to ask. I'll be there for ya." "Glad to do it, Marine; if you don't mind, I would like to pray with you and thank God for being there at the right time," Wit commented. "I'm glad too; are you Catholic?" he asked. "No, but we have the same God and it doesn't matter which avenue we take, we will still go to the same Heaven, if we accept him and live by his rules," Wit replied. "Are you willing to accept that?" "Yes!" he answered. Wit took him by the hand and gripped it firmly, "Lord God in heaven, master of all the universe, we thank you for your mercy and allowing us to be free from certain disaster and bringing us back safely to recover. Heal our wounds and make us whole so we may serve you whole heartedly. Be with us always as we pray, oh God, and keep us safe. Amen and Amen!" The Marine seemed pleased and yet puzzled, as he thought, "Who is this guy who slaughters the enemy and then prays to our God for mercy? Is he a prophet of sorts? I feel blessed to know him." The Nurses were standing behind Wit in awe of this kind and sweet man who was also a brave warrior. Then Wit added with a grin, "I can have Father Mike come over to see you, if you like. He may ask you when you had your last confession." "No, Corporal!" he quickly came back. "I think we're good for now." Everybody chuckled at that.

Wit then went over to the other bunk and visited with the big mouth Marine, "How are you doing, Big Guy?" he asked cheerfully. "You got a little headache? Sorry I had to do that to ya, but I had to get you back safely, so you could fight another day." "I had to have five stitches," he said mildly, "but I should be ok in a couple days." He then spoke softly to disguise his boisterous persona, "Soldier boy, if you ever need anything, don't hesitate to call. I don't care where I am, I'll come running." "I get the feeling you are a big-time football player," Wit followed. "When I get out, I'm gonna play for some big university," he said, "and then I'm gonna play in the NFL." "Then I'll tell you what you can do for me," Wit continued, "when you get to the NFL and you smear some poor little quarterback, stand over him and point your finger in his face. I'll probably be watching, and I'll know that's the big dumb ass Marine I once knew." He tried to laugh but was hurting. "Do you want me to say a little prayer with you?" Wit whispered; knowing he didn't because he didn't want to smear his image. "No! I think I'm good," he whispered back. "Well, you 'sea-going-bellhop' (referring to the marine blue dress uniform), I got to go and save some more Marines. Semper Fi," Wit laughed as he walked out. "I hear ya soldier Preacher," he yelled out as Wit and the Nurses left the tent to go for breakfast. When they entered the mess tent, they were met with applause to show their appreciation for what Wit and the Nurses did to save and treat the marines. Lieutenant Clark was already there and had breakfast and was finishing his coffee. He observed the greeting they all got, and his face turned a little red from embarrassment.

Wit and the Nurses went back to the treatment tent. Ev went to the latrine and while she was gone, Wit took Babs by the hand, pulled her behind the curtain, and kissed her gently and sweetly. She seemed to melt in his arms. They subsequently did this at every opportunity for the next couple months. She said, "You know I only have three months left and then I rotate home; my time is about up." "Yeah and I got four months left," he followed. "You going to come and look me up when we get home?" she asked. "You better believe it!" he answered. "And I'll never let you out of my sight. I'll love you till the end of time."

Ev and Babs formed sort of a pact. When the Marine Lieutenant showed up, he and Ev would go to the personal area and neck and smooch and make love and Babs would stand guard out front, in case someone came. When Babs and Wit had an opportunity, they would go to the personal area, neck and smooch, and Ev would stand guard. This was the norm for about a month. Then one day, when Wit showed up, he didn't see Babs. "Where's Babs?" he asked. "She's in the personal area waiting for ya," Ev answered. He went through the curtain and there stood Babs in a bath robe. He stood wondering what was going on. She then dropped the bath robe to the floor and all he could do was gaze at her. He had imagined what she would look like nude, like all males do. She was more than he imagined, she was an absolute goddess. She held out her hands, palms up, and said, "Well, you going to just stand there or are you going to do something?" He needed no more than that and had his clothes off in record time. He embraced her, holding her warm body against his and kissed her all over and rubbed her silky-smooth skin until he couldn't wait any longer. They were both breathing heavy as he lay her down on the bunk. He made love to her, and made love to her, and made love to her, and then they lay still embraced and out of breath. He said, "I could never love you more than I do right now. I just can't get enough of ya." She responded, "I will love you till the end of time and nothing or nobody will ever come between us." His reply was classic, "Till death do us part!" She commented softly, "Does that thing ever go down?" "What, WT?" he answered. "WT?" she asked. "Yeah, Wit's Torpedo. If I am with you, he rises to the occasion and is always ready." he answered. "When I leave, he goes down," Wit explained. "You named him? That's hilarious, ha, ha, ha!" she responded. "Tell him to do me one more time before you leave, and then I got to get back to work. When all this is over, and we go home, we can make love night and day, and we can start our own little family with little Wits running around fighting and screaming." He responded, "You mean '*half-wits*'." Wit did her as she asked and left the tent and Babs came out and said to Ev, "I am so in love with that guy I can hardly stand it. I've never felt like this before." "I know," Ev replied, "I can see it in your eyes. I hope when all this mess is over, it all works out for ya. He is a great guy and I don't think you could ever do any better."

A few days later, the Major commanded Wit to come and view the area map; pointing at the map, he said, "There's a battle going on over here about 10 miles to the west, at Hill 241. Take a run over there and see if you can be of any assistance. Don't forget your helmet and make sure you got plenty of ammo in case you run into something you have to fight your way out of." When he arrived, he found the Marines and the NK Army regulars really going at it. It looked like the Marines were outnumbered by 3 to 1 and it was a grave situation. The noise was deafening; machine guns chattering; mortar shells and bombs exploding; the strong smell of cordite burning the nostrils; napalm burning the hillside; rifles blazing away; grenades being thrown; one of the two damaged NK tanks exploding; men on both sides screaming. While scanning the situation to see where he would do the most good, one of the machine gunners got hit and slumped over the gun. Wit threw several grenades as he ran to the machine gun, jumped in behind the gun, pulled the gunner to one side while another Marine jumped in beside him with an ammo can, and feeding the machine gun, Wit started spraying Gooks and they started dropping in large numbers. The battle raged for about another half hour and then the Gooks, thinking they were getting the worst of it, pulled back and stopped firing. Wit then went to the badly wounded and prayed with them until they died and then began helping the injured. The Marine Corpsman (In the Navy and Marines, medical personnel are called Corpsman. In the Army they are Medics; all doing the same job.) was overwhelmed. There were just too many, so Wit loaded several of the worst injured into his Jeep and took off for the treatment tent. One Sergeant was heard saying, "Who was that guy?" Another said, "I don't know but I'm glad he showed up." Another comment was, "He had a Chaplain's insignia on his helmet." Then Lt. Clark said proudly, "I know who he is. That's Wit Whitson, the Chaplain's Assistant over at the Army outpost." Wit got the men the treatment they needed in plenty of time to prevent permanent injury; just another entry in the Major's private record of Wit.

That wasn't the only time Wit was seen. Whenever there was a skirmish or battle within driving distance, he would show up and get involved, pray for the dying, and assisting the Corpsman, or Medics, and haul some casualties back for treatment. It was a standard routine and soon the Army and Marines alike would recognize him on sight and cheered when he left to go back to the outpost. They came to believe he had divine powers to do what he did time after time and come out unscathed. In between battles he would go out at night and assassinate a few unfortunate commie soldiers. Father Mike worried about him and prayed for him constantly and thanked God every time he returned unhurt and made the entry in his record book.

After a couple months of lover's bliss and, as they were making love, Rollie rushed in and asked Ev where he could find Wit. She said he should be back anytime and asked if anything was wrong. He was excited when he said, "The Major needs him in a hurry. He said it was urgent!" She said, "I'll send him over as soon as he arrives." He left then and started looking around the camp. Wit had heard the conversation and quickly dressed and double-timed to the Chaplain's tent. The Major met him coming in, "I've got an important mission for you!" He led Wit over to the large map on the wall and pointed to a spot on the map. "There is a huge battle taking place about 7 or 8 miles northwest of here. Take the Jeep and get out there as soon as you can and see if there is anything you can do to help. Make sure you have plenty of ammo for the M1 carbine and you better take your side arm. My radio call name is 'Holy Grail 1, and you are Holy Grail 2. Keep me informed of what's happening." Wit grabbed his helmet and ran for the Jeep, jumped in, started the engine, and was on his way in split second time. As he got closer to the battle, he could hear explosions and saw jet planes flying over dropping bombs and napalm. He reached the crest of a high hill, looked down into a huge valley, and exclaimed, "Holy Caramba! I have just found the Korean War." The noise was deafening; the smoke choking; the smell of cordite burning the nostrils; jet planes dropping napalm and strafing; artillery and mortars shells exploding; he saw thousands of Chinese troops charging down the opposite hill like a swarm of locusts, over-running the allied troops in the valley. Artillery and planes were killing them at an enormous rate, but they just kept coming. He took out his binoculars to get a better look. There were burning tanks and trucks and it appeared that there were very few allied troops left standing. Just then an Army Sergeant jumped into the Jeep, and remarked, "I'm the spotter for the artillery and the planes." He then turned the frequency knob on the radio and started talking to the artillery, "Shorten 50 meters and 50 meters to the right." He then switched the frequency again and talked to the aircraft, "Bomb the leading edge to slow 'em down. Keep coming!" He then switched back to the artillery, "Shorten 50 meters and fire for effect." Wit then switched the frequency and called, "Holy Grail 1, this is Holy Grail 2, over." He never got a response and tried it again, "Holy Grail 1, this is Holy Grail 2, over." "This is Holy Grail 1, go ahead Holy Grail 2," was the response. "Holy Grail 1, alert the entire camp. Thousands of Chinese troops have overrun the allied forces and are heading for our camp. They should be there in about an hour. I repeat, alert the entire camp and prepare for the worst. Call for reinforcements. I repeat, call for reinforcements." The Major did just that. He set off the alert alarm and everyone scrambled to their assigned positions. They ran to fox holes and trenches and carried all the ammunition they could get their hands on. The artillery and planes kept pounding the Chinese Army and they were killing them at an alarming rate, but they just kept coming. They were rapidly approaching the Jeep and the Sergeant said, "Let's get the hell out of here." Just then a small jet had been hit and was approaching to make a crash landing very close to where the Jeep was sitting. Wit said, "Wait and see if that pilot is still alive." The Sergeant started to panic and said, "I'm taking the Jeep and getting out of here." Wit responded, sternly, "You take that Jeep and it will be the last thing you will do today," and he pointed his carbine in his direction. "You wouldn't shoot a fella American, would ya?" the Sergeant questioned. "In a New York minute," Wit threatened. The plane came to rest, and the pilot managed to open the canopy and tumbled out on the ground, and he appeared to be hurt. Wit ordered, "Let's get him into the Jeep. You lift under his left arm and I'll lift under his right arm." The Sergeant didn't like it, but he agreed, because Wit held the carbine in his right hand, and he knew he would use it. Wit yelled for him to hold onto the pilot as he hit the accelerator and it seemed that he only hit the high spots of the rugged terrain on the way back to camp. As they entered an area with huge boulders all around, they started receiving rifle fire. A few hit the side of the Jeep and a couple went through the hood. The Sergeant got nicked in the shoulder and it knocked him over against Wit. "You alright?" Wit asked, as he stopped the Jeep beside a huge rock. "Yeah I'm ok, just nicked me." he answered. "Well, we got to get 'em," Wit demanded. "I think there are a couple of them in the crevice of those two rocks about 60 yards out. Take the pilot's handgun, and you go around to the left and I'll go around to the right. We have to hurry but don't get careless." They worked their way around just like they planned and spotted two NK soldiers squatting in between the rocks with their burp-guns on the ready. They seemed confused as to what happened to the Jeep; it went behind the big rock but never came back out. Wit had the Sergeant in view and signaled him to take the one closest to him and Wit would take the other. Wit wanted them to shoot simultaneously so they would get them both at the same time, otherwise one might try to sneak away; they didn't have time to go on a search because they had to get to the camp. Wit motioned with his fingers up and counted one, two, three, and they both fired three rounds each, killing them both together. They proceeded toward the camp, and arriving at the camp, he sped to the trench on the perimeter and ordered the Sergeant to get out and man one of the machine guns. He then raced to the treatment tent and Babs came out and helped him get the pilot inside. The camp started taking artillery and mortar fire; it seemed like the Gooks had them zeroed in. He raced to the perimeter trench and a few of the machine gunners had been hit. He jumped into the trench and pulled a man away from the machine gun and started firing. Down next to the hit gunner sat a Private hugging the ground and holding his ears. Wit yelled, "Are you hit?" "No!" he stuttered. "I'm scared." Wit responded, "You want to be scared or do you want to be dead? When the ammo trucks pull up, start carrying ammo boxes to all the machine guns, and don't waste any time." The Private worked hard and did as Wit ordered. The enemy combatants came charging in, and the machine gunners shot and killed them as fast as they came into range. Another machine gunner was hit, and Wit yelled at the Private, "Did you train on a machine gun in basic?" "No!" he answered. Wit called him, "Come 're!" and he pulled him down behind a gun. "Watch what I do, and you can do the same." The Private got a crash course in Gook killing. Bodies were piling up and the ones that kept coming started tripping over them and slowed down their advance, which made shooting them a lot easier. The reinforcements he called for showed up and they joined in the killing. It was a slaughter and the piles of bodies that lay dead was impossible to count. Wit patted the Private on the back and said, "Now you are a combat soldier!" The Private just smiled and had calmed down completely. The Chinese then pulled back and ran the other direction, and soon all was quiet. Wit looked around and saw a lot of tents flattened and then he saw the treatment tent was destroyed. He ran as fast as he could to see if the Nurses were alright. He met Ev at the entrance of what was left of the tent, and she stopped him, "Don't go in there, Wit. It's not pretty." "How's Babs?" he asked nervously. "She's gone," Ev followed. "She never had a chance." Wit was shocked, "Oh, no," and he was speechless for a moment. "She was scheduled to go home next month." Then Ev said, "Yes, and to have your baby; she was pregnant. She never told you because she didn't want you to lose focus and get yourself killed." This made Wit sick. He went out to a big tree near the perimeter, sat down, and cried. In the meantime, the reinforcement unit must have been made up of some old vets that fought the Japs; they learned that when the Japs pretended to be dead, they would rise-up and shoot the Americans in the back so, they proceeded to go through the bodies and shoot any of them that were suspect of still being alive. Also, the Engineering Unit came in with a bulldozer and backhoe and began digging a huge cavity in the ground beyond the barbed wire and close to the wooded area to push the dead bodies into a mass grave. The sounds of the shooting and digging went on for hours. Wit was oblivious of all this as he cried the rest of that day until it started getting dark, and then his heartbreak turned into rage.

CHAPTER 14

It was almost like a switch had been thrown. He stood up, walked over to his tent, suited up, and slowly walked out of the camp, in an enraged state. The entire area for miles was crawling with Communist troops. Before now it has been war between nations; now it's personal; woe to the poor bastard that gets in his path. Somebody was going to pay for what he lost. For the next couple months, Wit stayed out in the wilds and never went back into camp. He slaughtered countless numbers of Communist troops, ripping out their throats, and leaving paths of death. He ate off the land whatever he could find and drank from the streams. He learned a few words of Korean and, if he should engage a citizen, he would ask, and they gladly accommodated him with something to eat and offered a little rice wine. He never touched alcohol in his life, but he learned to tolerate it to keep going. He roamed the area and killed without hesitation and left death in his wake. It was almost impossible to ascertain the total number of victims because they were so spread out over the area, but it was determined it was in the hundreds. Patrols from the camp that went out to scout around, came back and the reports said the same thing, "Large numbers found with their throats ripped out." Some prisoners that were captured called the area, 'THE AREA OF DEATH', and it was the home of a *demon* that killed anyone that entered. They refused to enter regardless of whether they were ordered or not. They would simply skirt around it.

Father Mike issued an order to all patrols that went out, "If you should run across Corporal Loren 'Wit' Whitson, tell him it is crucial that he come in immediately. This is an order." About a week later a patrol was out scouting and they ran across Wit just sitting and resting against a tree, cold and miserable. There were signs winter was setting in. "Hi guys," he said in a soft tired voice. Normally he saw all the patrols that were out, but they never spotted him. "Are you Corporal Whitson?" the patrol leader asked. "Yes!" he answered. "We have been issued an order by the Chaplain to inform you that you are to come in immediately. He said it was crucial and most important." "Tell him I'll be coming in," Wit responded, totally exhausted.

A couple days later, Wit appeared at the perimeter. The guards knew who he was and never bothered to ask for a password, even though he wouldn't know it anyway because he had been gone so long. They watched quietly as he entered the camp, slowly shuffling his feet along and paying no attention to anyone. What a bedraggled figure he was; unshaven, shaggy hair, shivering from the cold, dirty and bloodied clothes. Father Mike came out and embraced him for all to see, "Glad you are back! Come on in." The Major had come to think of Wit as a son and admired him immensely. They went in and sat down, and the Major said, "You look like hell. Are you alright?" "Yes, I guess," Wit responded, "I've been having sharp pains in my stomach, but I'll be ok." "It's probably because you haven't had a good meal or a good night's sleep," the Major remarked. "Rollie, run over to the mess tent and see if you can round up something for Wit to eat; meat, potatoes, milk, and anything not too spicy. Wit, you only have about a month to go before you rotate out of here. I can't let you go home looking like you do. You've lost a lot of weight and your eyes are sunk in your head, and you are just a pure mess. We must get you back in shape with the time you have left. I am ordering you not to leave the camp for the rest of your tour. Did the patrol tell you it was crucial that you come in?" "Yes, they did," he responded. The Major continued, "First, I never had a chance to congratulate you for your part in saving this camp during the attack a couple of months ago. The Sergeant that came in with you filled us in on taking out the two NKs and saving the jet pilot. He said he was impressed and would like to have you in his outfit. We would all have been annihilated, if you hadn't given us the warning. I'm putting you in for a medal." "No, please don't," Wit insisted, "I don't want to call attention to anything I have done, and you know how some will dig into it to get the gory details." "Alright, if that's the way you want it, but I am promoting you to Sergeant," Father Mike added. "Why?" Wit argued. "I don't have much time left and I'll be rotating out of here." "It will give you many advantages; more money, more opportunities if you should decide to stay in, less hassle to do dirty details, eating better food in the NCO mess hall, more authority; just to name a few. Get some Sergeant stripes the first chance you get .... What you have done, however, an ordinary person doesn't do unless he has been possessed, and, I hate to say it, Wit, I think you have a **'*demon*'** dwelling inside you that has control over you. I hope I'm wrong! I think we can beat this thing with a lot of prayer and trust in the Lord.

It'll be up to you, though. That brings me to the crucial point. Our top officials are scheduled to start negotiations with the Communist leaders for a ceasefire, not a peace treaty, but just to stop fighting and killing. They are aware of the fear you have put into the enemy with your exploits and they want to avoid the subject to keep it from becoming a point that will cause the commies to walk and not talk. The commies don't seem to be in favor of the negotiations, so it won't take much for them to call it off. If it should be brought up, our people are going to play dumb and swear they know nothing about it, and it is just a superstition among their forces. So, your activities have caused them to classify it as a secret of the highest order and it cannot be declassified for 40 years; it has been ordered to be sealed by the President," the Major explained. "40 years? Wit responded. "I won't even live that long." "That's exactly what they are figuring," the Major concluded, "and you are to swear to never speak of it. Ever! Of course, you can if you should be around when it is declassified. So, stick around camp and do your job and get yourself back in shape with the time you have left." As the Chaplain was walking out, he turned and said sadly, "Oh, uh, Wit, I want to tell you how sorry I am about the loss of Babs. I know how attached you two were. We lost a lot of good people that day and would have lost a lot more if it hadn't been for you." Rollie returned and Wit minced at the food but managed to get most of it down. He then lay down and fell into a deep sleep, dreaming about his most pleasant times with Babs and how beautiful she really was; his heart was broken because he knew he would never lay eyes on her again.

CHAPTER 15

Wit arose early. He asked Rollie to give him a close haircut and cut off most of the beard, so he could shave the rest of it. He rolled up a change of clothes, tucked them under his arm, and headed to the shower tent. It was different because the old one had been demolished in the attack, but he was able to get the job done, shivering from the cold. He applied all the smell good stuff and was now presentable. On his way to the mess tent, he stopped at the treatment tent. He had to muster up a lot of nerve to enter because the one he was used to seeing wasn't ever going to be there again. Ev and a new Nurse Lieutenant were sitting at the table. Ev introduced her as Lieutenant Christine and told her that Wit was the Chaplain's Assistant, the one she was always talking about. Wit mentioned that they agreed not to be formal unless officers were present but, if she had a problem continuing that practice, he would honor her wishes. She had no problem. "Then I'll call you Christy if that's alright," he said. She agreed that was fine with her. The tent was replaced after the old one was destroyed. It was similar in function, but the layout was slightly different.

Christy was a real carrot top. She had bright red hair, a lot of freckles, and bright blue eyes. She had an average build but well endowed, which was the first feature that met the eye when anyone met her. "Have you ladies had breakfast yet?" Wit asked. "No, we were waiting for the rush to settle down, so let's go," Ev said. When they entered the mess tent, all eyes were on Wit. He felt it but tried not to pay any attention. They had a different cook than when he was here before; as well as a lot of new faces from new troops. The cook came over and introduced himself and expressed how happy he was to be acquainted with the Chaplain's Assistant, being careful not to mention being acquainted to a true live hero. Falling back to the standard question that is most often asked in the military, Wit asked, "So, where you from Christy?" She answered, "I'm from Nebraska." "Oh, a corn-fed gal, eh?" Wit mentioned with a smile. "Yes, born and bred," she bragged. "I got my Nursing Degree from the University of Nebraska and went straight into the Army to do my share." "Good for you," Wit replied, "I'm proud of ya. With that and a nickel you can get a cup of coffee. I'm a factory worker from Ohio. I couldn't afford to go to college, but I could afford the draft. I never had a Father; we were just too poor." "Then Christy said, "Now I can see why they call you Wit." "Just like my Hollywood hero, Jimmy Durante, always said, 'I got a million of 'em'." And then facing Ev he continued, "Well Ev, looks like I'm going to be in your hair for a while. I have a month left in my tour in Korea and I need to get myself adjusted, mentally and physically, to enter the real world again. For the rest of my life, I will never forget Babs and what little time we had together. They will probably assign me somewhere to help train new recruits to finish out my two years. I probably will be in often to get my fill of that great coffee, if that's alright with you ladies." "Wit," she said, "you will be welcome anytime. In fact, it would please me if you would spend most of your time with us while you are still here. Me and Babs were like Sisters and I miss her terribly, and I will never forget her and what she meant to me. I only have a couple months left myself." "Are you getting out then?" he asked. "Most likely!" she replied. "Me and that Marine just might get married and start a family in Minnesota. I think he might want to make a career out of it. It shouldn't be too bad after this one is over." "What do you hear from him?" Wit asked, with interest. "The last I heard, they were crossing the 38th parallel and fighting toward Pyongyang, the capital of North Korea," she answered, looking slightly nervous. "I'm sure he'll be fine," Wit responded, trying to assure her. "I hear a severe winter is settling in a couple hundred miles north of here. Is he anywhere that far up?" "No," she explained, "but he mentioned the fighting at the Chosin Reservoir was brutal because of the freezing weather, a lot of frost bite, weapons jamming, and running out of ammo, and temperatures almost unbearable. They call it the 'Frozen Chosin'. They stumble over the frozen Chinese bodies buried in the snow. Sounds bad! We're lucky it hasn't gotten anything like that here. I feel sorry for those guys." "Being from Minnesota, you ought to be used to this kind of weather," Wit added. "This is nothing compared to home," she noted.

 Strolling back to his tent, Wit spotted a familiar face walking across the open area." Hey, Howard," he yelled. The guy continued and Wit yelled again, "Hey Howard Wilson!" The guy turned around and with a startled look on his face, he yelled, "Loren! Loren Whitson. What the hell are you doing here?" "I'm assigned here. I'm the Chaplain's Assistant," Wit replied. "Well, I'll be damned," Howard commented, "how the hell are you? I haven't seen you since high school." "What are you doing with that Ranger patch on your shoulder, Howard?" Wit asked, being pleasantly surprised to see him. "What are you doing here in our little outpost?" "We were up at the Yalu River when tens of thousands of Chinese came rushing across the border. We fired with everything we had until our guns burned up or we ran out of ammo, and they just kept coming. When we saw we never had a chance and never had anything to fight with, we ran. I ran 80 miles in four days. There are just a small number of us left and we came upon this place," Howard explained. "How long you think you will be staying?" Wit asked. "I don't know! We'll probably pull out tomorrow as soon as we get something to eat and get a little rest," Howard continued. "I'll tell you what, Howard," Wit suggested, "I'll go with you to the mess tent and get you something to eat and then you can get a good shower and then I'll take you to my tent and you can catch up on some sleep. Ok?" "That sounds great," Howard agreed, "I can't remember when I last had a good meal and shower, and when I was able to sleep sound." "I'll need to fire up some generators to run some heaters," Wit added, "otherwise it will be a mighty cold shower." So, Wit proceeded to do what he promised, and while Howard was eating, Howard asked, "Have you seen any action, Loren?" "Oh, it gets a little exciting around here once in a while," Wit answered coyly. He didn't want to get into any specifics. "What do you hear from home?" Howard asked. "Mail doesn't catch up to me very often out here," Wit answered. "I don't know what happens to it. Everybody, except my Mom, has probably forgotten about me." When they arrived at the Chaplain's tent, Wit introduced Howard to Father Mike and explained they had gone all through school together. The next morning, Wit had breakfast with Howard, and invited the Nurses and introduced them. After they ate, Howard shook Wit's hand briskly, thanked him and they said their goodbyes, and promised they would hook up when they got back home, then the Ranger team assembled, and moved out. He mentioned to the Nurses that he was really surprised and pleased to see Howard, "He's a real good guy!"

CHAPTER 16

Most of the major fighting was moving north and there weren't many casualties coming in, and the outpost, for the most part, was taking it easy. One night while those in the Chaplain's tent was bedded down for the night, Christy showed up with a report that a casualty had been brought in and it looked bad and Ev asked her to go for Wit. He dressed as fast as he could and hurried over to the treatment tent. Father Mike, aware of the commotion, dressed and arrived only a moment later. The young soldier had strolled into a mine field and stepped on one and was torn up rather badly. Ev said she wasn't sure how long he was going to survive, and she felt he needed Wit's services. Wit looked at the soldier's dog tags to learn his name, so he could talk to him as a friend. He took him by the hand, "Joe, my name is Loren. You have been hurt pretty bad and it doesn't look good." Wit said. He had a shot of morphine for the pain but was able to communicate weakly, at best. "Mom? Mom?" he uttered. "Listen to me Joe, do you believe in God?" Wit asked. "No, I'm an Atheist," he muttered. "Does your Mom believe in God, Joe?" Wit questioned. "Yes, she goes to church every Sunday," he replied. "But you didn't go because you didn't think you needed that stuff, right? And you thought it was interfering with your good times, partying and drinking?" Wit surmised. "Yes!" he said. Wit continued, "Well, Joe, it is time for you to start believing, if you expect to go to Heaven. I know you thought there was no such place as Heaven, but you can't go to your grave without taking a chance there isn't a Heaven. I'll call it good insurance and it doesn't cost you anything, but you can't afford to take a chance. God is keeping you alive long enough for you to confess your sins and ask for forgiveness. Your Mom will be pleased to know that you finally saw the error of your ways and started to believe. Do you understand?" "Yes!" he said weakly. "Are you ready now, Joe?" Wit questioned. "Yes!" he answered. Wit began, "I want you to repeat with me the 23rd Psalm and then I will say a prayer asking God to take you to be with him in Heaven, and someday you will meet your Mom there. She will be pleased to meet you there." Joe squeezed Wit's hand with his fading strength, and Wit continued, "Say what I say, Joe. The Lord is my shepherd, I shall not want." Joe repeated it. "He maketh me to lie down in green pastures; He leadeth me beside the still waters. He restoreth my soul; He leadeth me in the paths of righteousness for His name's sake. Yea, though I walk through the valley of the shadow of death, I will fear no evil; for Thou art with me; Thy rod and Thy staff they comfort me." The Nurses stood in back with Father Mike with their heads bowed and their hands folded. Father Mike turned and eased out of the tent and muttered to himself, "I think Wit is going to be alright." Wit continued, "Thou preparest a table before me in the presence of thine enemies; Thou anointest my head with oil; my cup runneth over. Surely goodness and mercy shall follow me all the days of my life; and I will dwell in the house of the Lord forever. Amen! This was written for guys like you, Joe. Do you now believe it? Are we ready to ask God to believe that you are sincere and ready to enter the kingdom of Heaven?" "Yes," he said, and he was fading fast. "Dear Father in Heaven. Accept the confessions of Joe and take him to be with you to be by your side in Heaven. Forgive and forget his past mistakes and give him the newness of life. Give this man your glorious blessing. Amen! and Amen!" Wit looked up and Joe had passed. He placed Joe's arms across his chest and struggled to stand up. He poured so much emotion into his blessing, he was wobbly. He turned around and the Nurses were standing there with tears in their eyes. Christy said, with emotion, "I never witnessed anything like that in my entire life. I would not have missed it for anything in the world." "Now, Christy, you see what I have been talking about," Ev said, referring to past conversations they have had about Wit.

Father Mike approached Wit and informed him that he had to go to the rear for a few days and he wanted Wit to preach the sermon in the church service on Sunday. "I never did anything like that before," Wit confessed nervously. "I think you'll do fine," Father said assuredly. "Pick your subject and post it so everyone will be notified as to what it will be." Rollie's tour was completed and he was hitching a ride to the rear with Father Mike. Wit shook his hand and wished him well. He also expressed his appreciation to Rollie for all that he had done for him since he arrived. Rollie was going to be hard to replace. He was a quiet and calm individual that did everything he was asked and never seemed to resent anything that was asked of him. Replacing him will be one of the Major's tasks while he was gone.

Wit thought long and hard and finally decided on a subject and posted it 'Go and sin no more'. Services will be conducted by Loren Whitson. When the word got out, most of the entire camp wanted to go to the Sunday services to show their support for the guy they felt had been blessed by the deity. They filled the tent and the overflow gathered outside in great numbers, standing in the weather, but they didn't seem to mind. Wit thanked them for coming and informed them of how nervous he was because he had never done this sort of thing before. Somebody yelled out, "Get 'er done, GI, we're behind ya." Wit began, "The Old Testament is filled with some of the baddest people you could ever imagine. They thought nothing of stoning someone to death or beheading them or sticking a sword through their heart or making a sacrifice of them by burning them or killing their babies, and on and on. Then a savior was born, and he came to be a light to the world, heal the sick, provide for the widows and orphans, and preach nothing but good and the newness of life for everyone. He and his disciples walked from town to town telling of the good news and people gathered in large numbers to hear his message. He was in one town, squatting down and drawing something in the dirt when a woman came running down the street and ran up to him. A loud and murderous crowd ran up with stones and rocks in their hands. 'Rabbi, this woman is a prostitute and she goes around town sleeping with anybody that will pay her a few coins and for this sin; we are going to stone her to death'. Jesus stood up and said, 'Let him who is without sin, cast the first stone'. The crowd became totally silent. They stood motionless for a moment and then each, one by one, dropped his stone and walked away. Then Jesus said, 'Woman, where are those that accuse you? Go and sin no more.' And she did. She never sinned again, and she followed him for the rest of his life. She was there when he was crucified on the cross and she was the first to go to his tomb to prepare his body for burial. He wasn't there, however, and she saw an angel sitting there. 'Where is my Lord'? she asked. The angel said, 'He is not here. Go and tell the others he has risen.' He said he was going to die on the cross and take all our sins with him. He left us with a clean slate but, if we sin after that, then it is up to us to be judged before we can enter the kingdom of heaven. In John 3:16 it says, 'For God so loved the world that he gave his only begotten son, and whosoever believeth on him, shall not perish but have everlasting life.' He gave his son to die for us on the cross, to take all our sins with him. The son said, 'Go and sin no more.' I say, go and sin no more and the gates of Heaven will be opened to you. Go and pray to the Lord and ask him to forgive you for whatever you may have done. You say you don't know how to pray? He was asked by one of his disciples, Teacher, teach us how to pray.' He said it is very simple and gave them the Lord's Prayer. So, join me in the Lord's Prayer: Our Father who art in heaven, hallowed be thy name. thy kingdom come; thine will be done, on earth as it tis in Heaven. Give us this day our daily bread and forgive us our trespasses as we forgive those who trespass against us. Lead us not into temptation but deliver us from evil for thine is the kingdom, power, and glory forever. Amen! Pray this prayer and then you may want to add anything that is on your mind, any concerns you may have, ask for a blessing for some friend or loved one, and above all, thank him for the blessings you have received. I guarantee he will hear each, and every prayer. Thank you for coming."

When the crowd dispersed, they were rather quiet, only speaking in low tones. When Father Mike returned, he received a lot of comments of the job that Wit had done, and the size of the congregation that showed up to hear his message. He had given them a lot to think about that they related to the Father in different terms. Father Mike told him he got high marks and was pleased with him.

They received word that the negotiations had begun. They squabbled over the shape of the negotiating table and every minor thing they could think of. They negotiated the exchange of prisoners and they fought over the terms. Battles continued, and people died on both sides while the top guys agreed to disagree. In other words, each side didn't want to admit they were not winning the war. They didn't want to lose face to the world and let the world know the stupid reasons they were fighting in the first place. The Russians didn't care. They had promoted the war for their own Communistic purposes and all they had to do was supply the North Koreans and the Chinese with arms and equipment. For the most part, there wasn't going to be a surrender like in all the past wars the Americans fought. All they had to do was negotiate a cease fire, but it certainly wasn't cut and dried, and it was impossible to determine when that was going to happen.

CHAPTER 17

A deuce and a half (2 ½ ton truck) pulled in late one night with a load of replacements. It was the truck that was dispatched to carry a load of men, including Loren, back to the point of debarkation; destination, United States. They assembled at the truck after breakfast and normally a few show up to see their friends off. This time a large group showed up to send Loren off, Nurses, cooks, mechanics, troops that would not have been there if it were not for him, and the Chaplain. The Nurses, with tears running down their faces, embraced him and kissed him on the cheek, everyone crowded around to shake his hand and wish him well. The Chaplain held his hand in both of his hands and was speechless and glassy eyed. That grizzly old Major showed emotion because his friend was leaving, and he may never see him again. Loren had a lump in his throat and only said his goodbyes softly. The driver yelled for everybody to load up because they had a long trip ahead, approximately 165 or 170 miles, so they were going to be on the road most of the day. They stacked their duffel bags at the front of the truck and then found a seat along the side of the truck. They arrived and unloaded and the first thing the men asked to do was visit the latrine. It had been a long trip and they all had full bladders.

A large number of trucks had arrived earlier, and some were still coming in. All the men started recognizing faces they knew, and it became a joyous reunion. Loren spotted a face he knew very well, and he was overjoyed, Corporal Bobby L. Williams. They were not shy about embracing each other and exchanged the thrill they felt to find their friend made it safely and were heading home. A group of non-coms held rosters of the men that were to form in their group and one Sergeant blew his whistle to get everyone's attention. Each Sergeant shouted out the names on his roster, and for the most part, they were in alphabetic order. One Sergeant's roster consisted of non-coms, which included Loren. He told Bobby he would catch up with him later and then joined his group. Father Mike was right; non-coms got preferential treatment. Loren's group seemed to get sleeping arrangements a grade level above the others. Loren, being aware of Sergeant rank, and above, and forbidden to fraternize with those less than Sergeant, only had Sergeant stripes sewn on half his uniforms, therefore he could associate with his friends of lesser rank by wearing his uniform with corporal stripes. It took a few days for everybody to arrive, so they took advantage of the time to eat well and rest up.

It didn't take long to get everyone loaded onto the ship and it got underway. The mood was a whole lot different than it was when they came to Korea. They were less nervous, and a lot more joking went on. They were bunked in accordance with the alphabet, however, and Loren and Bobby were near each other. They both asked about what was going on at home and they both indicated that, where they were, mail never reached them for long periods of time. Loren asked Bobby if the wedding date had been set and Bobby answered with a grin, "She says she has all the plans made and all I had to do was show up." They both laughed at that. "But I don't care," he added, I'm so damned tired of being away, all I want to do is settle down and have a family. If I have a son, I will forbid him to enter the Army. I'll make him go to college and make something of himself; how about you?" Loren explained, "I don't know what I'll find when I get home. I got letters from my Mom and a close friend and I got a few from a student Nurse I met before I left, so I guess I'll have to get me a new supply of women. I plan to investigate going to college on the GI Bill. It may be tough getting in because I never took academic courses in high school. I really don't know what's going to happen. I don't want to go back into the factory, but you never know, I may have to because I need money and I want to buy a car." Bobby indicated he was in some bitter battles in the mountainous areas and he saw a lot of the guys that they went through basic with, killed or injured. He added, "You remember Wessel and Wagner and Wright and Old Kantuck? They were injured and got a ticket back to the States. They made me a squad leader. I didn't want the job of being responsible for someone else's life, but I took it because some of the guys in the squad were not the kind I wanted to depend on if I was going to come out of this thing alive. How about you? When we split up, you were going to be a Chaplain's Assistant. How did that go?" "We went to an outpost made up of tents and then, after a couple months, we moved the outpost up near Wonju," he explained. "The going got pretty rough from time to time, after the Chinese got into the game. We weren't big enough to have a hospital, but we had a couple Nurses that did the best they could. In most cases, if a casualty came in that was borderline and needed surgery, the Nurses couldn't handle anything that serious, and we usually lost the guy. I would stay with, and assure him, I would not let him die alone and I prayed with him to the end. It was pretty taxing at times, emotionally." He wasn't about to go into details about what all he really did. "I see you finally got some nice shiny jump boots," Bobby said, amused. "Yeah," Loren answered, "I got them from a guy that never had any more use for 'em, like robbing from the dead. But they were just going to sell 'em or give 'em away and my old combat boots were getting thin on the tops where I burned the heck out of them trying to get a shine on 'em." Work details were handed out to all the lower ranked men and Bobby got his share of them. Loren was relaxing on his rack when a wise ass Corporal came up to him and ordered him to sweep the deck. Loren had his shirt on with the Corporal stripes on it. He got up and put on his jacket with the Sergeant stripes on it and the Corporal apologized and went off to pester someone else. He muttered to himself, "Thanks Father Mike, you were right, rank has its privileges."

After the boat docked and the troops went ashore, they went through the procedure of mustering out or getting reassigned. They all received physicals and filled out paperwork and, those that had completed their enlistment, were paid and received their separation papers, and left to board waiting buses to take them wherever they wanted to go. Those that had not completed their 2-year enlistment were interviewed for reassignment. Bobby L. was designated to spend his remaining time assisting in the training of new recruits. He asked to go back to Breckinridge, but what he didn't know was that

Breckinridge was destined to shut down. At the time they graduated from basic training, their company area was closed; companies before them and after them were closed as they graduated. Bobby was assigned to Fort Hood, Texas. During Loren's interview, he was asked if he wanted to stay in the Chaplain's Service and he said he would prefer it. He also said he wanted somewhere warm because he hadn't thawed out yet from the cold in Korea. The interviewer checked his lists for available vacancies and asked, "Do you like southern cooking to go with the warm weather?" "That sounds ideal. I love country cooking, hot biscuits and country ham. Mmm! Where is this glorious place?" Loren queried. "Fort Rucker, Alabama!" he responded. "I'll take it," Loren answered immediately. "You are entitled to some leave-time if you want it," he replied. "No!" Loren said, looking down at the floor. "I need to do some straightening out before I go to be with family, so I think I will go directly to Alabama and be their Chaplain's Assistant." "That's fine, Sergeant," he said. "I'll cut the orders right away and you should be able to get out of here tomorrow, or the next day at the latest. They have a lot of orders to cut."

Loren knew nothing about Fort Rucker, and he was surprised, after he arrived, to learn it was a pilot training base for small aircraft and helicopters. He settled in getting acquainted at the Church and meeting the Chaplain, Major Bill Golden, and his staff. It was a large church compared to what he was used to at home and it was certainly humongous compared to his tent church. His duties primarily were to work with veterans who had problems adjusting and new recruits with family problems. Some of them were messed up rather badly and it was difficult communicating with them. He would try talking to the bad ones and found their mind was somewhere else, so he decided their condition was beyond his scope. He chose to work with the milder ones, and they seemed to be more on his level and understood each other. General conversation on simple things between two young men, and sometimes women, that had similar experiences in a war zone went a long way getting the thinking back on track. In most cases they just needed someone to talk to that understood what they experienced and how they should go about readjusting to civilian life. Wit would also interject the power of the Lord and how He could give them strength when they became troubled. In his back and forth with those vets, he was feeling like it was helping himself too. The Chaplain asked Wit to work with a vet that had requested help, so Wit met with him and questioned what unit he was in and what his duties were and wanted more personal information, so he would know how to proceed. He became suspicious and later went to the records office and found the guy had lied to him. The unit he said he was assigned to didn't exist, so he couldn't verify his information. His next session, he told the guy he couldn't work with him because he lied and that was the worst thing he could have done. Wit explained it all to the Chaplain and that he didn't understand what the guy's intentions were, or what he intended to gain from it. The Chaplain thanked him and said he would handle it.

  His few months he had left went rather quickly and he was beginning to live with himself and calm down inside, except he still had a pain in the stomach occasionally. He went to see the doctor, but he never had an answer, so he gave Loren some pills for ulcers, although he never had ulcers. During his exit interview, the Lieutenant interviewing him tried to get him to re-up for six more years. "No!" Loren said. "I think I need a break; it's been a long time since I've been home." Just then a helicopter flew quite low and close to the window where they could see it pass by. "Now I would like to learn to fly one of those," Loren said, with a little excitement in his voice. "There were a few of them in Korea and I saw the importance of them in combat. I think they are the coming thing." "With your rank, it will be no problem," the interviewer said, "you can take a leave and, when you get back, you can start in the next training class." "I think I better get out," Loren said finally. "Ok," the interviewer replied, "but remember, you have six more years of obligation, and if you should decide to go active again, you can retain your rank, and we can get you into those helicopters. You'll graduate as a Warrant Officer, which is a pretty good place to be, somewhere between a non-com and a Lieutenant, and they will call you Mister Whitson." "I'll certainly keep that in mind," Loren responded.

CHAPTER 18

It was late in the day when Loren got off the plane at the Cincinnati airport. There wasn't much activity and the terminals were rather empty. As he was trying to decide how he was to get home, low and behold, he spotted his old friend, Bobby L. Williams walking toward him with his duffel bag on his shoulder and a big smile on his face. They dropped their bags and gave each other a spirited greeting and a firm handshake. "Looks like we made it, Whitson!" Bobby blurted out with a big smile. "We sure did, didn't we?" Loren responded. "They signed a cease-fire after we left." "I'm sure glad," Bobby followed, "a lot of good guys were lost in that worthless war." "Is your fiancé picking you up?" Loren asked, changing the subject. "I'd like to meet her." "Yes, and my future Father-In-Law and Mother-In-Law," he responded. "Anybody meeting you?" "No," Loren answered, quite solemnly, "I didn't tell them I was coming. I don't know if there's a bus this late and a cab will probably cost a fortune. I could hitch-hike, I guess." They walked out of the terminal and met Bobby's 'in-laws-to-be', and Bobby explained to them Loren's plight. Then his future Father-In-Law said the most satisfying thing Loren had heard all day, "We have no problem driving him home; it's in the same direction and only a little farther." Now that was a load off Loren's mind. His home was about 15 miles further north than the town Bobby lived in. Loren got out, retrieved his duffel bag and after trading parting comments, said their final goodbyes. As the saying goes 'parting is such sweet sorrow'. He never saw his good friend Bobby L. again.

The family was naturally glad to see him, and his Mom prepared a good meal for him the following night for dinner. He ate the best he could, but he still had the pains in his stomach, and it was difficult because he didn't want to disappoint her. When his old friends heard he was home, they came in to see him and welcome him home. They each had a car to run around in and they would take him to visit other friends and their families. That lasted a couple days. They had jobs and were attending schools and had steady girlfriends and had other interests than when he was a part of the old gang. He then made a major mistake. He needed his own car. What he didn't know was the money he was sending home for his Mom, she put into the bank for him. When he went shopping for a car, he found the price of cars had gone up significantly since he bought the old clunkers. With the economy improving after the World War, inflation also was increasing, so to buy a nice car, it took a significant amount of money, or go in debt. That means you made car payments and insurance payments and that meant you needed an income. He bought a rather nice late model Pontiac and went in debt. The first place he went was to see Josie. He had fantasies about Josie for a long time and now he was really going to get serious and make a move for her. He drove to her house, parked on the street in front, and started walking up the walk to the house. She was sitting in a swing on the front porch and when she saw him walking up, she stood up and "**AWWWKKK,** Josie's knocked up!" He stopped dead in his tracks, waited a moment, and continued to walk up onto the porch. She explained how she met this guy and they were married a year ago and yaddy, yaddy, yaddy, ... he never heard another word she said. Her Mother welcomed him in and was glad to see him. She still loved him and had his graduation picture sitting on her end table in the living room. He stayed a little while and made small talk and then, driving down the street he thought, "Good decision? Good thinking? That was the big questions two years ago and the answer now is ***hell no!***"

After a few days, with all his friends now having their own interests, he found himself, for the first time in his life, with nothing to do. He made a trip to one of the universities to apply for entrance in pursuit of a degree. The student advisor surprised him by telling him that, by not taking academic courses in high school, he was not qualified to tackle complicated courses because of the lack of algebra, plane-geometry, trigonometry, and physics courses he should have taken in high school. He then suggested that Loren take them in night school and then come back and try again. Naturally he was disappointed and depressed while driving home. The only answer was he had to go back to the factory and ask for his old job back, the one thing he promised he would never do. But that was what he did; after all he now had bills to pay.

Loren, by chance, ran into his old childhood friend, Charles. Charles lived across the street and he and Loren grew up together and were close until his family moved to the other side of town during their high school years. Charles was a year older than Loren and his family was more well off and therefore, he had all the good toys and sports equipment. His parents sent him to a military academy his senior year and then he joined the Air Force after graduation. He just got out two weeks before Loren. He started dating a girl a family acquaintance introduced to him and subsequently had a few dates. He suggested they go on a double date and he would ask his girl to fix Loren up with a blind date. Loren drove his impressive looking car and he and Charles picked up his girl whom he introduced as Maggie. Maggie was 19 but looked a lot older; had auburn hair and hazel eyes. She was well put together and very pretty. The blind date's name was Joanie. She was cute, had dark hair and was stocky built; she was a very happy sweet girl. Maggie and Joanie went through high school together and had been good friends for a lot of years. Everybody enjoyed themselves and became well acquainted. Loren and Charles had a couple double dates, Charles with Maggie and Loren with a different girl named Judy.

Loren went across town to where Charles lived with his parents, to see what plans he had for the day. Charles informed him he was leaving for California to make application to get into University of Southern California (USC) and asked Loren to go with him. Loren had to decline because he had car payments and needed to work. Charles never told Maggie his plans. About a week later Loren got a phone call from Maggie who was wondering if Loren had heard from Charles. He informed Maggie that Charles had gone to California to go to school. After a short conversation, Loren asked Maggie if she would like to go for a ride, since it was a nice sunny day. They learned a lot about each other on that ride. Maggie had attended Nurse's training for about a year and was now working for a Doctor, a General Practitioner. He told her he had just returned from the military and went back to his old job as a machinist in a local factory. That was the beginning of a serious romance. They started dating and soon become an item. About three months later there was a cut back in the factory and Loren became a victim of a lay off. His older Brother recently went to work at Frigidaire, a division of General Motors, which was about 35 miles away, and he was willing to introduce Loren to their management and therefore Loren became employed in the Future Engineering Model Shop of Frigidaire, working the weird hours of 4:30 in the afternoon to 2:00 in the morning, and half days on Saturdays. They drove that distance over back roads; he had to leave at 3:00 pm and never got home till 3:00 am. He was required to join a very powerful union, but the pay was good, and they had terrific benefits, because of the union. The hours caused a minor problem, however. Maggie worked days and, while she was working, he was sleeping or traveling and working and, while he was working, she was sleeping so they never had much of an opportunity to see each other. It was a very unorthodox courtship to say the least. They tried every way they could to connect. Naturally they had the weekends and they tried to get together just for a few minutes at lunchtime. He usually got up at 10:00 am and she would try to call a little after that just to talk a few minutes. Maggie's family wanted to meet Loren, so she invited him to come to Sunday dinner. They were a fine Kentucky family that came up north to Ohio many years before. She had two younger brothers, Gerald, the oldest, and Lonnie, who was about 10 years younger than Maggie. Her Mom fixed a fine southern meal; fried chicken, green beans, mashed potatoes, corn bread, sliced tomatoes, and for dessert she had cherry pie. They all liked each other from the very start and seemed to have a real good time, laughing and joking with each other. Loren offered to help with the dishes and her Stepfather teased him for being a 'squaw man', helping the women.

CHAPTER 19

Loren continued to have problems with his stomach. Sometimes the pain was so severe he couldn't eat and at times he had no desire to do anything. His Mom would prepare food that had no spice or anything that would cause indigestion. Loren's older Brother was dating a girl and the four of them planned a picnic at an amusement park. They packed a basket with a variety of food and a cooler of soft drinks. While they were spreading a picnic table and unpacking the food from the basket, Loren got a whiff of the food and it turned his stomach and he, therefore, spent most of the time with his head in trash barrel dry heaving. It goes without saying, it wasn't the most enjoyable picnic. They were all sympathetic and understanding, but that didn't keep Loren from feeling terrible about messing up their plans. Maggie arranged for Loren to see her boss, the Doctor. He never had an answer but thought if he drank some form of chalk water to line his stomach before eating, then he could at least keep it down. He also prescribed a little pill to calm the stomach. It seemed to ease the misery somewhat but never solved the problem;

he stayed with it a couple months to give it a chance. Maggie arranged for a second opinion with a Doctor friend of her boss, and he never had an answer. The second Doctor thought what he was doing was the best option.

There was no doubt they loved each other to go through all the misery of wanting to be together. They did simple things like going to church and drive-in theaters, or just spending time together. After about 8 months, Loren bought Maggie an engagement ring. When her Mom found out, she went ballistic. She wanted Maggie to marry someone of prominence, like a Doctor or Lawyer or a Land Developer, just anybody that could provide her with riches and a big house and fine jewelry and furs; not a factory worker. The disagreement became so bad, Maggie moved out. She found an elderly person who wanted someone to live in, so she wouldn't be alone, and the old woman's family felt better about the idea also. It is difficult moving into someone else's house trying to be accepted. Generally, the older people are set in their ways and feel like the live-ins are trespassing or interfering with their routines that they have had for many years. Maggie would stay a few weeks and then look for another place. Patients coming into their office usually knew of someone who needed a live-in. She did this for a couple months and it was becoming taxing on her so finally Loren said, "Let's just get married!" They hadn't planned to marry for some time yet. After they became engaged, they had gone to a furniture store and picked out their furniture and wanted to pay it down first. The situation with her Mom made it impossible to have a formal wedding so they decided to go to Indiana to tie the knot. They went one Saturday and visited a church of Loren's denomination in a small town. They talked to the Minister and he said a blood test was required and they had to wait three days after taking out a license. It looked like the following Saturday was the day, if everything worked out. Maggie extracted Loren's blood and her boss extracted her blood and sent it in for testing. They checked out an apartment in a complex close to where Maggie worked. It was laid out in a horseshoe fashion with 4-unit apartment houses on both sides of the street. All the buildings were exactly alike. It was a little more expensive than what they thought they could afford but it had all the positives they needed, so they signed the papers to take it. The next thing they did was to get someone to stand up with them, so Maggie asked her friend, and past next-door neighbor and her husband, to go with them and they were glad to do it. Everything worked out and 10 months after they met, the deed was done. As the old saying goes 'they were as poor as a church mouse' but they were excited and happy. They couldn't afford a honeymoon. They had told the furniture store it was going to be a few more months before the wedding. When they jumped up the schedule, the furniture store only had part of the furniture in the store. The rest had been ordered, so they delivered only part of the order. They had to sit on the floor to watch television because there was no living room furniture. Maggie was in the kitchen trying to fix some dinner one Sunday afternoon. Loren was watching a pro-football game on television. A big linebacker broke through the line and smeared some poor quarterback; he then stood over him and pointed his finger in his face. Loren sat straight up and said laughing, "Way to go, you big dumb-ass Marine!" Maggie yelled from the kitchen, "What did you say Honey?" "Oh nothing, I was just rooting for this team," he answered. There was no way he was going to explain it to her. They were happy together and more relaxed since they had more time together. They would lie in bed holding each other and plan the future. They dreamed of paying off the car and the furniture and then try saving enough to buy a little house, maybe get a dog, and later have a couple kids. They only hoped to have a simple and ordinary life together.

They had befriended a young couple, Don and Mabel, who lived in the apartment below theirs with their new baby daughter. The four of them would play cards or watched ball games or just shoot the breeze. At times Mabel would invite them down for supper. She was a decent cook and they enjoyed her meals and sometimes Maggie would cook the meal. Maggie would go down and visit with Mabel and play with the baby almost every night, just to pass the time and keep from being lonely while Loren was at work, and the two of them became close friends.

The hours were a little better after they married, but still a problem. Maggie was able to come home for lunch and they could eat together. At times she would tell him before hand to wake her when he came home so they could spend time together. It was not a good scenario for two young warm blooded newly-weds, but they had hoped it would get better in time. Loren's stomach was still giving him trouble. It seemed to be getting worse, rather than better. He never missed work, but he suffered every night, and this went on for about six months. One night the pain was so bad he asked his Supervisor if he could go home early. All he could think about was lying down and try to get the pain to ease up. The Supervisor understood because he had stomach problems in the past and had part of his removed, so he told Loren to go ahead and try to come back the next day. It was about 11:00 pm when he got home. He tried to be quiet in case Maggie was asleep. He quietly unlocked the door and eased in and closed the door behind him, he stood still for a moment. He heard some rustling coming from the bedroom. Thinking Maggie was having trouble getting comfortable, he quietly slipped to the bedroom door and got the shock of his life. Some big dude was on top of her humping as hard as he could. Loren went into a rage. He leapt onto the big dude with his knee in his back and, pulling his head back, he had his right hand on his throat ready to rip it out. He had flashes of Chinese and Koreans and ripping out their throats. His eyes were blood red and hollow and devil-like and he gritted his teeth, not mindful where he was or what he was doing. Maggie had a grip on his wrist and was screaming, "Loren, Loren, Loren, Loren." He couldn't hear her and was on the verge of ripping the man's throat when he came to his senses. He realized what he was about to do when he loosened his grip, got up and went into the living room, shaking and sick. He stood in front of the picture window staring out when the big dude came through the room carrying his clothes under one arm and holding his shoes in the other. As Loren opened the door, the big dude said, "I'll get you for this you son-of-a-bitch." Loren had a ball bat standing in the corner behind the door; one that he kept from his old softball days. He grabbed it and went out the door and, while the dude was standing at the top of the steps, Loren swung the bat and hit him across the shoulders as hard as he could, and he tumbled down the steps headfirst. He lay at the foot of the steps for a moment collecting himself, then got up, picked up his belongings, and yelled again, "I'll get you for this," as he ran out the door. Loren went back in and Maggie had put on her robe and came toward him, "Loren?" He interrupted sternly, "You better get out of here, quick." "Where can I go?" she asked, crying. "I'm sorry, Loren!" "Go to Doug and Betty's across the street," he answered bitterly, "tell them I'm on a rampage and you want to sleep on their couch tonight. You don't have to explain anything to them."

He paced in front of the window the rest of the night. His gut was really hurting him now and he was nervous to think of what he almost had done. He remembered what Father Mike had said, "You are possessed with a *demon* and hopefully you can pray hard enough for it to leave." "It looks like the *demon* was here to stay," he thought, "it's not safe for me to be loose in civilian society." Then he thought about Babs and started to really get emotional. Babs vowed she would never do anything to cause him pain. As he paced, his mind wandered, and it was full of what-ifs. Finally, he concluded the only answer was to go back into the Army and leave this life to those who deserve it. When the light of dawn came on, he got into his car and drove across town to his Mom's house because he knew she would be up. He knocked on her door and when she opened it, she said, surprised, "Loren, what are you doing here? Is everything alright?" She could see he was troubled. "Come on in and have some coffee with me and tell me what's on your mind." She poured him a cup as he sat down, and he started off by saying, "Mom, I think I'm going back into the Army." "What?" she spoke seriously. "Yes, I just can't get adjusted to this civilian life," he added. "I've tried but I'm just fighting it." "I knew that old Army would mess you up," she replied. "You haven't been the same since you got home. What about Maggie? What is she going to do?" "I don't know," he answered. "She can have a divorce if she wants it or, if not, I can get an allotment and send her some money." He knew his Mom was totally against divorce, so he didn't dwell on that idea. "She can have the car and furniture and that money will help her make payments. With my rank, I can get into Helicopter Pilot School and come out as a Warrant Officer. It should be a lot more pay and they are offering pretty good bonuses to reenlist. She can get medical benefits off me too; she should be alright. If she finds somebody else, and wants to go off on her own, that's ok too. I just got to go where I'm comfortable." "I had a bad feeling about this marriage from the start," she added. "I never thought you were ready for marriage and you two just had too many obstacles to overcome. Young married couples should always be together at first; sometimes love is not enough."

When Loren returned to the apartment, Maggie was sitting on the couch sobbing. Before he could speak, she said, breaking up as she tried to spit it out, "Loren, I love you and I am truly sorry. Let me explain, that guy was Don's brother. He started hanging around and seemed to be there whenever I went down to visit. One night I took my little record player down and we all were playing records and singing to the music. After that night, they wanted me to bring it down every time he showed up. He offered to help me carry the player and the records up to our apartment and then grabbed me and kissed me. I didn't object to it. He would carry it up every time after that and kissed me more and started feeling around and eventually we ended up in the bedroom. Do you think you could give me another chance?" She cried harder as she begged, "Please Loren, give me another chance. I'll do anything to make it up to ya." He was sitting down in the chair and listening quietly, looking at the floor, and stated, "No, it's over. You did the worst thing to me that you could ever have done. Remember when we first started going out and I used to be extremely jealous and you said, 'You got to trust me'. Now you want me to trust you again?" She couldn't get the picture out of her mind what she saw in his eyes and was truly afraid of him, even though she really loved him. "It doesn't matter now," he concluded. "I have decided to go back into the Army. I don't really care what you intend to do. I'm not going to divorce you, unless that is what you want. You can have everything; the car, the furniture, the apartment if you want it, and anything else you can think of. If you don't want a divorce, I will send you money to help make payments until it's all paid off. I'll get a pretty nice signing bonus and, since you are considered a dependent, I can get an allotment. With that money and your pay, you should be able to live comfortably, unless you let some dirt bag come along and spend it for you." "When will you be leaving?" she asked sadly. "In a few days or as soon as I can get everything cleared. I'll call work and tell them I'm quitting, and I'll give my Brother all my tools and he can take control of those. I'll need to make a trip up there to sign some papers and get my final check and settle-up whatever they may have. I still have my uniforms, so I'll only take a couple changes of civilian clothes. I'll donate the rest of them to the Salvation Army," he concluded. "You going to tell your old friends you're leaving?" she asked, trying to be helpful. "No," he answered, "they acted like they weren't too excited when I got home and never even came around after that first day. They have their own routines. I've never felt more disappointed and alone in my life, until you entered the picture. I hoped everything was going to be alright because I was starting over, but you really put a wrench in those gears." He took care of all his business and stopped to say goodbye to his Mother the night before he was to leave. The next morning Maggie stood and watched as he finished packing his duffel bag, and she asked, "Do you want me to take you to the airport or somewhere?" "No," he said firmly, "I don't need you for anything. I have it taken care of." "Are you going to let me know where you are?" she continued to ask. "No," he followed, "I will not be calling you or writing to you. We're done!" He lifted the duffel bag onto his shoulder and turned to her and said, "You know what is ironic? Your Mom thought you were too good to marry a low life factory worker. Good luck!" She watched as he went down the steps and out to the curb and got into an army colored car, and it sped off down the street.

She never saw him again. She never married again, or even dated, or asked for a divorce. After she paid off everything they owed, she bought a little house, just big enough for her, and lived a sad and lonely life. The only time she would go out was with family or friends, and that was rare. She continued to work as a Nurse, however, and that provided the sum-total of what little social life she had. It could be said that what she saw in those flaming eyes of a *demon*, that distorted face, and the terror that dreadful night frightened her so bad; it left her just a shell of a woman.

CHAPTER 20

The driver of the car was a Master Sergeant, the recruiter that signed Loren up for six years. Loren asked, "What is your plan to get me to Fort Rucker? I hope it ain't a 10-hour bus ride that stops in every little town." "No!" he replied. "I'm gonna take care of ya. I have arranged an 'Air Force hop' and I'm driving you to Wright-Patterson-Air Force Base." "Wow, Sarge, that's great!" Loren exclaimed. "The next time I have dinner with the General, I'll tell him how good a job you are doing." "Well, while you are at it, ask him to give me an extra 30-day leave," he replied. Loren responded, "Now you know if you had 30-days, you would just get into trouble and get busted." "Yeah, you are probably right," the Sarge remarked. "Just tell him I am doing a good job." He delivered Loren to a building at Wright-Pat and handed him an envelope and said, "Everything you need is in this envelope; your records and enlistment papers; just go in and report. The name of the pilot you will ride with is Captain Duval; I wrote his name on the envelope for ya. Good luck and if you ever get back in town, stop in and see me and let me know how you are doing." They shook hands and Sarge drove off. Loren went into the building and reported, and when he came out, he saw a familiar face walking on the sidewalk toward him. "May the Saints preserve us, Dick Sadler," Loren remarked. "Loren Whitson!" he responded. "What in the hell are you doing here?" "Well, look at you Dick," Loren continued, "wearing Sergeant's stripes and with a star in the center. What's that star stand for?" I'm a Tech Sergeant; I have been here ever since I enlisted. I work in a lab and we do research and stuff like that. Everybody is a Tech Sergeant where I work, so nobody can pull rank," he explained. "The last time I saw you is when we went to get our physicals. What happened to ya? Where did you end up?" "I was drafted into the Army and trained in the infantry and ended up in Korea," Loren responded. "I became a Chaplain's Assistant." "That sounds like an easy job; Did you just sit in a church all day?" Dick continued to ask, jokingly. "Not at all," Loren responded, "part of my job was to go out into the battlefield and when I found a feller that was at the point of death, I prayed with him until he took his last breath. It was extremely tough at first; it was guys like you and me with an arm or leg blown off; a big hunk of shrapnel sticking in his belly; a hole in his head; any number of things to gory to describe. It messed me up bad. I went back to civilian life for about a year and a half, but I could never adjust. Nobody understood me, and I didn't understand them. I would go to bed at night hoping to get a good night's sleep and wake up in the middle of the night with cold sweats and flashbacks of all the horror. I concluded that the only place where they understood me was the Army, so I re-enlisted." Dick seemed to share his pain, and said, "That's why I joined the Air Force, I didn't want any part of that; I'm a short timer now and I'll be getting out and it's all behind me."

"Let me give you a piece of advice, Dick," Loren added. "There's like a mini-recession going on and I suggest you check it out before you leave this nice setup. You will need a contact or know somebody to be able to get a job. You can't just walk into a place and say I want a job. You might consider extending a year if you don't have something lined up. Well, listen, Dick, I am supposed to get a hop to Fort Rucker, Alabama with a Captain Duval; I'm scheduled to start Helicopter Pilot Training," Loren injected. "Do you know where I can find him?" "Sure," Dick replied, "you remember Bob Duval that graduated with us; I'll take you right to his plane." "Yeah, I remember Bobby Duval," Loren responded, "he never went for that hoop-la stuff in high school; he was always serious and business-like." "He still is," Dick added. "He flew some missions in Korea and shot down a few Russian MIGs. He did like you, got out and said the world, as he knew it, wasn't the same, so he re-enlisted. Hop into my Jeep and I'll drive ya out to his plane." As they rode toward the airstrip, Dick added, "You are going to love those helicopters; the guys here that use them say it's like having a car. You walk out the door and get into your chopper, fly where you want to go and don't worry about red lights or traffic cops; then land in some parking lot and get out, just like car. The best thing would be if you could get your own chopper." The Captain was waiting by his jet plane, and when Loren got out of the Jeep, he said, "Loren Whitson! So, you are my special passenger." Loren responded, "Bobby, how the heck are ya? Long time no see; am I your only passenger?" "No!" the Captain said. "I'm waiting for two Engineers that I am taking to Titusville, Florida. After I drop you off at Fort Rucker, then I'll run them over there. They are going to some big defense plant and work on new kind of special rocket. What are you going to do at Fort Rucker?" "I'm getting into the helicopter pilot program," Loren answered. "The helicopter is the new wave of warfare for the future," The Captain added. "I hope the wars are over for a while," Loren replied. "Don't bet on it!" the Captain remarked. "Things are getting stirred up in Indo-China. The French are duking it out right now, but they are not winning, so you can bet Americans will be getting involved; it's all politics. Have you ever flown in a jet before?" "No, it will be my first time," Loren responded. The Captain continued, "We take off fast, go up to 30,000 feet and come down fast. I'll have you there in an hour or so." "That sounds better than 10-hours in a bus," Loren laughed. The two other passengers arrived; they all boarded the jet, and fastened their seatbelts good and tight, and they were off and shooting through the sky.

The Captain didn't lie; they observed the ground from a lot higher than Loren had ever been, flying in those prop puddle jumpers. It didn't seem like any time had passed when the Captain announced they were arriving at Fort Rucker. He said he would make a pass and then make a new approach, so the post could be viewed from the sky; then he landed and taxied slowly up to the hangar. A Corporal was sitting in a Jeep, that had a Chaplain's insignia on it, next to the hangar; the ground crew ran out and, when the Captain opened the door, they lowered the steps and Loren shook the Captain's hand and climbed down and walked over to the Jeep with his bag in his hand. The Corporal introduced himself as Gene Howard, the Chaplain's Orderly. Fort Rucker consists of tens of thousands of acres in the southeast corner of Alabama mostly in Dale County but branches over into other counties. It was named in honor of Tennessee-born Colonel Edmund W. Rucker, a Civil

War Confederate officer. It was called Camp Rucker until in 1955, it was then changed to Fort Rucker.

"Don't tell Chaplain Bill I said so, but he got excited when he heard you were coming back," Gene offered. "Are you going to be staying at the church?" "I re-enlisted for helicopter training," Wit responded. "I would like to help out at the church if I have spare time; I have no idea what the schedule will be. I had a nice little setup in the church basement when I was here before." They drove to the church and Wit got a welcoming handshake from the Chaplain. Something new had been added, a pretty little Army Corporal was sitting at a desk, and Chaplain Bill introduced her as his Secretary, Rose Herzog. She looked to be in her upper 20s or maybe 30; she had muddy blonde hair tied in a knot, she was slightly stocky built and well endowed. The Chaplain said, "Come on into my office and you can tell me what have been up to since you were here last." They went in, closed the door, and sat down, and the Chaplain began, "You are probably wondering about Rose; I got so busy I had to have someone to help with the clerical work. She is really messed up; her husband was killed in Korea; she put in a tour over there as a Company Clerk. I was hoping you could use some of your magic on her and try to get her straightened out." "Be glad to try," Wit replied, "it will depend on how my schedule will be and if I will have time. I need to report in and I'm sure they will give me the straight skinny. I was hoping to stay in my old place in the basement, but they may require all the trainees to stay together; we'll see." Wit reported and it was explained: The training is 18 months; there will be classes from fundamental skills to aviation medicine; final classes to be held in the cockpit of the helicopter. But first things first; you are to complete a General Physical Examination, plus including a class 1A Flight Physical Exam; all results to be approved by the Flight Surgeon at Fort Rucker. They are going to be busy, so make your appointment as soon as you can. Wit asked Chaplain Bill if he knew the Doctor and he said he is Doctor Lloyd Owens; he has a lot of years as a Field Doctor and will be very thorough, but fair. "He has a dry sense of humor and will try to put you on, hoping to tap into your nerve system." Wit replied, "I'm trained in that from basic training. They were as tough on mental endurance as well as the physical training. I was sensitive at first but developed the attitude I learned to live by; 'if it can be done, I can do it'."

Doc Owens never left a stone unturned; he and his staff ran tests that Wit never knew existed. After he finished, he called Wit into his office, and commented, "We have a heavy load right now, but we should have all the results in about a week. Are you having any problems right now?" Wit replied, "I have one that I've had since Korea. My gut kills me sometimes. When I was home, I dry heaved and gagged and couldn't stand the smell of food. I went to several Doctors, but they didn't have the answers." Doc leaned back in his chair, gazed at Wit with a squint, and asked, "Do you drink a lot of coffee?" "I drink my share; you are not a soldier unless you drink coffee." Wit responded. "And you drink some in the middle of the afternoon when your stomach is empty?" Doc continued. "And that is when it hurts the most?" "Yeah!" Wit came back. "I've been drinking coffee all my life; that shouldn't have anything to do with it." "Dammit, Sergeant, I'm the Doctor around here!" he yelled sharply and slammed his fist on the desk. "You got a nervous stomach and the caffeine is making it worse." Wit was surprised at this outburst, and he just stared at the Doc.

The Doc offered, "If you crave coffee, there's a new brand out called 'Sanka', but I think you can only get it in instant. Just put a spoonful in a cup of hot water. It tastes like crap, but you can adjust to it; it's caffeine free. Also, and this is important, when you feel hungry in the middle of the afternoon, go to the vending machines and get a pack of cheese sandwich crackers and a can of vegetable juice. Don't let your stomach get empty; that's when it starts getting nervous. Where you from, Wit?" "Ohio!" he replied. "Don't they learn to respect Doctors in Ohio?" he asked, as he relaxed back in his chair. "Yeah!" Wit came back. "And Doctors respect their patients!" The Doc cracked a little smile, and said, "I can see why they call you Wit! Try what I am prescribing, and I think you will start seeing results in a week. In a month you will never know you had a problem. But don't go back on coffee just yet. Give it several months and then you might try mixing the full strength with the decaffeinated; keep me posted." "Is this going to keep me out of training?" Wit asked. "No!" he answered. "This is fixable and not really serious."

CHAPTER 21

Wit passed all the physical requirements. He passed the Selection Instrument for Flight Training Test. He scored high on the General Technician Test on armed forces vocational aptitude battery. He was now ready to proceed to his classroom training. His training instructor was Captain Carl Lindell. For some strange reason, the Captain had a dislike for Wit. Strange because they never had a confrontation of any kind or even had a conversation of any kind. Wit was sitting in class, listening intently, and squeezing his little rubber ball. The Captain directed, "Whitson, do you have to squeeze that little ball in class?" "Sorry, Captain, if it's distraction, I can put it away," He responded. So, he put the ball in his pocket. "Well, why are you squeezing it anyway?" The Captain continued. "I was told by an old combat Sergeant in basic training, that taught hand to hand combat, that I needed to develop strong hands," Wit responded. "He emphasized that it could save my life and he suggested I squeeze the ball every chance I got." Wit later asked Chaplain Bill if he knew Captain Lindell. He said, "No, I have never met him, but I've heard a little about him. He is an Aeronautic Engineer and seems to know his stuff. Why? Is there a problem?" "I'm the last to complain," Wit continued, "but he started ragging on me from the very first day and I don't know why. He wreaks of alcohol and tobacco and sometimes he comes in with bloodshot eyes. I think he has a drinking problem. I'm not going to do anything to antagonize him; I just want to finish his course and move on." Chaplain Bill replied, "If it gets to be a problem, let me know." Unbeknownst to a lot of people, most Chaplains are Majors and pack a lot of weight.

The training class building was located next to the aircraft runway and Wit was sitting next to a large window. He noticed a small single wing airplane approaching for a landing, but he was coming in too high. Wit jumped up and yelled out, "He's coming in too high; he's gonna crash." The Captain ordered, "Whitson, stay in your seat!" Wit ran out the door of the room and then out the building and ran as fast as he could toward the plane. The pilot tried to over-correct and jammed the nose into the runway and it tipped up on its nose. Wit jumped on the wing and managed to pry the canopy open and started pulling the pilot to get him out. The pilot was dazed, and Wit started yelling at him to help get out. The fuel line ruptured and fuel was spilling out on the pilot's flight suit. Then Wit noticed a small blaze, probably from the sparks when the plane skidded on the runway. He managed to get him out and dragged him away from the plane but the fuel on his flight suit had started to burn. Wit laid on him to smother the flames. He then rolled him over and smothered the flames on his back. About the same time the firemen arrived and started spraying foam on the plane. The ambulance loaded the pilot and transported him to the hospital. Wit sat down, buckled his knees, and put his head on his folded arms. There were some burns on his hands and arms and his eyebrows were singed. He was thanking God for giving him the ability to save the man's life. Captain Lindell ran up and yelled, "I'm gonna have you court-martialed Whitson for disobeying a direct order." Wit just looked up at him and said, "I could never have saved him if I didn't have strong hands." The Captain just walked away. The Fire Chief listened to the whole thing and remarked, "That guy has really got it in for you. I saw the whole thing, and if you need a witness, don't hesitate to call. I think you did a very brave thing."

The Captain filed charges and a hearing was scheduled to be held in three weeks. A JAG Lawyer, Lieutenant John Fowler, was appointed to represent Wit and he recorded Wit's account of what happened, word for word. The Lawyer got depositions from the Fire Chief and several firemen and the emergency technicians. There was a Major, as the lead officer, and two Captains and two First Lieutenants on the panel. Captain Lindell sat to one side in a chair and Wit and his JAG Lawyer and Chaplain Bill sat together at a table in the center of the floor facing the panel. The Major made it clear this was not a trial but merely a hearing to get all the facts. Captain Lindell was asked first to give his reasons for filing charges, and when it came out, it sounded like a feeble attempt to discredit Wit. The JAG Lawyer read aloud all the depositions, and they were all in support of Wit and his actions. The Lawyer then asked the panel for permission to have Sergeant Whitson leave the room. That was music to Wit's ears because his stomach was getting empty and he wanted to go out for some cheese crackers and vegetable juice. Then his Lawyer called on Chaplain Bill Golden, and he took what looked like a report from his pocket, and said, "If the panel will allow me time, I would like to read a letter from Army Chaplain, Major Mike Molloy, that is pertinent to this case." He was granted permission: 'I first met Sergeant Whitson when he was just a Private and had arrived in Korea from the States and his group was waiting for trucks to transport them to the front. They seemed to have time to spare so Private Whitson went across the tarmac to where our boys were laying badly injured and dying and he started praying with them while they were taking their last breath here on earth. I had him transferred to me as a Chaplain's Assistant in our remote outpost made up of only tents. He started working with the Nurses in the medical tent, praying for the injured that had arrived badly wounded. He would go out into the battlefields and administer to the wounded, showing no regard to the dangers of shelling and fighting going on around him. We moved our tent city closer to the combat area and he continued to go out into what was now a more dangerous situation. While out doing his job, he saw hordes of Chinese soldiers charging and screaming, like they were insane, toward our outpost. He radioed to me the danger that was about to be upon us and possibly annihilate everyone in the camp. He said to get prepared and call for reinforcements. A spotter for artillery was running for his life to get away, but then a small jet plane was coming in for a crash landing, and Sgt. Whitson forced him at gunpoint to stay and help the injured pilot. As they were speeding back in their Jeep, they started receiving rifle fire from two North Koreans, so they stopped long enough to kill those two. They sped into camp and he directed the spotter to man one of the machine guns in the ditch on the perimeter, and he took the wounded pilot to the medical tent. He then raced back and manned a machine gun that was unattended by a wounded gunner. He personally killed hundreds of the enemy combatants and luckily the reinforcements arrived and turned the tide of the battle. When I suggested I put him in for a medal, he pleaded with me not to do it because he would have to explain why he got it, and that would only embarrass him. When he loaded onto the truck to rotate back to the States at the end of his tour, everyone in our outpost came to see him off, and even the toughest of them had a tear in his eye because they all knew they would not be standing there alive if it were not for Sergeant Whitson. In my 27 years as an Army Chaplain, I had never seen anything to come close to matching what happened that day. If he ran out of the building in defiance of a direct order, which I understand he did, and he saved a pilot from a burning plane, I can say unequivocally that he never did it for glory or be a hero. It is an internal instinct inherent to save his fellow man, and in the many months I was associated with him, I prayed hard to understand it, but never could. These are not things that were reported to me; I personally witnessed them first hand. I hope this will help you to understand the makeup of this true patriot that you are about to convict. Signed: Major Mike Molloy, Chaplain of the US Army. God Speed!' I hope this information will give you some insight of the actions of Sergeant Whitson." The room was dead silent; not a sound of any kind could be heard. Captain Lindell just sat and stared at the floor and showed no emotion whatsoever. Then the panel leader said, "We will retire to our room and discuss the facts as presented to us." They went into the back room and one started pouring three-fingers of Scotch Whiskey into each of their glasses. They all lit up a cigar and paused for a moment. Then the Major said, "I don't know about the rest of you, but

I could never hang a man that saved my life from a burning plane. I would be showering him with gifts and praise." One of the Captains said, "We have to take into account that Captain Lindell has been a credit to the Army, so we have to come up with a solution where everybody wins." One Lieutenant spoke up, "We have other classes teaching the same thing, so why don't we transfer Whitson into one of them? It seems we have a conflict of personalities. I know just the class. Lieutenant Chris Berger was awarded a battlefield commission and I know they will speak the same language." They all agreed and the Major asked if there was a better solution, and there was none, so he said, "Then that is what we will do." They emptied their glasses and snuffed out their cigars and went back to the hearing and dictated their decision and adjourned the hearing. Wit was told of the decision and he promptly asked permission to go to the hospital and pray with the wounded pilot, and it was granted.

CHAPTER 22

Wit got along great with Lt. Berger. Being that he had never taken academic courses in high school, he felt he was behind the other trainees, because they had taken those courses and a few of them had some college courses. He studied hard to keep up and never went anywhere or did anything but studied late into each night. Chaplain Bill said he was concerned about him and suggested he take a break, so one Friday night he asked Rose to take a walk in the park and she could point out a few buildings or landmarks, because he still hadn't gotten around enough to learn where things were; and too, it would give him a chance to work with her to see if he could help straighten her out. The park was a pretty place with lots of flowers and trees and walking paths. There were benches spaced along the paths and there were people just sitting and enjoying the evening. Rose rarely said a word unless he would ask her a direct question. They sat on one of the benches and he proceeded to find what her interests were: "Do you like sports?" he asked. "Not really!" she replied. "Do you like to cook?" he continued to ask. "Only when I have to!" she responded. "Do you have any hobbies?" he continued to ask. "No!" she answered bluntly. "Do you like music?" he asked, running out of things to ask. "I have a large collection of records," she remarked. Aha! Now we are getting somewhere. "What type of music do you like best?" he insisted. "I have all kinds; big bands; blues; country; classic; opera, I play them all depending on the mood I'm in," she explained. "Would you like to go up to my place and listen to some?" "Sure, I would love to," he replied. They went to her apartment on the second floor of her building, and she didn't lie; there seemed to be hundreds of records. He started looking through the collection and remarked, "I like slow, dreamy, soothing, and quiet music; I call it, 'music for lovers'." While he was searching for the ones he liked, she quietly went into the bedroom, and came out wearing pajamas and had let her hair down from the bun. He said, "I found a couple here, Tenderly, Al Martino, Connie Francis, Perry Como, Jo Stafford, Connie Smith, and a few instrumentals, and then said here is one of my favorite singers, Joni James." She stacked them on her record player with an automatic changer that held ten 78 rpm records; turned the volume down low to make them sound dreamy. He asked, "You want to dance?" She never said a word and stepped up to him and put her arms around him and they started moving with the music, holding each other close, body to body. She pulled her hair off her neck, as if to invite him to nibble, and he started kissing her on the neck and nibbled on her ears. She pulled him tightly against her and he could feel her hard nipples pressing through his T-shirt. He reached down and took hold of the cheeks of her butt and she tightened her muscles and started kissing him gently. She took him by the hand and led him to the bedroom and they proceeded to romp on the bed all night. Morning came, and she said, "I think we need a shower; we are smelling like sex."

They took a shower in her bathtub; it had a pull curtain across the tub and a shower head, but it was plenty good enough to get the job done. They dried off and he asked, "Don't you have anything to eat around here? The Doc said for me not to let my stomach get empty." "Yeah!" she answered. "There's stuff in the ice box." He went to the ice box and got out some sausage and eggs, put a frying pan on the stove, and started frying. She got out a mixing bowl and started mixing pancakes, and then asked, "Do you want coffee?" "No!" he replied, adamantly. "Doc Owens said to drink 'Sanka'." "What's that?" she asked. So, he proceeded to describe 'Sanka', but since he had never seen the stuff yet, he quoted the Doc's description word for word. "You have milk?" he asked. "Yeah, I have milk!" she responded. It was a sight to behold, they had not dressed; cooked and ate their breakfast in the nude. After eating, he went for a bathroom break and she proceeded to clear the table and started washing the dishes. When he returned, he helped her get the kitchen back in shape. Then, without further ado, she took him back to the bedroom for another day of romping. She put so much into it, by the end of the day, she fell into sort of a faint. He sat on the edge of the bed pondering what he should do about her situation, and then she started blinking her eyes and sat up. He said, "I think I need to get going; I don't want to get behind in my studies," so he got dressed. She walked him to the door and gave him a little soft kiss and said, "Thanks Wit, I really needed that." He responded, "My pleasure!" She now seemed different; she had color to her cheeks; she didn't have that hard stare; her hard nipples softened; she seemed totally relaxed. As he went down the steps of her building, he muttered, "I guess you do whatever works."

Wit continued to bear down on his studies; he had previously felt like he was behind the other men in his class, but now it seemed he was catching up with them; now he had a little more free-time. He made friends with a couple guys in his new class and they included him in their conversations. They laughed about going to the nearby town of Daleville and getting wasted in the Old Dutch Club; they invited him to go the next Friday night. He declined, of course, and he explained he didn't drink, so he would not fit in. Chaplain Bill noticed the big change in Rose and remarked, "I don't know what you did, or said, but she seems to be a totally different person." Wit explained, "I tried to find something she was interested in and she finally admitted she loved music and had a huge record collection. Brother, does she ever; she has every kind of music imaginable; she has an exceptional stereo system that has perfect sound, and can hold a stack of ten records. None of the methods I formerly used on the messed-up veterans would work because she just wouldn't express herself. Not to change the subject but, I wanted to ask you if I could borrow the Jeep Friday night to go to town. A couple guys in my class were telling me about going to a club in Daleville and end up getting wasted. I don't want them to do anything stupid and get into trouble where they might get washed out of the program. Since it's my first time off the base, I don't know where to go, so I thought I would ask Rose to go as my guide; hopefully she will." "Yeah, that sounds like a worthwhile gesture," Chaplain Bill replied. "It would be a shame if they couldn't finish and get their wings." Wit explained to Rose what he wanted to do and needed her help to guide him. He mentioned they would wait till about 10:00 and that would give the men time to get stupid and have enough to drink. She agreed and said she knew where Daleville was and where the club was. They parked in the lot as close to the door as they could, in case they had to assist a couple drunks. Two MPs (Military Police) hung around outside the door. Wit and Rose went in and the place was full; there was a live band playing and most everybody was dancing. The two friends from his class were at a small table being entertained by a couple Floozies. Wit wanted to keep an eye on them, so he asked Rose to dance, and he managed to dance and watch the guys. He noticed they were downing their drinks, but the Floozies were only taking a sip from time to time. One guy was kind of loose with his money and just shoving it in his pocket. Then Wit saw the kicker, one of the Floozies reached into his pocket and relieved him of all of what was left of his money; she then stuck into her bra. Wit told Rose, "That's it; they have had enough, let's try to get them out to the Jeep." They weren't exactly able to walk on their own, so Wit and Rose wrestled them out to the Jeep and managed to get them in the back seat. He told Rose, "Keep an eye on these two, I got to go back in for a minute." He walked back in and went straight to the pocket-picking Floozie, and demanded, "Hand over the money you stole out of that guys pocket." She responded, "I don't know what you are talking about." "Yes, you do, I saw ya," he said sternly. "There's two mean looking MPs outside and all I have to do is report it to them and you don't want that kind of trouble." She took the money out of her bra and threw it at him and said, "Take it you son-of-a-bitch." He picked up the money and put it in his pocket. When he got back to the Jeep, he had the two happy guys try to explain to Rose where they lived, and they delivered them home.

They managed to get them into their rooms and they fell on their beds, passed out. Rose asked, "You think they will be alright?" "Oh yeah!" he responded. "This is not the first time they got destroyed."

He took Rose back to her apartment and she asked, "You want to come in for some coffee? I bought Sanka!" "Really?" he remarked, "I need to try that stuff. It's already 1:00 o'clock, so I don't want to stay long. I need to return the Jeep to the Motor Pool." She put water in the tea pot and lit the stove to heat the water; he started reading the label on the jar. She wasn't gonna waste time on that; she turned off the stove and took the jar out of his hand and led him to the bedroom for another romp. It was of much shorter duration than the first time. He got the opportunity to try the Sanka and the Doc was right, it was awful. He said, "Doc knows what he's talking about; my stomach is not near as bad as it was." When Wit ran into the Chaplain, the Chaplain asked, "How did it go with your trip into town?" "It went great," Wit remarked, "the two guys were about to get into trouble and we wrestled them to the Jeep and took them home. Two MPs were standing outside and, if we hadn't gotten them out, they might have ended up in the clink. I might try that more often; go to other towns close by and rescue our military boys and get them home safely. Rose was a big help; if it weren't for her, I might still be wandering around the countryside."

On Monday morning, when he went to class, the two classmates were standing and talking, and he walked up to them and asked, "You guys alright?" One said, "Yeah, I vaguely remember you and some girl taking us home. We really appreciate that. It's hard to say what alley we would have slept in." Wit then asked, "Did you spend all your money, or do you have some left?" The one that got his pocket picked answered, "Nah, I'm busted till payday." Wit handed him his money and the guy's eyes got big, and he questioned, "What's this for?" Wit answered, "That's your money; that Floozie you were with, picked your pocket, and I made her give it back. Of course, I had to fight her for it and received a lot of cussing in the process." "Well that dirty bitch," he followed. "It's alright to have fun," Wit added, "but you two have got to use good sense. The shape you were in, you could have gotten into some serious trouble, and there would be a chance you might be washed out of the program. I would hate to see that happen." "You're right, Wit. I think we learned our lesson," one said. "We owe you one." "Better watch it!" Wit laughed. "I may want to collect sometime." The Instructor told them to take their seats.

CHAPTER 23

Wit mentioned his idea to Rose; to go out to other nearby towns, like Newton or Level Plains, and check the places the guys go and take them home safely. She liked the idea; gave her a chance to get out. So, whenever they had time, they would go to a town on a Friday night about 10:00, or so, look for guys in the facility, and keep an eye on them while they danced, and when the guys started getting loud or rowdy, they escorted them to the Jeep and took them home. Many times, they lived off the base, and when they delivered them to their abode, their Wife would be waiting and met them at the door. She thanked them and appreciated it, and Wit would say, "No problem, see ya in church." Most of the wives were understanding that their man needed to blow off a little steam but wanted them to come home safely. After all, this was the military. Wit and Rose were becoming well known and when the Jeep, with the Chaplain's insignia on the side, would go down the street, they would get waves, no matter who was driving. A few of the MPs appreciated it, but there were a few who didn't. It took away their opportunity to knock a man in the head and haul him to the lockup. Then one day, Chaplain Bill said, "I don't know what you are doing, but our attendance at church is up about 50%, and I get questions frequently from them wanting to know how Wit and Rose are doing, if they don't see you in church." "That's good!" Wit responded. "I wish we could go more, but my training is intensifying, and I'm usually tied up." Time was going by rather quickly and Wit was spending less time in the classroom and more time on the simulators and performing mechanical functions on the helicopters. It was explained that, if the ship has a failure and goes down, you better be prepared to fix the problem, because you certainly are not going to find a mechanic out in the wild somewhere.

Wit thought it was about time he told Rose about his wife, Maggie. They found a free night and went to a nearby town and, as usual, found a couple soldiers getting pissy-eyed. They delivered them home and ended up at Rose's place, and he asked her to heat the water for some Sanka. They sat at the table and he said, "You know, Rose, my training is winding down and I will be reassigned; I like Alabama a lot, but I want to go where there are mountains and lakes; new scenery; something different." She responded, "I was hoping to get a transfer and we could stay together." "When I came back from Korea, my mind was destroyed, so I came here to finish out my active duty requirements. I was assigned to the Chaplain and worked with other vets that came back in as bad a shape as I was. Working with them help straighten me out to where I thought I could go back into civilian life. When I got home, I found all my friends had moved on and I didn't fit in anymore. I met a girl and fell in love and we dated for about 10 months and we ran off and got married in a little church in Indiana. She was sweet and fun-loving and seemed to be someone I could settle down with. My stomach was in constant pain all this time; even went to a couple doctors but they never had the answers. Anyhow, it was like someone had thrown a switch, her personality changed, and she wasn't the person I thought she was. I was working second shift and she was working in a Doctor's office in the daytime, so we had to arrange time to be together; that is not the recipe for two hot blooded newlyweds. One night, at work, my stomach was really on fire and I asked my Supervisor if I could go home. Being he had a history of stomach trouble, he understood, and granted me the time off. I got home somewhere between 11:00 and midnight, crept in the door so I wouldn't disturb her sleep. I heard noises coming from the bedroom and moved silently to the doorway and saw some big dude and her going at it hot and heavy. I went berserk and jumped on top of him and was going to kill him. I had flashbacks of killing Koreans and Chinese and could have killed him in seconds. My wife, Maggie, was screaming at me all this time and I finally came to my senses. I went into the living room and stood in front of the picture window, shaking and hurting all at the same time. The big dude came out of the bedroom carrying his clothes and shoes and threatened to get even with me. Our apartment was on the second floor and when he got to the top of the stairs, I hit him a mighty blow with a ball bat I kept by the door. He tumbled down the stairs and lay on the landing at the bottom for a while, and then got up and went out the door cussing me with every word known to man. I went back in and Maggie was sitting on the couch apologizing, but she also realized I almost killed her lover, and when she witnessed the fire in my eyes, she was afraid of me. I told her she better get out quick; go to our friend's apartment across the street; just tell them we had a fight. I paced the rest of the night in terrific pain, but more so knowing I almost killed a man. I realized that I was not fit to live as a civilian; they didn't understand me, and I didn't understand them, so I decided the only people that I understood was in the Army, and that I must re-enlist. At daybreak, I drove across town to see my Mother and tell her I just was not able to adjust, and that I was going back into the Army. She replied, 'I knew that old Army would ruin you', and started to cry. Then she asked, 'What are you going to do about Maggie?' So, I explained that I was going to offer to give her everything and, if she wanted a divorce, she could do that too. I went to the recruiting office and signed up for 6 years with the guarantee that I would go into Helicopter Pilot Training, and they said with my rank that would be no problem. I went back to the apartment and Maggie was sitting on the couch, and looked a mess, so I told her flat out we were done, forever. She begged for another chance, that she was so sorry, and all that crap. I told her she could have the car and furniture and everything. We owed on all that stuff, and the apartment rent, and so to be fair, I told her if she did not want to get a divorce, she could receive an allotment from the Army, and with what she made from her job, she should be able to make all the payments; or if she found another stud to marry, it would be cancelled. She asked if I was going to let her know where I was or write or call and I said no, never. The recruiter pulled up in front in an Army car, I threw all my keys on the end table, walked out and never looked back." Rose listened intently through the whole story and remarked, "So, you are married?" "Yes!" he replied. "Kinda! But let me say this, as I was trying to help you with your problem, you helped me tremendously, and I feel I can move on, but not as a civilian. We have spent a lot of time together and I know we have feelings for each other, but it could never work out between us. You deserve better than the likes of me; you are sweet, kind, gentle, and beautiful, and there is a kind and gentle man somewhere out there that would be more than proud to have you and make a life with you. Father Mike, in Korea, said I had a *demon* inside me, and he was praying hard that it would leave me; he is right, and I will never commit again." She had tears running down her cheeks and she said, "I feel so sorry for you, Wit. I will never forget you." "Did you ever cheat on your husband?" he asked. "No! Never!" she answered. "I loved him so completely, I never even considered such a thing. I gave him all I had to give." "You must learn to love again!" he continued. "Be faithful and true and have a family and love your family with all your being; you will be happy again and it will be easier when you have someone to share it with .... is there more hot water so I can make another cup of decaf?" "Yes!" she responded. "But we ain't gonna waste time on that; we are gonna use every minute we have making love until you ship out." He laughed and said, "Copy that!"

CHAPTER 24

Graduation day finally arrived. Family members and close friends of the trainees were milling around the grounds; the band was playing, and it was a joyous occasion with the hot Alabama sun bearing down. Wit had only his close friends, Chaplain Bill, Orderly Gene, and of course, Rose. Lieutenant Berger approached Wit and said, "I was worried about you at first, but you buckled down and ended up near the top of the class. You are going to be a fine officer, Warrant Officer Whitson, or should I call you Mr. Whitson?" "Thank you, sir; got a nice sound to it, doesn't it?" Wit said. "And I would like to compliment you too; you are a fine training officer, and I was privileged to be in your class." Doc Owens walked up and commented, "Well, you Buckeye Hillbilly, what are you going to do next? Make General?" "Never thought of that; thanks for the suggestion," Wit joked. "Before I forget it, I really appreciate your advice to fix my stomach problem; them civilian doctors never had a clue. I'm having very little, if any, pain and I owe it all to you." "Told ya," Doc replied, "I'm the Doctor and you are the patient. Just keep doing what you are doing, and eventually you may be able to get back on the hard coffee but be careful on an empty stomach. You might try mixing half coffee and half decaf, if you want to get the coffee flavor." "You were right about the Sanka," Wit added, "it took some getting used to, but it served the purpose." "Where do you go from here?" Lt. Berger asked. "I don't know," Wit responded. "I requested some place that had mountains and lakes and pretty scenery, and I would like to stay in the Chaplain's Service."

The ceremony went well, and all the graduates were excited the long miserable spell was over but thrilled they had succeeded. They all got their orders and Wit got his wish, he was going to Straubing, Germany. He arranged for Air Force hops, so he wouldn't have to sit on a ship bobbing around on the ocean. They agreed to pick him up on base at the air strip early the next morning and fly to Iceland; then a cargo plane would fly him to Germany. He told Rose he was available for a short time and he would need to start packing, so they disappeared from the crowd and ended up at her apartment; just enough time for a rout in the sack. It was an emotional moment, after they finished, and he became really serious, and spoke from the heart, "Rose, it is important that you start living again; start associating with other people and get active." "How am I going to do that?" she responded. "The only time I have ever done anything or gone anywhere was with you." "I can make one suggestion, if you will allow me," he followed. "You are working for a man that is available; and he is single; and he is lonely." "Me?" she stammered. "With a Preacher?" "Why not?" he followed. "He is as decent a man as I have ever known, and he has an honorable profession. Get to know him; ask him to go to the towns like we did; ask him to go to the gym and work out; ask him to go to the movies; ask

haven
haven
Emden
Hamburg
Szczeci
Groningen
Oldenburg
Bremen
Elbe
Gorzo
Wielkopo
LANDS
terdam
Hanover
Potsdam
Berlin
Enschede
Frankfurt
Arnhem
Münster
Bielefeld
Brunswick
Magdeburg
Ziel
Go
Dessau
Cottbus
hoven
Duisburg
Dortmund
Halle
Essen
Kassel
Leipzig
Görlitz
Düsseldorf
Dresden
Bad
Hersfeld
Erfurt
Jena
Cologne
Eisenach
Aachen
Bonn
Gera
Chemnitz
Decin
Liège
Zwickau
Ústí nad La
M
Hof
Frankfurt
Prague
Wiesbaden
Cheb
Mainz
Bamberg
Plzen
LUX
Würzburg
CZECH
REPUBLIC
Mannheim
Nuremberg
Metz
Saarbrücken
Ceske
Budejovice
Karlsruhe
Heilbronn
Regensburg
Rhine
Nancy
Straubing
Stuttgart
Strasbourg
Danube
Passau
Ulm
Linz
FRANCE
Augsburg
Munich
Freiburg
AUS
Mulhouse
Salzburg
Konstanz
Garmisch-
Partenkirchen
Liezen

him to go bowling; ask him to come up and listen to music. You both have a sweet and loving disposition and probably have more in common than you think; might eventually click. Give it a shot." She looked at him like the wheels were spinning and thinking, "Maybe he has something there; never thought about it like that before."

The post at Straubing, Germany was an old German Air Force Base in the foothills of the Alps, about an elevation of 1400 feet; the Danube River flows through the center of the town; he admired the beauty of the country as they flew over and was anxious to get on the ground and get a closer look. The Army base was the home of the 6th Regimental Combat Team and located 3 miles from town; being a former air base, it had its own air strip. Corporal Jay Stewart, the Chaplain's Orderly, was waiting when the plane landed and introduced himself and then transported Wit to the Chaplain's office at the Chapel. The Chaplain, Major Ray Jones, greeted him graciously, and took him on a brief tour of the church. The base didn't have barracks; it had billets, which resembled a college dormitory with rooms which accommodated 2 to 3 occupants. Wit was to have his own room with the Regimental Headquarters Company, even though he was assigned to assist the Chaplain; also, on base was the 1st Battalion; there was a 2nd Battalion at a nearby town of Landshut; there was a 3rd Battalion in the nearby town of Regensburg. The 3 Battalions alternated patrolling the Czechoslovakian border, which is a Communist country, in 6 weeks increments. The Chaplain, like many of the married personnel, lived in town with his wife, and commuted to the base.

Wit asked Corporal Jay to drive him around the base, so he would know where everything was located, especially his quarters and the mess hall, and the CP (Command Post). The base was well equipped with a quite a few amenities; a movie theater; a swimming pool; a gymnasium; a snack bar; a bowling alley; a PX; and about anything that a person would want to spend his time off duty. He asked Jay what he was most interested in and he said probably the movie theater and the PX and snack bar. Wit explained, "You know, Jay, in the States, me and the Chaplain's Secretary started going to the nearby towns and any of the personnel that were partying too hard at the clubs or bars, and were just about to get into trouble, we would get them out of there and deliver them home. Saved a lot of them from getting in trouble and chewed out; even from getting dirty details. When they sobered up, and realized the favor we did them, they were really grateful and appreciated it. I would like to do that here and wondered if you would be interested in going with me. I would need directions where the hangouts were, and you most likely would know, and help with wrestling the drunks into the vehicle." "Yeah, that sounds like fun; give me something new to do," Jay answered. "There's a lot of them that get their pass pulled at the gate and I'm sure they would appreciate it; couldn't haul too many of them in the Jeep, so we might borrow the ¾ ton truck from the Provost Marshal Captain; he most likely would appreciate it too so he wouldn't have to deal with all the drunken soldiers." Wit mentioned it to the Chaplain, and he liked the idea and offered to contact the Provost Marshal Captain to explain the plan and ask to borrow his truck. Wit suggested the truck have a cover over it because the nights might get cold and he didn't want the passengers to be any more miserable than they already were from partying.

Wit went to the CP and introduced himself and showed his orders to the top officers and explained why he was sent there.

He explained that he would be required to complete a specified amount of flight time in the helicopter. They explained that he would most likely have to go to Freising Air Force Base, approximately 40 miles south, since they had no helicopters assigned here. He made a point of learning what hours the mess hall was feeding, and he developed a routine when to eat; then to go to the gym and workout to start his day, that is if there were no objections. He had to be careful not to give the impression he was here on holiday and cause dissention among the powers-to-be. He was basically still in Non-Com mode, and hasn't yet grown into Officer's Mode, so he was still acting like a Sergeant, not a Warrant Officer. He would report to the Chaplain each morning to see if he had anything needed to be done. Wit and Jay were kept busy on Friday and Saturday nights hauling inebriated solders back to camp; making several trips each night since it was only 3 miles from town. They saved a lot of them from getting their passes pulled at the gate and having to pay cab fare. They soon became well known among the troops and their truck was nicknamed 'The Drunk Mobile'. Those that became unruly or troublesome were the responsibility of the MPs.

After about a month, he asked the Chaplain if he had any objections of him driving his Jeep to the Freising Air Force Base to meet with the helicopter group and set a schedule for getting in his flight hours and any additional training on models he wasn't familiar with. The Chaplain had no objections and even mentioned that Wit might request acquiring his own helicopter. He drove down and presented his orders showing he was a qualified pilot and had a long heart-to-heart talk with Colonel Robert Rankin, Commander of the helicopter group. The Colonel explained that they were constantly getting in new models and he should put in a requisition for one of their used ones. He added that Wit make sure they had helicopter mechanics in the motor pool, and they had a supply of airplane gas. He mentioned there should be airplane gas on hand since it was an airstrip. He had a training officer take Wit up in one of the models he would most likely receive, and it was far advanced from the ones he trained on. With a few simple directions, Wit was flying like an old pro; he was elated, and the officer was well pleased with Wit's performance. Wit mentioned that a two-seater should suffice, but the Colonel strongly suggested a four-seater. He stated that Wit would eventually be spending most of the day transporting personnel to various locations in a lot less time than in a road vehicle, and once the convenience became apparent, he was going to be extremely busy. He gave Wit a box of log books to record all his trips and the hours expended on each trip. He stressed the importance of keeping a record of the hours because the chopper required specified maintenance at various intervals. He gave him a box of authorization forms and impressed strongly that no trip be made without an authorization from a ranking officer. This will also eliminate joy-rides at your expense. "I will call your Regimental Commander, Colonel Joe Krause, and tell him to get a requisition in ASAP. We are old golfing buddies; he can never beat me, though, but don't tell him I said that." And laughed.

Wit drove back to Straubing really jacked up. He remembered his school chum, Dick Sadler saying, "It will be great if you can get your own chopper." He went directly to the motor pool, introduce himself as Warrant Officer Loren Whitson, and asked the First Sergeant in charge, the important questions: "Do you have helicopter mechanics in house? Do you have airplane gas?" The First Sergeant introduced himself as Ralph Knudsen, and spoke directly, "You are the guy that drives The Drunk Mobile. I got a couple regular customers of yours," and he yelled for Dilly Duncan and Hap Gabbard to come over. "You have been bringing Dilly home every weekend. He can't stay away from the Straubing Schatzis; he's had the clap three times. They just give him penicillin and as soon as he is cured up, he is right back at it; but he's a good mechanic. Hap Gabbard is a trained helicopter mechanic, but he hasn't had any to work on for a while." "I will probably be getting one in the very near future," Wit said. "As soon as I get the word, I may see about sending a few of your men to Freising AFB to get you up to speed on the model I will receive; I'll start working on that because I think it will happen real soon." First Sergeant Knudsen added, "We have a large tank of airplane gas; this is an airstrip, you know, and planes fly in and out of here all the time, so we are required to maintain a supply. It'll be a break getting to go to Freising and associate with them fly-boys; right guys?" Of course, they responded with a resounding, "Yeah!" Wit then went to see Chaplain Ray and filled him in on what had transpired at the AFB. The Chaplain said, "If the Air Force is going to contact our Regimental Commander and have him send in the request, I'll just sit and wait to hear from him. I got a feeling you won't have to wait long."

CHAPTER 25

Ten days later the Chaplain told Wit the requisition had been approved. He added, "Go to the motor pool and get the names and serial numbers of three mechanics that will go with you and inform them to prepare to spend from three days to a week training on the helicopter you are to get. We need to cut orders for TDY (temporary duty). The Colonel has been informed and we asked them to provide the necessary quarters and anything else you might need." Wit rushed over to see Sgt. Ralph and told him what the Chaplain said and informed him that they would plan to leave as soon as the orders came through. Sgt. Ralph said, "I won't be going; I can't be away that long, but I will send my Staff Sergeant, Dave Kelly, and Dilly and Hap. They are all good mechanics." Sgt. Kelley signed out a ¾ ton truck and he drove; Wit rode in the jump seat and the other two rode in the back. Before they departed, Wit explained the seriousness of applying themselves to learn as much as they could. He explained the difference of a land vehicle breaking down on the road to a malfunction in the air a couple thousand feet up; it was serious business. It didn't take long to travel the 40 odd miles and they were cordially welcomed; they were soon settled-in and introduced to their counterparts that would work closely with them.

The mechanics went through all the maintenance checks numerous times until they thoroughly understood all of them. A training officer accompanied Wit for the first day and a half, and then he soloed for the next couple days until he was totally comfortable with the chopper. He remarked how much improved this model was from the ones he trained in; how much easier everything was. The Air Force work day ended at 5:00 pm, so they had some free time. The airmen took them to the local Gast Haus for a few Lowenbrau (German beer, about 12% alcohol). Wit didn't drink but he went to socialize and see the local establishments. They were laughing at Dilly talking about how hot the Chaplain's wife was, and how he would like to get his hands on her. They explained she was definitely not the run of the mill Straubing Schatzi (commonly referred to as 'bunny fart'). Wit warned them that they better stick with the Schatzis; if they got caught messing with the Major's wife, they could spend the rest of their lives in a stockade; it would not be worth that. One asked Wit, "Have you met her?" "No!" he said. "I've never even seen her. They live in town and I never go to town except with the Drunk Mobile." After a couple beers, the airmen suggested they go back to the base and sack out; they needed to be fresh in the morning. They were serious about their jobs and Wit hoped that attitude rubbed off on the Army guys. They completed their mission and Sgt. Kelly was given the manuals, which contained the maintenance schedules, and they strongly emphasized the schedules be adhered too. Wit said, "I'm flying this big boy back; any of you brave enough to ride with me?" and he smiled, really excited to have his own chopper. Hap said, "I'll ride with ya. I can only die once." They received certificates for their training, and it was entered into their files when they returned.

Wit went to the Chaplain's office to see if any authorizations had been turned in, and low and behold there was one. He was to take a Sergeant from the records section to Nurnberg. The Sergeant said, "I've never rode on one of these things; how long you been flying?" Wit said, "You are my first passenger." The Sergeant reemarked, "Oh, shit!" When they returned safely to Straubing, Wit remarked, "Now that wasn't so bad, was it?" The Sergeant said, "It beats bouncing around in a land vehicle for two hours." There continued to be more trips and more satisfied passengers that liked cutting the travel time, and Wit was feeling a lot more confident with each trip. Soon it was like his old buddy Dick said, "You will be like walking out and getting into your car." It was fast becoming like Col. Rankin said, "Once they find out how nice it is to travel by air, the busier you are going to be." He was starting to get runs every day; sometimes two a day if they were close.

One day the Chaplain said, "You have a special passenger flying in today, a Congresswoman from Utah. Take the Jeep and pick her up at the airstrip. Bring her back here when she is finished, and she will stay at my house with me and my wife tonight." She got off the plane carrying a small suitcase and what looked like a cosmetic bag and her purse. She appeared to be in her mid to upper 50s, and average build, and had a very pleasant smile, and was well dressed. Wit introduced himself and asked, "Where is it you would like to go?" She answered, "I am, Gloria Banks, and part of the Armed Services Committee, and we have a contingent that are reviewing military facilities. I was unlucky to draw this part of

Bavaria and need to go to where the troops are patrolling the Czech border." "Ma'am!" he replied. "I don't think you are dressed properly to go out there; that is too rough for someone wearing a dress and high-heels. Are they expecting you? You know the Army; they like a little notice so they can clean up and straighten things to make it presentable. I have an extra flight suit that might fit ya. You might have to roll up the sleeves and cuffs, but I think they will work." They drove to his billet and went up to his room. He said, "I'm sorry but we don't have facilities for women in this building." He proceeded to remove the flight suit from his wall locker, then turned around, and she had already stripped off down to her bare essentials; bra, panties, and garter belt holding up her nylons. He stripped down to put on his flight suit. She wasn't looking all that bad, and she noticed a bulge growing in his boxers. He carried the suit to hold up to see if it was alright, and she reached in the opening in his boxers and grabbed WT (Wit Torpedo). Then the strangest thing happened, she looked into his eyes, and her eyes rolled back into her head. She started saying, with desperation, "Do me, Wit! Hurry! Hurry!" He didn't know what was happening, but he rapidly removed her bra and panties, and she fell backwards on his bunk, and he buried the torpedo up to the hilt. After 5 or 6 strokes, he thought she was done, but she kept ordering, "Don't stop!" After each half dozen strokes, she continued to order, "Don't stop!" Finally, after about 5 times, she made one last squeeze and seemed to faint. He proceeded to put on his flight suit and then she sat up. She remarked, "I don't know what happened; nothing like that has ever happened to me before. I've been divorced for 30 years and have never had any desire to have a man; never!" He said, "Put on the flight suit and we can go over to the Officer's

Mess Hall for lunch; there is a lady's restroom over there and you can clean yourself up; shouldn't be any ladies in there this time of day." They carried her bags and sat at a table next to the wall so they could talk in private. She took her cosmetic bag and went to the lady's room. Wit motioned to Smokie, the black cook, to come over, and he asked him if he had caesar salads made up and he said he did. Wit asked him to bring one with turkey and one with ham. Bring a couple bottles of Coke and glasses with ice. "We don't want to ask the lady to drink from the bottle. What do you have for dessert?" "Pineapple upside down cake," he replied. "Great!" Wit said. "That's my favorite." Smokie went for the food and the Congresswoman returned to the table. "I did the best I could, but I think I will be alright," she commented. "I want to apologize to you for being in such poor condition; I am kind of embarrassed of how poorly I must look undressed." "Don't give it a second thought; I didn't think you looked bad at all," he replied. "The main thing is if you were satisfied." "More satisfied than I have ever been in my whole life," she responded. Smokie brought the food and drinks, and Wit said, "Smokie, this lady is a Congresswoman from the great state of Utah. Smokie is the best cook in the Army and we are lucky to have him. He is from New Orleans, or do you say Nahlens? He cooks all that Creole stuff and his Jambalaya will curl your hair. He is going to bring us the best of the best; Pineapple upside down cake." She replied, "Pleased to make your acquaintance; why do they call you Smokie?" He laughed and said, "When I started into cooking school, I burnt everything I cooked and had the whole place filled with smoke." "That's a good story," she responded, and they all laughed.

They were just finishing eating when Colonel Joe and his wife came in. They walked over to the table and sat down, and the Colonel said, "So this is the little lady from Utah that is gracing us with her presence. This is my wife, Priscilla." Wit had never met her, and he introduced her to Wit, "This is Warrant Officer Loren Whitson, aka 'Wit'." Wit stood and shook her hand. "What do you two have planned?" the Colonel asked. "She wants to view the Czech border and the troops patrolling it," Wit replied. "I told her she was too well dressed to go there, so I lent her one of my flight suits." "Very becoming!" Priscilla remarked. "I hate to put the rush on," Wit said, "but we have to get going and get back before dark. I don't have night flying instruments. Congresswoman, you better make a pit stop before we go. They don't have lady's rooms up there. Of course, we could find you a big tree to get behind." Prim and proper Priscilla shot him a dirty look. The Colonel remarked, "That's a good one Wit." She then shot the Colonel a dirty look. "Not enough humor in this world," he said, "everybody is too serious." The Congresswoman returned from the restroom, and Wit continued, "I wouldn't want to hang that chopper in the top of a tree; it would be hard to explain what a Congresswoman from Washington was doing in the top of a tree in Bavaria." And Priscilla put her two-cents worth in, "And without a restroom!" Then the Colonel added, "You've heard the superstition never to walk under a ladder; well you wouldn't want to walk under that tree." That brought a boisterous laugh and everybody in the mess hall looked their way wondering what was so funny.

CHAPTER 26

They returned from their trip to the border none too soon; darkness and cold was setting in. He suggested she put on a jacket because once the sun went down, the temperature here drops rapidly. He mentioned the Chaplain had planned for her to stay at his place in town, but he had no idea where that was, so he would have Corporal Stewart take her; but first they needed to eat, because he didn't know what kind of cook the Chaplain's wife was, so it would better to be safe than sorry. She put on a jacket over the flight suit and they went to the Officer's Mess where she hurried back to the lady's room. They found a table off to one side where they could speak privately. He said adamantly, "Don't you dare look into my eyes. When I speak to you, I will look over your shoulder. I don't know what happened, but I don't want it to happen here." She asked, "Are you married, Wit?" "Well, yes and no!" he replied. "What do you mean?" she continued to ask. "Either you are, or you aren't; it's like saying you are a little bit pregnant." They ordered their meals and he tried to explain, "When I was in Korea, I was a trained killer; I could kill with weapons or with my bare hands; it didn't bother me; I could kill and lay down and go to sleep like nothing happened. The Chaplain said he felt there was a *demon* inside of me and he was going to pray hard that it leaves me and find a new home. It must have changed from the *'Demon of Death'* to the *'Demon of Love'*; I thought it was gone. I had three months left, so I went to Fort Rucker, where I got the hankering for the helicopters, and I worked with messed up vets that had returned; I felt like straightening them out was good for me too; I soon felt like I was good enough to go back to the civilian world. I met a girl and we fell in love and got married. We would lay in bed, holding each other in our arms, and plan our future; I was going to try and go to college and then we could buy a house and have a couple kids, and live happily ever after. After six months I came home from work early and found some big dude humping the heck out of her, and she was enjoying it. I jumped on him and came within a hair of killing him and directed her to leave immediately for her own safety, which she did. I paced the floor all night, nervous and scared, that I almost killed a guy, and realized I didn't belong in the civilian world because they didn't understand me, and I didn't understand them. The Army was where I belonged, so I went the next day to the recruiter and signed up for six years, providing they would put me into helicopter training. My wife, Maggie, apologized repeatedly and wanted another chance, but I said it was over for good, and I would never call her or write to her, ever. We owed on everything and I told her if she didn't want a divorce, she could get an allotment from the Army and from what she made as a Nurse, she should be able to pay everything off; and if she found another stud and wanted to marry him, the allotment would stop. I haven't seen any divorce papers, so I guess I'm still married."

Their food was served, and while they were eating, Wit asked, "How did you get into politics?" She explained, "I was raised as a Mormon in Ogden, Utah, and Mormon men are allowed more than one wife, so I was one of two wives my husband had; we were married for five years. He favored the other wife over me and treated her better and loved her more. She got pregnant and I thought, now I should be favored, but it didn't happen. He had his eyes on a sweet young girl, about 17, that was developing rather nicely. I had a talk with him and told him I wanted a divorce. He begged how much he needed me and wanted me to stay. He needed me alright; I did all the cooking, cleaning, laundering, and anything else that needed to be done. I told him I had made up my mind. He went to the church council and they came down on me hard; threats of all kinds; going to Hell was their strongest argument. I packed my bags and left for Salt Lake City where I was lucky to get a room at the YWCA. I got a job that didn't pay much but I was able to eat. I met a couple girls that introduced me to a Lawyer that had won divorce cases against the church and we won. The girls were doing volunteer work for some political campaign and ask me to join since I didn't have much to do. I did and it was fun; socializing and believing I was helping some cause. I started going to rallies and parades and listening to speeches; they were all saying the same things; more jobs; less taxes; promising anything the voter wanted to hear. I started to believe I could be a politician, so I registered to be put on the ballot. I didn't have any money for signs or bumper stickers or posters, so I started going from door to door. All my opponents were so boring and dry, I thought of something different; I bought a joke book and selected jokes that pertained to politics. When I would hold a small street corner rally, I would put a little humor in it by telling a few jokes, and soon I had everybody laughing, rather than falling to sleep. I didn't win the first time because nobody knew my name, but the second time around, voters remembered me and soon I was receiving donations, which accelerated my campaign, and I was elected. I have been elected ever since. I make it a point to do whatever I can to help my constituents, and they remember that, and are my best campaigners."

They finished eating and he said, "I'll drive you to the church where Corporal Stewart lives; he has a little apartment and is usually there most of the time. What are your plans for tomorrow?" She answered, "I want to go to Regensburg and Landshut, your other battalion camps, and then on to Freising AFB where they will take me by jet to Berlin. I will meet up with the rest of our contingent and we will fly back home." He responded, "I can take you to the battalions and Freising. The Chaplain will already be back in his office early, so I'll have the Corporal pick you up, and we can leave about 10:00." "I won't have time to get your flight suit cleaned," she added. "Don't worry about that," he responded. "I have a German lady that picks up my laundry at the gate and I can just add a couple packs of cigarettes for her trouble. American cigarettes are as good as gold around here." He took her to the church, and he rousted out the Corporal, and while they were waiting for him, she squeezed Wit a real tight hug, and said, "I wish I was going to stay with you tonight." "Ha!" he remarked. "That would really create an explosion." The Corporal took him back to his billet and then took the Councilwoman to the Chaplain's home in town.

Wit took a shower and had a good night's sleep and a good breakfast and was ready to go when the Corporal arrived, and then they went to the motor pool. Sergeant Knudson came out and said, "Wit, the way you are racking up hours on this bird, it is going to need a major overhaul real soon." "How soon?" Wit asked. "Probably in the next few weeks," he replied. "What does that mean, Wit?" the Councilwoman asked. "That means I'll be grounded for 2-3 weeks. They must change bearings, belts, hoses, overhaul the engine, and anything that looks worn or has aged. It's all for my safety," he sadly responded, "but that's not now, let's get aboard." They flew to Regensburg and she met with the Upper Echelon of the 3rd Battalion, and they then flew to Landshut where she met with the Upper Echelon of the 2nd Battalion. He suggested they eat lunch at Landshut because, by the time they reached Freising, it would be too late. They arrived at Freising and Wit escorted her to Colonel Rankin's office, and he proceeded to introduce them. The Colonel remarked, "Wit is the most popular guy in Bavaria." The Congresswoman came back and responded, "And the most loved." "The Colonel added, "I wouldn't know about that. How's your chopper holding up? I understand you are in the air more than on the ground." Wit remarked, "My guys tell me I am due for a major overhaul in a few weeks; the hours are starting to add up." "Maybe we can find one to lend ya," the Colonel continued. "We get new ones in and there are a few older ones that are just sitting out there. They may not be the same model as yours, so your mechanics will need to come back and get familiar with them. Let me know when you are ready, and I think I can help you out." "I got to get back to Straubing," Wit commented. "You all can solve the problems of the world," and he started for the door. The Congresswoman followed him and extended her hand to shake goodbye and said, "Thanks Wit, I really enjoyed your company." He looked over her shoulder but could read her lips saying, "I love you, Wit."

About a week later, when Wit returned to the motor pool from a trip; Colonel Joe was there and talking to Master Sergeant Knudsen. Wit walked up and the Colonel said, "We have a deuce and a half broken down about 25 miles north of town. Take a mechanic with you and go out there and bring back the Captain that's with the driver. The Sergeant can load his tool box and he will try to get it running." Wit replied, "We will need to hurry before it gets dark." The Sergeant commented, "The tow truck is on the way, but we can get there quicker." They arrived at the truck and the Sergeant unloaded his tool box and Wit instructed the Captain to hurry and get on board because the darkness was fast upon 'em. They arrived back at the motor pool and the Captain said, "Come on Wit, I'll treat you to dinner." They walked to the Officer's Mess Hall and the Colonel came out and said, "Go on in and eat, Captain. I want to talk to Wit a minute." The Colonel's car was sitting there, and Priscilla was sitting in it. "I want you to do me a favor, Wit," he asked, "I have an officer's meeting and I want you to drive Priscilla home." "Yeah, I can do that," Wit responded, "but she will have to give me directions because I don't know anything about getting around in town." He got into the driver's seat and, it was obvious, she wasn't too happy about it; and the Prim and Proper Priscilla was now meaner than a snake. "That sombitch promised to take me to dinner, and he's gone off with the boys. Well, you will have to take me because I'm not going to miss out because of his crap. He does this all the time," she threatened. She directed him to a rather fancy restaurant, compared to the Gast Haus he normally went to pick up the boys in the Drunk Mobile, and he remarked, "I'm not dressed properly for a place like this." "You are just fine," she responded. "Have you eaten yet?" "No!" he replied. "I've been on the go all day, and my stomach tells me I better eat soon." They walked in and were met at the door by the head waiter and she asked for a table along the wall. There were numerous non-coms in there with their wives or girlfriends, and they were dressed in their Class A uniforms, and that made Wit more uncomfortable. She was in control, "I'll order for you; what do you want to drink? Beer?" "No!" he answered. "I don't drink; I'll have water with a slice of lemon, if they have it." She ordered their meals, and it didn't matter what it was, for as hungry as he had been for hours, it all tasted good. There was an old German Oompah Band playing different tunes, mostly waltzes. After they ate, she insisted, "Let's dance!" He responded, "I can't dance to that kind of music." She said, "Yes you can; just hang on to me and move your feet." They just danced the old two-step, no matter what the tune was. They went back to the table and she knocked down a couple shots of cognac. "You better watch that stuff," he warned, "it's rather potent." They danced another dance; came back to the table, and she knocked down a couple more cognacs. She stood up to dance again, weaved a little, and commented, "I think I'm getting a little tipsy." "We better get you home," he said, "while you are still able to give me directions to your house." He parked in the driveway that ran alongside the house; helped her out of the car, and half-carried her into the house. They went into the bedroom, that had two 3/4 beds, and she stood beside one and extended her arms out, weaving back and forth, and said, "Undress me and put me to bed." He thought, "Uh-oh, how do I get out of this? I warned Dilly, if he messed with the Chaplain's wife, he would get the stockade. If the Colonel walks in and I am undressing his wife, I'll get the firing squad." "I got to get back to camp," he blurted out. He was saved when a younger woman walked in, and her seeing what was taking place, said, "Prissy, what are you trying to do?" She slurred, "What does it look like I'm doing?" The younger woman said, "I'll help you get into bed," and proceeded to undress her and get her into her night gown. She looked to be more Wit's age and must have just bathed, because she appeared to be wearing only a bathrobe. After she got Priscilla settled, she asked Wit not to leave yet; she wanted to talk to him; and she would percolate a pot of coffee. She wanted to know about what the latest trends were in the States; what they were wearing; and the kind of music that was popular, and things in general that was happening over there. They talked through the entire pot of coffee, and he got up to leave. He said, "My day started at 0500 and it is now getting mighty late, and I need to get back to camp. She thanked him for talking with her and walked up and gave him a juicy kiss. She made the fatal mistake of looking into his eyes; her eyes rolled back into her head, and she started, "Do me, Wit! Hurry! Hurry!" She dragged him into the adjoining room, which was her bedroom, unzipped his flight suit, grabbed the Torpedo, fell back on the bed, and he buried the Torpedo up to the hilt. After about six strokes, he thought she was done, but like the Congresswoman, she kept wanting more, and she went eight times before she went into a faint. He was dressing when she sat up in the bed and remarked, "What happened?" He responded, "I don't know; I can't explain it, but I got to get out of here before the Colonel comes home and sees what I've done." Then she said, "Please don't go. I'm frightened of what just happened, and I don't want to be alone right now. I'll put on another pot of coffee and we can talk awhile." Priscilla was now sound asleep and lightly snoring. They sat down at the kitchen table and Wit said, I have to ask, "Does Priscilla do these things often? I mean somebody bringing her home and undressing her for bed?" The young lady answered, "Not often; usually when she gets upset with Joe." "Who usually brings her home?" he continued to ask. "Most of the time it's the Provost Marshal Captain; do you know him?" she responded. "I know who he is," Wit replied, "but I don't really know him. He lends us his truck on weekends; do you participate when he brings her home?" "No!" she said. "I think he's an asshole and I can't stand him; she only uses him as a convenience. I am confused by what happened tonight. Can you explain it?" "No!" he responded. "It's something that just started happening recently, and I find it just as weird as you do. Were you satisfied?" "That's the next crazy thing; I have never been more satisfied in my whole life," she remarked. "That's the important thing, I guess," he added. Then she wanted to talk about what was happening in Germany; when he was going back to the States; what his future plans were; anything to delay his leaving. Then he stated sternly, "I got to get out of here and get back to the base." She gave him a wet kiss on the mouth and thanked him, and he left. He was driving down the street and saw two Privates walking down the sidewalk, laughing and staggering, holding each other up. He pulled over and said, "Come on boys, it's time to call it a night." One slurred, "We sure are having a good time." And they both laughed, and Wit said, "Get in the car; I'm taking you back to camp." They got in the back seat and giggled all the way to camp. Wit asked, "What billets are you in and what is your room number?" They were in 1st Battalion billets on the second floor. He managed to get them upstairs and took them directly to the latrine and told them they better take a whiz before going to bed; he then took them to their rooms, and they flopped on their bunks and fell asleep, still giggling.

CHAPTER 27

The next week, for the first few days, he transported personnel with authorizations to various destinations. He stopped in at the Chaplain's office to see if there were any authorizations, or if he had any instructions. The Chaplain said, "The Provost Marshal Captain wants to see you and Colonel Krause wants to see you and you are to report to the Infirmary." "What does the Colonel want?" Wit asked. "I don't know what any of them want; they just asked to see you when you came in." Chaplain Ray responded. Wit went to the Provost Marshal's office and the Captain was leaning back in his chair and he said, "I haven't had time to get acquainted with you, Mr. Whitson. You seem to be on the go so much." "I know," Wit responded, "sometimes I meet myself coming and going." "You seemed to have time to take the Colonel's wife to dinner and dancing," he smirked. Then Wit recalled what the young lady said about the Captain, so he became cautious of the questions the Captain was asking. He responded, "That's right; I did what the Colonel asked me to do. She had too many cognacs and got a little woozy and I took her home. A young lady came in and helped her get into bed, and she soon fell asleep. I don't know who the young lady was; I assumed she was their Daughter. When I was about to leave, the young lady asked me to stay; she made a pot of coffee and she wanted to know about what the latest trends were in the States. I don't know how long we talked, but I do know we drank up two entire pots of coffee." "That young lady was not their Daughter; she is Priscilla's Sister, Lisa," the Captain clarified. "Then you picked up two soldiers and took them back to camp." "That's right, Captain," Wit answered, getting a little agitated. "Are you tracking me, Captain? You must have a lot of time on your hands worrying about my whereabouts." "Don't get insubordinate with me, Mr. Whitson; I outrank you, you know. I could have you busted," the Captain remarked, angrily. Wit responded, very calm and collected, "You know, Captain, what I went through in Korea, I vowed that nothing was ever going to bother me again if I survived that mess. You could bust me to Private and it would not bother me. I am a career soldier and I know I will get 3 squares a day, a place to sleep, and clothes to wear, and even a little spending money. So, you can threaten me and even take action, I don't care." "I heard you did some big secret thing in Korea," the Captain continued. "What was that?" "Nice try, Captain," Wit quipped. "You would have to go to the Pentagon to get that, and I doubt you would get it then. Our President had that sealed and it will not be unsealed for 40 years, if then…if we are done here, I have to go see the Colonel. If you want me to hand carry any documents, I can do that for ya." "What are you going to see the Colonel about?" the Captain questioned. "I have no idea," Wit answered. "The Chaplain said to go see you and then the Colonel and then the Infirmary. I don't ask why; I just go and find out when I get there." Wit got up to leave and the Captain laid out a couple documents and said, "I want you to sign these." "What are they?" Wit asked. He said, "They are charges against the two boys you picked up. They violated the curfew." "Those boys did nothing wrong; they were just out having fun and lost track of the time. I don't even know what time it was; I didn't look at my watch," Wit argued. "Who signed them?" He looked at the signature and it was far from being legible. "I thought only Doctors wrote where you couldn't read it," he continued. "Lieutenant John Weikart!" the Captain responded. "I'm not going to sign these trumped up charges." Wit complained. "What does Weikart have to do with these boys?" "He's their Platoon leader," the Captain answered. Wit had him by the short hairs now. "I know Lieutenant Weikart; I have transported him on several occasions to various places," Wit remarked. "His office is in the CP and those boys are in 1st Battalion, so you got the wrong information. If you have any problems with me, see Major Ray; he's the one I answer too." The Captain tried one last ditch effort, when he asked, "You borrow my truck on weekends; do you want to continue that?" "Yes, I do, and I appreciate it, and the boys I bring back to keep them out of trouble appreciate it more than me," Wit responded, "but if you want to discontinue that, say the word, and it will end right now. I can spend my Friday and Saturday nights at the movies or in the gym and go to bed early. I just thought it was a nice thing to do, and personnel all the way to the top thinks so too, and they commend you for lending it to us." He thought it would degrade the Captain somewhat, then the Captain said, "That's all Mr. Whitson."

On the way to the Colonel's office, Wit was to pass the Infirmary, so he stopped in. He saw a PFC sitting at a desk and remarked, "Hey Private, I thought I recognized you; I've brought you home a few times on weekends." "Yeah," he said, "I like that German beer and sometimes I drink too much. The best thing about it is, it makes my bowels move regular." "That's probably the only thing it does for ya," Wit responded, smiling. "What did they want to see me about?" "They just want to give you your booster shots," he replied. Wit got his shots and went to see the Colonel. The Colonel explained, "Wit, there is a very important conference being held at the Wald Hotel in Stuttgart and I want you to deliver some valuable information; it's all in the briefcase and I want you to personally hand it to a WAC Lieutenant named Shirley Weller. It is a highly classified conference, so after you put it in her hands, you can't stay, but we have reserved a room for you so you will spend the night. Then tomorrow fly back after the conference concludes, bringing the WAC Lieutenant here so she can relate all that transpired to all our top Regimental Officers. Then your job is completed. Take luggage with all your personal items and a dress uniform, and civilian clothes in the event you are invited to dinner and socialize and dress accordingly."

He landed at a military base, introduced himself, and asked them to look after his chopper and refuel it; he was planning to leave the next day. He then asked to be transported to the Wald Hotel, where the conference was being held. They all were apparently aware of the conference, so they accommodated him on everything he asked. He entered the hotel and registered at the desk and asked the desk clerk to hold his luggage until he returned, and then asked directions to the meeting facility. There were two MPs standing at the door to the meeting facility and one said he would take the brief case. Wit made it clear he was to hand deliver it to Lieutenant Shirley Weller. They allowed him to enter and he had never seen so much brass in one place at one time. The Lieutenant saw him come in and she went directly to meet him and introduced herself and he introduced himself. She directed him, "Go check into your room and put on your dress uniform and come back at 1800 hours for dinner." He watched her as she walked back to her seat; her uniform was a perfect fit and not a thread out of place; her hair was equally the same with not a strand out of place. He got his luggage and went to his room on the top floor with a view of the courtyard and the city. It goes without saying, he was impressed with the hotel and his room; he had never had accommodations to equal it. He took a shower and shaved, watching the time so he wouldn't be late. After he dressed, wearing his Class A uniform, he didn't bother with all his ribbons, but he pinned on his Combat Infantry Badge, the one thing of which he was the most proud; he went down to the meeting facility and the meeting had just concluded for the day.

Lieutenant Shirley met him and took him by the hand and led him to the dining room where they found a table for four. Every feature of Shirley was striking; beautiful with dark hair and an hour-glass figure; a pleasant smile with perfect white teeth. Wit commented, "Everything about you is perfect, so I looked for a flaw, and I found one." "What?" she asked, surprised. He grinned and said, "You have a runner in your nylons." "Damn!" she said, as she looked at the back of her calves. "That's the second pair today." She asked, "Do you like your room?" "Gosh yes," he commented. "I've never had a room as grand. Do you have a room here or are you staying somewhere else?" She answered, "When I arrived, it was booked solid, so I guess I will go out to a military camp and try to find a bunk in a barracks." "No way!" Wit exclaimed.

"You are staying in my room with me. It has enough amenities for both of us, and more. You are not going to stay in an old barracks with a bunch of smelly men." That pleased her and removed some of the obvious tension. A 2-Star General came to their table and asked if he could join them. He introduced himself as General Kevin Kaiser and Wit introduced himself. The waiter offered drinks and Shirley asked for a Slow-Gin-Fizz and the General asked for Bourbon on the rocks and Wit asked for his usual, water with a slice of lemon. The General commented, "Is that all you're gonna drink?" Wit answered, "I don't drink alcohol; I'm in the Chaplain's Service." While they were eating, the General commented, "I check out everybody that attends these conferences and I found your record. You had an impressive tour in Korea. You must have seen a lot of action?" "More than my share, General," Wit replied. "You must have killed a lot of the enemy?" the General continued. "More than my share, General," Wit repeated. "When did you get into helicopters?" the General asked. Wit explained, "I tried civilian life, but I just didn't fit in anymore, so I re-enlisted if they would guarantee me helicopter training. There weren't many in Korea, but I was impressed with the ones I saw and thought if I ever should come back into the Army, that's what I wanted; I took my training at Fort Rucker." "Did you run into a Lieutenant Chris Berger down there?" the General queried. "Yes, he was my training officer. We got along great and I learned a lot from him," Wit responded. "I gave him his battlefield commission," the General said, "he was a non-com and one of the bravest men I ever knew. Your Regimental Commander is, Colonel Joe Krause, a mighty warrior in the Argonne Forest in the big war; puts his men first. The way things are stirring up in Indo-China, you might prove very valuable, being a chopper pilot. That's the quickest way to get around in those jungles." "As long as I can stay in the Chaplain's Service," Wit replied. "Not to change the subject, but what time tomorrow will the conference conclude? I don't have night flying instruments and I need to get us back by dark." "We need to go through the information you brought and if we start by 1000 hours, we should finish by 1500," The General explained. "Will that give you enough time? This little lady is extremely valuable cargo and I want her to get to Straubing tomorrow." "I think we should be alright, if we leave immediately after the meeting," Wit finalized.

"Are your bags at the front desk?" Wit asked. "Yes!" she answered. "I asked them to look after them until I came back." They got her bags and he said, "Come on Louie, follow me upstairs." She responded, "Yes sir, Mr. Whitson, I'm right behind you," They entered the room and she stopped and remarked, "You only have one bed!" He replied, "That's all we need; look at it; it's big enough for 3 or 4 people." She asked him to call for room service and have her uniform pressed and said she was going to take a shower. Room service responded quickly, and Wit handed it out the door and instructed them to have it back by 0700 in the morning. He proceeded to put her other clothes away when she yelled, "Wit, I need you! Now!" He hurried into the bathroom and there she stood dripping wet and shivering, "I forgot the towel." He grabbed a towel and proceeded to dry her off as fast as he could. When he got to her beaver, he continued to rub it with the towel, while looking at her nipples starting to firm up. She smiled and said, "I think it's dry, Wit." "Oops, sorry," he replied, with an ornery grin. "I just wanted to make sure." He told her to wrap the towel around her wet hair. He led her to the bed, and turned out the lights, because he didn't want her to see the *Demon of Love*, at least not yet, and said, "There is only one rule and that is, 'there is no rule'; do whatever you feel like doing." He had it in his mind he was going to work this Goddess over, if it took all night, and he was going to satisfy the Wit Torpedo. They did it all for about 2-3 hours and stopped for a bathroom break. That was a mistake! She turned the lights on and when she returned, she saw the *Demon of Love* in Wit's eyes. Here we go again; her eyes rolled back into her head and she started the routine, "Do me, Wit! Hurry! Hurry!" After 5-6 strokes, he thought she might have had enough, with all they had done already. No way! She kept saying, "Don't quit!" and they continued for a record of 10-11 times and then she went into a faint, like all the others. It was now about 0300 hours, and she sat up, like all the others, and said, "What happened? I couldn't control myself, but I loved every bit of it." He answered, "I can't explain it, but you saw the *Demon of Love*."

Wit concluded, "We are all sweaty and we both should take a shower; we need to try and get some sleep; you have a big day tomorrow and must be at the top of your game." She found a shower cap and they got into the shower and she started blabbering, "Me and my fiancé have been living together for about a year and he wants to get married; I'm not so sure I am ready. He has never satisfied me like tonight and, when I get home, I'm gonna break up with him." "Wait a minute!" Wit exclaimed. "This was a one-time occasion; it is a fantasy; it will never happen again; after tomorrow we will unlikely never see each other again. Don't judge him by what we did; give him more time. Think of it more positively; you could have a family, as well as a career. If you shoot him down, then he is likely to look somewhere else, and maybe start a family with a new woman. Time will pass by and when you reach 45, you will wonder what happened and will consider yourself to be beyond child bearing age, and who knows what desperate measures you will take. You are an intelligent woman, so use that intelligence where it counts; planning your future." "Sometimes I think he just uses me, and he's not serious," she continued. Wit said, "I don't know about that; maybe that's a good reason to re-examine your situation, but just don't jump to conclusions. Think about it and do what you think is best for you." They finished their shower and dried off, and Wit said, "We got to try and get some sleep; we only have a few hours left." "Well I get so mad thinking about it," she continued. "You haven't heard a word I said," Wit scolded. "Maybe I should give you a good spanking." She smiled and responded, "I would like that!" "Yeah, I would like to see you explain to your fiancé the bruise hand prints on your cheeks," Wit joked. "Now you lay on your side facing the far wall and go to sleep; I'll lay on my side facing the other wall. We have a wake-up call for 0700." He fell asleep thinking how he could really love this woman, but she wouldn't be a 'Babs'.

The wake-up call came at the same time there was a tap on the door; delivering the freshly pressed uniform. They got dressed and went down and had breakfast, and it was nearing time for the meeting to start. Wit said, "I'll go back up and pack our bags and check out and make sure we have transportation back to the chopper." The meeting concluded at 1430; Shirley came out and General Kaiser right behind her. The General shook Wit's hand and said, "Nice meeting you Mr. Whitson; you get this little lady to Straubing safely; she still has important work to do before she goes back stateside." "Nice meeting you, General," Wit concurred, "and it was a pleasure breaking bread with ya last night. You have a safe trip back to Washington." Wit had bought some snacks and cokes for their trip back because they skipped lunch. The weather was good, and the sky was clear, and they arrived at the motor pool with daylight to spare. Sgt. Knudsen transported them to Colonel Joe's office. There was plenty of brass attending that meeting as well; even Priscilla was there. Wit introduced the WAC Lieutenant and turned to leave and said, "My job is finished." The Colonel interrupted, "How was your room at the hotel, Wit?" "It was great; I was on the top floor and had a great view of the city. I didn't realize Stuttgart was that big," he explained. Then Priscilla asked, "And how was your room, Lieutenant?" She answered softly, "I had a great view, as well." When Wit reached the door, the WAC Lieutenant stopped him and gave him a little peck on the cheek, and said quietly, "Thanks, Wit!" Priscilla remarked, "Hey, that's conduct unbecoming an officer." She took Wit by the arm and said, "Come on, Wit, and I'll buy your dinner." He responded, "I'm not going to town; I've had a couple rough days; we can go to the Officer's Mess." While they were eating, Priscilla asked, with a little jealousy in her voice, "What was that all about with that cute little WAC?" "Oh, she is living with her fiancé in Washington, and he wants to get married, and she is all nervous about it. I tried to counsel her that marriage was a serious commitment and she better be sure before she makes the leap," he explained. Priscilla then said, "You sound like you are experienced." "I am!" he replied, "I had a failed marriage that lasted about 6 months." "What happened?" Priscilla kept prying. "She couldn't keep her pants on," he responded sternly. Priscilla knew she hit a nerve and settled down and just made small talk. "Now that we are on the subject," Wit began, "I want you to end your extracurricular activities with the Provost Captain." She turned a little pale, and remarked, "Do you know about that?" "I get around," he said, "and I know a lot of stuff that goes on. You are risking everything and he ain't risking anything; he is a very evil and devious man and no telling how many wives he has used his influence on to get what he wants. He might even try to black-mail you someday, if he thinks you will bow down to him. You've been married to a great man for 25 years and if he ever got wind of that kind of stuff, your lifestyle, as you know it, would be over."

CHAPTER 28

About two weeks later, Chaplain Ray informed Wit that Colonel Rankin had a replacement helicopter for him, "It's not the same model, so you better take your mechanics with you to get trained on it. I'll get the orders cut for TDY to Freising and you can leave day after tomorrow." Wit went to the motor pool and informed Sgt. Knudsen of the plan, and he wanted the same 3 mechanics that had been servicing his present chopper. He informed Sgt. Knudsen that he had put the three mechanics in for an additional stripe, since they had been doing an outstanding job keeping his old bird in the air. All four rode in the old chopper this time; it was the first time two of them were ever in it; it was a lot smoother than bouncing on the road in a truck. They landed at Freising and Wit instructed the men to get settled in their quarters; the airmen were cordial as usual. There sat a brand-spanking new helicopter with a Chaplain's insignia on the doors and written across the boom was the letters 'CHOPPER CHAPLAIN'. Wit was stunned! It was so beautiful he even got tears in his eyes. Colonel Rankin came out and said, "You must have been rubbing elbows with the right people; it's all yours! A brand new 'BELL UH-1H IROQUOIS', more commonly called, 'HUEY', It has all the bells and whistles available, and now you have to spend the week learning how to use all those bells and whistles. Your mechanics will spend their time learning how to service it." That evening the mechanics and Wit went to the local Gast Haus with the airmen, and while the boys were downing a couple beers, Hap said, "You couldn't fly at night before, now they will have you flying around the clock." "You are right, Hap," Wit responded. "I'm gonna need to put in a requisition for another chopper pilot." Dilly said, "Won't be long and you will have your own Air Force." They all laughed because it was truly a joyous occasion; Wit even bought the beers.

Wit flew with a training officer for the first three days, learning about all the controls and radio, and even went up at night to learn how to use the night instruments. He commented to the training officer on how sweet and smooth the chopper handled, and the vast improvement it was over his old one. He soloed the next two days, following a required routine, which familiarized him with the use of everything in every possible situation. The mechanics spent their time being instructed on a like-model performing all the maintenance procedures and requirements. When their duties were completed, Wit said, "Ok men, let's take this Big Boy to Straubing and show off a little, but not too much, we don't want anybody to be jealous and frown on us." Colonel Rankin came out to see them off, and commented, "We will overhaul your old machine for ya and when you get a second pilot, let us know. I spoke with Colonel Joe several days ago and he put in a requisition to Fort Rucker for a pilot out of the next graduating class, which I understand will happen in the next few weeks." "Thanks

Colonel!" Wit replied. "You have gone above and beyond for us and I really appreciate it." They took off and Wit radioed ahead to Sgt Knudsen their ETA (estimated time of arrival) and landed at the motor pool close to the time, and all the motor pool personnel were out waiting to see the new chopper. Also waiting were Colonel Joe and Priscilla, Chaplain Ray, and Corporal Jay. Wit just beamed with pride; this had to be the happiest day of his life. The Colonel informed Sgt. Knudsen that he had prepared a luncheon at the Officer's Mess and for him to bring the three mechanics for a little celebration. Tables were pushed together with ten chairs around them and the nine sat down and the Colonel motioned for Smokie to sit and join them. Several KPs served the food and drinks, and after Chaplain Ray gave the blessing, there was a lot of laughing and joking among them. Then Sgt. Knudsen distributed certificates to the three mechanics for completing the Helicopter Maintenance Training and iterated that they would go into their files. Then the Colonel asked Wit, "Do you want the honors?" Wit stood and said, "You three mechanics have done an outstanding job of keeping the old chopper fine-tuned and safe for me to fly around Bavaria and I sincerely appreciate it. Sometimes you had to put in extra time and effort so I could meet my schedules, and there were times, even Dilly had to sacrifice and not go to town and be with the Schatzis." They all laughed at that because they all knew Dilly. "I felt you should be rewarded, and all here agreed with me and allowed me to add another stripe to your uniforms, so Colonel Joe has honored me, and allowed me, to present to you this promotion." This was truly a joyous occasion, mainly because they all had the highest regards for Wit for what he had brought to Straubing; like the Congresswoman said, "He is the most loved man in Bavaria."

The next morning, while on the way to the Chaplain's office, Wit stopped in the PX for some shaving cream. He was passing a rack of sunglasses, stopped suddenly, and muttered to himself, "There's exactly what I need." He saw sunglasses that were mirrors on the outside where his eyes were not visible to the person trying to look into his eyes. He lifted them from the rack and examined them and they were perfect for his purpose; the ladies could not look into his eyes and see the *Demon of Love*. He bought two pairs, one to wear, and one to keep in the chopper, in case he should misplace one, or lose it. He wore a pair, relieved that he found a solution to his problem; he didn't have to feel weird looking at their shoulder, or past them, avoiding eye contact. He proceeded to the Chaplain's office and, when he walked in, the Chaplain said, "Good morning Wit, have you ever met my wife, Helga?" Whoa, what the motor pool boys were saying is right. She walked over and extended her hand to shake, and said, "Pleased to meet you, Wit, I've been hearing a lot about you and now I get to meet you in person." He got a whiff of her expensive perfume and he was temporarily speechless. She certainly was not a typical Schatzi but gave him the first impression she was a high-priced whore. Everything about her was high class from top to bottom and she was truly beautiful. Trying to recover from the shock, his first thought was, "How did Chaplain Ray end up with an Amazon like this?" "Pleased to meet you, Helga. Are you from Straubing?" he asked, after coming to his senses. Chaplain Ray said, "No, she is from Munich. She goes down there occasionally on weekends to visit with her family. Since you haven't been to Munich, maybe you could go with her sometime and she could show you around. It's about 2 to 3 hours by train and you could get a close look at the countryside." Wit's head was abuzz, "Eh, what? This guy is sending his wife, arguably the most beautiful woman in Germany, on a weekend trip with another man? Does he have a screw loose? Just has to be something wrong with this picture!" After he finally collected himself, he responded, "Why, yeah, I would like to see Munich. When I was a kid during the war, I heard Hitler made speeches to hundreds of thousands of people there. From the newsreels at that time, it looked like a very large and busy city." Then Chaplain Ray added, "I'll let you know the next time she plans a trip, and if you aren't too busy, you can get away for a few days." Wit said, "Not to change the subject, but are there any authorizations for today?" The Chaplain answered, "Yes, there is a Captain that wants a ride to Nurnberg," and he handed him the document, and Wit walked out. Walking to the motor pool, he muttered out loud, "I don't care how busy I am, I will definitely be available for that trip. Sure, glad I kept my new sunglasses on. That could have been a disaster."

A few days later, the Chaplain informed Wit that the Colonel wanted to see him; he didn't know why or how important it was. Wit went to the CP and everybody greeted him cheerfully, which lifted his spirits considerably. The Colonel greeted him and said, "Have a seat, Wit. I keep getting glowing reports about you, as far away as Washington, and I started thinking that I don't really know you, and I mean really know you. Have you always been in the Chaplain's Service?" "I never got into the Chaplain's Service until I arrived in Korea. I was trained at Camp Breckinridge, Ky in the 101st Airborne Infantry; trained, as we were told, to be replacements. To make a long story short, the Chaplain observed me praying for the severely injured that were destined to die, and I prayed until they took their final breath, hoping God would hear me and accept their souls into Heaven. He asked if I would be interested in being his Chaplain's Assistant, working with the medical tent when casualties came in. We were in an outpost close to the front lines made up of tents, so we could be mobile and move on short notice. I would race to the battlefield and assist wherever I could to try and save the injured and pray for the dying." "So, you saw action?" the Colonel asked. "Yes!" Wit replied. "More than my share." "Did you kill anybody?" he continued to question. "Yes! Wit answered. "More than my share. How many is hard to say; hundreds, at least." "Did it bother you to kill?" he asked. "Not at all, because I was trained for it," Wit responded, "and in a lot of cases, it was to kill or be killed. At first, I was nervous because I never hurt anybody in my whole life, and the more I killed the more relaxed I became, and did what I had to do, so actually it became easy. I had three months left in my enlistment and could have gotten out, but the horror of it all stuck in my mind and I went to Fort Rucker where I worked in the Chaplain's Service. There were troops that returned from the war that were confused and mixed up, so I worked with them, hopefully to help straighten them out. Working with them helped get my mind straight; I thought enough to go back into civilian life. I met a girl and got married and discovered after six months that I did not fit in anymore and decided to go back into the Army where they understood me and I understand them, providing they would put me into Helicopter Pilot Training. So that's the long and short of it. I had an Uncle that told me when I was a teenager that *'it doesn't cost anything to be friendly'* and I learned to live by that. I try to go out of my way to help people whenever I can and have a kind word for everybody I meet; doesn't mean everybody likes me, but that's ok, I do my thing and feel good about it." "I think I got the picture," Colonel Joe said. "Colonel Rankin said you are the most popular guy in Bavaria, and I believe it. Keep up the good work." The Colonel threw a couple documents on his desk and said, "Let me ask you about these?" "What are they?" Wit asked. "The two boys you picked up the night you took Priscilla home, like I asked you to do, violated the curfew, and the Provost Captain brought these charges against them. They have your name on them, so what can you tell me about 'em?" the Colonel requested. "Colonel!" Wit began. "The night I took your wife home, she insisted we go to a restaurant and eat dinner, which I agreed to because I hadn't eaten since breakfast. She had a few cognacs and we danced to a couple tunes, and she said she was feeling a little tipsy, so I told her we better go, because I didn't know where she lived. I don't know what time it was when we got there. Your sister-in-law, Lisa, came in and put her to bed, and I said I had to get back to camp. Lisa begged me to stay and talk and she would make a pot of coffee. She wanted to know what was happening in the States and what my future-plans were, and just normal conversation. I thought she was just wanting to talk to someone, so we talked through two pots of coffee. I never looked at my watch when I left so I don't have the slightest idea what time it was. I saw the two boys walking down the sidewalk, laughing and singing, and having a good time. I picked them up and said it was time to go back to camp. Their rooms were on the second floor of the 1st Battalion billet, so I wrestled them upstairs, insisted they visit the latrine, and then took them to their rooms, and they flopped down and fell asleep, still laughing. The Provost Captain said the signatures on those documents were Lt. John Weikart and if you look at them, you will see they are not legible. I refused to sign them when he said Lt. Weikart was their Platoon leader and brought charges. I explained to him that I knew the Lieutenant from our numerous trips, and his office was in the CP and he had nothing to do with the 1st Battalion, so he had false information. I also explained, in my opinion, that these boys didn't do anything wrong and didn't warrant a blemish on their records, that they were just out enjoying themselves and lost track of time. He accused me of insubordination and threatened to bust me, since he outranked me. I politely told him to do what he had to do, that it would not bother me in the least. He then threatened to stop letting us use the Drunk Mobile if I didn't reveal to him the highly secret event that took place in Korea that was sealed by the President and not to be declassified for 40 years. I told him good luck with that, and he excused me. I say again, Colonel, those boys didn't do enough wrong to warrant a court-martial. Extra detail like cleaning the latrine or KP or something of that nature is sufficient." The Colonel just sat and looked at him, absorbing all he was saying. "Let me say one last thing," Wit added, "and I hope you don't take it the wrong way. General Kaiser paid you quite a compliment when he said, 'Colonel Joe always took care of his men'. I am not going to sign a trumped-up charge against those boys." The Colonel folded the two documents and threw them in the trash can, and said, "Nice talking to ya Wit; have a nice day!" Wit got up, thanked him for his time, and walked out.

CHAPTER 29

For the next couple weeks, Wit continued to transport personnel in his new chopper and received positive comments on how much it was improved over the old one. This pleased him because he was obviously proud of it. He went to the Chaplain's office to see if he had received any authorizations. The Chaplain informed him that Helga was planning a trip to Munich and was leaving the following Friday; if he thought he could get away and wanted to go, she would make all the arrangements. He responded that he definitely wanted to go. The Chaplain suggested that he dress casually and look like one of the locals, because Helga would dress likewise, and it would be more relaxing than wearing a uniform. He went to the barber shop and got a trim; checked all his toilet articles to be sure he had enough of everything; laid out all the clothing he would wear and/or take; informed the men at the motor pool that he was going on a 3-day pass.

Corporal Jay transported him to the train station and Helga arrived within a few minutes after he did. He hardly recognized her because she dressed as normal as a local would dress. Her hair was tied in a pony-tail; she wore petal pushers and a button-up blouse; her shoes were saddle-oxfords with low cut anklets; she wore very little make-up. She looked every bit like an American teeny-bopper. Despite all her efforts, she couldn't completely camouflage that superior figure, and still got the attention of lusty eyes. They boarded the train and had double seats facing each other and she sat with one leg folded under her and jabbered like an excited teenager all the way to Munich; her conversation was directly to the point, her desire to go to the States. Wit eventually got the impression that her number one goal was to get to the States, and he felt she was going to get there by hook or crook, even if she had to use Chaplain Ray Jones as a stepping stone. Too bad, because he thought Ray was a terrific guy and didn't deserve to be conned like that; or is he too blind and stupid to think she really loved him? It's like an old movie and you watch it all unfold and can't wait to see how it ends.

They hailed a taxi and were transported to the hotel; Wit's eyes bugged out. It had to have been the most expensive and glamorous and fanciest hotel in Munich. When they walked through the huge lobby to the front desk to register, she put on a little extra twist with her hips, and all the hotel personnel greeted her by her first name. He immediately realized that he hit the nail on the head when he first met her; this was her place of business and the price here for one night was equal to the Chaplain's monthly pay. A bellhop carried their bags to the elevator and pushed the button to the 10th floor. "How have you been Helga?" he asked. "Just fine, Siegfried, how's the family?" she responded. They arrived at their room, and the first thing he noticed was one huge bed. His mind clicked into gear, "Loren Whitson, you are about to get the adventure of your life." She went into the bathroom while he proceeded to unpack his bag. She came out wearing an amber colored satin robe with a sash tied around her waist. His immediate thought was, "She never bought that thing at the PX for 5 bucks." She glided to about the center of the large room; untied the sash; threw open the robe; cocked one hip off to one side, displaying all the tools of her trade; and she had it all. With an inviting smile, she had him undressed and in the bed before he could take a second breath. She used all the tricks of the trade, like in a rehearsed sequence, first to the last. The only thing he could think was some rich business man would gladly pay a $1000 a night for what he was getting for free.

Finally, she said, "Get dressed and we will go down to the dining room for dinner." The dining room was huge with dimly lit crystal chandeliers spaced throughout the room over a spacious dance floor. A small combo band played soft and soothing dinner music, meant to relax the dining guests. Helga ordered a bottle of an expensive dinner wine and Wit had his usual, water with a slice of lemon. She must have worked up a thirst because she wiped out over half the bottle while they ate. After they ate, they just sat and listened to the music for a while, and then she suggested they dance. This was the next puzzling part; she held him so close that he could feel her heart beating through their clothes; she closed her eyes and rubbed her cheek against his, and periodically gave him a gentle kiss on his mouth. This was a totally different character than when they were in the room. It was like she had two personalities; was this the one Major Ray fell in love with? They sat down and she wiped out the rest of the bottle of wine, and then ordered another one. They danced some more, and she drank some more until she suggested they go back to the room. The first episode she made love to him; the second episode he made love to her and it was totally different; she was receptive to all his moves and she was enjoying every bit of it.

They slept in the next morning and decided to order in a brunch since it was late. While they were eating, Wit thought it would be a good idea to go out and walk around and see the sights; Major Ray would certainly ask what they saw in Munich and they would need to tell him something that was not a lie. They took a shower and it was a little after noontime when they started their walk. They sauntered around, holding hands like a couple tourists, looked at various points of interest and conversed about the busy traffic and crowded streets. She knew about the area close to the hotel, but when they got a few blocks away, she didn't know any more about it then he did. He became aware of it but elected not to say anything. They strolled for a couple hours and then stopped and got something to drink at a sidewalk café; making small talk and commenting on things they observed that were interesting; continued their walk until it was nearing dinner time and then returned to the hotel when she suggested they eat before returning to their room. They listened to the music while they ate; they didn't dance because she said her feet were tired.

They entered their room and startled an intruder who was rifling through their luggage. Wit automatically went into action; jumped on the guy and forced him to empty his pockets, and he threw everything on the bed; Wit had nothing of value, but Helga had some expensive jewelry. He was on the verge of ripping out his throat when Helga saw the *Demon of Death* in Wit's eyes and she yelled at him continuously to stop and let him go; she said she got everything back. He came to his senses in the nick of time, an instant before the intruder was doomed to die. The intruder raced out the door like his pants were on fire. She reacted exactly like his wife, Maggie, had done when she saw the flaming red, unhuman-like eyes. She shook with fright and showed fear like she had never known. She never spoke another word and Wit sensed it, and it goes without saying the love making was over. He was a little shaky from what he almost had done, and knowing the *Demon of Death* remained. He had hoped it transformed into the *Demon of Love*, but that obviously wasn't the case. She remained quiet, put on her night clothes and lay on her side of the bed with her back to him, and he did likewise; she shifted positions all during the night, apparently to frightened to sleep.

The next morning, she stated that the train was scheduled to leave for Straubing at noon and suggested they order in their breakfast, shower, and get there a little early because, being Sunday, most likely a lot of people would be traveling. They didn't look up while they ate, and he then asked, "You are not from Munich, are you?" She spoke quietly and responded, "No, I am from a little town about 30 kilometers outside of Munich called Andechs," "You don't have any relatives here, do ya?" he continued. She answered "No, I don't." "Then how did you end up here and perform your activities?" he insisted. Then she opened up and explained, "I was a young teen age girl when our town was bombed and totally destroyed during the war. We had nothing; no food; no money; no shelter; just imagine what it is like to have absolutely nothing. I decided to come to Munich because it was a prosperous city and there must be work, any kind of work. I was noticed by the young men and they offered me 40 Deutsch-Marks ($10) to have sex with them, and that provided the meals and money to buy a few clothes. It was easy and doing it more often, I was able to take money and food to my Mother and family. As I grew and became more attractive to men, I raised my price to 80 Marks ($20), and business increased. When I took food and money to my Mother, she condemned me for my activities, but never refused any of it. I noticed the Prostitutes around the big hotels, the way they dressed and conducted themselves, and how they attracted the men of means. I bought a couple expensive outfits, some tantalizing perfume, painted myself up, learned how to walk to call attention to my body, raised my price to 4000 Marks ($1000) a night, and started making some real money. I became acquainted with the hotel staff and offered them a commission if they could line me up with rich business men. I learned what it takes to please them and now they ask for me specifically when they come to this hotel." Then Wit asked the big question, "Do you have a plan for when Ray finds out? You know somebody is going to learn about it and think it would be exciting to tell him just to see what happens; the world is full of those types of people." "Are you going to tell him?" she asked, nervously. "Never!" he exclaimed. "Your secret is safe with me; it will destroy that man if he finds out and I hope I'm not around when it happens. He is one of the greatest men I know, and it would be cruel to drop a bomb on him like that."

She never spoke another word; they boarded the train and she just stared out the window; he cat-napped all the way to Straubing. When they arrived, they climbed into one of the waiting taxis; the driver got out and threw their luggage into the trunk; she gave him her address. When the cab pulled up to her house, he carried her luggage to her door; she got out and never said goodbye, kiss my ass, or nothing. He thought it was just as well and knew his adventure with Miss Helga had ended; for good. He instructed the driver to take him to the Army base and was dropped off at the gate. He had the gate guard call Corporal Jay to come and pick him up and take him to his billet. The next morning, when he went to the Chaplain's office to see if there were any authorizations waiting for him, Major Ray asked, "What did you think of Munich? Did you enjoy your trip?" "I'll tell ya, Major, there is so much to see there, that it would take a couple weeks to see it all; and all the traffic and people hustling around, I can do without. I'll just stick with little old quiet Straubing," he explained. "The hotel was great; the music was great; I ate till I could barely walk; now I'm ready to get back to work." Major Ray didn't mention Helga; she probably never acted any different. She is such a professional 'faker', she most likely just picked up where she left off; poor guy!

A couple weeks later, on a Friday night, a Staff Sergeant, came back to the base, exceedingly drunk and raising a ruckus. The gate guard pulled his pass; he went to the armory and broke in and stole weapons and ammunition and then went to the ammo dump and commandeered an ammo truck, went back to the gate and shot and killed the gate guard. The guard only had 10 days left before he was to go home. This created a real uproar and so every guard post had to be manned around the clock, requiring every soldier to stand guard. They captured the killer, but they didn't relax the guard duty. Morale hit rock bottom for the next couple weeks. Wit mentioned that if that Sergeant would have returned to the base in the Drunk Mobile, the entire incident could have been avoided.

A couple weeks later, after everything seemed to cool down, a call came in to the Staff Duty Officer from one of the line companies, that a Platoon of Czech tanks had crossed the border into Germany. The Staff Duty Officer, who was normally a Lieutenant, thought it might be a joke, so he disregarded it. (Ala, Pearl Harbor). When Colonel Joe found out about it, he became furious, and ordered, 'henceforth the Staff Duty Officer would be no less than a Major'.

CHAPTER 30

The hierarchy must have gotten wind of it because S-2, the intelligence group, made a study and determined that, if the base at Straubing should be attacked by the Communists with jets and missiles, it could virtually be destroyed in 10 minutes. Enter General George Schafer; the gruff speaking; hardnosed disciplinarian; cigar smoking; snarl lipped; take no prisoners Commander of the Vll Corps. He called an unannounced Muster-Alert for all the bases under his command at 0400. Talk about stirring things up. Loud speakers started blaring and whistles blowing, rousing everybody out of their warm bunks. Wit had never experienced an alert like this. He ran out into the hallway in his t-shirt and boxers trying to find out what was happening, when a Staff Sergeant, who was putting the push on his troops, tried to explain it in as short a time as possible. Then the Colonel's Orderly approached him and said he was needed in the Colonel's office immediately. Wit responded, "I will get there as soon as I can, but first I have to take my daily constitutional, and that has higher priority." So, he whisked into the latrine, tried to rush his business, then dressed, and then hot-footed it to the Colonel's office. When he entered, Colonel Joe was talking with a mean-ass looking General. "This is our helicopter pilot, Chief Warrant Officer Loren Whitson," the Colonel introduced to the General. "He knows more of the whereabouts of Bavaria than anyone else and he will transport you to any destination you ask." Then he continued, "Wit, this is General George Schafer, our Supreme Commander of Vll Corps. I want you to stick with him like glue and take him wherever he asks to go." The General, trying to act tough said, "Yeah, and when I say shit, you better squat." That come on didn't bother Wit, and he responded, "Sorry General, you are too late. I went before I came over here." Colonel Joe knew Wit was not going to be phased by this big mouth General and just smiled.

All the sections of Headquarters Company in the CP had their own assigned deuce and a half, and a driver from each section. The first order of business for those drivers was to go to town and drive a predetermined route and pick up all the personnel that lived in town. Meanwhile all the personnel in the sections of the CP unloaded all the files from the file cabinets and packed them into banker boxes; then loaded the boxes into the trucks on their return to the base; the personnel then boarded the trucks. The trucks were directed to leave the base in a predetermined order in a convoy that traveled what seemed like an eternity to a designated area. As they passed through small towns, the women would run out and throw water on the road to hold down the dust and keep it out of their houses. When they reached the heavily wooded area, more like a forest; referred to it as the Bavarian Forest, which was so thick that very little light filtered into it; they set up camp. The cooks set up first because the troops had not been fed, and they proceeded to form the serving lines for breakfast and coffee. Some of the non-coms tried to flex their power and have the troops dig fox holes, but very little of that materialized. It was all planned to simulate an actual attack by enemy forces and all the personnel would know how to function if such an attack should occur. An important fact was mentioned, 'the personnel living in town with their families might think it more important, and their first priority would be to see that their families were safe'; if it was for real.

The General suggested they fly over the convoys of each of the bases to view their exiting procedures. He then wanted to fly over the bivouac areas to see their camouflage techniques and if they were setting up proper perimeters surrounding the areas. When he figured the cooks had plenty of time to set up their field mess, he made the suggestion of Wit's liking, "Let's find a place to set down and have breakfast with the men; are you hungry?" Wit responded, "I can eat anything that can't eat me first." They looked for a clearing big enough for the chopper to set down, and they found one, but it was going to be tight. "Can you set down in that small space, Wit?" the General asked. "General, I can thread a needle with this thing, so just hang on," Wit bragged. He set it down gently and smoothly, and the General congratulated him, "Good job, Wit!" The General walked around, inspecting the area, with Wit right on his heels; he just shook his head to the affirmative, like he was satisfied with the setup. As they strolled through the area, the men saluted and a few said, "How's it going, Wit?" "Fine, is everything alright? If you need any help, let me know," he responded. "Why would they need help?" the General asked. "That's what the Chaplain's Service does," Wit replied. "These boys are 5000 miles away from home and they have families that may have problems and they worry about them, so we do what we can to ease the situation." "Do they all have problems?" he asked. "No, I try to be friendly with everybody and they appreciate it," Wit replied, "I had a dear old Uncle that would tell me when I was a young teenager, *'it doesn't cost anything to be friendly'*," The chow line was moving quickly and when the General had seen all he wanted, they selected mess kits, and got in line like all the other troops, where the cooks served them generously with food and coffee.

They sat under a big tree and the General got a little more personable, and a lot less intimidating, when he asked, "Wit, nothing much bothers you, does it?" Wit replied, "General, I made a vow that if I should get out of Korea with all my skin, nothing was ever going to bother me again, and I have stuck to that vow." "I noticed you have 'CHOPPER CHAPLAIN' painted on your chopper, are you in the Chaplain's Service? Have you always been in the Chaplain's Service?" "I took my basic training with the 101st Airborne Infantry at Camp Breckinridge, Ky and the very first thing they told us was that we were training to be replacements in Korea. When we landed at Pusan,.........and he proceeded to relate his story as he told Colonel Joe. Chaplain Mike Molloy was one of the finest men I had ever known, and we related as close as a Father and Son could possibly be, not like an officer and a lowly soldier. He taught me how to love your fellow man and do whatever it takes to instill the love of God. He said not to take every case to heart, it will drive you crazy; do your best and be satisfied, and then move on to someone else that needs you. I am a career soldier and I will stay in the Chaplain's Service until I can't function anymore. Then I will know I have done my best and will be satisfied." "Did you see action in Korea?"

he asked. "Yes! General," Wit replied. "More than my share." "Did you kill anybody?" he continued to ask. "Yes! General," Wit replied. "More than can be counted; in the hundreds, maybe thousands." The General seemed to be feeling things out, when he asked, "What do you think of Colonel Krause." Wit sensed it and answered, "Colonel Krause, and even his wife, Priscilla, have treated me admirably and it has been an honor to serve them. I agree with General Kaiser when he said Colonel Joe was a great warrior and takes care of his men." "You know General Kaiser?" the General asked, sounding surprised. "Why, yeah," Wit replied, "we broke bread together in Stuttgart at that big conference." "I was at that conference, and I didn't see you," the General followed. "I didn't take part in the conference, I only delivered a briefcase of information, and transported the WAC Lieutenant Shirley Weller back to Straubing." Wit explained. "General Kaiser is the most feared officer in the Pentagon," the General commented. "What else did he have to say?" "He said that the way things are heating up in Indo-China, with my skill as a chopper pilot, I would probably prove more valuable there than here," Wit explained. The General laughed and remarked, "Then I suggest you better start packing your bags." The General changed the subject, slightly, "Do you know Colonel Rankin from Freising AFB?" "Yes, Sir, he has been of most valuable service to me and my chopper mechanics," Wit answered. "I don't know how we would have functioned without him and his men."

After seeing everything to the General's satisfaction, they flew back to the base and landed at the motor pool. Wit instructed Master Sergeant Knudsen to have the men check the chopper good and fill her up; she was pretty dry from being up all day. The General instructed Sgt. Knudsen to drive them to the Officer's Mess; Colonel Rankin, Colonel Krause, and Priscilla met them there and Smokie served them an elaborate meal. Colonel Joe asked, "Well, General Schafer, how did you get along with our Chopper Chaplain? Did he take you to all the places you wanted to see?" The General was quiet, like he was thinking, and said, "You know what amazes me? This guy knows where everything is, and everybody knows him by name; I've never known anybody like that in all my years in the service." Colonel Rankin remarked, "He's the most popular man in Bavaria, and the Congresswoman said he was the most loved." Priscilla just beamed when she heard that, and added, "I agree with that whole heartedly." "He would be an asset to my staff," the General suggested. Colonel Joe spoke up, "I don't think that is possible, General, he is dedicated to the Chaplain's Service, and I doubt any offer would sway him away from that." Wit wasn't paying attention to much of the conversation; his mind was on hitting the sack and getting the sleep he lost early that morning. The General then finalized, "Colonel Joe, the S-2 boys said this base would be annihilated in 10 minutes if attacked by the Communists by using jets and missiles. From what I've seen today, I don't agree with that. They would get some of it, but certainly not all of it. You have a well-trained unit that is commendable. I will send in my report and you will get a letter of accommodation." That was pleasing to hear because everybody was naturally a little nervous. It took about a week for everything to get back to normal.

Wit asked Colonel Rankin how the overhaul of the old chopper was progressing, and he said it might take another couple weeks. He said the chopper was so outdated, some of the parts were discontinued, so they had to resort to parting out some of the other choppers of that model to get the parts they needed. Colonel Joe informed Major Ray that a new graduate from Fort Rucker was due in a few weeks following a leave that he had accrued and wanted to use up; visiting his family. Major Ray called Wit in and wanted his opinion of whether the new man should be attached to the Chaplain's Service or attached directly to the CP. Wit suggested, "Wait and see what kind of man he is, and if he is worthy of being attached to this office. If he is, then I will need to spend a considerable amount of time getting him on board, and trained to fly our choppers, which are different than the ones on which he trained. It would be counterproductive for him to resort to a new system and not stick with our present one which is working quite well." Wit asked to review the file of the new man, WO Russell Lambert, to learn a little about his background. Mr. Lambert ranked high in his training class and met the major requirements to be in the Chaplain's Service, which made it a whole lot easier for him to be included. He was tall with blonde hair; had a pleasant disposition and seemed to always have a smile on his face; a very likeable person. He was assigned a room in the same billet as Wit, which made it easier to communicate.

Corporal Jay completed his enlistment and rotated back to the States and Major Ray requested a replacement and his new orderly's name is Corporal Leon Brown. As soon as Cpl. Brown arrived, Wit introduced him to 'The Drunk Mobile', and he agreed to make the weekend runs to town and bring back the party animals. He acclimated the Corporal to the base and where all the facilities were located; the CP; all the billets; the all-important motor pool; places he should be familiar with, and where to deliver the partiers. When Mister Lambert arrived, he agreed to continue the weekend runs, also, so he was included, and in just a couple weekends, they were both handling the job admirably. Wit took Mr. Lambert to the motor pool and introduced him to Sgt. Knudsen and the mechanics. He suggested to Sgt. Knudsen that he begin a training program for more chopper mechanics; once Mr. Lambert completed his training in both choppers, and they started flying at the same time, the mechanics were going to be overloaded keeping them in the air. Colonel Rankin contacted Wit when the old chopper overhaul was completed and ordered Wit to fly Mr. Lambert to Freising for training in both choppers with the assistance of his Air Force training officer. While there, Colonel Rankin informed Wit that the word he was getting was the unrest in Indo-China was escalating, and the number of advisory troops were increasing, and they were starting to look at all the experienced chopper pilots and mechanics in all the branches of the services.

After the word got out that two choppers were available, it didn't take long for the authorizations to increase accordingly. Wit passed on the information of what Colonel Rankin had said to Major Ray and suggested they requisition an additional pilot, because he may become a short timer. Seeing how well Mr. Lambert had taken to the job, Wit felt it was an opportune time to take a vacation, since he hadn't been out of Bavaria for the last year and a half. He asked Major Ray for a week leave and thought he would go to The Netherlands to start with, and proceed from there, while the weather was still good. He took a scenic train ride to Amsterdam, and had a taxi take him to a decent hotel. The hotel desk clerk said there was a circus in town, and they were booked solid; people coming from all directions. He asked Wit if he would be willing to share a room and Wit answered, "It will depend on who I must share it with." He gave Wit the key to room 231 on the second floor. Wit went in, and not seeing anyone there, yelled out, "Hello, is anybody here?" A swivel rocker was sitting to one side and it spun around, and there sat a little lady midget. She wasn't short on words when she said, "I told them I didn't want to share the room with some old stinking woman." Wit responded, "I told them I didn't want some old smelly man." She laughed and said, "My name is, Libbey." He said, "They call me, Wit." She explained, "The circus comes to town once a year and people come from all directions; the hotels are always full. I am one of the performers in the circus and have been for many years. My husband did a high wire act and we tried to persuade him to use a safety net, but he said people come to see thrills, so he performed without it. 15 years ago, he fell to his death, so I am a widow. Before you ask, I am 55 years old and 40 inches tall." Wit asked, "Are there any other little people, besides you, that are with the circus?" "Yes," she answered, "there are four other couples, but they won't associate with me, because I asked the women to share their husbands with me." "Now, Libbey, you know that wouldn't work," Wit responded. "You are smart enough to know that could turn into a disaster; one of the husbands may find you more satisfying than his wife, and that could really get ugly. People have been murdered over such as that. Is it possible that one of them has a Brother or Brother-In-Law or a Cousin they could fix you up with?" "They have never offered to find me a mate," she answered. "What do you do, Wit," she asked. "I'm in the United States Army," he replied, "and I am stationed in Bavaria in Germany, and I thought I should see other countries while I had the chance." The Dutch people love Americans," she stated. "When the Nazis occupied our country, they brutalized the people and raped the young girls and made us work for them for nothing. Then one day the sky was filled with paratroopers; fine strong young men from the 101st Airborne. They sent the Nazis running for their lives and we cheered; sad part was a lot of the young men were killed. We never forgot that and will always be grateful."

Then she stunned him with a question when she brazenly asked, "I was getting ready to take a shower; do you want to have sex before we shower, or after?" He answered, jokingly, "We can do both!" Well, she wasn't joking and started to peel off her little outfit. He then kicked his brain in gear and thought, "Boy, you better get out of here, so think of something fast." He did, when he asked, "Would you do me a favor, Libbey?" She replied, "Yes, if I can." He asked, "Could you shave off the long hair in your armpits and on your legs? It's grossing me out!" She responded, "Yeah, I can do that." When she disappeared into the bathroom, and out of his sight, he put on his sunglasses, grabbed his bag and ran like a scared rabbit down the hall to the stairs and went down, two at a time, to the crowded lobby. He then walked nonchalantly out the door. Taxis were lined up at the curb bumper to bumper. A taxi pulled up, double parked to let out the fare. The driver got out to get their bags and carried them to the door where a doorman carried them in. The taxi door was left open and Wit climbed in and instructed the driver to take him to the train station as fast as he could. He was dropped off at the Ticket Master window and asked, "How soon is the first train out of here?" The Ticket Master said, "There is a train leaving for Copenhagen in 15 minutes." Wit said, "Great, give me a one-way ticket." He no sooner found an empty compartment and sat down when the train jerked and was soon rolling down the tracks.

He sat gazing out the window, watching the landscape whiz by relaxed him; and dozed off to sleep. A jolt woke him up and he saw a beautiful blonde sitting opposite him. "I'm sorry, I didn't hear you come in," he remarked. She replied, "I saw you resting and tried not to disturb you. Are you traveling to Copenhagen?" "Yes," he responded, "I went first to Amsterdam to do some sightseeing and it was so crowded, I had to get out of there." She continued, "The circus comes in once a year and people come in from hundreds of miles around; it's not usually that crowded. My name is Anna Lisa Anderson; what do they call you, and where are you from?" He answered, "They call me, Wit, and I am in the United States Army; stationed in Bavaria in Germany. Are you going to Copenhagen?" "Yes," she said, "I live there." "Well, good," he came back, "Maybe you can recommend a nice hotel, not too fancy." "I can do that," she added. "There is one within walking distance of where I live." "When I hear the name, Anderson, I think of the famous Hans Christian Anderson; are you by chance a distant relative?" he asked. "I wouldn't know about that," she answered. "Anderson has been a very common name for centuries in Denmark. What do you do in the Army, or what is your job?" "My primary duty is in the Chaplain's Service," he explained, "and my secondary duty is a helicopter pilot. You speak better English than I do, so you must have a pretty important job yourself." "We were required to learn 5 languages in our schools, and it becomes very useful in my job as a model; I model evening gowns. In fact, we are having a huge style show in Paris next month; they will show all types of wearing apparel and shoes; there will be buyers from a lot of different countries attend and place orders," she explained. "Not to change the subject," he remarked, "but does the train stop any time on the trip? I haven't eaten for quite a while and I could sure use some food. How about you?" "Yes!" she said. "I could eat; the train will stop in Hamburg for ¾ of an hour and there are several diners close by."

The train started to reduce speed as it entered the city, and she commented, "We want to hurry and get off because most of the passengers will get off and the diners will be busy." They were standing at the door when the train came to complete stop and they jumped out and hustled to one of the diners. The menu wasn't in English, so he asked her to read it to him; she asked what he had a taste for. He suggested a sandwich of flaky white fish, if they had it, with lettuce and cheese and mayonnaise; and a Coca Cola. She ordered it and, like a model would order, a salad and beet juice. She explained, "They get really mean if a model gains one pound!" He noticed her more closely as they hurried to the diner; she was the same height as him and she wore a short tight-fitting skirt and she was a little more on the skinny side for his liking. After they got back to their compartment, and taken their seat, her skirt was well up on her thighs and her legs were spread enough so he could view her red panties. She then smiled and asked him a direct question, "Would you be willing to pay for a little entertainment?" "Absolutely not!" he answered directly. "I don't have any problem getting all I want whenever I want." Little did she know that all he had to do was take off his sunglasses, but this wasn't the time and place for anything like that. He looked out the window for a while and dozed off for another nap. She alerted him, "You may want to start waking up because we will be rolling into town pretty soon." He looked out and there was water on both sides; he saw boats and ships of all sizes, types, and shapes; there was a strong smell of fish in the air. He remarked, "I've never seen that many boats in one place at one time in my whole life."

The train came to a stop and she said, "You are now in Copenhagen! There are over one million bicycles in this city; it is the easiest way for people to get around." She led him to the hotel, and he registered, and she stated, "I'll take you to your room and get you settled in." The room was very nice and clean; she looked it over completely and it met with her approval; she acted like it was her room. She seemed to linger like she had nowhere to go, so he just walked up and kissed her. He took off his sunglasses and she had her eyes closed, but opened them suddenly, and saw the *Demon of Love* in his eyes. She started yelling, "Do me, Wit! Hurry! Hurry!" He yanked the tight skirt up over her hips and pushed down the pretty red panties, and commented, "Holy cow, even her beaver is yellow. She must die it to match the hair on her head." The WT was ready, and he laid some pipe. She lasted about 8 times and then went into a faint. She finally awakened and said something in a foreign language, and he said, "Speak English!" She was shaken and asked, "What happened?" "You just met the *Demon of Love*," he answered. "Were you satisfied?" "Oh, yes," she replied, "more than I ever had in my whole life." She tried to stand, but was a little wobbly, so he suggested she lay awhile, but then clean out that yellow beaver and take a shower. She stayed with him for four days and four nights; half the time in the bed. She held his hand as they toured the city, visiting the famous statue, Little Mermaid, at the wharf and spending a day at the famous amusement park, Tivoli Gardens. There was the church made up of all bricks, outside and inside walls; everything. They ate at nice restaurants and enjoyed each other's company. The thing about her he didn't like was she flirted with all the men and they flirted with her and she seemed to be infatuated by it, but he thought when he leaves her, he will never see her again, so he didn't let it bother him. On the fourth day, he said, "I'm leaving in the morning; need to get back to camp." She responded, "I need to get to work, too. I have that big style show next month and there are a lot of dresses to be fit and made up in preparation for it." He boarded the train for Germany, found his seat, looked out the window, and saw Anna walking hand in hand with a Marine down the sidewalk and chuckled, "Go get 'em, Anderson, the Marines have landed."

CHAPTER 31

The train ran along rivers much of the time and there were many scenic sights; he could see ancient castles on mountain tops that were probably built as early as the 1500s, or before. It then headed southward toward Straubing, and after arriving, he called Cpl. Brown to pick him up and transport him back to the base and hoped he could get something to eat at the Officer's Mess before going to his billet. There were some men still in there cleaning up; he pecked on the window and they let him in. They were well acquainted because he hauled them back to camp from town in the Drunk Mobile on more than one occasion. He said, "I was hoping there would be some food left that I could chow down on." One said, "Yeah, I think there is some in the kitchen; go help yourself." He found more than enough and stuffed himself, and drank a big glass of milk, because he hadn't eaten much since morning. He thanked them kindly and went to his room and sacked out. He showered the next morning and then went to the Chaplain's office for an update of what was going on. The Chaplain asked about his trip and he responded, "Saw a lot of nice scenery and statues, went to some museums; spent a day at Tivoli Gardens in Copenhagen; met some nice people; and ate some delicious fish; it was very relaxing." Major Ray said, "Mr. Lambert is on a run and I have two more authorizations, but they are scheduled for the same time, one going east and one going west." Wit looked at them and noted, "They both have Lt. Weikart's hen-scratching on them, so I better go see which has the highest priority." "It's now Captain Weikart," the Chaplain said, "he got promoted." "Glad to hear it," Wit replied, "he's a good man and well deserving of it." As he approached the Captain's office, he could hear someone yelling in a high-pitched voice, seeming to be upset about something. When the Captain saw Wit, he asked him to come in, "Explain to this young Lieutenant that a helicopter can't fly in two different directions at the same time." "I'm afraid that's true, Lieutenant," Wit responded. "If you have the answer to that, I'm listening." Colonel Joe, hearing the ruckus, walked into the Captain's office, and not too happy at what he was hearing, asked, "Do we have a problem here?" The Captain chimed in and said, "There's been a mix-up, Colonel, and it's my fault. I scheduled two chopper trips, but I inadvertently marked them the same time. The Lieutenant wants to go to a line company on the border and a Captain needs to go to Vll Corps, at the request of General Schafer." "And what is it you need to go to the border for, Lieutenant?" the Colonel asked. "I promised the Platoon leader that I would bring him some updated procedures, today," the Lt. answered. Colonel Joe just shook his head, and was starting to get pissed off, and commanded, "Stand at attention, Lieutenant, when you see a superior officer enter a room, and you are in here raising hell with another superior officer over something that doesn't mean a rat's ass. A request by a General outweighs anything a little Lieutenant with one shiny gold bar has to say." The Lt. started to get the hanged-dog look and slumped his shoulders. The Colonel continued, "I said stand at attention, and stay that way until I tell you different. When it comes to the helicopter crew, Mister Whitson has full authority, and answers to no one except me. I'm sure he or Mister Lambert will accommodate you as soon as they can. Now give me a snappy salute and hold it until I return it." He returned the salute, and as he was walking out, he asked, "Can I take you to lunch, Wit?" "I better get that Captain to see the General," Wit replied. "He's liable to bite that old worn out cigar in half, if he gets mad enough; maybe dinner if I get back in time, if that's ok?" "That'll work," the Colonel responded, "and I'll tell Priscilla so she can join us." "I want to congratulate you Captain on your promotion," Wit offered. "You certainly are deserving of it." "Thanks, Wit, coming from you that means a lot," the Captain offered. "That young Lieutenant is just out of OCS, (Officer's Candidate School) and that little gold bar on his shoulder makes him think he's hot stuff." "I know," Wit said, "we always called them *'90-day wonders'*." He met the Captain that was going to Vll Corps at the motor pool, just as Russ was coming in. "Have the men gas ya up and go get something to eat. Then go see Captain Weikart about taking a Lieutenant to the border," he instructed. "Try to get back in time for dinner at the Officer's Mess and I'll introduce you to the Colonel's wife. You will love her." So, it all worked out!

Priscilla arrived first and selected her usual table near the wall, Wit and Russ joined her, and Wit introduced them. Then Wit said he had to make a pit stop and went to the restroom. "How did you happen to get assigned to Straubing?" Priscilla asked. "When I was training at Fort Rucker, I worked in the Chaplain's Service," Russ answered, "and the Chaplain informed me that there was a requisition received asking for a helicopter pilot to work in conjunction with the Chaplain's Office in Straubing, Germany. He said it would be an excellent opportunity to work and learn from, arguably, the most respected man in the US Army, Chief Warrant Officer Loren Whitson. From the time I arrived at Fort Rucker, everybody that I met, sang the praises of Wit Whitson, so I talked it over with my wife and we agreed I should jump at the opportunity." "Well, they got it right," she replied. "Not only is he the most popular soldier from Bavaria all the way to Washington, DC, but he is loved by everybody." Her lower lip started quivering, and she added, "I am afraid we are going to lose him." Just then Wit arrived and broke the spell, "When I first came here and met Priscilla, she sort of adopted me, and ever since, she has made sure I was well fed; and I have learned to love her more than anybody else in Bavaria." She put her hand on his and squeezed, endearingly. "He goes all day helping other people and doesn't eat right," she remarked. "I guess I've missed a meal or two," he replied. "Did you tell Russ about the Congresswoman who was afraid we were going to hang the chopper in the top of a tree, and she would be up there without a restroom?" "That was funny," she commented, "but no, I didn't get a chance." "Congresswoman?" Russ questioned. "Yeah," she added, "I told you he was loved all the way to Washington; he had dinner with Generals; spent two days with a pretty little WAC Lieutenant from the Pentagon; she even kissed him when he left; all the women falling at his feet." "Not exactly," he responded, "I don't see many women; I see you more than any of them; I see the Schatzis in town when I bring back the party boys to camp." Colonel Joe arrived and joined them; he had already met Russ when he arrived from the States. "How do you like things, so far?" the Colonel asked. "Is Wit treating you alright?" "Almost," Russ responded, jokingly, "if I could just get him to spit-shine my boots." "Ha!" Wit remarked. "You'll have a lot of sleepless nights worrying when that's gonna happen."

They were waiting for their meal they ordered, and Priscilla asked, "How was your vacation, Wit? Did you meet any sexy women?" "Let me tell you about the midget I met in Amsterdam," he explained. "She was 55 years old and 40 inches tall and hadn't had sex for 15 years, since her husband was killed." He proceeded telling the whole story, including the conversation he had with her, and finalized, "When she said we were to take a shower and asked if we were going to have sex before or after, I jokingly said both, but she wasn't joking when she started to peel off her little outfit. I thought, I got to think fast and get out of here, so I asked her to shave off the long hair under her arms and on her legs. When she went into the bathroom, I grabbed my bag and ran like a cat with its tail on fire, down the hall, down the steps two at a time, out the front door, jumped into a cab and instructed him to get me to the train station quick as he could. He dropped me off at the Ticket Master window and I said I want a one-way ticket on the first train leaving town. He gave me a ticket to Copenhagen, leaving in 15 minutes. I didn't breathe until the train was rolling down the tracks." They all laughed till their sides ached. He didn't want to go into meeting the blonde model, so he added, "Copenhagen is really nice with a lot to see. I saw unique architecture, statues, museums, and a great amusement park called Tivoli Gardens, and ate some really good fish."

"Sounds like you have fun wherever you go; and where do you plan to go next?" Priscilla asked. "I have had a number of people tell me I didn't want to leave Germany without going to Garmisch," he replied, "so I may plan to go down there for three or four days." "That's my most favorite place in the whole world," Priscilla remarked. "I've been there five times and I know all about it. I could go with ya and be your tour guide." Wit glanced at Colonel Joe to see what kind of reaction he had to that, but he was busy eating and his mind was elsewhere. "Well, Russ, you think you might bring your wife over here?" Priscilla asked, getting him into the conversation. "I would like to," he replied. "I wrote and told her this was mighty pretty country and she would enjoy herself and we could be together." "How did you end up in the Army and helicopters?" she continued to ask. "I went to college, hoping to play basketball and get a scholarship. New players came in that could run faster and jump higher, so I didn't make the team. An Army recruiter came to our campus and he explained some great opportunities; pushing helicopters as the new way to go; better than slopping in mud in the infantry. I met my wife in college, and we had just gotten married, and money was tight, and that made the bonus money look even better, along with becoming a Warrant Officer; making good pay. With the bonus money she would be able to finish school and become a teacher, like she planned." "Do you think there might be a chance you will be called to Indo-China?" she continued to ask. Wit chimed in and responded, "I don't think that is likely. From what I understand, they won't be calling any married men; the thinking has changed since the last wars; like having brothers in the same unit. The politicians are shying away from causing unrest among the voters that may result in them losing their cushy jobs."

As Wit and Russ walked back to their billet, Wit said, "There are a lot of good people on this base, some that will like you for who you are, and some that will not because they are envious of you having a more glamorous job; that's their problem. Don't let it become yours. Be friendly with everybody and treat them all the same; do your job willingly and to the best of your ability; don't show favoritism. If you get two authorizations, one for an officer and one for a non-commission officer, and the officer tries to pull rank to put his in front of the other, just kindly remind him that your instructions are to take them in the order they are received, and Colonel Krause is the only one that can alter that directive. The cream will come to the top; the ones that give you the most respect will greatly outnumber the ones that don't, and those are the ones that will enhance your position. You want to stay on the good side of Priscilla; she packs a lot of weight; nobody is stupid enough to oppose her. After I ship out, you will find there are a handful of people that will make sure you are taken care of; Major Ray; Colonel Krause; Colonel Rankin, and of course, Priscilla. Stay on good terms with the men in the motor pool; treat them with respect and dignity, regardless of their rank; they are the ones that are going to keep you safe while you are flying. Keep the Drunk Mobile rolling; you will soon know all the men by name, and they will know you by name; they will give you unlimited respect because you will have saved them from possible headaches. These are some of the basic rules to start with, but in time you will find your own way. The main thing to remember, and it's what I always preach, *'it doesn't cost anything to be friendly'*."

CHAPTER 32

There was a lot of excitement at the motor pool when Wit returned from a run. "What's going on?" Wit asked, curiously. "Mr. Lambert had to make a forced landing about 40 miles from here. He was able to radio in his coordinates and no one was hurt," Sgt. Knudsen explained. "Does the Colonel know this?" Wit asked. "No, we just got the message," the Sgt. answered. Wit went straight to the phone and called Colonel Joe and explained what he knew about the incident and he was going there to bring Russ and his passenger back. "I'll call you later when I get back and give you the details," he offered. He knew from the coordinates exactly where the site was and wasted no time getting there. Russ and a young Lieutenant were standing at the wreckage when he arrived. "Any of you hurt?" was the first thing he asked. Russ walked around the wreck with him and said, "No, my hydraulics went out and I had trouble controlling the thing, so I decided to set it down, rather than try to go any further. I tried to set it down easy, but it hit rather hard. It's the first time the Lieutenant had ever ridden in a helicopter and he's pretty shook up. He looks like he may start to cry." "Are you sure you two are not hurt; no scratches or bruises or broken bones," Wit pushed. "No, we are ok, but he is shaken up," Russ continued. Wit said, "Look at me, Russ, can you fly my chopper back? I'll radio Colonel Rankin and have him send a big chopper with a hoist to haul this junk back, and I'll just go with them." He could see the doubt in Russ's eyes, and he said, "Get everything out of the old chopper and put it in mine. I'll go talk to the Lieutenant." He approached the young officer and introduced himself and said, "Get all your stuff out of the old chopper and get into mine and I'll take you back to the Infirmary and get you checked out." He could see the young officer was scared to death, when he said, "I'll never get into another helicopter as long as I live." Wit got a little short with the officer when he said, "There's an old saying that if you fall off a horse, you get right back on it, otherwise you will be too scared to ever ride again. Now get your stuff and get in that chopper, unless you want to walk 40 miles." The young officer started shaking and said, "I don't think I can." Wit got right up into his face and said sternly, "You are an officer in the United States Army, act like it. Now get into that helicopter. Now! Russ, get all your stuff; I'm taking you both back to the Infirmary and get you checked out."

He arrived back at the motor pool, borrowed a Jeep from Sgt. Knudsen, and drove to the Infirmary. There was only one Nurse in there when he walked in with Russ and the Lieutenant. "These two men have just survived a helicopter crash and I want them checked out. They claim they have no scratches or bruises or broken bones," he instructed. The first thing the Nurse did was take their blood pressure and temperature and listened to their heart with a stethoscope.

She said, "Their blood pressure is sky high and they have a rapid heart-beat. Since there are no physical damages, that I can see, I can give them a sedative and they should be alright in the morning." "Not good enough!" Wit exclaimed. "With their blood pressures that high, they could go into cardiac arrest and die overnight, and nobody would know about it till morning. I want them to stay here and be monitored all night." The Doctor entered and responded, "I don't think it's necessary, and besides that I don't have anybody to do it." Wit about blew his stack, "Then you better start calling somebody!" The Doctor countered with, "This is my hospital and I outrank you, so you don't demand anything here." "What's your name, Doctor?" Wit asked. "Captain Bradley," he answered. Wit went straight to the telephone, instructed the operator, "Connect me with Colonel Joe Krause's home in Straubing." Priscilla answered, and Wit tried to explain to her the situation, "Russ and a Lieutenant had to make a forced landing, and I have them here at the Infirmary; and nobody is hurt, but their blood pressure is sky high, and I think they should be monitored here overnight, but I'm getting opposition from Bradley, and he's pulling rank on me." She responded, "I'm coming in! Colonel Joe is not here right now." "That's not necessary, Priscilla, I can handle it," he directed. Click, she hung up.

"Ok, Bradley, give them the sedative, and make it strong. I'm staying here all night. If anything happens, I'll yell loud and clear," he instructed. The two crash survivors went immediately sound to sleep. Wit sat in a chair; couldn't find a comfortable position and squirmed around till about two or three in the morning; his eyes got so heavy, he had a hard time staying awake. Then he thought about laying down on one of the other cots, after he made one last check of the men. He was soon sound asleep. The next thing he knew, some sweet voice was saying, "Mr. Whitson, the Colonel called, and wants to see you right away." He opened his eyes and said, "Did I die and go to Heaven? You are the most gorgeous creature I've set my eyes on in a long time. Did anybody ever tell you that you were gorgeous?" She said, "Yeah, my husband!" She resembled the closest person to Babs and brought back memories. "That figures," he said. "What is your name?" "Mimi Monroe," she answered. "Is he in the Army?" Wit continued to question. "Yeah, he is a Staff Sergeant in the Headquarters Company of the 1st Battalion, Monty Monroe," she replied. "When was the last time he told you that you were gorgeous?" Wit pressed on. "I'll have to admit, it's been 4 or 5 months," she answered. "If you were mine, I would tell you every day," he replied. She said, "I hate to push you out the door, but I don't want the Colonel to get mad at me and think I didn't tell you." "How did the other two men do?" he asked. "They were fine; got up and said they felt great and went to have breakfast," she answered. "Good!" he exclaimed. "I guess old Bradley knew what he was talking about. I better splash some water on my face; I'm having a hard time waking up. I want to be good and alert when the Colonel chews me out."

He walked into the Colonel's office and knew right away it was going to be rough. He stood at attention and snapped off salute and said, "Chief Warrant Officer Loren Whitson reporting, sir." He held the salute because the Colonel hadn't yet returned it. The Colonel just sat quiet for a bit, and then said, "Ok, Whitson, I want a full report of the accident, and don't leave anything out." Wit went through the sequence in its entirety, even being harsh with the Lieutenant. The Colonel then returned a sloppy salute, "Not all officers are combat soldiers. Some have equally important administrative jobs like drawing maps, writing procedures, record keeping, etc." Wit added, "I felt really bad after I spoke harshly to the Lieutenant. Here was a young guy who never rode in a helicopter before and it crashes, and naturally he is going to be scared and shook up. I was hoping to snap him out of it and told him he had to get back in or he would always be afraid. The Doctor gave them a strong sedative and I insisted they remain in the Infirmary all night in fear they could go into cardiac arrest with their extremely high blood pressure. They slept through the night and then got up this morning and went to breakfast. I staid all night to make sure they were going to be alright."

"What time did Priscilla leave?" the Colonel asked. "Priscilla!" Wit exclaimed. "I never saw Priscilla!" The Colonel continued, concerned, "She left me a note saying she was coming in to help you." They both got excited and the Colonel called the front gate to find out who was on guard during those hours. They told him the soldier's name and the Colonel ordered them to contact that soldier and find out if she came to camp. The soldier informed them that he never saw her. Wit advised, "Let's get the chopper and fly over all the streets in Straubing. We might see an accident or something that may give us a clue." They flew as low as they could covering one street after the other, and then Wit got an idea. "Do you know where the Provost Captain lives?" "Yeah," the Colonel answered, "he's the next street over at the 'T' intersection." They flew over and spotted the Captain's car still in the driveway. "Shouldn't he be at the base?" Wit asked. "Yeah!" the Colonel exclaimed. Then Wit remarked, "He's got her in there. I'll land at the end of the street and we can run back, and you go in the back and I'll go in the front." The Colonel said, "No, you go in the back and I'll go in the front." Wit crashed through the back door into the kitchen and there stood the Captain in his boxers and 'T' shirt, and blood all over them. He leaped on the Captain like a cat on a mouse, and the *Demon of Death* appeared; his eyes were fiery red and he had flashbacks of Korea; he was on the verge of ripping out his throat when the Colonel entered from the front and saw what was happening. The Captain was paralyzed with fear when he saw those eyes. The Colonel starting yelling and pulling Wit's arms and saw the *Demon of Death*. Wit immediately relaxed his grip, and yelled, "Where is she? Where is she?" "In the bedroom!" he managed to mutter. The Colonel went into the bedroom and when he saw Priscilla all bloody and her clothes ripped nearly off, he turned and came back and began pummeling the Captain with both fists till his face looked like hamburger. "That's enough, Colonel," Wit ordered. "Call the Straubing Polizei (Police) to come get him and lock him up. We've got to get her to the Infirmary quick. I'll run and get the chopper and you wrap a blanket around her and carry her out." He set the chopper down in the intersection and they loaded her in, and he lifted it straight up and then off to the base. The Doctors and Nurses took her back to the treatment room immediately and all of them started working on her. Wit and the Colonel sat in the hallway waiting for a diagnosis. The Colonel asked, "How did you know to suspect the Provost Captain?" "Your Sister-In-Law first gave me the heads up about him because she despised him and warned me to be on my guard and never trust him. She had him aced out. Then I found out he was tracking me and when I told him he must not have much to do, he became irate, and threatened to bust me down to a Private. I really started paying attention and concluded he had an evil and devious mind. I felt there was no limit he wouldn't go for his own personal gain, but I never dreamed he would go this far." "When did Lisa tell you this?" the Colonel asked. "She went to the States months ago." "Remember when you asked me to take Priscilla home? Lisa put her to bed and asked me to stick around and talk. We talked through two pots of coffee in the kitchen while Priscilla snored in her bedroom. Don't tell her I said that!"

The Doctor came out and reported, "We cleaned her up and we didn't see any broken bones. She is so cut up and bruised and traumatized, I can't say she is going to make it. It is just too early to tell!" Wit asked, "Can we go in and see her?" "She needs to rest and maybe later, when we see how she is," Bradley responded. Before the Doctor got it out of his mouth, Wit was on his way in, and the Colonel right behind him. He looked at her with a heavy heart, sat on the edge of the bed, put her bloodied hand in between his hands, and asked, "Priscilla, can you hear me?" She could barely move her bruised and cut lips, but managed to say, "Yes!" "I am going to pray for you, and I want you to listen carefully; understand?" he added. She managed to say again, "Yes!" Chaplain Ray heard about it and rushed to the Infirmary, and he and all the Infirmary staff came in, from the least to the greatest. He began, like he did years ago in Korea, praying for those on the threshold of death. "The Lord is my shepherd; I shall not want. He maketh me to lie down in green pastures; He leadeth me beside the still waters; He restoreth my soul. He leadeth me in the paths of righteousness for His namesake. Yea, though I walk through the valley of the shadow of death, I will fear not evil, for Thou art with me. Thy rod and Thy staff they comfort me. Thou preparest a table before me in the presence of mine enemies. Thou anoinest my head with oil; my cup runneth over. Surely goodness and mercy shall follow me all the days of my life; and I will dwell in the house of the Lord forever." Everybody standing around had their heads bowed, and it was dead silent. Priscilla's swollen eyes were shut when Wit asked, "Are you still with me?" She managed to say, "Yes!" He continued, "Lord, I want you to have mercy on my good friend; she has a good heart and was on her way to lend a helping hand to aid a couple soldiers but was intercepted by an evil and insane minded man. She didn't ask to be brutalized and tortured so severely that she is now on the verge of dying. She now needs your mercy and blessing and your healing hand, and I beg you now; hear me, oh Lord and answer my prayer. Amen! And Amen!" She managed to ask, "Am I going to die, Wit?" He answered, "Absolutely not! The man upstairs assured me that you will live, so don't even worry yourself over that. You will be sore for a few days, so do everything they tell you; they are good at their jobs." He put her hand under the blanket and pulled the blanket up under her chin, and said, "You have always taken care of me, so now I am going to take care of you." She managed a little smile, and muttered, "Have you eaten today?" He replied, "Now that you mention it, I haven't eaten since early yesterday morning. You know how I get busy and skip a meal. I want you to sleep now, and I will be back later to check on ya." There wasn't one person there that wasn't shedding a tear. Wit tried to stand up and his knees wobbled because he put so much into his prayer, it drained him of his strength, and Chaplain Ray took him under the arm and sat him down in a chair. They all dispersed to their jobs. They had just witnessed the real Loren Whitson, not the happy, joking, chopper pilot.

In a few minutes, he was able to get up and walk, and Bradley asked, "How can you in good conscience give someone false hope like that?" Wit said, "The Bible says that Faith can move mountains, and Bradley, we have just moved a mountain." "I don't believe in that mumbo-jumbo," Bradley remarked. "Sometimes it takes more than pills to heal the sick. Are you an atheist, Bradley?" Wit asked. "Or is it you don't believe in anything?" "When you going to call me who I am?" Bradley asked, irritably. "It's Doctor or Captain!" "No disrespect, Bradley," Wit responded, slightly mused, "some people look like their name, and you don't look like Captain, but you certainly look like Bradley. I like you Bradley; you are intelligent and a good Doctor, and I respect your position. Just look at Mimi; she fits her name. If she were a big breasted, red head, with freckles, she wouldn't look like a Mimi. Do you like to sing, Bradley?" He responded, "I've been known to belt out a tune or two; what does that have to do with anything?" Wit answered, "I would like for you to come to our Chapel on Sunday; we have hymn books full of good tunes." Then Bradley ordered, "Go on and get out of here; I got work to do." Wit smiled and said, as he was walking out, "Amen brother!" He went to his billet; shaved and showered, put on a clean flight suit; and went to the Officer's Mess. Smokie came up to his table and asked, "Is Miss Priscilla going to be ok? I heard she was going to die." "Smokie, take it from the horse's mouth," Wit replied. "The Lord said she was going to live, and I say she is going to live." He responded, "Praise the Lord!" "Now, Smokie, I haven't eaten a meal for two days, and I feel like I could eat a big piece of ham and eggs and hash browns with some hot rolls," Wit requested. "You got it coming up, Wit," Smokie answered. Just then Mimi walked in and Wit motioned for her to come sit with him, "I just ordered a big plate of ham and eggs; let me tell Smokie to fix you some too." "I usually don't eat like that," she remarked. "Nonsense!" he exclaimed, and he motioned to Smokie, holding up two fingers, to make it two. "Where you from, Mimi?" he asked. "I'm from Pittsburg," she answered. "You have an uncanny likeness for I girl I loved and adored deeply, but she was from Indiana," he remarked. "What do you mean, 'was'?" Mimi asked. "She was a Nurse Lieutenant in Korea and we fell in love. We planned to marry after the war, buy a little house, and raise kids, and live happily ever after. Then in an attack, an artillery shell hit her treatment tent and blew her to bits," he explained. "That's awful," Mimi replied, sadly, "I feel like I want to cry for you." "No need," Wit added, "I have cried enough for both of us. You look like you could pass for her Sister. That's why I thought I died and went to Heaven." "I don't have a Sister; I have two Brothers," she explained. "Was your Dad a traveling salesman, by chance?" he asked. "He might have ventured to Indiana and had an affair," he joked. "I wouldn't know about that," she replied. "I know he was gone a lot."

CHAPTER 33

Wit was getting better acquainted with Mimi. Whenever he would go to the Infirmary to check on the progress of Priscilla, he would complement her and tell her she was gorgeous. He would always ask first thing how Priscilla was and one morning Mimi remarked, "She had a rough night; she wakes up screaming. I figure she is re-living the awful experience; probably natural." Wit went in and said a little prayer, like he did every time he went to see her. "You've been up all night," Wit offered. "Let's go get some breakfast." She replied, "If I keep eating like that, I'm gonna gain weight; I'll just eat some cereal." "Cereal doesn't stick to your ribs; you will feel hungry in an hour," he explained. She said, "Ok, if you insist." After they ate, she asked, "Would you walk me to my suite; I want to talk to you." They walked to her building, which was close to the Infirmary; all the Doctors and Nurses had their own little suite. They were nice; bedroom, living room, eat-in kitchen, and a bathroom, all the comforts of home. She plugged in the percolator to make a pot of coffee, and while they waited for it to percolate, she went in and changed out of her uniform, and into her pajamas. They sat at the kitchen table; she poured the coffee; and he waited for her to tell him what was on her mind.

"I think my husband is having an affair," she offered. "That would be tough to do around here," he responded. "There are very few women on this base." "He's not here," she continued. "He's in Frankfurt training with the Army Olympic Team." "Really? What events is he in?" Wit asked. "I didn't know they had an Olympic team." "Well, they do," she answered, "and he throws the shotput; discus; and javelin." "He must be a big strong guy to be in those events," Wit remarked. "He's 6-ft 5-in and weighs 250 pounds," she continued, "and he has been over there for several months. When he comes home, he shows no interest in me at all; says he is too tired, and just wants to lay on the couch." "That's pretty strenuous training so I can understand him being tired," Wit replied. "Let me finish!" she said. "I went over there to one of the track-meets and he didn't hang with the other men, but with one of the female runners. They stood over to one side away from the others, until they were called to their events; then they went back together." "Maybe you are reading something in there that's not true," he responded, "like they could just be good friends, same as me and you are friends." "Sounds like you are taking his side; like all men stick together," she inferred. "I was going to ask you to take me over there next Saturday to the next track-meet, but if you don't want to, that's ok. Maybe I can find another way to get there. I was planning to go without him knowing I was coming and sit in the stands like a normal spectator and spy on him." "I'm not saying I won't take you," he explained, "but that's about a 300-mile ride and I would have to ask Captain Weikart to authorize it, and we would need to stop about halfway and refuel, so you are asking a lot." "I have to know," she said seriously. "It's effecting my eating and sleeping and preventing my mind from concentrating on my work." "I'll talk to Captain Weikart and let you know," he finalized. "I have to try and get some sleep, if I can," she remarked. "I have to pull a 12 hour shift tonight, so go on and get out of here."

He went to Captain Weikart's office and explained that Mimi wanted to go to Frankfurt on Saturday and watch her husband in the track-meet and would need his authorization. The Captain surprised Wit when he said, "I've been wanting to go over to that track meet; I have a lady friend that is a runner, and I have never seen her run. I understand she is pretty fast. Do I know this Mimi? What time are you planning to leave?" Wit explained, "Mimi is the Nurse that has been taking care of Priscilla. It's about a 300-mile trip so we would have to stop and refuel about halfway, maybe in Nurnberg; I would think we would need to leave about 0700." The Captain wrote out and signed the authorization. Wit reported back to Mimi that the trip was ok, and they would leave about 0700, and that should get them there around 1000 hours. She agreed that would be fine and that would get them there in time for the first event, which was at 1100. The trip was uneventful, and they elected to sit high in the center bleacher so they could view the entire field. All the athletes were stretching and loosening up and practicing their starts prior to their events. Wit sat in the middle between the Captain and Mimi. Wit asked the Captain, "Do you see your lady friend?" "She is over there on the side talking to that real big guy," he answered. Wit then turned and said to Mimi, "That's the Captain's lady friend over there on the side talking to that big guy." She turned blood red with anger, and he realized he made a mistake, so he grabbed her arm and squeezed it hard, indicating she dare not say anything and make a scene. Her husband and the runner seemed to be rather chummy and enjoying themselves. They separated when he performed his events and when she performed her events, and then they got back together. It was difficult to assume something was going on because all they did was talk and laugh. The return trip was rather quiet; the Captain dozed, and Mimi seethed most of the way.

When they landed at the motor pool, Wit suggested he get a Jeep and take them to their respective living quarters. The Captain offered to buy their dinner, and Mimi said because it was her first helicopter ride, she felt a little queasy and couldn't eat right now. The Captain said, "I'll walk and get the kinks out; you two go ahead." Wit and Mimi got into the Jeep, and she started, "You saw him; I knew it; he never giggled like that with me." She was madder than an old wet hen. Wit went in with her and said, "I want to see you eat something; you are going to make yourself sick if you don't eat; what do you have here?" She responded, angrily, "I'll make a peanut butter and jelly sandwich. Do you want one?" "No thanks! I know a lot of people like 'em, but to me it's like putting ketchup on ice cream. Well make it and eat while I am here, and then I'm going to take off," he remarked. She asked, "Would you like to have sex with me?" He responded, "I would run across red-hot coals bare-foot to have sex with you; but I won't. That would be the worst thing you could do at this point. If you find out that you have been wrongly accusing him, and then with a guilty conscience, you confess it to him; if he is anything like me, he will kiss you goodbye. If you find he is guilty, and file for divorce, the first thing the Judge is going to ask you is if you ever had sex outside of marriage? You will be under oath to tell the truth and you say yes, then he is likely to rule for you both just to go see a counselor. You need to stop thinking negative thoughts and start planning how you are going to save your marriage, in any case. When he comes home, tell him to look you straight in the eye and answer one question, 'are you having an affair, yes or no'? If he gives you an adamant 'no, how could you think of such a thing?', then you get over it and move on. You are smart enough to know if he is guilty by how he reacts. I've got to get going; I'll see ya sometime time next week; I've got to get back to Army business."

The next morning, he had an early breakfast and then went to visit Priscilla. She was sitting up eating oatmeal. "Well, look at you!" he remarked, surprised. "You have made my day. You are looking a whole lot better; the swelling in your face is going down and the cuts are healing; you will be up and at 'em in no time. Ole Bradley is doing a great job on ya." "You make my day every day, Wit," she commented. He said a little prayer with her, and kissed her hand; said he would see her later, and left for church. He met Russ outside the church and informed Russ that on Monday they need to go see Colonel Rankin about getting a chopper to replace the wrecked one. Russ looked up and said, "Well, look coming here." They saw Bradley walking toward the church with a lady on his arm, "Wit and Russ, I want you to meet, Virginia," he introduced. "She is a Doctor over in Nurnberg and comes to visit on some weekends and I go over there some weekends, that is when we can get away." "She's very pretty, Bradley; she even looks like a Virginia," Wit commented. Virginia looked at him kinda funny and Bradley said, "Don't pay any attention to him; he's sorta whacky; that's why they call him Wit." Wit introduced them to Chaplain Ray, and he was overjoyed to see the two

Doctors in church. Bradley could be heard singing above the congregation, and Virginia was holding her own too.

Monday morning Wit and Russ had an early breakfast; visited and said a little prayer with Priscilla; then flew to Freising. He approached the Crew Chief and asked to talk to the men that brought the old chopper back. They were standing close by and he yelled for them to come over. Wit asked, "I would like for you to show us the big chopper you used to bring the old wrecked chopper back, and exactly how you hooked onto it; and exactly how you unhooked it." They explained there were two men, in addition to the pilot; and they all proceeded to ride out in a Jeep to the huge chopper. They demonstrated how they used the wench mounted inside the side door, with the cable rolled up and a hook attached to the end of the cable. They crawled inside and were amazed at how much more complicated the controls were and how spacious it was. They then rode to the scrap heap and the airmen demonstrated how they hooked up the old one. They then went to visit Colonel Rankin and asked if he had a chopper they could borrow. He said, sadly, "The powers-to-be transferred a few of my pilots to Vietnam. They are increasing their advisory forces and need more helicopters, and pilots." "Vietnam?" Wit asked. "I thought it was Indo-China." "Indo-China split into three countries; Cambodia; Laos; and Vietnam, and our problems are with Vietnam," the Colonel explained. "There are a couple out there that are the same model as yours and they are lucky if there are more than a hundred hours on 'em. Take one with ya and I'll contact Colonel Krause and try to get it transferred." "One last thing, Colonel," Wit continued, "I have a wild idea that's been brewing in my mind and I am going to talk to Colonel Krause about calling a meeting, to include you and hopefully General Schafer, because it will cost some big money; just a head's up. Thanks for the chopper!" They saluted and Wit and Russ each flew a 'copter back to Straubing. Wit visited Colonel Krause and asked if he would call a meeting and explained he would describe its purpose at that time.

CHAPTER 34

Colonel Joe agreed to hold the meeting which included him, Colonel Rankin, General Schafer, Major Ray, Russ, and Wit. Wit started out thanking them for taking the time to come and listen and stated, "I've been thinking about this wild idea for some time, but when Priscilla experienced her unfortunate incident, then it became more realistic than ever, at least in my mind. The helicopter has added a new dimension to the military, as well as to the civilian community. When I landed my chopper in the intersection in town, which I admit was risky because of the tight space, we were able to get Priscilla out and loaded, lifted straight up, and headed for the Infirmary, and landed at the front door, and the medical team responded quickly, and it all happened in about 10-minutes. If I was not able to get to her and had to call for an ambulance, by the time they would have driven to town and back, we could very well have lost her. When Russ had a malfunction and had to make a forced landing, I went out and was able to land at the sight. They fortunately were not physically injured, but were naturally frightened and shook up, and I made the decision to get them to the Infirmary as soon as possible to get them checked out, and again the medical team responded quickly. It took approximately 20-minutes to load them and unload them at the Infirmary. Colonel Rankin's team was able to go out in his huge chopper, equipped with a wench and hook, lift the wreckage, and transport it back to the scrap heap in less than an hour. If a road wrecker would have been dispatched, it would have taken hours, not counting the time to disassemble it so it could be transported on the roadways. What I'm saying is we need to be thinking about equipping ourselves with a large and powerful helicopter that is capable of rescuing anyone from anywhere. You have seen the skiers going to the mountains on weekends. If there happened to be a skiing accident, it takes rescue teams hours, and possibly all day, to get to the skier and get him, or her, down the mountain, and they may die in the process. We could go in there and pluck that skier off the mountain and have them at the hospital in an hour. If one of our trucks should run off the road and have some injuries, we could hover over the sight, drop down a basket or stretcher, lift them up into the chopper, and transport them quickly to an aid station. The same thing with Priscilla; if I were not able to land, our rescue helicopter could have hovered over the intersection, dropped a stretcher, and done the same thing.

  The next part of the wild idea is, we need to get the Germans involved. I would bet there are veteran German pilots that live around Straubing that would love to get into the air again. They could help us the same as we could help them. They would need to agree to construct a landing pad on top of their hospital, where a helicopter could land with the victim, and their medical team had the convenience to run out and tend to that victim, immediately. We need to add a landing pad at our Infirmary also, right at an emergence entrance, because time is of the essence. I had to park in the parking lot and was thankful I had space available. We would need to train people for this purpose, in the military as well as the civilians. I would bet the ranch that Fort Rucker is already working on this application; and Fort Benning also, because this is the future. I know what you are thinking; what is it going to cost? Probably a lot, but the big and only question is, *what is the price of a life?* You can replace equipment and money, but not a life. I want you to think about it; Russ and I are willing to help however we can. If it sounds too far-fetched, throw it in the can, but remember, you are on the cutting edge, and it could be a feather in your caps in the European Theater. Wit and Russ snapped to attention and saluted, and Wit added, "Thank you gentleman for your time and for listening. Come on Russ, I'll let you buy my dinner." Every officer sat and listened intently and never said a word through the entire presentation. After they walked out, Russ asked, "Do you think they will buy it?" Wit responded, "Who knows! You know the Army; they will think about and then talk about it; and then pass it on upstairs; and if they get a positive reaction; they will claim it was all their idea. You will know when they call you in and pin gold bars on ya and make you an officer in charge of it."

Wit told Russ he was going to press his luck and ask for another pilot and the other chopper that Colonel Rankin said was just sitting idle. He didn't want to go over Major Ray's head, so he started with him, and hoped he would agree. "Major Ray, our transport business has really taken off. The personnel that use it have found the time-saving benefits of it far outcry the land travel. It sometimes is a strain trying to accommodate everybody, and we don't like to turn anyone down or make them reschedule their trip. Colonel Rankin said he has another chopper just like ours that is just sitting idle, because they transferred his pilots to Vietnam. We can get that chopper, but we would need to requisition another graduate pilot. I suggested to Sgt. Knudsen that he start training more mechanics because they are feeling the strain also. If you should agree and would want to keep the chopper crew in the Chaplain's Service, then make a contact to Major Bill Golden, at Fort Rucker, and ask him to recommend a pilot that is suitable for our purpose. I think you will agree that Russ has worked out extremely well." "I think you are right. I will talk with Colonel Krause and see if he concurs, and if he does, we can get the wheels in motion," he responded.

Priscilla was improving nicely and started getting around a little with the aid of a walker; trying to get some exercise. The prediction was, if she continued to improve, she could go home, providing they could find someone to be of assistance to her. A new Provost Captain arrived, and Major Ray suggested that Wit and Russ go introduce themselves and welcome him to Straubing. He was a lot more personable than the last guy, and easy to talk to. Wit explained, "We use the truck that is assigned to your office for our Drunk Mobile, and if you have no objection, we would like to continue that service. We know the men really appreciate it; keeping them from getting into trouble. Of course, if any of them become unruly, then we alert one of your MPs, and let them handle it." He commented, "I have no objection, and from what I understand, other camps are copying the idea." "If I might be so bold to ask," Witt continued, "what happened to the last Captain? He just seemed to disappear and never heard from again." "He is in Fort Leavenworth Prison in Kansas, and from what I'm told, he is insane. He sits and stares and keeps saying the Devil is going to get him." Wit knew what he meant; he saw the *Demon of Death*.

A couple weeks later, Major Ray said the requisition had been approved and they can get the third Bell Helicopter. A pilot had been chosen and he would be coming, but his class hadn't graduated yet, so it may be a while. Russ and Wit went to Friesing to get the chopper and Colonel Rankin joked they were building their own Air Force. Wit asked, "Have you heard anything about the rescue service I talked about?" "I haven't heard anything," he answered, "the last I heard of it was General Schafer took it and ran with it. You know how the military works; they will need to study it to death before they make a decision." Sergeant Knudsen asked the C & A (Classification and Assignment) Department to keep an eye out for mechanics when they interviewed new troops coming in; he asked for 6. He explained the road vehicles were suffering because the helicopters were requiring most of his mechanic's time.

Russ and Wit were up early, as usual, and went for an early breakfast, and Russ said he was going to the Chaplain's office to see if any authorizations had come in, and Wit said he was going to visit Priscilla first, and then go to the Chaplain's office. He found she was progressing nicely, said a short prayer, and then proceeded to see Major Ray. "Do we have any authorizations?" he asked. "We had one," the Major answered, "and Russ took it. But we have something more important to do; the Colonel wants us in his office macht schnell (fast)." They hopped in his Jeep and were there in record time. They walked in and there sat General Schafer, Colonel Rankin, and Colonel Krause.

Wit saluted and they asked him to sit. His first thought was they wanted to talk about the rescue team, but that couldn't have been more wrong. Colonel Krause started, "Wit, you have made a lot of friends in a lot of places and they have learned to respect you and what you have accomplished in your two years here. But now it's time for you to move on to a new assignment. Normally they don't ask, but tell you where you will go, and you go; that's the Army way. They have decided to give you a choice of four assignments; staff position with General Kaiser, staff position with General Schafer, helicopter training officer at Fort Rucker; all of which will require you to take a commission of Lieutenant. The fourth choice is Vietnam." They all sat and watched him as he was giving it some thought. "Gentleman, all those positions are greatly appreciated, and would be welcomed by an ordinary person to be so honored," Wit remarked. "I guess I am not an ordinary person; I am a career soldier well trained as combat soldier; I am also a trained killer; I am also a trained helicopter pilot; and I am also active in the Chaplain's Service. Therefore, I think I would be more useful in Vietnam, a dangerous place I know, but I think they would benefit more from my talents and experience. I am truly grateful to have had the opportunity to serve under you gentlemen, and you have allowed many of my dreams to come true, and for that I am also grateful. How much time do I have?" Colonel Krause said, "We will try to buy you as much time as we can, but probably a couple weeks." Wit responded, "Good, that will allow me time to work out a few loose ends and prepare Mr. Lambert for the takeover; and I would like to take a few days to go to Garmisch." General Schafer remarked, "We hate to lose you, Wit. You have been a good Ambassador for the Army; and we respect your decision and wish you God-speed." Colonel Rankin commented, "I am going to arrange a series of hops from Freising to Da Nang in Vietnam with the Air Force; probably a number of stops because it is approximately 5000-miles." Major Ray seemed a little bit emotional and never said anything going back to his office. Wit went to the motor pool and told them the news and thanked them for their loyal service keeping the choppers in the air. He told them they were going to be busier because they were going to get the third Bell helicopter. Dilly said, "I predicted you were going to have your own Air Force someday," and laughed. Hap responded, "Yeah, but he won't be here to see it." Russ returned from his trip and Wit said, "Come on, Russ, let's go to lunch; I have some news for ya." They sat down to eat, and Russ was antsy waiting to hear the news. "I have just been informed that I am shipping out within the next two weeks," Wit stated, "and now it's your ballgame." "Where are you going?" Russ asked, acting a little surprised. "Vietnam, they say. So, if the rescue idea is a go, you will have a great opportunity to build on your career. You can bring your wife over; get a little house in town; buy a car; and raise some kids. You will get a commission which will be decent pay, and they will bring in more pilots, and you will be in charge and let them do the transporting. When your enlistment is up, you will probably get the opportunity to go to Fort Rucker and be a Training Officer. When you get your 20-years in, you can retire with a nice pension." "What if it is not a go?" he asked. "Then you ride out your enlistment, go home and go to college on the GI Bill and get your degree, and get a good position in some big company," Wit continued. "You have the best of both worlds; it is a win-win situation for you, and I sincerely hope you win. If the problem in Vietnam escalates into big shooting war, then it is likely they won't want to spend the money here but on the war effort." "How do you know all this stuff?" Russ questioned. "Like I used to tell the guys in basic training, the Army is not brain surgery; it's common sense. We had some young officers then that just didn't have a clue, and they were going to lead us on the battlefield." "I hate to see you go," Russ commented. "It makes me a little nervous." "Don't get nervous, just roll up your sleeves and attack it head on. You will do fine," Wit added. "Not to change the subject," Russ remarked, "but does Priscilla know yet?" "I'm not sure," Wit replied, "and I have to be very careful how I tell her. She is not going to take it very well."

After they ate, Wit went to see Priscilla and told her he was planning a trip to Garmisch for three or four days. "Do you think you could handle a trip like that? Probably early next week?" he offered. "You really want me to go?" she asked. "I can talk to Joe and see what he thinks." "Ask him to go along, too," Wit answered. "He needs to get away for a couple days. We won't do anything strenuous; just hang out and enjoy the scenery; eat a big ole wiener-schnitzel; I hear they have a rather nice ice show. Don't try it if you think it's going to be too taxing on ya. The last thing I would want is to cause you pain and discomfort." She talked to the Colonel and he talked to the Doctor to get his opinion. He said she never had any broken bones, but she had lost a lot of blood and they were trying to build her up and get her strength back. He thought she should take it slow and easy and rest frequently, but might do her good, emotionally. Colonel Joe decided to go with them so he could share a room and look after her, and that would give him a chance to take a break. The Colonel made all the reservations and they rode the train to Garmisch and checked in. The Colonel thought Priscilla should rest a bit from the trip, so they just hung out for a couple hours. The scenery was everything that everybody said it was. They had rooms with a view that showed the best sides of the mountains. It was a relaxing few days; they ate good; went to the ice show and enjoyed the music; walked around the lake and just made small talk. The final evening, Wit and Priscilla were sitting on the veranda; it was quiet and serene; a memorable moment, and Wit said, "We have a new pilot coming in after he finishes his training. I want you to do what you do best, be a friend and see that he is taken care of, like you have with me. He's gonna be young and probably the first time away from home, so he's gonna need time to get adjusted." She squinted her eyes, and looked straight at him, and said, "Wit, are you trying to tell me you are leaving?" She started to tear up. "Now don't do that," he commented. "Not for another week. You knew that it was going to happen sooner or later." "Yeah, but I hoped it would be later," she replied. "Maybe I can pull some strings." "No, no, it's a done deal," he responded. "I have a lot of good friends around Bavaria, but you have been my best friend, and I will never forget you. You need to concentrate on a full recovery and devote your time and energy taking care of Colonel Joe. He's probably nearing retirement age, and you two might want to renew your vows, and stick together like glue, loving each other with all your heart and soul."

The final day was spent saying his goodbyes; and a lot of tears welled up in a lot of eyes; even Smokie had a hard time and couldn't say a word; just shook Wit's hand. Major Ray said, "It's been a pleasure having you here, Wit, and I pray that the Lord will watch over you and keep you safe." He handed Wit an envelope and said, "I contacted the Protestant Chaplain in Da Nang, Captain Jim Shoemaker, and he is expecting you, so report to him as soon as you arrive and give him this envelope. It contains all your records that he will need. Jim and I went to the seminary together and you will find he is a quality guy. They also have a Catholic Chaplain and a Jewish Chaplain and I'm sure, knowing you, it won't take you long to get acquainted with them. It might please you to know that he has arranged for you to have your own helicopter." "Thanks Major, you have been a stellar individual in my eyes, and I am thankful that I was able to serve under you," Wit replied. Colonel Joe reported, "Priscilla wants to cook supper for you tonight." "Cook?" Wit questioned. "I didn't know she knew how to cook." "Sure," the Colonel responded, "you don't grow up in a family of 8 kids and not learn how to cook. She just doesn't like to make a mess fixing it and cleaning up afterwards, so we eat out." "I'm sorry, Colonel, I just don't have time," Wit answered with regret, "The jet leaves at 0400 from Freising, and Russ is taking me down there at 0300, and I got some last-minute things to do; I probably won't even go to bed. Apologize for me because I know she had her heart set on it. I'll say goodbye now, Colonel; it's been a pleasure serving under you and I could not have had a better Commander." "Take care of yourself, Wit, and God-speed," the Colonel replied, and they shook hands, firmly. Russ got him there in plenty of time, and loaded his duffel bag into the waiting jet, and he had tears welling up in his eyes, and Wit said, "Don't you start that! You are now in charge, so do what I told ya; you will do fine. I'll be praying for ya." Russ watched the jet disappear in the dark sky. It is said it is bad luck to watch a flight till it's out of sight, but that is just another superstition.

VIETNAM

CHAPTER 35

It took about 12-hours with the number of stops and changing planes to travel the 5000 miles to Da Nang. The last pilot apparently radioed ahead because there was a Jeep waiting for him that had a Chaplain's insignia painted on the sides. The driver introduced himself as Corporal Robert Hall, Chaplain Jim Shoemaker's Orderly, and he said, "Welcome to Vietnam!" They went to the Chaplain's office in the Chapel and Wit saluted, introduced himself; and handed him the envelope. The Chaplain was tall and well groomed, dressed in fatigues, and smiled and welcomed him to the Chapel. He said, "I don't stand much on formalities, so you can dispense with the saluting. Some of us officers would rather it was not obvious we are officers because it is like having a bullseye on your back. We have accommodations here at the Chapel, and Corporal Hall will show you to your quarters. You probably noticed a lot of construction going on at the air strip and things seem to be in disarray, but the Seabees are working hard and will get it done in due time. The heat takes a toll on them and you will get used to that too. Get settled in and we will have something to eat and I'll fill you in on what we are faced with. Believe me, it is not pretty. It is about a 180-degree difference than what you were used to in beautiful cool Germany." His quarters were not spacious, and sparsely furnished with the bare necessities but seemed to have everything he would need, especially a small table fan. Corporal Hall introduced Wit to a Vietnamese couple, man and wife, and explained they take care of our needs; cleaning, laundry, preparing meals, and maintenance work; or anything else that he may want. He explained they speak enough English and French to communicate with anybody. Wit struggled pronouncing their names, so he settled on calling them, "Mr. and Mrs. Dink." He unpacked his duffel bag and arranged his belongings in some crude fashion to where he could access anything in a moment's notice.

I've scanned your file briefly and see you have had a varied career," the Chaplain remarked. "Are your quarters satisfactory?" "They will be fine," Wit answered. "I don't usually spend much time inside; I am usually out and about. I spend most of my time helping someone or rescuing someone or praying with someone; any way I can that will add aid and comfort." "Have you eaten?" Jim asked. "I ate some at the various stops on the way; those Air Force boys eat pretty good." "I got a little something here, so sit and eat while we talk. Robert, you are welcome to join us," Jim directed. "Do you have any idea of what goes on here?" "Not a clue!" Wit remarked. "I didn't either when I came here," the Chaplain explained, "so I tried to do a little research and get an idea of what we were up against. It is a mess that the politicians created, and it is a most dangerous place, and I don't see it improving anytime soon. At the end of World War 2, the Soviets and Chinese indirect support in the Indochina War from 1946 to1954 helped the Ho Chi Minh Communists drive the French from their former colony. In 1954, the 17th parallel was established as the dividing line between Communist North Vietnam and anti-communist South Vietnam. Hanoi, the capital of the north regime resumed the war through infiltrations and insurgents. In 1955, Saigon, the capital of South Vietnam, started retaliating and killing the Communists Sympathizers, which prompted the North Vietnamese terrorists to start killing the South Vietnamese officials. In 1957, 1500 US Military Advisors came in to train the ARVN (army of the republic of Vietnam) Rangers, so they could protect themselves. After the first two Americans were killed, the NV increased their raids and demonstrations, which resulted in an increase of Advisors to 3200. Now the US Special Forces, namely the *'Green Beret'*, and the CIA have begun instructing and organizing the ARVN. Meanwhile the Advisors have steadily increased in number. I advise you to be observant and conscience of everything and everybody around you and be careful who you trust." "Sounds like I am going to need to learn about the jungle as quick as I can; I may need to go out where I can be of assistance and lend a helping hand," Wit responded. Chaplain Jim added, "Then I suggest you go out and learn from the best, the Green Beret. A few of them come in to the Chapel on Sundays and I will introduce you to them. You are going to need your chopper to get out there because there are no roads to drive a vehicle. Chaplain Jones told me of the one you had in Germany and I have managed to get the same model for you. It belonged to a Colonel and it has been used very little. The heat and humidity made him deathly ill and he was forced to transfer back to the States. Robert can drive you out to see it and then you might talk to the mechanics at the air strip and have them convert the wheels to skids. Wheels will do you no good in the jungle. Again, I suggest you only wear your Chaplain's insignia on your uniforms; nothing else."

"Thanks, Chaplain, I'm sure I will have a lot more questions arise, but for now I'm anxious to see the chopper," Wit responded. "Come on, Robert, let's go check it out." They drove out and it was everything the Chaplain said it was; it was clean and practically new looking. They drove to see the air mechanics and Robert introduced him; they said it would be no problem converting it to skids, and they would make sure it was serviced. He then asked for a special favor, and he drew a sketch to demonstrate; paint on it 'CHOPPER CHAPLAIN', and the Chaplain insignia. They smiled and one said, "Copy that, Wit." He had Robert drive him around and show him where everything was. It was a spacious area with a lot going on; it was obviously in build-up mode and appeared to be setting up for some serious business. He asked to see the hospital because he planned to spend a considerable amount of time there visiting the sick and wounded. Robert drove to the front of the hospital, and stopped, "This is Da Nang General in all its glory!" he exclaimed. They were constructing pre-fab housing just walking distance from the hospital for the hospital personnel; Doctors, Nurses, etc. After a couple days, and giving it some thought, he decided to go to the hospital and get acquainted, so he drove over and walked in and met a Colonel and introduced himself, "I'm Chief Warrant Officer Loren Whitson and I am new at Chaplain Jim's Chapel, and you will probably be seeing a lot of me. I thought I best look around and get familiar with the hospital." The Colonel responded, "I'm Doctor Matthew Ashby, and I oversee all the goings on at the hospital. Glad to have you aboard. Let me have someone show you around." He called a young Nurse over and asked, "Annie, would you give Mr. Whitson the grand tour of the hospital?" "Everyone calls me, Wit, so you might as well too," Wit remarked. Annie was a cute little Nurse, looked to be in her early to mid-twenties. She said, "Sure, come on and I'll treat you to a coffee and a donut." "I haven't had a donut in a long time; sounds good," Wit remarked. They had their snack and toured the main areas of the hospital, and he asked, "Where are your living quarters?" "They are building those pre-fab units as fast as they can and I have one of the first ones, number 16. Let's walk down and I'll show it to ya," she offered. They went in and the first thing she did was turn on an oscillating fan in the kitchen and then in the bedroom. She commented, "I'm so hot I feel like taking off my clothes and standing in front of the fan." Wit replied, "Don't let me stop ya; I'm gonna look at the appliances in the kitchen." He checked them out and went back to the bedroom and there she stood, nothing on but her panties and bra, holding her arms out and letting the fan blow on her. "Would you do me a favor?" she asked. He thought, "The last half-naked woman asked me to do her a favor, I ended up in bed with her." So, he answered, "Yeah, if I can." "Would you introduce me to that good-looking boy that drives the Chaplain's Jeep?" she asked. "I never get to meet any decent guys; those airmen get drunk and are so vulgar and foul-mouthed." "He is Corporal Robert Hall, and a very decent young man; he doesn't smoke or drink or use foul language; he doesn't go to the bars or brothels. I'll do you one better, I'll bring him to the hospital, and you can treat us both to a donut and coffee. I might suggest you don't stand in front of the fan, at least till you get to know him better," he added.

She chuckled and replied, "I know what you mean. I don't do all those things either, and that is why it gets so lonely."

A couple days later, Wit said, "Come on, Robert, I want you to go to the hospital with me; I got someone I want you to meet." "Who?" he questioned, trying to figure out who it would be. "You'll see; I think you will be pleasantly surprised," Wit answered. They drove to the hospital and Wit introduced Annie and Robert, and said, "Annie is going to treat us to a donut and coffee." The young couple's eyes met, and you could feel the sparks. While they were enjoying their donut, Wit volunteered, "When I was a kid, the city bus would stop in front of my house. We would take the bus, which only cost a nickel, and get a transfer, and open the windows and go for a cool-off ride. When the bus reached the end of its line, we transferred to another bus and got another transfer, and rode all over the town cooling off on a hot summer night. You two could go on a cool-off ride in the evening through Da Nang in the open-air Jeep." They really liked that idea and planned to go that very night. "Keep your eyes on the sky and don't get caught in a rain storm," Wit laughed. It became a regular event for the young couple to go out on a hot steamy night for a cool-off ride. Wit wasn't a sound sleeper and he could hear Robert come in around 11:00 each night, and then he would relax, knowing they had no problems. One night, Robert came in around 3:00 in the morning and so Wit questioned him at breakfast, "You and Nurse Cooper getting along alright?" "Yeah, she's a great girl," he responded. "We were caught in the rain last night and we were soaked to the skin and went to her unit to dry off." "The fan dry you off?" Wit asked. "Yeah, how did you know?" Robert admitted. "Just a guess!" Wit replied, with a slight smile.

CHAPTER 36

The second Sunday later, after the services at the Chapel, Chaplain Jim addressed Wit, "I want you to meet Staff Sergeant Mike Staun, the lead instructor of the **'Green Beret'**. This is Chief Warrant Officer Loren Whitson and he is assigned to our Chaplel, and he is more commonly known as, Wit. His desire is to learn all he can about the jungle and jungle fighting, so I suggested the Green Beret would be the best training he could get along with the ARVN Rangers." Mike looked at him and remarked, "Whitson! That name sounds familiar. Did you by chance fight in Korea?" "Yeah," Wit answered, "seems like many moons ago." "I remember you!" Mike replied. "You were the one that called for reinforcements when the Chinese hordes were about to attack your outpost. You were one of the machine gunners that killed so many their bodies stacked up like cord wood. I was one of the reinforcements. They sure made a mess out of your tent city; then you disappeared." "Yeah," Wit responded with a stern look in his burning eyes, "but I made 'em pay." Mike noticed it and regretted bringing it up because it appeared to be a sore spot, and he hit a nerve.

That was something the Chaplain didn't know about Wit and he just stood quietly and listened to the conversation, but he also noticed the eyes. Mike continued, "This is a totally different kind of war. A wise man once said that, if any nation attacked the United States, they couldn't win because they would have to conquer the people, as well as the military. The British found that out in the Revolutionary War; with all their power and might, they were beaten by Patriots fighting Indian style from around trees and ambushes and a spy network that included women and kids. George Washington had his armies that faced the British army and outsmarted them in every big battle. This is going to be a war just like that; I'm not saying we can't win because we are surely gonna try. These people have been fighting for years and defeated the French, even with us providing the French with the latest weapons. You are welcome to join us, and we will teach you all we can; we are training the ARVN Rangers, and you can learn a lot from them about the jungle. I suggest you bring about a dozen canteens filled with good water, and a case of your favorite C-Ration. You will learn why when you get there. Bring something to wear that is more suitable for the jungle than what you have on now." "Will you be going back soon?" Wit asked. "I will need to follow you since I don't know where your training camp is." "I'm gonna eat a good meal and pick up some supplies," Mike replied, "probably be a couple hours." "Good," Wit responded, "that'll give me enough time to get my stuff together."

The camp was a large cleared area with underground bunkers, with sandbag barriers stacked all around each of them, and watch towers and redoubts around the perimeter, all manned with machine guns. Wit parked his chopper on the outer edge so as not to interfere with the training. Mike introduced him to the other training personnel and the ARVN officers, and they all welcomed him whole heartedly. Mike offered to share his bunker, along with another Sergeant; he took him inside and explained the setup, "The bunks are crude canvas on frames cantilevered from the sides about 3 feet off the ground to prevent snakes from crawling in with you. You want to keep your flashlight handy to shine on the floor before you get up in case one happens to get in; we have some deadly varieties that can do some serious damage. We alternate guarding the bunker during the night; the other bunkers do the same; since we now have three in ours, we can do 4-hour shifts. We try to keep a good supply of good water and whatever food we can get, but sometimes we can't get in to resupply, so you may need to rely on what you brought; and use yours when you go on missions. That is where your subject is, 'Jungle 101'; you will learn more there than we can tell ya because you will experience it for yourself."

Mike and several other Sergeants were standing with Wit, when he asked where he took his basic training. "I trained with the 101st Airborne Infantry at Camp Breckinridge, Ky," Wit replied. "The weapon of choice back then was the M-1 Garand. We now use the M-14; 7.62 mm NATO round, and has a 20-round magazine. It can fire 750 rounds per minute at an effective range of 500 yards; it has an automatic or semi-automatic selector. You fired the M-1 up to a 1000-yards, but as you can see, we don't have a target at that distance, here in the jungle," Mike explained. "I think the first thing you want to learn is to be proficient, in all respects, with the M-14; firing in all positions; assembly and disassembly, and cleaning. Learn to use it the way that is the best is for you; you may not have the luxury of stopping and aiming, because more chances than not, your target will be moving." He spent about a month, firing thousands of rounds and, in the mean-time, when his shoulder got sore, he disassembled the rifle and gave it a good cleaning. They had simulated targets of the enemy jumping from behind trees and he only had a quick glimpse to take a shot. Wit concluded that the best shot was from the hip on semi-automatic and he practiced endlessly until he hit the target perfectly every time. The targets were jumping out at random and he learned to anticipate where they were, which gave him an additional split second. The Green Beret instructors and the ARVN Rangers assembled around him and marveled at his skill.

Mike then suggested he go on a short mission with the Rangers and get a firsthand look at the jungle and what he would be faced with. "This is their home turf where they grew up; so, learn from them all that you can. Learn to rely on your own instincts, however, because that will become your best weapon; stay *focused* or you could become dead. The officers are dependable, but the others not so much." The officers spoke enough broken English that he could communicate, but the regular troops were a different story. They were good about warning him about the dangers to watch out for, like signaling to circle around anthills; there were black and red ants that could sting like a hornet and inflict quite a bit of pain. The officers were serious, but the rest of guys didn't seem to take things as serious, so Wit decided to hang back and let the squad lead the way. He would follow their path and find a dead snake from time to time on the trail where they killed it, which didn't hurt his feelings none. They avoided the swampy areas and walked the dikes around the rice paddies. He got the picture in a hurry about what Mike was talking about with the water not worth drinking. Men, women, kids, and water buffalo working in the paddies would squat and take a dump, and then proceeded to work. He took a drink from his canteen and said, "Boy that tasted good!" They hiked most of the day thru tall grass and bamboo, and a rare clearing from time to time, and then entered through a bamboo gate into a village area. All the people came out of their hootches and stared at the American. The ARVN Major introduced Wit to the Ancient, who appeared to be the old senior leader of the clan and the Major was the interpreter between them. A dark cloud blew in and it started to rain, so the Ancient invited them inside, and offered Wit a mat to sit on; all others squatted. It looked larger from the inside than it did from the outside; plenty big enough for the entire family with none of them reaching an estimate of over 80 to 100 pounds, and they sat around a small fire in the middle of the room. An old woman offered a cup of rice, which Wit accepted gladly, since he was feeling hungry after hiking all day. Then she offered him a fish; now that was a different ball game; after seeing their dirty water and knowing the fish had to come out of that water, he didn't want to hurt their feelings, so he cut off the head and tail, sharpened a stick and ran it through the fish lengthwise, and held it over the fire till he thought it was thoroughly cooked, then proceeded to eat it, carefully picking out the bones. The kids grabbed the head and tail and enjoyed eating those, so nothing was wasted.

The Rangers and the Villagers conversed in their own language and Wit concluded that it would take a hundred years for him to learn how to talk with them. Finally, the rain stopped, and the Major said, "Rain stop, we go." They all stood and started bowing to each other. Wit stuck his hand out to shake with the Ancient, but he didn't know what Wit wanted, so Wit urged him to take his hand and shake. The old man started shaking slowly and then started shaking faster and grinning from ear to ear. The old woman, that gave them the food, was a tiny woman, even smaller that Mrs. Dink, looked at him with her big eyes, and reminded him of a kewpie-doll, so he put his arms around her and gave her a hug. She stiffened and then the Major said something, and she then smiled showing what teeth she had left. As they left the village, Wit asked the Major, "What did you say to the old woman?" "I tell her you work in big temple, was Messenger from Holy One," he replied. They returned the same way they had gone out and it took a lot less time, and he was tired; he hadn't hiked that much in several years. He wanted to eat and get a big drink of water and offered to take the last watch in the bunker, giving him time to rest first.

The next morning, Wit made a little stove by filling an empty C-Ration can with dirt and soaking it with gasoline. It burned slow but managed to heat a can for breakfast. Mike had fresh coffee he made in a French Cocotte, like a Dutch Oven, that he found, apparently left by the French Army when they departed. He filled his mess kit cup and sat down next to Wit, "Help yourself to the coffee. The Rangers said you did quite well for your first time out and impressed the Villagers you visited. You may have missed your calling; maybe you should be an Ambassador for the US Government," and smiled. "I don't even know what an Ambassador does," Wit responded. "Mike, I've been thinking," Wit began. "I've been here for over a month and maybe I should go back to the Chapel to see if there is anything I should be taking care of. I know the Chaplain is probably worried; wondering what may have happened to me. I think I have learned a tremendous amount, and I can see I have a long way to go, so I plan to return in a week, or two. Make a list of any provisions you may need for me to bring back, that is unless you are planning to go in yourself." "I intend to go in myself," Mike replied. "I need to attend church, and I can get whatever we may need. There are a couple things you need to do; get your hair cut into a burr, like mine; go to the hospital and ask for some dusting powder for lice and fleas and dust yourself good and the clothes you have been wearing; then wash them in GI soap. Most all these people have lice and, if you are going to be hugging them, we don't want you dragging lice into camp."

The first one he ran into at the Chapel was Robert and asked, "Robert, do you have a pair of hair clippers?" "No, I don't," Robert answered. "You will have to go to the Airmen Barber Shop." Wit entered the Chapel and let the Chaplain know he was back for a couple weeks and he was going to the barber shop and then to the hospital and see about getting some lice preventive powder. "Glad to see you are back, Wit," the Chaplain remarked. "You go take care of that first because that is one thing we don't want to get started here. Then you can tell me what you have been doing for over a month." "You have anything good to eat on the stove, Chaplain?" Wit asked. "I'm craving food." The Chaplain handed him his pay that he missed getting while he was gone, and said, "While you are over near the hospital, pick up a sack of cheeseburgers at the diner, and bring them back and treat us. We have different kinds of soda and coffee, and of course water." "Do I just get enough for the three of us, or do the Dinks eat them too?" Wit asked, so he would know how many to buy. "They are becoming more Americanized, so they eat them, too," the Chaplain commented. The hospital staff checked him over good and determined he never had lice or fleas, but suggested he dust himself good when he went out in the jungle. He carried in the bag of burgers and, while they were eating, he described in detail his mission trip with the ARVN Rangers. He then took a much-needed shower and put on clean clothes. He asked Mrs. Dink to use the strong soap when she did his laundry.

Wit went in and sat down with Robert and the Chaplain, and he asked, "Mrs. Dink seems to have a little baby bump; is she pregnant?" "Yeah," the Chaplain responded, "I think she is due in four or five months." Wit added, "I wouldn't want to bring a baby into this world, the shape this country is in." "Can't stop Mother Nature!" the Chaplain exclaimed. "So, Robert, how are you and Nurse Cooper getting along?" Wit asked. "We are getting along great," Robert replied. "She will have enough points in two months, and she can go home." "How about you, Robert, how long do you have?" Wit continued to ask. "I'll have enough points in three months. We've been talking about re-enlisting so we can stay together," he answered. "Don't you dare," Wit barked sternly. "Don't even think about it. Get out of here as quick as you can while you are still living. This is going to become the most dangerous place in the world, and you could both die here; and for what? This is a politician's war and there is not going to be a quick end to it. She can get a job at any hospital in the States and you need to go to school and get an education. Pick your school and she can work near your school. When you get a little money, get married; buy a little house; and raise a family. I know what I am talking about; I've been there. A Nurse in Korea and I fell in love and we had plans to do just that, and then the worst thing happened, an artillery shell hit her tent and blew her to a million pieces. It has haunted me ever since. If you want me to talk to Annie, I will, but you better use your heads and take my advice. This is not a game we're playing here, it's a game of life and death. I don't know what the Chaplain thinks about it, but if you are smart, you will go home and don't look back. You will read about it getting ugly and how you could have made the biggest mistake of your young lives. Now go take her for a cool-off ride and tell her just exactly what I said and start making real plans." The Chaplain listened to the conversation quietly and finally said, "What Wit says makes good sense." After Robert left to go see Annie, the Chaplain asked, "Is that what you were talking about with Mike Staun when you said you made them pay? Is that what that highly classified document, sealed by the President, is about?" "Yes! And Yes!" he answered, and he could feel the *Demon of Death* stirring inside of him. The Chaplain watched his expression closely, and what he saw made chills run up his spine, so he elected not to pursue it further.

For the next couple weeks, Wit rested and ate decent food and made regular visits to the hospital. He offered to pray with any of the patients and hoped to give them comfort, while being many miles away from home. He became well acquainted with the hospital staff, and especially Dr. Ashby, whom he had discussions with about his past experiences praying with the dying; also, his experience working with disturbed veterans, trying to get them conditioned to go back into civilian life. He stocked up on the provisions he would need at the Green Beret camp, and then flew out to rejoin Mike. "Anything exciting happen while I was gone?" he asked. "Yeah," Mike responded, "I guess you heard President Kennedy was assassinated?" "Yeah, I heard that." Wit replied.

"Then you know Vice-President Johnson was sworn in to take over?" Mike continued. "Yeah, so?" Wit questioned. Mike explained, "Well, Johnson is saying he intends to ramp up the military activity here, and that means America is going to be in an all-out war in Vietnam. That will filter down to us, and we will need to accelerate our training of the ARVNs. The ARVN's friends from the north say the assassination has prompted Hanoi to try to push the US out, and they have increased their violence activity. Since you were worn out on your last short mission, I suggest you try to get yourself back into fighting condition, like you were at one time. We are stepping up our physical training and I suggest you join in; we are going to have more demonstrations of actual combat which I think will benefit you also." Wit agreed, remembering back to the days of basic training and the Airborne Ranger trying to toughen them up so they could survive in combat. He had softened up some living the good life in Bavaria, but now it was time to buckle down again. The little ARVN guys were fit, and he had to push himself to keep up; at the demonstrations he would squeeze his little rubber ball, one hand and then the other, while he intently watched the technique of the GB. He applied himself vigorously, huffing and puffing, and after several weeks, he started feeling more like himself.

"We have an added problem," Mike explained, with concern. "The Viet Minh, that whipped the French in the Indo-China campaign, have formed a guerrilla unit that is growing fast; we hear they are now about 35,000 strong. They are now called Viet-Cong, or VC, meaning Vietnamese Communists; that is in addition to the 80,000 regulars of the North Vietnam Army, or NVA. They are crossing the 17th parallel and infiltrating into the south. I'm forming a new mission, and I suggest you go along, to scout the area and see if they are closing in on us here in our camp. I have alerted all personnel to be prepared to fight if necessary; our former instruction was to fire only when we were fired upon, but I am cancelling that instruction and do whatever it takes. Keep *focused* and watch your back; I hear the South Vietnamese soldiers may run to the north and join them, so the ones that you are fighting with today may be fighting you tomorrow; be ready for anything." Wit let the ARVN lead the way, like before, and it wasn't maybe an hour when they walked into an ambush. Two ARVN were killed, and two ran, but not far, because the Major shot 'em. They started spraying bullets on automatic, in the direction of the attack, but the VC seemed to have disappeared. Wit got a glimpse of them and they were not in uniforms, but dressed in what looked like black pajamas. The VC snipers had them pinned down, and the Rangers couldn't see what they were shooting at; they just sprayed bullets. Occasionally a VC would run from one tree to another, so Wit set his M-14 on semi-automatic, and just like the simulated targets, he started to pick them off one at a time and he shot 4 of them. Then all got quiet, and it was thought they retreated somewhere in the jungle. They examined the places in which they were shot and found blood but no bodies, so they assumed their casualties were carried away.

CHAPTER 37

The ARVN carried their two dead comrades back to the camp and were all excited to tell about their fight. The ARVN Major reported the entire event in detail to Mike, and Mike listened intently to all the information he was getting. The rest of the ARVN troops were chattering away in their own language, still all excited, and Mike smiled like he was pleased with what they were saying. Wit asked, "What are they saying?" Mike answered, "You have a new nick name, **'*Jungle Rat*'**." "That's funny!" Wit remarked. "I just picked them off one at a time, like I did while practicing on the simulated range. The Major shot two of his own men that tried to run away, and they are still out there; the VC dragged their dead away." Mike was quiet for a moment and then said, "The word is going to spread through the Communist ranks about a killer American going by the name of The *Jungle Rat*, so you are going to need to be careful they don't associate that name with The *Chopper Chaplain*, or *Wit*. It will be like 'Clark Kent going into a phone booth to become Superman'. If they connect the two as one, then you won't see the next light of day. When you move around in town, you must dress normal and act like you normally do when you go to the hospital or the diner, or where ever. That's what the Communists do; they work in town where they can find jobs, or are farmers, and then, at night, they become guerrillas causing mayhem, terrorizing and killing Southern Sympathizers. Don't tell anyone, not even the Chaplain, unless he starts to suspect something, then you can explain it to him, only if he swears to secrecy. If you encountered them as close as you did, then it is a matter of time before they zero in on our camp, so we are going to tighten up our security. We got the word our aircraft were fired upon by Soviet and Chinese anti-aircraft artillery, so that's an indication that it is accelerating. Do you want to go on another recon patrol?" "Yeah, but I think I want to go alone and meet the (PM) Pajama Monkeys at their own game," Wit replied. "I'll dress as light as they do, and move around like they do, and not carry a heavy weapon. All I will need is my sidearm and K-bar (knife), so I can move around swiftly. If I catch one of them, I'll kill him with my bare hands." "I hope you know what you are doing?" Mike responded, concerned. "Where do you plan to go?" "I'll go to the same place we went the last time; I got some unfinished business I want to take care of," Wit replied. "If you could manage to bring back a prisoner, we can learn more about them," Mike suggested. "I can't fool with prisoners," Wit responded. "They will only slow me down. I'll just kill 'em!"

He moved swiftly toward the place where they were ambushed and then slowed to a methodical pace, where he advanced from cover to cover, taking time to observe and look for movement. He remained concealed and careful; he then detected movement. A young pajama monkey (PM) came carelessly up the trail, seemingly not expecting any activity, like a teenager roaming around a town on a Saturday night. When he reached the tree where Wit was waiting, Wit reached out and grabbed him by the hair and proceeded to tear out his throat. The PM didn't know what happened; Wit searched him for any documents, and finding none, dragged his body off the trail into the tall grass. He picked up the rifle the boy had dropped, intending to take it back to camp. He waited and observed and then, out of the corner of his eye, more movement; he was registering in his mind how these guys moved about. He waited for the second PM to come by, and when he reached the tree where Wit was, Wit swung the rifle, holding the barrel like a baseball bat, mashing the face, killing him instantly, and then did the same thing; search and hide the body. He left the rifle this time with the body. He continued to move forward, slowly and stealthily, watching for another poor soul destined to meet his maker. He was well hidden in a good spot, like a deer hunter waiting for the big buck, and another PM came into view. It was obvious he wasn't aware of his buddies' demise, or he wouldn't have been so nonchalant. He still moved warily, not showing himself in the open. Wit observed how he moved about and got a quick lesson on jungle movement. He wasn't coming in Wit's direction, so Wit moved toward him, and when he got in position, he snatched him like a toad snatches an insect, and tore out his throat. He heard chattering of two or three as they walked up the trail. He thought he would follow them to see where they were going, or where they would hide. They approached an old temple with a cemetery along the side, lifted a grass covered trap door, and four of them dropped into a hole and then pulled the lid over the hole. They left one standing guard about 25 feet from the hole behind a grave marker; Wit looked closely around to see if there were more. Satisfied there were no more in this gang, he crept up and sent the unfortunate little man to the great jungle in the sky. He hastened back to camp to report to Mike, taking the rifle with him.

Mike said, "That's a Russian made AK-47, and it is used throughout by all of them. Don't think it is an inferior weapon; it is an excellent rifle." "Show me how to disable it," Wit requested. "I don't like leaving them out there for them to use again." "I'll show you how to remove the firing pin," Mike offered. "I doubt they carry around extra firing pins." Wit responded, "They don't carry anything except the rifle, and two of them I killed had a knife." "How many did you kill?" Mike asked. "I killed four of 'em," he answered. Then he described the scene at the old temple; how they dropped into a hole and disappeared. "I can take you right to the place if you should want to send some men and drop a couple grenades or smoke bombs down the hole," Wit suggested. Mike was becoming more impressed with Wit and all he had accomplished in such a short time, and he asked, "Are you ready to go out again?" "Not yet," Wit replied, "I want to rest up for a few days and replenish the water I've been sweating out, and eat regular; then I'll go out again, if you want me to." In his down time, he squeezed his rubber ball and sharpened his K-bar, keeping it to a razor's edge; and napped occasionally.

After a few days, he felt recuperated enough to go out again. Mike asked, "Where are you going this time?" "I think I will go more west and search the area. I was thinking about what the ARVN Major said to the villagers about me, and they seemed to accept it. If I enter a village, I will try the same explanation, but since I don't speak their language, I thought I would take my cross with me, and hopefully when I show it to 'em, it will have the same impact," he explained. He donned the 'Jungle Rat' attire and went out with no big weapon, just his sidearm and knife. He moved cautiously through tall grass, bamboo, trees, and under heavy trees that made a canopy so thick, it was almost pitch dark, blocking out the light. He stopped momentarily to get his night vision and then moved through, carefully. He saw a limb hanging down which he almost ran into, grabbed it, and realized it was a snake looking him in the face; he grabbed his knife and sliced its head off. He thought, "That thing almost gave me a heart attack; I need to be extra careful. Like Mike said, 'there are things out there that are hunting you in addition to the Commies'." He never saw anything in over an hour, and then walked the dike next to a rice paddy and came to a bamboo fence with a gate in front. He concluded there must be a village behind it but wasn't foolish enough to go banging on it, so he went around the fence and there was no fence on the sides. The grass and trees were extremely thick, but he managed to work his way through and entered the village. He stood in an open space in front of a hootch; only saw some chickens and pigs, but no people. Then someone noticed him, and they all came out and gathered around, and he asked, "Speak English? Speak English?" Two men said, "Me speak!" He wanted to let them know he meant no harm, he said, "Me work in big temple." He took both arms and moved them in a circle, indicating big. One of the men interpreted to the villagers. He took out his cross and showed it to them and said, "Me messenger from the Holy One." They interpreted that and were relieved and smiled. He then asked, "VC? VC?" "No VC," they said. He wasn't carrying a rifle or wore a helmet or carried a back pack, so they concluded he wasn't military; an old woman brought him a small bowl of rice, and while he ate, the small kids came up to him. He patted the little boys on the head and pinched the cheeks of the little girls, and they all giggled. As he was finishing his rice, there was a commotion outside the fence, and one yelled, "VC! VC!" He darted to the hole in which he entered and dashed through the foliage to get around behind them. He looked back and there appeared to be about 25 or 30 of 'em in a frenzy, and he began hearing screaming and yelling, and he surmised they were killing the villagers. He moved swiftly down the trail in which he came to get space between them. He saw a PM hot footing toward him and figured he must be a straggler, so he lay in wait for him; the PM wasn't paying any attention to anything but seemed destined to get up the trail. Wit grabbed him by the hair and lifted him off his feet, and methodically ripped out his throat. He dragged the body into the grass but kept the AK-47 rifle because he figured he might have to shoot his way out of there. He left the trail and made a bee-line for the camp, going through wet grass and creeks and streams, and he could hear thrashing behind him because they were now chasing him. It was like Old Daniel Boone being chased through Kentucky to the Ohio River by some irate Indians. He turned and started picking them off, with the rifle on semi-automatic, and they stopped to hunker down, which gave him a few seconds to proceed running again. When he got close to camp, he started yelling, "VC! VC!", to give them a heads-up, but they were already prepared. The Green Beret and ARVN troops rapid fired all their weapons and lobbed mortars and killed a good number of the Commies. The VC dragged their dead and retreated into the jungle.

The battle left two Green Beret wounded and three ARVN soldiers killed. Mike stated, "It's time we shut it down here; we don't have the manpower to withstand a major attack." "Where will you go?" Wit asked. "There are other training camps south of here, so we might join up with them until the US Army arrives, and then we will split up and help train them. They will be young and green as gourds and won't have the foggiest idea what is going on here." Wit said, "I think I better go back and re-establish myself as a Chaplain's Assistant for a couple months, so they don't get the idea I'm the Jungle Rat. I can take the two wounded men to the hospital, but first I need to change back into my 'Clark Kent' outfit." Mike stopped him, and said, "Hold on a minute; you got a leech attached to the back of your arm, and a couple on your pant legs." Mike removed the one on his arm with his knife and shook off the others and stomped them. "When you go to the hospital, have them treat your arm so it doesn't get infected. Wash your jungle outfit yourself; you don't want the maid to see what you wear, just to be safe," he added.

CHAPTER 38

He flew the wounded directly to the hospital, and the Doctor said the wounds were not life threatening and treated his leech bite. He went to the Chapel and Captain Jim welcomed him with a big smile. "You look like death warmed over," Captain Jim commented, humorously. "You better take time to become Old Wit again." "I intend to," Wit responded. "Anything new going on?" "Yeah, lots," the Captain continued. "Robert and Annie went back home. He said he would have liked to have said goodbye and thanked you for all your advice and being a good friend. We have a new Orderly, Corporal Ernie Allen, and I will introduce you when he gets back. They are building a new hospital on the beach south of here about three miles, called 'Naval Support Activity Hospital'. I get the impression something big is going to happen sometime soon." Corporal Ernie walked in and Chaplain Jim introduced them. "Where you from, Ernie?" Wit asked, which was common place. "Dallas, Texas," he answered. "Dallas, eh?" Wit continued. "Were you there when the President was shot?" "No," he responded, "I was in basic training at Fort Leonard Wood,

Missouri, so I missed all the excitement. I trained in motor transport; also, was assigned as a Chaplain's Assistant. They said there was an opening here, so I jumped on it; thinking it was better than getting shot at." "Do you know how to cut hair?" Wit asked. "I'm afraid not," Ernie replied, and laughed, "and I would hate to see the mess I would make of that." "Well, come on Ernie," Wit requested, "let's go and get me a haircut and then ride down to see the new hospital they are building. You watch closely how they cut it and then you will know how to do it the next time." "I have a list of items I need you to pick up at the Commissary while you are out joy riding," the Chaplain requested. As they rode to the barber shop, Ernie said, "The Chaplain said you have been training with the Green Beret." "Yes," Wit replied, "I've been training with them well over a year. Part of my job is to go out wherever there has been trouble and do what I can to administer what help I can to aid anyone that has been injured. I knew nothing about the jungle, and that is one place you better know what you are doing if you want to survive. There are more things out there that can kill ya, not counting the Commies, that want a piece of an American's scalp." "Did you ever hear of the Jungle Rat?" Ernie asked, curiously. Wit had to play dumb and responded in a way where he didn't lie. "There are a lot of big rats in the jungle, and probably as many in the back allies of the towns," Wit explained. "I haven't encountered too many rats, but I sure have the snakes; now there is a nasty bunch." "I mean a man called, 'The Jungle Rat'," Ernie clarified. "A man that looks like a rat?" Wit laughed. "Where are you getting that stuff?" "The airmen tell about him," Ernie said. "Airmen!" Wit remarked. "What would they know about anything like that? The only time they get out of their hammocks is to party.

Do they talk about the man-eating tigers? I haven't seen or heard any yet, but the ARVN boys say they have heard them roar at night."

After the haircut, they stopped at the Commissary, and while Ernie was shopping, Wit looked around and stopped suddenly. He stopped at a rack that had baseball caps, so he picked out a Cincinnati Reds cap that fit nicely, and remarked, quietly, "That's what I need to look like I am just a regular guy." He put it on his head backwards and showed it off as he walked to meet Ernie. They rode to the new hospital construction site and parked up close to where most of the activity was taking place. Wit approached a man that looked like the officer in charge, and introduced himself, and asked, "Do you have a scheduled time when it is supposed to be finished?" "Yeah!" he exclaimed. "Damn quick, or sooner. Marines will be arriving soon, and we are ordered to be finished by that time; looks like the war is gonna begin sooner than we think and gonna be serious. We are doing what we can, working around the clock, and this heat and humidity doesn't help matters." Wit reported it all back to the Chaplain.

"I noticed Mrs. Dink is getting quite big," Wit related to the Chaplain. "Is she about due?" "Yeah," the Chaplain replied, "I would say she is getting close, so we need to keep an eye on her." A couple days later, Wit was looking for Mrs. Dink to give her his laundry, and she was nowhere to be found, so he started a search, and found her laying on her cot in a fetal position, holding her belly. "Need help?" he asked her. "Baby coming?" She shook her head to the affirmative; her eyes were big like she was begging for help. "I'm taking you to the hospital," he remarked, and she showed a little fear in her face, and he said, "Don't worry, I will stay with you." He had no idea where Mr. Dink was. He picked her up and carried her to the Jeep and drove to the Emergency Room entrance. Two Nurses saw him pull up and came out with a wheel chair, and he said, "I think she is in labor!" "Does she belong to you?" one asked. "No," he answered, "she and her husband work at the Chapel." He parked the Jeep and went inside where they were taking her directly to the Delivery Room. "She is scared!" one Nurse remarked. "You think you could go in with her, or would you pass out?" "Honey, if you have seen half of what I've seen in my time, you wouldn't ask such a question; this should be a piece-a-cake," he responded. She had fear in her eyes, so he held her little hand to let her know he was gonna stay with her. She never made a sound through the entire delivery and the Nurses thought that was unusual. After they cleaned her up and cleaned the baby, they gave her the baby. It was a tiny thing and weighed 4 pounds and Wit commented, "He looks like a little mouse so I will call him Mickey, like Mickey Mouse." The Nurse asked, "Is that what you want on the birth certificate?" "Oh no," Wit quickly responded, "he needs his own identity; I call his parents Mrs. and Mr. Dink because their real names are a mouthful." One Nurse said, "Maybe we can name him Baby Dink." The other Nurse said, "Maybe Rinky-Dink." Wit quickly said, "Ladies, we need to be more respectful; they are humans just like we are. I'll bring Mr. Dink in and he can give you all the information you need; he speaks good English." Mrs. Dink thought she was done and started to get up to leave. One Nurse urged her to stay down and held up 3 fingers, and said, "3 days!" Dr. Ashby came in and asked, "What's going on?" Wit answered, "I brought this little lady in to have her baby; she works at out Chapel." "He sure is a little tyke, ain't he?" the Doctor commented. "Yeah, and I learned something today," Wit remarked. "You think you could deliver a baby now?" the Doc asked. "I probably could," Wit replied, "but gosh, I hope I don't have to."

Wit went back to the Chapel and explained everything to the Chaplain and Ernie, and said he didn't have time to hunt them down, so he rushed her to the hospital. They both admitted they didn't know where they were, or anything about it. Wit said, "I didn't see Mr. Dink, and I knew I had to hurry, so I just carried her to the Jeep and took her to the Emergency Room. It was a good thing, because they wheeled her directly to the Delivery Room, and it happened quickly. I need to take Mr. Dink because they need a lot of information I couldn't give 'em. He is as little as a mouse, so I nick-named him Mickey." He finally found Mr. Dink, and informed him, "You are a Papa; a big bouncing baby boy." Mr. Dink wasn't sure what a Papa was, and he gave Wit a strange look. Wit rephrased it, "A Father; a Daddy!" "Oh!" he finally caught on and started jumping up and down and laughing hysterically. Wit then said, "Come on, we go to hospital and you tell them names." Wit and the Doctor became close friends, and they exchanged information whenever they had some to share. While Mr. Dink sat with one of the Nurses and explained to her what she needed to know, Wit sat with the Doctor and asked, "Have you heard when things are gonna start happening? The new hospital is going up fast, like they are pushing the schedule." "I heard the Marines are coming in very soon; how soon, I don't know," the Doctor replied. Wit responded, "I don't like the sound of that. I'll check with the Green Beret to see what they know." He returned to the Chapel and ran into Ernie. "Ernie, do you have a gun? What did you fire in basic?" Ernie replied, "I fired an M-1 Carbine and they issued drivers a .45

Cal Grease Gun, but I never fired it. I don't have a gun now." "When I go to the Green Beret training camp, I want you to go with me and learn how to use a .45 Semi-automatic hand gun. You must learn how to defend yourself because we are on the verge of a major war and you absolutely must know how to use one. I'll see that you get one, and we better check to make sure the Chaplain has one," Wit commented.

Wit spent about a month catching up on sleep and decent food; he made routine visits to the hospital, praying with anyone that was sick or stressed out. A couple weeks later, Sgt. Mike Staun came in for church service, and afterwards, Wit cornered him for what information he may have. He said, "We closed down the camp we occupied and joined with another camp about 15 Klicks further south. We had two of our instructors from another unit killed, so we can see things building up fast. The Commies are increasing faster than we are, and the ARVN boys are trying to keep pace, which means we are pressed to the limit training them." "I want to follow you out and know where you are located, so let me know when you are ready to leave," Wit replied. "I want to bring our new Chaplain's Orderly, Ernie, with me to learn how to use a handgun, and I would appreciate personal instruction and target practice for him from one of your instructors. I don't know what they are teaching them in basic training these days; he is like a sitting duck that doesn't know how to defend himself. And oh, don't mention the term 'Jungle Rat'; he's been hearing it from the airmen and has asked about it. We will only stay one day, and I will bring him back. I will then return in a few days to sharpen my skills, if that is alright with you." "Yeah, no problem," Mike responded, "we have learned a lot about their booby traps that you will need to know." Ernie had a very patient instructor and he learned quickly; he became proficient hitting the targets, so the last thing to learn was, how to clean the gun. He was instructed how to disassemble, and clean it, but he fumbled around trying to re-assemble it, and after a few tries, he managed fairly well. Mike gave him the gun as a gift, with a holster, so he could wear it, if, and when, it should become necessary. Mike remarked, "I hope you never have to use it!"

CHAPTER 39

A couple days later, Wit went back to the camp; he took enough C-Rats and water to last a couple weeks; he took his Jungle Rat attire with plans to go on a couple lone expeditions in the jungle. He joined the ARVN Rangers in their PT (physical training) to tighten up his muscles, since he was lazing around for a month. He shot targets with his .45 and the M-14 until he felt confident again, like he was previously. He impressed the new Rangers like he did with the old, shooting from the hip. His knife was sharp, but he wanted to make sure it had the razor's edge, in case he needed it. Mike had boobytraps that they discovered and brought back for training; punji stakes coated with human dung that could cause infection if one was unlucky enough to step on one in the swamp; explosives that could go off with the slightest jar, normally hung on gates or doorways. He had large sketches of punji pits that contained sharpened bamboo about three feet long that could impale you if you should step on the grassy mat cover and fall through. He made sketches of trip wires that could set off an explosion or release a spear mounted in a nearby tree. And worst of all, a child or woman that carried a grenade where they could walk up to ya and set it off, killing you and either of them. Mike reiterated what he said since day one, "If you lose '*focus*', you are dead. They are increasingly insane with one thought in mind, kill the Americans and Rangers, however way possible. I hear they bombed the USS Maddox, and that has gotten the ire of President Johnson." It was a shuttering thought.

When Wit thought he was ready, he told Mike, "The Pajama Monkeys (PM) have thought of ways to get me, but I am going to make them know what it feels like to be hunted like an animal. I knew an old Marine who fought the Japs in the Pacific, and he said, 'If you want to live, you have to get down to their level; be as brutal as they are and treat them the same as they want to treat you'. He said, 'They cut their heads off and mounted them on the windshields of their Jeeps and let them know we are as bad as they are; and you survive'. His name was Leon Farmer, and he was so tough, when he got a toothache, he took a pair of pliers and pulled the tooth out." Mike thought, "This guy is a true Jungle Rat; and a Chaplain?" It gave him chills. Wit suited up in his jungle attire and set out early in the morning. He wanted to learn more about the boobytraps, and he searched for anything obvious that might contain them. After about an hour, he spotted a PM just sauntering along, like he never had a care in the world, and he winnowed through the jungle. Wit thought, "I am going to follow him and let him teach me where the boobytraps are." He soon noticed a pattern that the PM moved in; what bushes to go around; what trees to avoid; when to get off the trails and when to get back on. "They can't all know who set the traps, but they had to know where the traps would be, so they could avoid them, and it makes sense that certain bushes, trees, and trails were similar so that any one of them could identify the trap and avoid it. Very clever!" he surmised. He worked his way back to camp and explained it all to Mike. Mike was impressed, and asked, "But how would *we* know where the traps are?" Wit responded, "I want to go out again, and I will try to cut a twig off the bush or tree, and if I spot a trip wire, maybe I can cut it and bring back the explosive with a piece of wire attached. This is what I learned from one PM, so maybe I can follow another one and see what other items are used, but I'll do that another day. All the VC units in Vietnam may not use the same identifying marks, so this might just be particular to the unit in this location. Until I can learn more about it, I would suggest the Rangers don't go crashing through the jungle in a group, especially at night. Of course, that is not my call." It rained during the night and was quite foggy the next morning, so he decided to wait until the following day, hoping it would clear up. He told Mike he wanted to scout in a different direction, and if he was lucky, he might find another PM to follow, and that would tell him if the traps were set in similar places, or different, to prove his theory. The following day, it did clear up but with a slight mist, which made moving around better and with less noise. He crept slowly, avoiding what he thought might be a trap, and spotted a PM moving cautiously around the similar places as before, so he followed him, and the PM met up with another of his friends. They jabbered for a bit and then continued. One place the first VC yanked the other one away from the direction he was going, which meant he saved him from almost walking into a trap. When they avoided a bush or tree, he cut a sprig of each and stuck them in his belt. Then they got off the trail and he examined where they got off and found a twine running to the edge of the trail, so he followed the twine to a buried mine along the edge. He carefully cut the twine, and, with his knife, he managed to dig under the mine, and headed back to camp with the unexploded mine.

Now Mike was really impressed. He not only said he would deliver, but he did just that. Mike displayed the items Wit brought back and gave instructions to all the men and the Rangers of how to avoid all these things. Wit was surprised when a Colonel and a Captain emerged out of a bunker, walked over and viewed the items Wit brought back. Mike introduced them and said, "This is the Jungle Rat you have been hearing about!" "Really!" they both said at once, with somewhat a shocked look. They looked at him standing there, not a big man like he was perceived to be, and dressed in his jungle attire, although appearing to be menacing. The Colonel said, "You are becoming famous in this part of 'Nam. Does that little helicopter with Chopper Chaplain painted on it belong to you?" "Yes, sir," Wit responded, "I'm in the Chaplain's Service." The Captain said, "You could have fooled me." "That's the idea," Mike remarked, "he can come and go as he pleases in town and go out into the jungle and be a killer later. As you can see, he has been very useful to us; he has been training with us for over a year and a half. We joke like he is 'Clark Kent' going into a phone booth to change his clothes. He will change when he gets into the chopper to go back to the Chapel to look like a Chaplain's Assistant." "Have you killed any Gooks yet?" the Colonel asked. "Yes, my share," Wit responded. "I went out with the Rangers at first, and then found I was more effective going alone. I meet them on their own ground, do 'em in, and throw their bodies into the brush. I don't carry a weapon, except my .45 and knife. Mike showed me how to disable their AK-47 so I don't leave them a weapon to pick up and use later. Now gentlemen, I want to get back and watch the Marines land. The war is about to begin in earnest." "Have you considered transferring to our unit?" the Captain asked. "No thanks!" Wit replied. "You guys are too tough for me." Mike snickered as Wit saluted and walked back to his chopper and changed his clothes and was off for Da Nang. They never said anything and just watched him and shook their heads in disbelief.

"Ernie let's go and watch the Marines come in," Wit suggested, and they rode to the waterfront. The 9th Marines made an amphibious landing and came ashore carrying so much equipment they almost drowned. "Look at the fresh faces on those kids," Wit remarked. "They don't have the slightest idea what they're in for; some you are seeing alive for the last time." "They are trained, ain't they?" Ernie questioned. "They ain't trained for this," Wit answered, "and besides that, they are outnumbered 30 to 1." Funny thing was, when they came ashore, young boys were waiting and offered to sell them Coca-Colas; school girls made lays and greeted them. Certainly, different than when the Germans greeted the Army at Normandy on 'D' day. Another group, the 3rd Marines, about 800, flew in and landed at the air strip. "Look around and watch the men just standing and watching while the younger people are happy to see them come in," Wit remarked. "Those guys are VC and are here spying. If you should follow one, you will see him meet up with one of his fellow PM (pajama monkeys) and report." "How do you know that?" Ernie questioned. "I've seen enough of them to know how they act and what they are thinking," Wit explained. "The town is full of 'em. It's hard to tell the good guys from the bad guys, except when you find one mysteriously died; he is the good guy." Ernie just looked at him wondering how he became so bitter. The Marine Compound opened the next day. The 9th Marines' mission was to defend the air strip and bridges and the perimeter around Da Nang from any aggression or infiltration to destroy US planes and military property. The 3rd Marines branched out more southerly in defense of US interests, especially along the beaches.

Wit returned to the camp and reported to Mike about the arrival of the Marines, and how they were so laden down with equipment, when all the weapons the PMs carried was a rifle and possibly a knife. The Colonel approached him and asked, with a grin, "What are your plans for today, Jungle Rat?" He seemed to be amused that this Chaplain's Assistant was a cold-blooded killer. "Well, Colonel, I thought I would go out and do some more scouting and kill as many as I can before they can kill those young men that the Politicians have thrown into the fire." The Colonel was speechless when he saw the seriousness in Wit's face. Wit went to his chopper and changed into his jungle attire, and when he returned, the Colonel remarked, with concern, "Be careful out there!" For some reason, Wit felt anger because of the turn of events, and he proceeded to kill PMs. He grabbed them and tore out their throats before they knew what happened; he threw them into the brush and disabled their rifles. In time, he became well acquainted with friendly villagers, when at first, he was stared at because he was an American, but they soon paid no attention when he entered their hamlet or village. People went about their business and the kids never stopped playing when he arrived; an old woman would treat him to a bowl of rice for a hug. The VC were finding their comrades killed with their throats torn out, and the word spread throughout their units that it was the Jungle Rat. He became enemy #1 and they put out rewards for his capture or his dead body.

CHAPTER 40

The Marines began sending out patrols and they soon got a taste of death in firefights with the VC. Ambushes increased and the Marines soon became smarter and learned how to detect them and defend themselves. If they didn't stay together, and one or two would venture out away from their unit, the VC would kill them and mutilate their bodies, and leave them hanging upside down from a tree for the others to find. It was total '*barbarianism*'! When Wit came across such heinous crimes, he would report back to the Fire Base that he thought they came from, so they could go out and retrieve the body or bodies. He became well known to the Marines, and they appreciated his efforts. On one scouting mission, he heard a firefight in process where the VC ambushed a Marine patrol, and several Marines were hit. The Marines were spraying magazine loads of ammo at whatever looked like a PM, but the PMs ran from tree to tree. Wit arrived and picked up an M-14, put the selector on semi-automatic, positioned the rifle on his hip, and started picking off the PMs one at a time, just like he practiced at the Green Beret camp. They quickly realized they were beaten; dragged their friends away and faded into the jungle. A Corpsman quickly started examining and treating the wounds of the ones that were hit. A Corporal, the patrol leader, approached him and remarked, "I've never seen shooting like that before; sure, glad you showed up. We were in deep shit." "You'll learn in time!" Wit replied. "I just hope you do before you lose a lot of your men. You better get your wounded back soon for treatment. Good luck to you boys; maybe we'll run into each other again sometime." The patrol was all excited when they got back to their Fire Base and couldn't wait to tell the platoon leader what happened. When the Medevac arrived to pick up the wounded, they told the door gunner, and he said, "Boys, you have met the Jungle Rat; sounds like he saved your asses."

Wit had one more stop he wanted to make before returning to camp; a small hamlet with about 10-12 families, enough to tend their few rice patties; in a serene setting, normally quiet and peaceful; chickens aimlessly pecking around; pigs rooting and grunting; water buffalo munching on grass. The people were always friendly and accommodating, offering him a bowl of rice whenever he came. He became sort of attached to this small group, and the feeling seemed mutual. What he saw pierced his heart; dead bodies everywhere. Children with their heads bashed in; men lying in pools of blood with their throats cut and their brains knocked loose; women with their bellies cut open and their intestines laying on the ground. He muttered, "Whoever did this is not human!" Then he went into a hut and saw the worst of the worst. A pregnant woman had her guts cut out and her baby and afterbirth spilled on the floor next to her in a pool of blood and matter. He stared at her in disbelief, and then he saw it, the baby was still alive and moving; its little arm was sticking up out of all that mess. He pulled it free, tore off a strip of cloth and tied the umbilical cord about two inches from the baby's body, and cut the cord loose from the mother. The baby was a mess, so he picked it up and went outside and doused the baby in a basin of water, wiping it clean with a cloth, wrapped it in another cloth and placing it in the crook of his arm, like a running back carrying a football, hastened toward another hamlet he was familiar with about a mile away. He prayed all the way, "Lord help me get this baby to another hamlet without any delay." When he arrived, he went straight to the hut where the old woman and old man always welcomed him. He placed the baby in the old woman's arms, and she quickly ran out with it. He said to the old man, "VC killed entire village; all dead." The old man replied, "VC come here; looking for you." Just as quickly as the old woman ran out with the baby, she returned, and quietly handed him a bowl of rice. Wit asked the old man, "What she do with baby?" "Took to younger woman," he responded. While he was eating his rice, he asked the old man, "Who will bury the dead in the village?" "We go!" the old man answered. Wit worked his way back toward the camp, killing a PM here and there on his way; feeling good he was able to save the baby, but sad about his friends.

He returned to camp covered with sweat, and blood on his hands and clothes. The Colonel and Captain and Mike noticed his condition and approached him, and the Colonel asked, "Busy day today, Wit?" He explained everything in detail to them; only because it was information they may use. He said, "I think those young Marines are gonna be alright. They are learning the hard way, but they are learning fast. I think they have become aware of what they are faced with and they are smart enough to adjust to it. Slaughtering all those people was totally inhumane. I'm gonna get extra special pleasure with each one of them I kill from now on." "We believe ya!" Mike responded. "Gentlemen, I hate to leave good company, but I need to get back to civilization," Wit remarked. "I want to visit those injured Marines and pray with them. You fellers hold down the fort." He walked over to his chopper, opened the door, changed into his 'Clark Kent' outfit, and was up and away. The three of them didn't say a word as they watched his every move and disappearing into the sky.

He returned to the Chapel and removed all the filth and put on clean clothes. Chaplain Jim asked him to come into his office for a few minutes when he got time. He went in hoping it was not going to take long because he wanted to take a short nap. The Chaplain got right to the point, "I have been promoted to Major and you have been promoted to CWO4; congratulations!" "Congratulations to you Major; you sure deserve it," Wit responded. "Sgt. Staun tells me you are doing miraculous things out at their camp. I hope you aren't endangering yourself," Major Jim remarked. "Just another day at the office," Wit replied, "you know how war is? They brought in a couple injured Marines and I thought I would go and pray with them, after I get something to eat and take a short nap. If there is anything you want me to pick up while I am over that way, make a list and I'll stop at the Commissary."

He checked on Mrs. Dink and she was breast feeding little Mickey; when she saw him, she just grinned, and Wit patted him on the head. He chowed down on some decent vittles and then took a short nap. He picked up the list from the Major and then went to Da Nang General to see the wounded Marines and ran into Doc Ashby. "You wondered if I could deliver a baby?" Wit asked. "Let me tell you what I did." Doc was a tough guy, but he was almost sickened by Wit's description of what took place with the baby. He asked Doc about the Marines and Doc said, "They weren't brought here, so they must have taken them to the new Naval Hospital." "I see you are getting some new Doctors and Nurses," Wit commented. "Must be expecting your business to pick up." "Yeah, we got some new ones, and I am told we are going to get some more," Doc replied. Wit stopped at the Commissary and filled the list for the Major. While he was there, he went down the baby aisle and picked up a teething ring and a rattle for little Mickey. He then drove on down to the new Naval Hospital, and when he went in, he ran into the Corpsman, a Sergeant, that he saw in the jungle taking care of the wounded. He said, "Sarge, my name is Loren Whitson, nicknamed Wit, and I want your promise that when you speak of me, that's the name you use. Any other name you may hear, if it is suspected of being connected to the Chaplain's Service, could get me killed, and maybe even the entire Chapel staff, because I wear two hats, one you see here and one you may see elsewhere. Understand? And you might pass the word on to the other guys that were with you in the jungle." "Copy that, Wit!" he agreed. "What room are the injured Marines in?" Wit asked. "I want to offer a prayer with them." He went in and they didn't recognize him, mainly because they were taken out of the fight by the time he got there. He introduced himself and asked if he could pray with them. One had taken a bullet in the shoulder, up high, but not too bad. The other had some shrapnel in his leg that was removed. They both didn't get the ticket home, and in time, would probably return to their unit. It was a scare and they gladly submitted to a little prayer. When he returned to the

Chapel, he gave the teething ring and the rattle to Mrs. Dink; she had no idea what they were and what they were for, so he demonstrated for her, and then she caught on, and seemed pleased that he gave Mickey a gift.

Wit started to visit the hospitals daily because casualties began to arrive rather often, and he let it be known that his function there was to pray with them to help improve their healing. He ran into the Corpsman again at the Naval Hospital, and the Corpsman introduced Wit to the Director of the Hospital. When the Director began to realize the value in Wit's efforts, they became better acquainted and conversed more freely. It didn't take long for all the staff to appreciate the benefits and friendliness that Wit displayed, and soon, like in the past, "Everybody loves the Chopper Chaplain." He stayed out of the jungle for about a month to allow the bitterness he felt to sooth somewhat, because of the brutal slaughtering of his friends, and that could cause him to lose *focus*. Visiting and praying with the injured was helping him also to get his mind straight. He felt he was ready to return, and he had a score to settle. He went to the camp and Mike met him coming in. The Captain and Colonel joined them, and the Colonel asked what his plans were? "I was planning to do a little pay-back," Wit replied. The Captain spoke up, "Let me warn ya! The Rangers got some info from the locals that the NVA (North Vietnamese Army) have started filtering down across the DMZ. They are smart and organized, as the French learned the hard way, and they don't run around loose. If you should encounter them, they will most likely be a squad or patrol or even a platoon, and you can't pick them off one at a time. So now you will be faced with two enemies, the VC and the NVA. We haven't gotten the word they are this far south in our area, but we know there are heavy concentrations about 50 miles to the west, mostly moving along the Ho Chi Minh Trail getting ready to engage the US Army, which is arriving in a large scale. We still have a lot of VC to contend with for now, so if you still plan to go out, you better be extra cautious." "Thanks!" Wit replied. "I'll still go out, and if I run into anything like you say, I will get back and alert ya."

He went into areas where he was familiar, and killed any lone PM he encountered, but he saw no indication of the NVA. He went into one of his friendly hamlets along a river, that was small with enough people to tend their rice crops, and he was shocked to see the VC had been there and brutally slaughtered all the people, like the previous hamlet. He looked into each hootch for a sign of life and found none, but as he was about to leave, he heard a weak moan, and he looked to see where it came from. He found his friend, the wise Ancient, laying in the space between two huts, and he was still alive. He had a bad cut on his head, apparently from a blow by rifle butt, and his throat had been cut and it was bleeding, but it didn't appear to be cut deep enough to kill him. Wit made a quick decision to try and save him because he could prove to be valuable; from previous conversations he learned the Ancient could speak French and English. He found a piece of small rope and tied the man's wrists together, looped his arms around Wit's neck and hoisted him up on his back, like piggy-back. He returned to the camp and went straight to his chopper, explaining everything to Mike and others as he walked. He changed into his 'Clark Kent' outfit as quick as he could, and took off for Da Nang General, where he landed close to the Emergency Room door. Two people ran out with a gurney and helped put the old man on and wheeled him inside. The chopper blade was still spinning slowly, so Wit lifted over the living units and landed in an empty lot behind the units, and then hurried back to the hospital; Doctors already started working on the old man. Doc Ashby met him as he entered, and asked, "Are you the one that brought in the old man?" "Yes!" Wit answered. "I hope you can save him; he can be very valuable to me."

"I see you have a new Doctor that looks very familiar to me," Wit commented. "Doctor Betty West." "She hasn't been here very long, and I must say she is a very competent Doctor," Doc continued. "Where do you know Captain West from?" Wit explained, "When I returned from Korea, I didn't feel I was ready to go back into society, so I spent my last three months at Fort Rucker working for the Chaplain. He thought I could understand better the ones that were returning that had emotional issues, so I worked with a good number of them, and one of the worst cases was Doctor West. She was a Lieutenant then and had been in a hospital unit in Korea. One of the badly wounded Marines she doctored became like a pet project. They fell in love and started making plans, and each day the first thing she did was check on him to see if he was making progress. One day, when she went to check on him, his bed was empty, and she was informed that he took his own life during the night. That absolutely destroyed her. I worked and prayed with her as much as I could; she even went into the Chapel to pray every day on her own. I was afraid she might even try taking her own life to join with the Marine; it was that bad. Finally, she started responding and I found her to be a very good person with a good heart, and she became well suited to go back into civilian life; she left a week before I did. I must say I am surprised to see her back into this environment."

Wit went to speak with Doctor West, and she said, "When I saw you come in, my heart skipped a beat." She put her arms around him and kissed him on the cheek. "You look and smell awful," she commented. "Take my key and go to my unit, number 16, clean up a bit and come back about 6:00 o'clock, and I will buy you a double-decker-cheeseburger." "I knew a little nurse that lived in number 16," Wit said. "Did you make love to her there?" she questioned. "Oh, no," he replied, "I was curious to see the inside of one of the units and she showed it to me. She was a very nice and sweet young lady and I introduced her to our Chaplain's Orderly, and they fell in love and went home together." He went to the unit, stripped off his clothes, filled the bathtub with hot water and took a much-needed bath. When he finished, he didn't drain the tub, but proceeded to wash his clothes in the water using the hand soap. He wrung them out good and then rinsed them in the kitchen sink. He put on Betty's robe and carried his clothes out on the small back porch to dry. She had a clothes line on a pulley that ran to a tree in the back with a pulley, and with the clothes pins from a bag on a lawn chair, he pinned his clothes, and pulled them out to the center of the small yard. He muttered, "This is pretty neat, and with the hot sun and air blowing in this hundred-degree weather, it should all be dry in an hour." He went back in and using her safety razor, knocked off some whiskers. He then laid down on the bed to take a nap, with the fan oscillating, and soon dozed off.

CHAPTER 41

He napped about 2 hours and then checked his clothes. He had it figured right; they were dry and smelled a lot fresher than they did when he flew in. He walked to the hospital, and in a few minutes, she came out, and as they walked to the diner, he asked, "How is the old man doing? Is he going to make it?" "To early to tell," she replied. "He lost a lot of blood and we are giving him fluids; we should know more tomorrow." As they enjoyed their burgers and Coke, he asked, "What happened to you since we last saw each other? I figured you went home and found some handsome man and got married." She responded, "I went home and worked in a hospital for a couple years, but I wasn't satisfied. From all that I had gone through, something seemed to be lacking, so when this came up, I jumped at the chance to get back into the game. How about you?" "I went home a week after you left, went in debt for a car, got a job; met a girl I thought I loved, and we got married and made plans for the future. I had a real problem with my stomach; I would even gag at the smell of food. I was working second shift and my wife was a Nurse working in a Doctor's office during the day, and it became a problem finding time to be together. One night, at work, I was in so much pain, I went home early, and I caught some big dude humping her and I went into a rage and almost killed him. It scared me so bad that I realized I wasn't fit to be in a civilized world; that only the Army could understand me, so the next day I re-enlisted for 6 years, and told her we were done forever, and left. We were in debt up to our eyeballs, so I thought the only fair thing to do was give her my enlistment bonus and set her up with the Army spouse allotment, and with what she was making, she should be able to pay off everything, and live comfortably, unless one of her lovers should cheat her out of it; but that was up to her if she chose to live than kind of life. I haven't heard from her since; I'm still married, as far as I know; haven't seen any divorce papers to sign."

When they returned to her unit, she said without hesitation, "I want you to do me a favor." "Of course," he replied, "if I can." "Back at Fort Rucker I developed deep feelings for you, but I was afraid to say anything because you seemed so serious," she commented. "I want you to make love to me." "That wouldn't be a favor," he concluded, "that would be a pleasure." After they removed their clothes, he looked at her, all of her, and said, "I always thought you were beautiful, but you are absolutely breathtaking." They made love most of the night, well into the wee hours, and he asked, "Was that alright?" She answered, "That was wonderful!" He followed, "You better get some sleep, if you plan to report to work in the morning." "I start at 7 in the morning, and I finish at 6," she added. They slept until her alarm clock went off, and she got ready for work. They ate cereal for breakfast, and she ordered him, "You go back to bed and get more rest." He slept to just before noon, and then went out and sat on the front steps, all the while squeezing his little rubber ball, and to get some fresh air. Down the sidewalk came a sexy little number, wearing short shorts and a halter top, advertising her wares. "Are you waiting for someone?" she asked. "I'm waiting for Dr. West," he replied. "She doesn't get off work until 6, so why don't you go with me to my unit and I'll give you a cold drink and keep you company for a while," she offered. He followed her home, went in and was ejecting ice cubes from the ice tray, filled a glass with water and gulped it down. Then he hears, "Are you coming, or what?" He turned around and she was standing in her birthday suit, so he went into the bedroom with her and laid some pipe. When they finished, she said, "Get up and get out of here; I got to get ready and be at work by 5." He walked back to Betty's unit and thought, "That little gal has been around the block a time or two, and that wasn't her first rodeo." Then he remembered his old Company Commander, Captain Jack, saying when he addressed the troops, "If you have to stick your ying-yang in something, take a leak afterward as soon as you can to hopefully prevent a disease." He hastened his pace and went straight to the bathroom. He then laid down on the bed and went into a deep sleep.

He awoke when he heard Betty shuffling round changing her clothes. He sat on the edge of the bed, rubbing his eyes, trying to wake up. She said, with a nasty tone in her voice, "Heard you had a good time today. She couldn't wait to spread it all over the hospital when she came in to work." Now that snapped him awake, fore he knew he made a mistake, and now was on the bad side of Doctor Betty West." He never said anything, but got dressed, put his arms around her and kissed her on the cheek; she just stood with her arms down and didn't respond. He said, "I've got to get back to the war." She watched him walk out the door and down the sidewalk, and he then turned into the gap between the units, climbed into his chopper, and was gone. She watched him from her doorway till he disappeared, and muttered, "Be safe out there."

He flew to a Fire Base, and landed off to one side, where he changed out of his 'Clark Kent' outfit into his jungle attire. It was dwelling in his mind that he had hurt Betty, and she was the last person in the world he would ever want to hurt. He went into the jungle and saw movement and heard voices, so he hunkered down in the elephant grass, thinking he was concealed. He looked up and there was standing on each side, an NVA soldier, and they poked him in the ribs to get moving. He yelled out, "I hear you, Mike; I lost '*focus*'!" They moved about a couple hundred yards to a clearing, which he suddenly realized was a mini-POW camp with bamboo cages and an American captive in each one. They let the captives out and were lining them up, apparently going to move them to the north. The NVA said something to three young VC, and they faded into the jungle, leaving the VC to march the captives north. The VC guards looked like teenagers that were new and didn't realize they had captured a real prize, the Jungle Rat. One of the captives was Captain Carl Lindell, his old nemesis from Fort Rucker, and Wit quickly remarked, "Captain, what are you doing here? Are you nuts?" He answered, "Whitson, why are you dressed like that? Are you one of them?" There were nine captives, besides Wit, and he said to the Captain between his teeth, trying not to move his lips, "Pass the word to watch for my break, and overpower the guards." The Captain said, "Whitson, you are going to get us all killed." Wit was still angry that he had lost *focus*, and he said, "Captain, you are in my classroom now, so do what I say, or I'll kill you myself. Now pass the word!"

They were lined up in two columns and Wit was in the left column. The three VC teenagers were having a good time; laughing and poking the captives with their gun barrels; all excited. One of the captives was a young soldier, about eighteen or nineteen years old, and appeared to have symptoms of Malaria. He was weak and wobbling and sweating and then went down on one knee. The one VC raised his AK-47, about to smash the young soldier in the head, when Wit snatched it out of his hands and crushed the VC's head with repeated blows. The other captives overpowered the other two guards; one was laying and still moving, so Wit ran up and smashed his head till his brains burst out. He was still furious with himself for losing focus. He said to the captives, "Follow about 100 feet behind me; we must move fast; as soon as they discover we have escaped, they will be hot on our tails. Don't cough or sneeze or even breath hard. Watch me close; if I hunker down, you hunker down." They reached an LZ (landing zone) that was in the process of being set up. When they entered, Wit asked, "Who's in charge here?" One soldier pointed toward a sandbag bunker, and a spit and polish Lieutenant came out; his bars were shining and his boots spit-shined and his pants and shirt was creased. Wit thought of the first bone head officer he had in basic training, totally in love with himself. Wit said, "I just rescued these men from captivity. Get on the radio and call for a couple Medevacs to come pick them up." "Now see here," he responded, "I'm in charge." Wit was still seething, and he demanded, "You call for Medevacs right now or I'll put this rifle in your mouth and blow your brains out." His radio man was standing beside them and, with a smile, handed the Lieutenant the receiver, and he called without hesitation. Then Wit said, "The snipers love to shoot officers and you are a perfect target with all your shiny stuff pinned on. I suggest you get out of that garb while you still can." The Commies had caught up with them and were entering the perimeter, and the shooting began. The two Medevacs arrived coming in at tree top level and one landed and they rushed to load the captives; Wit ordered them to take the sick boy first. While they were loading the first one, the door gunner of the second one was spraying bullets into the Commies, and then the first one lifted off. They loaded the second one with the remaining captives and Captain Lindell and body bags, and it started to take off when an RPG was fired into the open door and another one fired into the cockpit, which caused the 'copter to explode and burn and fall to the ground in a pile of rubble. No way anyone could have lived through that. Wit turned around and the spit and polish Lieutenant was laying on the ground with a bullet hole in his head and chest and blood running down his sparkling uniform.

A Master Sergeant came up and said, "I tried to tell the dumb bastard, but he wouldn't listen." Wit responded, "Don't worry about it! Are you in charge now?" Yes," he said. Then Wit ordered, "You better set up for another attack. The 'copter gunner slowed them down, and as soon as they cart off their dead, they will be back, maybe not tonight, but in the morning for sure. Set your men in pairs around the perimeter, so one can rest while the other stands guard. Make sure they have extra loaded magazines and a pile of grenades at each station. Make sure your mortar pits are well stocked. You better call in and let them know what happened and ask for help; you are going to need it. These guys you are fighting are trained NVA and they will come in with fixed bayonets, with one thing in mind, kill the Americans. I'll stay until help arrives, but for now, I'm going to use that bunker and try and get some sleep." It remained quiet through the night and in the morning, a dense fog had rolled in, which was a guarantee they would attack under the cover of the fog. It was also going to hinder the 'copters coming in with fresh troops. The Sergeant alerted all his men to be ready at any time, and it didn't take long for the shooting to start. Machine guns started chattering and mortars shells were sent flying hoping to catch some from their rear. Incoming mortars were causing some casualties, and after a machine gunner was hit, Wit manned the gun. The fight continued for about an hour and the sun started to come up which caused the fog to dissipate. That allowed the gunships (firing helicopters) to come in with guns blazing, strafing the Commies. That turned the tide of battle; the NVA ceased firing and retreated into the jungle. Fresh troops arrived in slicks (troop carrying helicopters), and flew in and the first one hovered about two feet off the ground and the first man off the first slick was a grizzly looking soldier; dirty and torn camo fatigues; unshaven; scuffed up boots; cigar, partially chewed in half hanging out of his mouth; shouted as his men dismounted, "Spread out men!" Wit was amused by the sight of him, and remarked, "Sergeant, there is a real soldier!"

The old soldier approached Wit and the Sergeant, and the Sergeant started to salute, and the old soldier said sharply, "Don't you dare salute me; you know better than that. I'm Major Shelton; is there an officer in charge here?" The Sergeant responded, "We had a Lieutenant and he is laying over with the casualties to be Medevac'd out." Major Shelton looked at the body and remarked, "My God, he looks like he was dressed to march in a parade; his family will think he died a hero. Wit, what are you doing here? Don't you have anything else to do?" "Well I did for a while; I rescued nine captives from a mini-POW camp, and we escaped to here, and got involved in a shootout with the Commies," he responded. The Major then ordered, "Ok Sergeant, fill me in what's going on here." Wit then said, "I'm gonna leave this war in you gentlemen's hands." And he started walking away. The Major asked, humorously, "Where are you going? The fun is about to begin." "I've had my fun for the day," Wit answered. The old Major said, "Sergeant, there is a real solder!" The Sergeant responded, "He said the exact same thing about you." That brought a smile on the old soldier's face.

CHAPTER 42

Wit went back to the Fire Support Base (FSB) where he had left his chopper and changed into his 'Clark Kent' outfit, and returned to the Chapel. He asked Major Jim, "Anything new happening?" "The only thing I know is they are bringing in a lot of wounded and dead," he replied. "I'll clean up and eat and rest up a bit, and then I'll go to the hospital and pray for them," Wit responded. The Chaplain suggested, "You better get yourself back together. You are looking mighty poorly again." He looked in a mirror and agreed, "The Chaplain is right; I look like I'm getting old." For the next three days, all he did was eat and sleep and play with little Mickey. He then went to the hospital and found it to be a very busy place. Medevacs were shuttling in at a regular pace, and the casualties were unloaded. The KIAs in body bags were placed in trucks to go to the Mortuary; those injured, that had a chance, were taken directly into the hospital; a great number of 'almost dead' were placed under a huge tent to protect them from the hot sun and rain. Wit concentrated his efforts praying for the 'almost dead'. They were coming in so fast and dying so quickly, that he had to cut his prayers short, in order to administer to as many as he could. He knelt between two at a time, one on his left and one on his right; most were a gory sight to look at and he ended up with blood all over him, but he never faltered. He prayed with tears and sweat running down his face, putting in all the emotion he had, asking the Lord to be merciful, and take their souls into Heaven. He remained out there for hours on end, non-stop, but refused to give up, and was on the point of collapse. Someone told Doc Ashby and he went out and ordered Wit, "Stop and go home; you can only do so much; you are killing yourself. That's an order!" He staggered to his Jeep, sat behind the wheel, and prayed that the Lord bless those he couldn't, and then drove back to the Chapel. Doc Ashby called the Chaplain and told him what was happening, so the Chaplain was waiting for him when he arrived; helped him to his room where he collapsed on his bunk. He slept about 24 hours before he awakened, got up, and looked into the mirror again, and remarked, "I think I am 10 years older than I was the last time I looked."

The Chaplain called him in and gave him a good talking too, "You are too close to death, and getting away from reality. You are always preaching common sense, but you aren't practicing what you preach. It's gonna be a long war, but the rate you are going, you are not going to be around to see the end of it. Find something beneficial to spend your time on and get yourself back on solid ground. When was the last time you checked on the old man you brought in? You might start there." He thought about what the Chaplain had said and agreed with every word of it; he lazed around for about a week, getting his thinking straight and resting his body. He felt much more relaxed and collected, so he went to check on his friend, the Ancient (old man). He approached Doc Ashby and asked, "How's the old man doing?" "He's coming along nicely," Doc responded, "they take him outside in a wheelchair to get some fresh air and sunshine, so that's where he probably is right now. He speaks with a whiny voice, and I imagine it's because of when his throat was cut, something was damaged." Wit went out and sat with him and they talked for a while; he did have a whiny voice, so Wit named him Whiny. "They think that you are getting well enough, so I think in a few weeks, I'll be able to take you home," Wit offered. Whiny said, "I like it here; they feed me good and I sleep a lot. I don't have a home to go to." Wit responded, "You can't stay here forever; I'll take you to live at the Chapel until you are strong enough, and then I want you to go with me and teach me about the jungle." They were served lunch and got better acquainted before Wit went back in to talk with Doc Ashby. While they talked, he observed a lady Doctor getting all over the rest of the staff, cussing and acting disrespectful, like she was overworked and stressed out. "What's with the Major?" Wit asked. "She looks like she is about to crash; worse case maybe working on a stroke." "She is Doctor Susan McElroy, an excellent Doctor," the Doc answered. "She thinks she is invincible; she doesn't stop to eat or sleep." "If she has a breakdown, she is not going to do anybody any good," Wit offered. "She could be laid up for weeks and maybe never come out of it." "Do you have any suggestions?" Doc asked. "I have worked with a lot of returning vets that were confused and mixed up, and I managed to straighten them out, like Dr. West. Let me have her for three or four days and see if I can make any progress with her." "She's too valuable to lose," Doc remarked. "I want to take her home to her unit, but you may need to give her a direct order." Wit added. Doc agreed and Wit went up behind her and put his hand on her shoulder to introduce himself. She snapped, "Get your f***** hand off of me." He said, "I am Loren Whitson with the Chaplain's Service, and I want to take you home." "Are you some kind of Holy Joe, or something?" she continued. "Yeah, something like that," he responded. He took her by the arm and said, "Let's go; Colonel's orders." She was too exhausted to fight him, so he put his arm around her waist and helped her walk to her unit.

He said, "I am filling the tub with hot water and I want you to soak to open the pores so I can massage you with lotion; your skin is like parchment paper. Strip off your clothes and get in the tub." "I will not!" she said angrily. "I outrank you and I can order you to get out." "Yes you can, and I will leave," he said sternly, "and when I come back in a couple weeks, I'll go to the Mortuary and watch them load a box with a flag draped over it, with a tag that says, 'Major Susan McElroy, Doctor in the Medical Corp'. I will be saddened because I think I could have helped you. You are a good Doctor and you know what happens when a person is divergent from reality and crashes with mental exhaustion. Now get undressed and get into the tub while the water is hot." She sat on the edge of the bed and started to shake and cry. He had been stern with her but now he was becoming sympathetic, so he put a hand on each side of her face, lifted it up, and kissed her on the forehead. "Come on, now, I'll help you get undressed," he offered. "Not while you are here," she remarked. "You don't have a thing different that I haven't seen a hundred times before, so let's not waste the hot water, and get started," he insisted. She was too distraught and weak to argue anymore, so they removed her clothes. She got in the tub and said, "Boy this feels good;

I could go to sleep." "No, you won't," he said, "you can sleep when I massage you." He brought a chair from the kitchen and sat down beside the tub, and she remarked, "You going to sit and watch me?" "Yes, I am," he answered. "I'm not going to take my eyes off of you." She washed with a sponge while she soaked, and he stared at her. "You keep looking at my tits; is there something wrong with them?" she questioned. "No, no, they are fine," he explained. "I was just thinking about Dr. West." "What?" You look at my tits and think about another woman? What kind of a pervert are you?" She questioned. Then he explained about treating Dr. West some years ago, telling about the same event he told Doc Ashby. That seemed to satisfy her. He told her to hand him the sponge so he could wash the back of her neck and shoulders to open the pores.

"I put towels on your bed so we wouldn't get lotion on your sheets. Get out of the tub and I'll help dry you off, and we can go to the bedroom, and I'll start massaging and you will feel a lot better," he explained. She lay on her stomach and he massaged in the lotion, starting at the back of her neck and shoulders, and then down her back, and by the time he reached her lower back, she was sound asleep. He finished massaging and then let the fan blow the lotion dry, and then covered her with a sheet, and she slept till the middle of the next morning. He went into the kitchen to see if she had anything to fix to eat. She had some moldy bread and sour milk and the frig was empty. He checked to see if she was still asleep, and she was, so he hurried to the Commissary and bought up some food to cook for breakfast and dinner the next day. When she awoke and walked into the kitchen, he was frying sausage and eggs and making toast, and she asked, "Well, did you molest me while I slept?" "Of course not," he replied. "I wouldn't enjoy anything like that unless you were awake. I prayed for you and then ran to the Commissary. Go do what you need to do in the bathroom and your breakfast will soon be ready." "You prayed for me? I can't wait for a good cup of coffee," she remarked. "You are not drinking caffeine to keep you awake; you are drinking Sanka, decaffeinated," he made clear. "It will taste awful at first, but you will get used to it." "I think I can go back to work," she said. "No way," he replied. "I got you for several more days to get your body and mind back to normal. I didn't finish massaging last night, so today I'll massage your front, and then you can sleep some more."

He started massaging her front, and she commented, "I never thought I would ever let a man do what you're doing." "Were you ever married?" Wit asked. "I was married for three years," she answered. "He was a Doctor and we met in medical school and started dating and decided to get married." "Let me guess," Wit said, "you were both married for convenience, and not love. You were both married to your professions." "That's exactly right," she concurred, "but how would you know that?" "I just know," he answered. He started massaging her neck and then her shoulders, and then her chest and worked down from there. She said, "You are making me hot!" "Well, you can just get unhot. Get your mind on other things. Let me finish my story about Dr. West and that will give you something to think about. I was surprised to see her at the hospital, and she said I looked awful and smelled awful. That was because I just came in from the jungle and brought the old man in. She suggested I go to her unit and clean up and come back when she got off work and she would buy me a big double-decker-cheeseburger. I did that and then we went back to her unit, where she asked me to make love to her, and we did most of the night. The next day she ordered me to stay in her unit and rest up. Well, I did for a while and then sat on the front steps when a sexy little Nurse came by and offered me a glass of ice water and keep me company. I found out what she meant by keeping me company. She went to the hospital and blabbed all over the hospital what we did, which really upset Dr. West," he explained. "I remember that," Dr. Susan said. He continued, "Betty didn't want any more to do with me, and it really bothered me that I hurt her, because she is the last person in the world that I would want to hurt, so I left and went back to the jungle, but I couldn't get it out of my mind, and I did the number one worst thing, I lost '*focus*'. If you lose *focus* in the jungle, you are dead. And because of it I was captured by the NVA. I am enemy number-1 and there is a big reward out for me, but they must have been new in the area, and didn't realize the prize they had caught. There were nine other captives, and I told them to follow my lead and I would get them out of this. Without going into much detail, we killed all our guards and escaped. I will never lose *focus* again, for no reason." "You say you are enemy number-1?" she asked. "Why don't they just come and get you?" "Because they don't know me as 'The Jungle Rat', and they haven't connected the dots," he explained, "and you must never let on if you ever hear that term. You must just ignore it like it means nothing, unless you want me dead." By the time he reached her lower legs and feet, she had fallen asleep. He allowed the lotion to dry; covered her with a sheet; lay down beside her and caught up on some much-needed sleep himself.

CHAPTER 43

She was still sleeping when he arose, so he let her sleep as long as she could. He started preparing breakfast and she came in and said, "That smells good! Can I have coffee with that?" "Only Sanka!" he replied. "Go to the bathroom and do what you have to do, and it should be ready by then." They sat down to eat, and he remarked, "You are really looking better, more relaxed and clearer." "I am feeling a lot better. I feel like I could go back to work," she stated. "Not yet!" he remarked. "We are going to spend the day massaging and napping, and tonight, after supper, I want to try something I had a vision about. We are getting your body back in shape, but now I want to clean up your mind. As a Doctor, you know the mind controls the body, so if this works, you can write it up in a Medical Journal and become world famous. I had a vision during the night, and if you thought I was crazy up to now, you are really gonna think I'm nuts." After supper, he suggested they use mouth wash to freshen their breath because they were going to get really close in each other's face. He then closed all blinds to shed out any light, and he turned the fan on to the lowest speed. He wanted everything totally quiet and dark. They lay down together and he instructed her, "Press your body as close against mine as you can so I can feel your heart beat. Put your face up to mine and give me a soft tender kiss to help get you in the mood. Now kiss me again with more feeling. You do not say anything, no matter what; you try to clear your mind of all thoughts and only think of what I am saying to you. I am going to speak very softly, and I want you to concentrate totally on what I am saying to you; again, do not speak or react, except when I tell you to." The mood was set, and the only sound was the fan purring. He continued, "Imagine you and I are on a very small island, all alone. We are laying on a blanket over the warm sand, and the warmth is coming up through the blanket. There is a very gentle and cool breeze blowing, and there is a soft sweet sound of music that seems to be riding in the breeze; it has a soothing sound to it and your mind is drifting with it. You can feel your neck and shoulders are feeling limp and relaxing; the breeze and the music are causing you to think of nothing else. Now your arms and upper body are feeling limp, and just let them relax. Now your lower body and back are feeling limp, so just let them relax. The breeze and music are so soothing, your mind is thinking of nothing else. Now your hips and legs are feeling limp and relaxing. Your mind is quiet, and your body is limp, and now all you can think of is sleep. So, sleep and dream of our little island and how wonderful it is to not think of any worldly things that would disrupt the serenity of our little island. Sleep! Sleep!" And she did; she was sleeping more quietly and peaceful than any time since they started several days ago. He eased away from her, hoping not to disturb her, covered her with a sheet, and then laid down beside her to catch a little sleep himself.

He slept later than usual, and she hadn't moved all night; still totally limp. At one point, he lifted her arm slightly and let if fall back down, and it was still limp. He went to the bathroom and then went to the kitchen to start cooking breakfast. She emerged from the bedroom and went straight to the bathroom, and then came out wearing a robe, and said, "I have never slept so soundly in my whole life; I must have died. I don't know what you have planned for today, but I got some bad news for ya; I have started my period." He replied, "Well, you can't stop Mother Nature. Breakfast will be ready shortly, so set the table." "I think I could probably go to work," she stated. "Not yet," he responded. "I was planning on spending the day massaging and napping; I'll even let you massage me," he suggested, grinning. He massaged her upper body and legs and feet and then he laid on his stomach for her to massage him; it was feeling mighty good, and then she said, "Turn over!" He turned over and the Torpedo was standing straight up like a flagpole. "What's this?" she remarked. He answered, "That's WT, Wit's Torpedo!" She replied, "You named it?" She started laughing and laughed so hard she got tears in her eyes, and said, "That's hilarious; you named it!" She finally got control of herself and said, "I'm sorry, Wit, you probably had other plans for today and I messed them up." He replied, "I'll take an IOU! You go check your calendar and tell me what days you are not fertile, and I'll come back and collect."

They napped most of the day, and while they were eating supper he said, "You are 100% better than you were when I brought you home. You have not spoken in a nasty tone or said one cussword, and that is the way you must conduct yourself when you go back to work. Those other Doctors and Nurses are in as much stress as you are, and your brow-beating them only makes their stress worse. Not only that, they must despise you for it because this is not a game we are playing, and they are performing the best they can to save lives, and they need your support, not your criticism. The Bible says, 'do unto others as you would have them do unto you', so you would not like someone downgrading you." "You must think I'm a terrible person," she responded sadly. "Not at all," he continued. "Doc said you were too valuable to lose, and I agree with that, and I think together we have saved you from self-destruction, and you have a big heart or you wouldn't be in the business you are in. When you go back to work, do your job professionally, and work with the others as a team, being the sweetheart, I know that you are. You are the senior member, so part of your job is to instruct and assist those of lesser rank, and you will be commended for the increase in efficiency; it will be noticeable and the atmosphere will make working conditions more pleasant, if there is anything pleasant about it. If you feel like you are falling back again, think of our little island or talk to Dr. West; she's been on the brink and understands. By no means, let it fester. If you need me, contact the Chapel. Do you want another day because of your condition? You might want to lay around and feel more like going to work the next day; the long hours can be taxing; whatever you feel like doing. This has helped me take a break, so now I think I will go back to the jungle and kill Commies, after I check on my old friend." "You never did say where you found him," she remarked. "His village had been very friendly to me, and the VC came and slaughtered them all, because they were sympathetic to Americans. The old man wasn't dead, so I decided to try and save him; he can teach me a lot about the jungle I don't know. He speaks French and English," he explained.

Wit returned to the Chapel and the Chaplain addressed him, "Haven't seen you for a few days; what have you been up to?" He explained, "There's a Major Susan McElroy, a Doctor at Da Nang General that was overworked and stressed out and on the point of collapsing; she was out of control. Doc Ashby knew that I worked with returning troops from Korea that suffered with combat-fatigue and he asked me if I thought I could be of help. He said she was an excellent Doctor and too valuable to lose. She was on the brink of total collapse, and I knew if she crashed, she might be admitted to a psychiatric unit. I agreed to try, so he ordered her to allow me to work with her, and that didn't set too well with her. She fought me and cussed me and threatened to pull rank and ordered me out. I worked with a lot of military returnees the last three months at Ft. Rucker and each one had his/her own hang-up, so what I did was try to get into their mind and find what their problem was, and that was what I concentrated on. I had a pretty high successful rate, and all I worked with was able to return to civilian life. This Doctor was a different case; she hadn't slept in days and tried to live on a diet of a donut and coffee that she got at the hospital in the mornings. I had to get stern with her and convince her she was borderline for total collapse, or maybe even a stroke. What she really needed was rest, sleep, and food. I was able to get her calmed down and finally go to sleep. While she slept, I went to the kitchen to check the food supply so I could cook her a decent meal. All she had was stale bread and sour milk, so I went to the Commissary and bought food. For days there was a lot of prayer, sleep, and good meals. I never had a case like her before, so I had to pull out my bag of tricks, and I finally found something that worked, and she began to respond. She will likely go back to work tomorrow, a new woman." Major Jim remarked, "Wow, that is a great story. What do you plan to do next?" "I didn't get a lot of rest because I dared not to leave her alone, so I think I am going take it easy for a few days, and then go to Mike's camp, after I pick up the mail. That poor Mail Clerk is petrified at the thought of going out there. Mike picks it up when he comes in, and I usually take it with me when I go. The load is increasing because the Advisors have increased to about 25,000 in country; although they are spread out and Mike's camp got a lot of them because the ARVN Rangers have increased to 300,000, but again they are all spread out throughout South Vietnam.

He lazed around for a few days, eating, napping, and playing with Little Mickey. He went to the hospital to check on his old friend. Doc Ashby approached him, and remarked, "I don't know what you did, but Doctor McElroy is a totally new person; she has a new attitude and her work ethics have impressed everybody; she is a kinder and more personable, and the atmosphere has improved tremendously." "Well, thanks, Doc," Wit responded, humbly, "I'm glad it all worked out. I came to check on the Ancient, Whiny, and see how he is progressing." "He is doing really well," Doc commented, "being as old as he is; it takes longer to heal than a young person. He went through a bad ordeal, but I think in a few more weeks, he should be dismissed." He saw Dr. West and she completely ignored him; she was still hurt, apparently.

He picked up the mail and went out to the Green Beret camp, and told Mike, "I brought the mail; there's been an increase in bags since you have grown. Send a couple of your men out to my chopper, bring the bags in, and they can have 'mail call'. He did some target practice to retain his shooting skill and talked with Mike. Mike informed him about the increase in hostilities, which has resulted in an increase in casualties. "That crazy President Johnson is planning to send a half a million troops in here and has increased the bombing raids. The Cobra gunships have saved us more than once. You thought it was a playground before, but it has become an extremely dangerous place. The NVA is getting more involved since they started infiltrating further south." "I know about the NVA," Wit responded. "They captured me along with 9 other captives and were planning to move us to the north. They made a major mistake, and the Jungle Rat took care of that situation, and we escaped. I lost *focus*, but that will never happen again." "I would have loved to have seen that," Mike remarked. "That would have been something to tell my grandkids about." "All I can say," Wit continued, "there are three PMs with their heads smashed in. I met a grizzly old soldier named, Major Shelton; do you know him?" "I've met him and know who he is, but I've never worked with him," Mike answered. "I've heard he is a soldier's soldier." "That he is," Wit added, "and then some."

CHAPTER 44

Wit gathered up the mailbags, emptying what was coming in and taking back what was going out, and flew back to the Chapel where Chaplain Jim called him in, "I received a message from the Red Cross, and they said it was important that you come in to their office right away. They didn't give a reason why." "As soon as I drop off the mailbags, I'll see what they want," he responded. "I'm not giving them any of my blood." He went to the Red Cross office, having no idea what they wanted, but it didn't take long, and they said, "We received a message from your wife that her brother, Pfc. Lonnie Combs, has been listed as MIA, and she hopes you can possibly find him." "What unit is he in, did she say?" he asked. "He's in 1st Battalion, 3rd Marines and that is all we know." He went to the Marine Compound to get more details. He spoke with a young smart-mouth Lieutenant, "I am Warrant Officer Loren Whitson, with the Chaplain's Service, and I was informed by the Red Cross that you have posted a Pfc. Lonnie Combs is MIA. I want you to tell me where he was the last time you were in contact with him." "Well, now, what makes you think an Army Preacher can do what the United States Marine Corp can't do?" the Lieutenant bragged. Wit was in a hurry and had no time to listen to some shave-tail officer, so he stated sharply, "Show me on the map where he was; time is of the essence." "You can't go out there all alone; we'll send a squad of Marines with ya to protect ya," the smart-mouth spouted off. "If you don't want to help me, maybe my friend Colonel Willoughby will tell me what I need to know. He is a tough no-nonsense Marine that doesn't tolerate inefficiency," Wit offered. That got the attention of the lackadaisical officer in a hurry. "What exactly do you need to know?" he asked, now being more serious. There was a Captain sitting across the room and listening to the conversation and seemed to be amused by Wit's lack of patience, and commented, "I'm surprised that information was circulated that fast; we just posted it a few days ago. There are four men missing, Pfc Lonnie Combs, PFC Eugene Colvin, PFC Donald Helton, and PFC Duane Donohoo. They were ambushed on patrol and we found all the bodies of the ones killed, but we never found these four, so we assumed they were taken captive. We sent out search parties, but they never found any sign of them. Lieutenant, show him on the map the exact location of the ambush." "I will be flying my chopper out there, so is there an LZ or FSB close by where I can land?" Wit asked. "One last question; were the bodies of the dead mutilated?" "No, they were not, just shot up," the Captain responded. "Why?" "If they were mutilated, then the VC got them and they are probably dead already," Wit replied. "If they were not, then the NVA captured them and are planning to take them north, so there is a good chance I can find them. They may be in a mini-POW camp, but the jungle is most likely congested with

Gooks, so if we can get free, we may need support, because they are going to be madder than a hive of hornets." "To answer your question there is LZ-Amelia about five Klicks from the ambush site, and FSB-Clermont is about 12 Klicks back. If you can make it to the LZ, there will be a Platoon, or more, set up for action. If any are wounded, the Medevac will be nearby. Good Luck!" the Captain explained. "What makes him think he can find them when the Marines can't?" the Lieutenant smirked. "He will be able to find them if anybody can," the Captain responded. "He's the Jungle Rat!"

He flew to the LZ and landed on the back side, staying clear of any action that might damage his chopper. A Sergeant approached him, and introduced himself as the Platoon Sergeant, and Wit introduced himself and explained his purpose for being there, to try and find and rescue the missing Marines. "I want you to tell me anything that will help," Wit asked. "The pumped-up Lieutenant at the Marine Compound wasn't willing, or didn't know enough about it to be much help. This is LZ-Amelia, isn't it?" "I don't know where they get those people to make officers; and yes, this is Amelia" the Sergeant answered. "We sent out search parties in the direction of the ambush, and we even flew over the entire area, trying to find some trace of them. The patrol went out toward the west, and the ambush was about five Klicks out; that's where we found the bodies of the killed. When we flew over, I found the terrain became more rolling and small hills with some open areas, so you would want to stay around the edges of the open areas; you don't want to get caught out there during the daylight hours. I'm guessing they are smart enough to have stayed in the wooded areas so they couldn't be spotted from the air; also, they appeared to be traveling westward, by chance to hook up with other Gooks, and transport the men up the Ho Chi Minh Trail to Hanoi. We couldn't cross over into Laos; that is forbidden. It's been four days, so, it is hard to say how far they would be; they may have encamped in a wooded area, and not gone far at all; that's what I'm hoping. Do you want me to send some men with ya?" "No, thanks," Wit responded. "I do better alone. You might have your men keep watch for when we get back; they may be madder than hornets when they find out your men escaped, and we are going to be running for our lives."

He went to his chopper and changed into his jungle attire, checked to be sure his canteen was full, checked his side-arm, put his knife in its scabbard on his leg, walked back to the Sergeant, and asked, "Is that the place the Platoon entered the brush?" "Yes," the Sergeant answered, and then asked, "are those the only weapons you are taking?" "I don't want anything to slow me down, or add to the noise," Wit replied, and disappeared into the brush. He eventually left the wet areas, and reaching higher ground, he was able to move faster, puffing a little, climbing the upward grades. He periodically checked his compass and identified landmarks to remember on his way back. He moved along the wooded edges to remain concealed, and that was where he found the ambush site. He looked for signs and tracks to find the direction in which they traveled; most of the tracks went in various directions, but he did find the trail that a larger group used, so that was the one he followed. The Sergeant may have guessed right; going to hook up at the Ho Chi Minh Trail. He went for about three or four hours and stopped to rest at the summit of a small hill. He took a swig of water and started to survey the area around where he was, and he saw movement in a wooded area about two Klicks away. He made a quick decision to explore the location, and hopefully that was the one he was looking for, but he would only go so far, and then move in closer with the cover of darkness. A light rain began to fall, and that was good; it would make his movements quieter through the heavy brush and grass that concealed the location. He lay quietly in the grass and waited and rested.

Light began to fade, and he was able to move in closer. It must have been mealtime when he began to smell food cooking. He didn't recognize what they were cooking but would like to have a bite or two since he hadn't eaten since early morning. It was a small open area with cages around the edges, which he concluded was a mini-POW camp, like the one he was in when he was captured. It looked like only three of the cages were occupied; the rest being empty. The Gooks took small trays of food to the prisoners, and the one seemed to get pleasure in tantalizing one of the captives by kicking the cage. The one inside the cage yelled out, "I'll get you, you son-of-a-bitch!" The Gook laughed a high-pitched squeal of a laugh. Wit counted six Gooks and began to plan how he was going to take care of that many. He was surprised to see what they did after they ate; light up cigarettes that smelled like marijuana, and then break out a flask. After a bit they were getting high and drunk, laughing and grab-assing, which caused Wit to think this was going to be easy. They were squatting around a fire in the middle of the clearing, and all at one time, lay down and went to sleep near the fire. He snuck in and unlatched the cage doors, telling each captive he was an Army Chaplain, and not to make a move until he gave the word. Just then another Gook came in, paying no attention to his sleeping buddies, proceeded to dish up something to eat; he then squatted down near the fire. Wit, making sure there were not more of them coming in, snuck up behind the Gook, pulled his head back by the hair, and the Gook saw the *Demon of Death*, and he ripped out his throat. "Ok, men," he instructed, "keep quiet and get your rifles," which they did, without hesitation. The one Marine, the Gook was hassling, went over and smashed his head in, and said, "I told you I was gonna get you, you Gook Bastard." "Kill 'em all!" Wit ordered, and they got their revenge. "They said there were four of ya," Wit commented. "Yeah, Duane Donohoo," one replied, "tried to escape, and they shot him." Which way did he run?" Wit asked. "We need to try and find him to take his body back." They directed Wit and found him in tall grass, but he was still alive. He was shot in the leg from behind, and then crawled into the grass. Wit did a quick assessment of his injury, and said, "Looks like the bullet shattered the bone, but I think he will be alright if we get him back for treatment. He's got the million-dollar wound. Two of ya help him, and let's get going; as soon as they discover you have escaped, they are gonna be hot after us. Stay with me in a single file, and move fast, I can avoid any of their booby-traps." They didn't waste any time, and it went fast, going downhill most of the way. The Gooks discovered they had escaped and started chasing after them and shooting at the same time. Bullets were whizzing all round them, and soon they reached the LZ, where the Marines were set up and ready, and when the Gooks got in range, the lead started flying back at them. Wit told the Sergeant to call for the Medevac, and it appeared instantly, because they were sitting close and nearby, as requested.

 The Medevac started receiving fire, and the door gunner was giving all he had, so Wit picked up an M-14, put the selector on semi-automatic, and started shooting from the hip, picking off a Gook with every shot. He yelled for another magazine and reloaded and kept firing. Then two Cobra gunships approached at tree-top level and gave the Gooks a dose of American lead-poisoning. The Gooks backed off and the firing ceased. While they loaded Donohoo, Wit asked, "Which one is Combs?" One answered, "I am!" Then Wit said, "You were only a kid the last time I saw ya. Call your sister and tell her you are alright; she's worried about ya." The rest jumped in and one said, "I don't know who that guy is, but he sure saved our asses." Another said, "Did you see him shoot that rifle from the hip, standing out there with bullets whizzing around him?" Combs said, proudly "He's my Brother-In-Law!" They all said, "No shit!" The gunner said, "You boys have just met the Jungle Rat!" As the 'copter lifted off, you could hear, "Ooh Rah!" After the fact, Wit handed the M-14 to the Sergeant, and said, "That's a good rifle; it shoots straight and true; I'll let you clean it. I'll leave the war to you men; it's my suppertime, so we may meet again." He walked back to his chopper, changed into his 'Clark Kent' outfit, and lifted off for the Chapel. They all just watched him; well pleased and appreciative of what he had done and saved some of their own.

About a week and a half later, Wit remembered Dr. Susie's IOU, and went to collect. He met Doc Ashby and asked how everything was going and he asked about the old man. Doc said, "He's coming along just fine; in fact, I think you can take him home to convalesce in another week or so." Dr. Susie walked up and said, "Hey, Wit, have you rescued any captives lately?" Doc Ashby looked at them quizzically, and just waited for the answer. "Yeah, as a matter of fact, I did," Wit responded. "Four Marines! One of them was my Brother-In-Law. He was just a kid the last time I saw him, and now he is a Marine." Then she said, "I planned to cook supper for tonight; want to come?" "Can you cook?" he asked, surprised. "What are we having?" "We are having spaghetti and meatballs with garlic toast," she replied. "I'm making my dear old Grandmother's recipe." "Grandmothers I know cook meat and potatoes," Wit said, jokingly. "Did you make the meatballs?" "No," she said, "I bought frozen ones." "Did you make the sauce?" he continued to ask. "Not exactly," she replied, "I bought it in a can; but I'm cooking it." "Sounds good to me," Wit said. "How about you Doc, does that sound good to you?" "Yeah, it does," he responded. "I haven't had that in a long time." "Why don't you join us tonight?" Wit asked. "Then I want you to leave afterwards; I got a couple more days of therapy planned that I thought of, if you can spare her." "Not a problem!" Doc replied.

Doc Ashby came and they all enjoyed the spaghetti and meatballs with garlic toast, and then he left. Susie said, "I could have killed you when you asked him to come and eat. I've been dying for weeks till the day would come when I could get the WT. We can clean up the kitchen later; I can't wait any longer." "You ever had an all-nighter?" he asked. "Are you kidding? All I ever got was a quick in and quick out," she answered, and began stripping off. "I'm collecting on the IOU and the therapy is going to take a couple nights and a couple days, and that should have you walking on air," he promised. The next morning, they got up and bathed and cooked breakfast, and while they were eating, he asked, "How is Betty doing? I want you to watch her close, so she doesn't fall back into the rut she was in a few years back. When I first started working with her, I suspected she would want to join that Marine that took his own life; she was that bad." "You don't have to worry about her," Susie responded. "We talk a lot and have become best of friends; we talk mostly about you. I told her about you getting captured and she feels awfully bad about that. When I start feeling stressed, I talk with her, and sometimes I think of our little island. I'm good now and I know how to stop it. I am so grateful, and I will love you forever for saving me."

CHAPTER 45

Wit flew out to see Mike, and Mike informed him that he had to go back home. He said that when you get five years in country, you are required to rotate out. He asked Wit how long he had been in country and he said he had about six more months yet, and he had no idea where he would go after that. Then Mike said, "We received a new rifle, an M-16, and we are going to test it because they are forcing it on us, and we don't know how good it is. The Air Force uses the AR-15, and it is supposed to be modified from that for jungle warfare. It is a lot lighter and fires a 5.56 mm NATO round with a 20 or 30 round magazine. Instructions are they never need cleaning and so they don't supply cleaning kits with them. It fires 800 rounds per minute at a range of 550 meters. We received crates of them, so we are giving them to the ARVN Rangers to test, and while you are here, you might as well see what they can do. Let me introduce you to a GB who knows them inside and out, but I want to warn you, he is mean, angry, and has a nasty disposition. I had to call him down from time to time because he starts trouble with the other men. Wit, this is Randy Ross."

Randy was big and black, and when Wit stuck out his hand to shake, Randy ignored it. Mike insisted, "Randy, take Wit over to the sight bench and instruct him all about the M-16." As they walked to the bench, Wit asked the most common question in the military, "Where you from, Randy?" "Why? You ain't never goin' there," Randy remarked, speaking nastily. "You are right," Wit replied, in his normal easy-going style. "I will never return to the States until I can be of no further use to the Army." That seemed to soothe Randy somewhat, and he explained, "I am from the black section of the town, south of the railroad tracks, and the further down the street you go, the meaner the people get, and I lived in the last house." "Now, let me guess," Wit continued, "I bet that street had a little white church and your Mama went to church every Sunday, and every night she prayed and cried because of her love for you, and you still never went." "That's right!" Randy remarked. "How did you know that?" "The Lord told me," Wit answered, "and I believe your Mama is the sweetest and kindest person in that whole town, and is loved by everybody that knows her, and you can't understand that, and that boggles your mind. She probably got down on her hands and knees and scrubbed floors just to make a little money to buy food so you and the family could have a decent meal." Randy looked at him, slightly confused this man, that knew nothing about his family, hit the nail on the head. Wit continued, "I can only imagine what it would be like to be a black man in a white man's world, but I can say, being angry about it, doesn't change a thing. I also can say that we are here together in the rottenest place in the world, and we trust each other to have each other's back, because we are all Americans and wear the same uniforms, and eat the same food, and share the same living quarters.

Fighting and hating each other is not the answer, fighting and killing the enemy is the answer, but we must do it together, if we intend to win. Now, do one thing for me, write your good Mama a letter and tell her you are alright, and send her a little money; I'm sure she could use it, and you don't have anything here to spend it on anyway." Randy sat and looked down at the ground absorbing everything Wit was saying. They sat quiet for a few moments, and then Randy said, "First, we need to learn how to disassemble and assemble the M-16, and practice handling them." He gave detailed instructions and soon Wit mastered that exercise. Wit took one and fired four, 30 round magazines, rapid-fire, as fast as he could, and it got so hot, it had to be cooled down, or it jammed. The group simulated actual combat conditions, and a lot of them were jamming. It was no comparison to the AK-47 the Commies were using. So, if it jammed while you were in a fire fight, you are dead. How long and how many dead men would it take for the powers to be to correct its shortcomings? Scary thought! Wit thanked Randy, and stuck out his hand to shake, and this time Randy willfully shook.

Mike asked Wit, "What did you say to Randy? He seems different." "I didn't say anything he didn't already know; I just had him look at himself in a looking-glass," Wit explained. Wit thanked Mike for all his help and told him he would be missed. He added, "Let me tell you about the rescuing of four Marines. I tracked them for 3 or 4 hours, and finally caught up with them in a wooded area where they had a mini-POW camp. The Marines were in bamboo cages; it had been four days since their capture. There were six NVA soldiers guarding the camp. I slipped up close, with the cover of darkness approaching, and waited for the opportune time to make my move; question was how do I overcome six Commies? The Lord stepped in and showed the way; they started drinking and smoking weed, and soon passed out. One loan Gook appeared, and I politely killed him, pulling his head back, so he could see the *Demon of Death*, before he met his maker, and then ripped out his throat. I released the captives from their cages, and we ran for our lives. The mystery of it all was them getting drunk and what were they drinking?" Mike explained, "The French tried to get the Vietnamese to develop a taste for Rice-Liquor, and they were going to produce it and start a big business and make a lot of money. They also created their own brand of beer to get the people to develop a taste for that too, and they built large distilleries. I would say they were drinking Rice-Liquor; I've heard it was rather potent. I'm not surprised about the weed; I'm hearing our own troops are using it to get high. Can you imagine a bunch of doped up troops trying to fight a war? I think I am going home at the right time; I have had enough, and rather tired of it all." "What are your plans?" Wit asked. "First, I'm going home and hug Pam and the kids," he answered, "and then I most likely will train new recruits and try to teach them how to stay alive in this miserable hole."

Wit flew back to the Chapel and informed Major Jim that Mike was shipping out for the States. Then he asked, "You've been here a long time; aren't you required to leave?" "Nobody has said anything," the Major responded. "Maybe that rule is only for combat personnel." Wit went to the hospital to get Whiny released, and he brought him back to the Chapel to continue convalescing. Wit thought Whiny could help the Dinks with their chores and baby-sit with Mickey. Wit spent a considerable amount of time at the hospital visiting and praying with the injured; he even wrote letters for those that were handicapped. He made short trips to the jungle with Whiny, so Whiny could instruct him on various ways to survive, and what were traps that he could inadvertently walk into. Then Major Jim informed him, "Wit, you are going on R & R." "What? Why? Where?" he remarked, surprised. "You have a reservation for three days and three nights at the Continental Palace Hotel in Saigon. Your room number is 202." "Who did that?" he responded. "It might be a set-up." "It's no set-up." the Major replied. "Do you know a Congresswoman from Utah named Gloria Banks?" "Yeah, I met Gloria in Germany; a bunch of them came to inspect the military bases in Germany and I transported her around for two days; a very smart lady. Saigon is 400 miles away. I'll try to get a hop with the Air Force, if they have a flight going down there. When do I go?" he questioned. "I'd say you better hurry and get a flight arranged; you leave tomorrow," the Major informed him, and handed him the notice he was reading from.

He caught a jet and was in Saigon in about an hour. He registered in at the hotel and went to his room, and while he was hanging his clothes, there came a knock at the door, and there stood Gloria. She grabbed him and kissed him, and said, "I could hardly wait to see you again." "How did you know where I was?" he asked. "I'm in the Government, remember? We have ways of finding things out," she replied. "I came with a group from the Armed Services Committee to check out what was happening here. The menfolk went to the battle zone with the high-ranking officers, but said it was too dangerous for me, so I thought I would spend my time with you. Remember when I told you I was embarrassed by how I looked, being out of shape? I want to show you something." She began stripping off her clothes, and he looked at her, and remarked, "Wow, look at you! You have a streamlined body." She explained, "After I returned home, I joined a gym, and have been working out with one thing in mind, to look good for you. I met a Congressman from Massachusetts at the gym, and we became an item, and got married. He's older than me, and can't get it up like WT, but he is a fine fella and we get along great together. So, you and me and WT are going to spend three wonderful days and nights together. Is the *Demon of Love* still around?" "Nah!" Wit answered. "I think he transformed back into the *Demon of Death*." She said, "I can't wait any longer; put WT to work," and she hit the sheets. He figure, since she went through all that trouble, being in her 60s and now, except for a few wrinkles, looking more like she was in her 40s, he was going to give her the full treatment, which lasted for several hours, and then satisfied, she informed him, "Let's take a break, clean up, and go to the dining room for dinner; I have a lot to tell you."

While they were eating, she explained, "When we were in a conference at Wright-Patterson Air Force Base, I remembered you telling me you were from a little town not too far from there. I put my Secretary to work and tracked down your wife, and then I took the liberty of riding down to pay her a visit. She was very sweet and humble and welcomed me in and we drank a pot of sweet tea. She said you didn't like tea, and she didn't like coffee. I could see that she was, at one time, a very pretty woman, but now she has aged to where she looks 20 years older than you. She has a very tidy small house and a medium size car and said, with the Army allotment and what she makes as a Nurse, she has no debt and lives very comfortably. She has had no desire to date any man since you left, and the only time she goes out, is with some of the Nurses from the hospital, of which they may take in a movie or go to dinner. She is in close contact with her family, and that is all she lives for. I think she has accepted the fact that she made a grave mistake with you and has tried to live with it on her conscience ever since. I told her I met you in Germany, and you were the most loved man by everybody in Bavaria. She started to tear up, and I gave her hug, and bid her farewell." He remarked, "When we got married, I told her I was extremely jealous, and the worst thing she could ever do to me was cheat on me. She said that I was gonna have to trust her, and I did. Then I caught her in the act, and almost killed the cuckolder with my bare hands, having flashbacked to Korea, until she finally stopped me and brought me to my senses, but she saw the *Demon of Death* in my eyes, and that is what has plagued her all these years, thinking she saw the *'Devil'*. The thought of what I almost did made me realize I could never live in a civilian world again, so the next day, I signed up for six years with the promise I could go into helicopter training, and never looked back. She chose the way she wanted to live, but it wasn't the way I was going to live."

Then she added, "Let's order some dessert and I'll tell you about Helga Jones; remember her?" "Oh, yeah!" he replied. "I could never forget her. She had one goal in life, and that was to get to the States." "I went to a style show while I was in New York, and I was surprised when I saw her directing the models, like she was in charge," Gloria explained. "You remember I stayed at the Chaplain's house when I was there, so I invited her to dinner to return the courtesy. Not knowing how she happened to be there, I asked her about Major Ray, thinking he may have returned to the States also. She said they were divorced, and she went to Munich and started working for a modeling agency, and then was noticed by a representative from a large agency in New York, and he offered her a position, which she accepted, and is now Director of the New York office. I asked her why they divorced, and she pulled no punches. Colonel Joe and Priscilla were sitting in the lobby of the big hotel in Munich reading the newspaper, when she came in on one of her weekends, greeted the staff as usual by their first names, got on the elevator to go up to her favorite room. Priscilla was suspicious enough to instruct Joe to ask the elevator operator how much she charge for her services, and he told Joe, 4000-Deautsch Marks ($1000-dollars), and if he was interested, just ask for Siegfried, and he would set it up. When they returned to Straubing, Colonel Joe informed Major Ray that, what she was doing was a bad image for the United States Army, and he was to consider divorcing her and transfer to a different unit in a different town. Ray was crushed and embarrassed and apologized to Helga and said it wasn't his idea and he had no control over it but had no choice. I think he really loved her. She said after the weekend with you, she never offered her services again, to nobody. She said when she saw the *Devil* in your eyes, she swore it had ended, and avoided you the rest of the time you were there. She said she wasn't at the hotel for that reason; she had an appointment with the Modeling Agency the next day, and the hotel, not knowing any of that, offered her free accommodations, so she accepted."

"She knew that I knew what she was, and I knew her to be a fake," Wit responded. "She led Ray to believe she was going to meet her family, but she had no family in Munich, and I confronted her with that. She admitted it and then explained how she got into the business, and how she learned how to use her beauty to make a lot of money. I agree that she was arguably the most beautiful woman in Germany, but she had a devious mind. The last night we were there, we returned from dinner, and caught an intruder in the room trying to steal her jewelry, or whatever he could find that had value. I jumped him and made him empty his pockets, and was about to kill him, when she saw the *Demon of Death* in my eyes. From that point on, she distanced herself from me. I asked her, while we ate breakfast, if she had a plan for when Major Ray would find out, and he would eventually find out. She asked me if I was going to tell him, and I said her secret was safe with me because it would destroy a fine man, and it would never come from me. I'm glad she got what she wanted, and he is rid of her, but my heart goes out to Ray, a very fine man, and I hope, in time, he can find love again, but I doubt it. You ready to go back to the room?" "No, I want to walk around and see a little of the city while I am here," she replied. "No way, Hosea!" he remarked. "This is the most dangerous place in the world right now, and to walk out there would be suicide. We are at war and you can't tell the good guys from the bad guys because they all look and act alike, until the bad guys find an American to kill, and then you will know while you are being slaughtered. They assassinated the entire Saigon Government. We might venture out for a short spell in the morning while there a lot of people milling around, but definitely not during the night. Let's go to the room; WT is not done with you, yet."

About mid-morning, after they ate breakfast, Wit suggested they wear the roomiest shorts they got with big pockets and try to look as much like a tourist as they could; to go out along the shops and food stands; hoping to mix in with the normal people. He put his handgun in his right pocket and his knife in his beltline under his floppy button-up shirt to conceal them. He suggested she not take her big purse, but just a little hand size purse that she could slip into the front pocket of her shorts and keep her hand on it as much as possible, to keep it from getting picked. She enjoyed the sidewalk stands with the handmade trinkets, and she bought a few souvenirs. He tried to hide being antsy and his eyes rolled constantly looking for anything out of the ordinary, so he wouldn't get caught off guard. After a couple hours, he nervously insisted she had seen enough, and it was time to eat lunch. She thought he was just being paranoid, and over-reacting; he relaxed when he convinced her to get off the streets.

CHAPTER 46

They spent three wonderful days together; she was satisfied she got what she came for and he was glad to get a break from the horrors of war. He flew back to Da Nang and went straight to the Chapel. Major Jim was on the phone, and when he saw Wit, he remarked to the person he was talking to, "Here he is now! I'll tell him!" Wit responded, "Tell me what? I hope it's good news!" "Doesn't sound good, Wit. LZ-Carol has been overrun and there are a lot of casualties," the Major offered. "I never heard of LZ-Carol; can you show it to me on the map?" Wit replied. The Major pointed it out and Wit remarked, "I know where that is; it's the old Green Beret training facility. That's my old stomping ground; they must have settled on it and named it." He rounded up Whiny and said, "Come on, Whiny, duty calls." They flew to the LZ and he landed on the back side like he always did. There were bodies lying everywhere, and he walked over to the officer, that appeared to be in charge, and was surprised, "My gosh, Chris Clark," he spouted, "I thought I'd seen the last of you in Korea, and you are now a Major." "Hey, Wit, you still carrying your Bible under your arm?" the

Chopper Chaplain | 341

Major joked. "Yeah, only now I fly it around in my chopper," he commented, and pointed to his chopper marked 'Chopper Chaplain'." "I've heard of Chopper Chaplain, but I had no idea that was you," the Major added. Then Wit got serious, and asked, "What's going on here? bodies lying all around." "They were overrun by the Commies," the Major informed him, "but the worst thing is, they took a black Nurse captive." "That's not good!" Wit responded. "They will have a lot of fun with her. What is a Nurse doing out here anyway; any color? What lame-brain would send a woman out here?" The new Marines were running around all excited and nervous, preparing to go searching for the Nurse. "It's starting to get dark, Major," Wit added. "As excited as they are, they will end up shooting each other. Let me go in, and if I'm not back by dawn, then you can send them in. I've got my old friend, Whiny, and he can guide me. I didn't bring my jungle attire, is there a special forces casualty out there? He will have some items I will need." "We just got here, but I think there are a couple Green Berets lying out there," the Major answered. Wit found the black Green Beret, Randy Ross, and he examined him, and said, "Randy, it's Wit. You have been shot up pretty bad, but I think if they get you to a hospital quickly, you might just make it." "Just let me die," Randy responded. "Listen to me, Randy, they have taken a black Nurse captive, and I must try to rescue her, but I need what you have in your back-pack. I must hurry before it gets too dark, so I am taking out what I need. You promise me you will hang on until I get back. I should be back by dawn, and I will help load you myself into the Medevac. You promise? Hang on!" He took what he needed and dressed for the jungle, and told Whiny, "Gather up the big rifle and ammunition, and fill your pockets with grenades. Take a knife in case you need it," Wit instructed. They went into the jungle where they thought the Gooks went in, and he told Whiny, "I think they are going in the direction of your old village." Whiny wasn't strong enough to keep up, so Wit told him to hide in the tall grass and keep the weapons, in case they had to fight their out, and he would pick him up on the way back.

He was familiar with the area and was able to move swiftly, and he arrived at the village where he found the newborn baby. They left the bamboo gate open and there were cages all around, like a mini-POW camp. He was beginning to doubt these were the Gooks that had the Nurse, unless she was inside one of the hootches. It was getting darker and a rain began to fall, which he considered his aid. He had to look inside to be sure, so he crept to the opening of one and it was empty. He crept to the second one and it was empty also. He heard noises coming from the third one, and as he crept up to it, he heard a weak moan; he looked around outside and saw the Nurse tied to a tree. He went around to the back of the tree, and said, "I am an American Chaplain. Do not make a sound. I am going to untie you, but do not move. I want you to look like you are still tied." She was stripped naked down to her waste and shivering from the cold rain and sniveling, and he hit her on the shoulder, and said, "Stop it! It's time to get tough and mean. I'm going to try to get you out of here and you can cry later." He crept to the opening of the next hootch, where the noise had come from, and saw three Gooks inside. He had to know if there were more, so he continued to creep around and looked into two more, and they were empty. He concluded that there were only three, and he could kill them quickly, and make their escape. He rushed in and surprised them, and all they could do was look up, and he rapidly ripped out their throats. He took the shirt off one and took it to the Nurse, and told her, "Don't you get weak or faint, because I can't carry you; take hold of my belt at my back and don't let go because we are going to be moving fast. Don't cough or sneeze or make any sound whatsoever because those Gooks can hear a pin drop in this jungle. As soon as they discover you are gone and their buddies are dead, they are going to be hot after us, but they are not going to catch us. Got it?" And fast they went, and they could hear the Gooks thrashing through the grass behind them, but they managed to keep their distance. They reached the hiding place of Whiny, but discovered he had been found and slaughtered, and the weapons were gone. So, they had to run for their lives; the Nurse was out of shape and far from skinny, and she was starting to pant hard, and struggled to breathe. Dawn was approaching and he knew they were close to the LZ, and he yelled at her, "Suck it up! We are almost there!" A Medevac was loading casualties, and they could see the LZ, and Major Clark and another Marine ran out and grabbed the Nurse under her arms and practically carried her collapsed body and loaded it into the big 'copter. She managed to look down, as it lifted off, and saw the little helicopter with the writing on it 'CHOPPER CHAPLAIN'. The Gooks caught up, but the Marines were ready for 'em, and after a brief firefight, the Gooks faded back into the jungle.

The first thing Wit did was to go to the lister bag hanging on a tree limb and dip a cup of fresh water; drank it down and dipped another and drank it down. Major Clark came up, and Wit remarked, "I don't know what they add to the water, but it tastes like Iodine, but it is still better than the Gook sewer water." Then the Major asked, "Where is your old Vietnamese friend?" "I left him hiding in the grass guarding the weapons we took, and they found him and butchered him," Wit said, sadly. "Is the black Green Beret still hanging on?" "Yeah, he was on that 'copter that just took off; the Corpsman said he thought he would survive, but his fighting days are over," the Major replied. "He managed to say, 'tell Wit I got his back', whatever that means." "There's a story behind that," Wit added. "I thought I saw the last of you in Korea. I figured you and Ev went back to Minnesota, got married, and had a house full of kids." The Major commented, "We went back and got married, but I stayed in the Marines for the benefits. She had a baby, a son, and we named him, Loren, and then she got pregnant again, and I shipped out; of all places, to this rat hole. Didn't you get enough of Korea?" "I went home, and thought I was in love, got married, but it didn't work out very well because I couldn't adapt to civilian life, so I re-enlisted for six years if they promised me Helicopter Pilot Training, and that I would stay in the Chaplain's Service, so I left and never looked back," he explained. "This is the life where I belong, and I am a career soldier, and I will stay in it until I am of no more use to the Army." "You will get a medal for what you just did," Major Clark remarked. "I don't do stuff for medals; I'm just happy to do the Lord's work," Wit commented.

CHAPTER 47

Wit remained close to the Chapel, and for the next few months, spent most of his time visiting the hospitals and administering to the wounded patients, doing whatever he could, like praying with them or writing letters for them, or just talking with the ones that were traumatized by combat. He bumped into the Marine Captain at the Commissary, and the Captain asked, "I've been meaning to ask you, if we ran into each other again, how well do you know this Colonel Willoughby you mentioned to the Lieutenant in my office?" "Never heard of him!" Whip replied, grinning. "I had to make up something at the time to get going. Did those captive Marines do alright?" "Well, yes and no," the Captain responded, "Donohoo got the ticket home because his leg was shattered; Combs, your Brother-In-Law, finished his tour and went back to the States for re-assignment. Colvin and Helton didn't fair too well. The three went back to their unit and were in an Amtrak convoy where Marines were stuffed inside; Combs rode inside, but Colvin and Helton wanted to ride on top. Their Amtrak got stuck in the mud, and the Gook snipers picked them off like sitting ducks. The Marines inside escaped, but there was nothing they could do to help the two on top. They were so close to finishing their tour." "I'm sorry to hear that," Wit remarked, "they had been through enough and I hoped their luck would hold out," "I want to thank you for what you did," the Captain continued. "You did something we failed to do." "Your Platoon Sergeant was a ton of help," Wit remarked. "He provided me with valuable information that made it possible."

The Chaplain had been working with little Mickey, teaching him English, and he would say funny stuff like a young child would say, and everyone enjoyed having him around. Wit returned from the hospital one day and Mickey said, "Wassup, Wit?" He had heard the adults saying that, and picked it up, and everybody thought that was really funny. The Chaplain said, "Come into my office, Wit, I got a couple news flashes for ya." They went into the office and sat down, and the Chaplain didn't waste any time, and said, "You knew your time here was limited, so you are required to transfer out of country. It wasn't suggested where you were transferred to, so I suppose they are leaving it up to you where you want to go. You often said you would never go back to the States, so that leaves the entire world wide-open." Wit replied, "I guess I can go to Okinawa and work with injured vets at the hospitals, and then after a year, I may return here, where I know I can help out." "That sounds like a plan," the Chaplain responded, "and that will give you a chance to recondition your body. You have let yourself get into miserable shape. You think you can catch a flight?" "There are regular flights that go back and forth; I should be able to catch one." Wit replied. "I should be of service to the Chaplain's office there; can you notify them I'm coming?"

He caught a hop to Okinawa, and they landed at Kadena Air Base, and then caught a ride to Torii Station Army Base where he checked in at the Chapel. The Chaplain introduced himself as, Major Tilford Storm, and said, "I got the word from Major Shoemaker that you were coming, and I've been expecting you. You can stay here until you find more suitable quarters. I'll show you where you can settle in, and then I would like for you to fill me in on what's been going on in your life. He didn't tell me a whole lot. My Orderly shipped out, so I don't have one at the present time." "Appreciate it," Wit commented. "I don't need a large area because I spend most of my time out and about, so whatever you have will be alright, I'm sure." He unpacked his bag and returned to the Chaplain's office to describe his history, "It would take a library to collect all that I have gone through since I entered the Army; I took my basic at Camp Breckinridge, Ky with the 101st Airborne Infantry, training to be a replacement for troops in Korea. When we arrived in Korea, I began praying for the dying soldiers that layed spread out over a large area, when the Chaplain noticed me and asked me to be in the Chaplain's Service, and I remained there completing my required time. I had several months left in my enlistment, so I spent them at Fort Rucker working with troubled vets that had emotional problems from their traumatic experiences. I must say I had a good success rate getting them ready to return to civilian life. My toughest project was a Doctor Lieutenant that I thought would be impossible to turn around. I worked with her and we prayed a lot, and finally she started to respond; she went home a week before I did. I was a mess myself but helping them helped me too. I went back to the civilian world and realized I didn't belong there anymore, so I re-enlisted, providing I could get Helicopter Pilot Training, still being in the Chaplain's Service. I graduated and went to Germany for 2 years, assigned to the Chaplain's office and set up a transport service with the helicopter. I then went to Vietnam and was assigned to the Chaplain's office in Da Nang, where, at that time, they only had Advisors. In order for me to continue being of service administering to the wounded and dying in the upcoming war, like I did in Korea, I had to familiarize myself with the jungle, which was new to me. Major Shoemaker suggested I train with the Green Beret and the ARVN Rangers, so I would occasionally fly my little chopper out to their camp and spend some time with them learning weaponry and jungle knowledge. I spent considerable amount of time at the hospitals praying and working with the emotionally troubled. The Doctor I mentioned I worked with, showed up at the hospital in Da Nang, and is doing fine; a great Doctor, and is now a Captain. Then the Hospital Administrator asked me to try to help one of their finest Doctors, a Major that was on the verge of total collapse, and I thought could possibly have a stroke. She was not in agreement to that and fought me until I convinced her, that she was borderline on disaster that could end her life and career, so she relented, and miraculously in just a short time, with a lot of prayer, she responded and went back to work, with a brand new personality. The Colonel was amazed at the transformation, and naturally I beamed with pride with having success. I have found everybody is different, and I must get into their mindset to figure what's bothering them, and that is the toughest part, because most of them clam up and won't express their feelings.

 I am only here on hiatus until I am permitted to go back to Vietnam, and I plan to go back, because I feel I have unfinished business there and can be useful. If it is possible, I would like to be assigned a helicopter so I can fly to various hospitals to administer to the sick and injured and work with the troubled." "I don't think there would be a problem getting a helicopter; there should be some available at our air strip; you can use my Jeep in the meantime," the Major replied. "You mentioned helping troubled vets, and I have one you can begin with. He is the Nephew of Lt. Col. Roger Ivey, the Hospital Administrator, and he has concerns, since the boy has returned from combat in Vietnam. He seems to be in another world and has no interest in anything. Drive to the hospital and introduce yourself, and let the Colonel explain it all to ya." The next day, Wit drove to the air strip, and talked to the helicopter mechanics, and they indicated, since this was the training facility for Special Forces, personnel come and go constantly, and there were always choppers available. He requested a Bell, like he had for years, and they said there were several; just take your pick. He selected one that looked in good shape and had low hours and asked them to service it, which they gladly agreed to do. He drew a sketch of how he would like them to paint on his chopper the Chaplain's insignia and the words, 'CHOPPER CHAPLAIN'.

He drove to the hospital and went to see Colonel Ivey, who was very personable, and welcomed him, and offered a cup of coffee while they talked about Little Scottie. Wit asked to see Little Scottie's file so he could familiarize himself with what the boy's background was, and what his interests were. The first thing that jumped out at him was that both parents were Doctors, and to him that meant they were well-to-do, and he was most likely a pampered brat, but he decided the best thing to do was to let the boy describe himself in his own words. The

Colonel called him and had him come to the hospital, where he introduced him to Wit, but he didn't say anything about what his reasons were. Wit started, "Scott, I just arrived here yesterday, and I haven't the foggiest idea where anything is. If you don't have anything to do the rest of the day, I would appreciate it if you would drive me around and show me the places of interest." "I don't know too much about it; I don't get out and do anything," he replied. "How long have you been here?" Wit asked, surprised he didn't know much about it. "I don't know, four or five months I guess," he answered. "I have the Chaplain's Jeep, so let's go scout around and see what's around here," Wit insisted. "I want to see where the movie theater is, where the gymnasium is, where the swimming pool is, and let's see if we can find a hamburger joint; I'll treat ya to a double-decker-cheese burger."

They drove around and found all the places; everything was located on the base and that made it easy to find, so they went in for a 'burger and a Coke. While they were eating, Wit asked, "Did you play any sports as a kid, or for the school?" "No, nothing," he responded. "I was a 'Nerd'." "I don't think I know what a Nerd is," Wit replied. "I think of that as being a person that does nothing and not interesting in doing anything." "That's me," Scott explained. "I just hung out and my Nerd friends hung out with me." "Did you consider going to college when you graduated?" Wit asked. "Nah, I barely graduated, and I failed the college entrance exams," he answered. After they ate, Wit said, "Let's drive down to the beach; I hear the water is crystal clear." "It is unless there was a storm out to sea, and then it's a little murky," Scott explained. They found a place to sit and the water was a beautiful bluish color. They sat and looked at it for a bit, and Wit asked, "Where did you take your basic training?" "Fort Knox, Ky," he answered. "That's where my older brother took his basic during the Korean War. We all went down to visit him, and it was the middle of winter, and everybody down there was sick with pneumonia. Those drafty old barracks were like being outside. Did you learn about tanks?" Wit continued to ask. "Yeah, it was ok I guess; it beat walking," he answered, unconcerned. "Do you like to swim?" Wit asked. "Why don't we go up and take a dip in the pool?" That perked him up, "Now that I know how to do; we had a pool in our back yard, and I learned to swim before I could walk." They got their trunks and went to the pool. It was crowded, so it made it tough to swim, so they found an empty table with an umbrella, and sat down to watch the people. "There's some nice-looking ladies around here," Wit commented. "You like looking at the girls?" "They're ok," he said. "I never could get too interested in them." An attractive young lady, probably in her twenties, looking good in her bathing suit, was strolling by like she was looking for a place to sit, and Wit said, "If you are looking for a place to sit, we have plenty of room." "She said, "I've never seen it this crowded; thank you. I'm Mary Ann." "I'm Wit and this is Scott. We tried swimming but it is too crowded, so we thought we would just sit and enjoy watching the people." Scott seemed disinterested, so he said, "I'm gonna get going," and he got up to leave, and Wit said, "I'd like to get with ya tomorrow, if you ain't too busy?" "Yeah, sure," he replied, and threw up his hand as he left.

So, Wit, never being short on conversation, asked, "What do you do, Mary Ann?" "I'm a Nurse at the hospital," she answered, and spoke freely. "I was a Nurse in a field hospital near Saigon for about 9 months, and it almost drove me crazy, so I am on kind of a medical leave; I have terrible nightmares and can't sleep very well." "I put in five years up at Da Nang in the Chaplain's Service and they made me leave, so I am on a hiatus until they allow me to go back. Why don't we get dressed and I'll treat ya to a milk shake or something?" Wit offered. She responded, "I'm gonna need more than that; I haven't eaten since this morning." "We can get whatever you want. I'm new here so you are gonna have to show me where to go," he offered. They got dressed and went to a small diner, and when they finished, she asked, "Would you mind walking me home? It's not safe at night; people get mugged or attacked, and I'm afraid. It's about a mile from here." "That's not a problem," Wit replied, "and I thought Da Nang wasn't safe at night." She gripped his hand tightly as they walked down the sidewalk, until they reached her house. They walked in and she introduced him to her Brother. He was dressed in an Air Force uniform, and she explained, "He's in Air Security and has to be on duty all night." "Get him something to drink, Mary Ann; that's the least you can do since he walked you home," her Brother remarked, as he walked out the door. She started mixing her a soda and whiskey and asked him, "What would you like, I need false courage." "I don't drink!" he remarked. "Coke is fine, if you have it." She drank it down and mixed another and drank it down, and said, "Now I am relaxed, would you like to kiss me?" "Would you like for me to kiss you?" he returned the question. Then she asked, "Would you mind if I put on my pajamas?" "It's your house, wear whatever you want." She went to the bedroom and put on her pajamas and came out and turned on the record player, "What kind of music you like?" "I like soft and soothing music for lovers," he responded. "Here's my Mom's favorite, Joni James, 'Why Don't You Believe Me'; let's dance." They started dancing and she said, "Now you can kiss me." He kissed her and rubbed his hands over her tender body, and she started to get excited, so she led him into the bedroom, and he laid some pipe.

They loved for a while, and then just lay holding each other when there was a noise like someone came in. She said, very softly, "That's my Mom with her Air Force Captain boyfriend. He takes her to nice places and brings her back and they hit the sheets. He doesn't satisfy her, so she fakes it, then he gets up and leaves. Now she goes into the bathroom and cleans herself and comes back all frustrated." That was exactly what happened. Then she asked, "You more than satisfied me, would you be willing to go satisfy her? Wait till you see her, she's gorgeous!" "Wow, what a question?" he thought. "What would she think about that?" he asked, just out of curiosity. "Oh, she's ready," Mary Ann said, "that Captain only primed her. Hey Mom, you want me to share my boyfriend with you? He more than satisfied me." She yelled back, "Bring him on!" He went into the bedroom and she was lying there ready; and she was truly gorgeous. So, he banged the Mom, over and again, and that solved her frustration problem. Mary Ann yelled, "I want some more, but I need some more false courage."

Wit thought he hit the lottery, and when it was getting quite late, he remarked, "I need to get home; I got to get up early in the morning, but I'm not sure where I am." Mary Ann asked, "Do you know how to get home from the pool? I can give you directions from here to the pool." There were streetlights spaced along the street where it would be light and then dark and light again. As he entered a dark place, someone jumped out and it felt like he stuck a gun in his back, "Give me your money!" Ah, the good old days at Camp Breckinridge when the boys practiced such situations until they perfected it. He spun around and in one fluid motion, disarmed the robber and slammed him to the sidewalk. He was about to rip out his throat when the robber saw the *Demon of Death* and was paralyzed with fear. Lucky for him an MP Jeep came patrolling by and stopped. Wit said, with a smile on his face, "I don't think this fella is feeling too good." "What happened?" the MP asked. "He tried to rob me!" Wit replied. The robber was lying there as stiff as a zombie. "What happened to him?" the MP continued to ask. "I don't know!" Wit remarked. "Ask him!" "There has been a lot of crime lately, what are you doing out this late?" the MP asked. "I just walked a young lady home; she said she was afraid. Her name is Mary Ann and her brother is in Air Security; I just met him as he was going on duty." "Yeah, we know Mary Ann," the MP said. "We've warned her before to stay off these streets at night." "I'm new here and not sure where I'm going. I'm in the Chaplain's Service so why don't you boys give me a lift to the Chapel?" Wit requested.

CHAPTER 48

Wit met with Scott the next day and said, "Let' go to the gym and work out." "I'm not interested in that stuff," Scott replied. "Come on, a little work out will make you feel better," Wit remarked. Scott reluctantly relented and went along. When they went in, Wit asked who the head trainer was, and they introduced themselves and Wit said, "This is Scott Ivey and I want you to take him under your wing and teach him how to do exercises and learn how to use the equipment. His Uncle is the Hospital Administrator and he wants him to get into shape. Start him out easy so he doesn't strain himself." "What about you?" the trainer asked. "I don't need a trainer, I know how to do it all," Wit answered. He started out with loosening up exercises, and then started gradually on the various equipment, and then increased to where he was in a flurry and working the equipment to its maximum. The trainer said, "He's attacking the equipment with a vengeance; I hope it holds up." Wit put everything he had into each exercise, going from one to the other, and then finally quitting; drenched with sweat, and panting hard. The trainer asked, "What are you trying to prove? Do you hate somebody?" He responded, "I just spent five years in Vietnam, and now I am on hiatus, and as soon as I am allowed, I'm going back. I got some unfinished business there, and I got to be in top shape." "You could go out and train with the Special Forces Unit; they stress being in shape," the trainer suggested. "I might just do that," Wit added. "I trained with the Green Beret for two years before the war started, and I don't want to lose my edge."

An apartment became available two streets away from the Chapel, and well within walking distance; that got rid of another hurdle. He met with Scott and they went to sit on the beach, trying to get a little privacy. "Scott, what part of 'Nam were you stationed?" Wit began. "I was down in the southwestern part about 20 miles from Cambodia near, what they called, The Ho-Chi-Minh Trail," he answered. "Were you involved in any big battles?" Wit continued to ask, trying to get to the root of his problem. "I don't want to talk about it," Scott remarked. "If it is bothering you, you need to talk about it with someone, to get it out in the open," Wit explained. "As long as you harbor it in the back of your mind, it will cause you problems the rest of your life." "We were in Operation Junction City, and it was a huge mission, about 25,000 troops spread out over 50 miles, to search and destroy and to eradicate the stronghold of the VC and NVA. It lasted almost 3 months and it proved to be a big victory, killing 3000 enemy to only 300 of ours, and wounded 1500. I was scared out of my mind and thought it would never end; a few of my best friends were killed and we made a pact that the ones that survived would visit the families of those that didn't make it. I could never gather enough strength to face those families, so that is why I am staying here. How do you explain why you were lucky, and they weren't?" he questioned. "Let me explain something to you," Wit iterated. "You make your own luck, but it wasn't luck that you survived, you were spared. Why? Nobody knows! God spared you because he has another plan for you, and only he knows what that plan is. It might take years for that plan to materialize, or it might take months. You can't walk around with your shoulders drooped and looking at the ground; you are better than that. You are a veteran combat soldier of the United States Army, and you must feel that pride and walk with your head up and your shoulders back. Nobody, and I mean nobody, can take that away from you. You are no longer Little Scottie or Nerd Scott; that little kid is gone, and you are a man, and you must start believing and acting like one. Maybe you need to help God with his plan. I will talk to the Chaplain and see if he would be willing to assign you as his Chaplain's Orderly; there is a vacancy since his old one shipped out; it would give you a purpose. What do ya think?" "I don't know," he replied, "what would I do?" "Do whatever he asks you to do," Wit remarked. "He can't be in a lot of places at one time, so you would fill in a lot of the duties and lighten the load. I can ask him to talk to you, and then you decide. You will learn to be kind and friendly to everyone, and when you drive around in his Jeep with his insignia on it, people will look at you with respect, and respect by your peers is worth a million bucks. Remember to walk tall and look straight ahead; the future is yours."

The Chaplain took Wit's advice and talked to Scott and agreed he was a good fit for the Orderly job. Wit continued to work with Scott, taking him to the gym and changing his mindset to make him believe in himself, which he never did in his whole life because he never had too. The trainer was helping him with his workouts, and he was becoming more fit, which resulted in helping him feel better physically, as well as mentally, and it began to show. Wit went to the hospital, like always, and ran into Mary Ann; he had been working with her to rid her of her nightmares but didn't seem to be making much progress. "Hey, Wit," she said, "Mom is cooking a nice supper tonight and wanted me to invite you, so can you make it?" "Yeah, a home cooked meal sounds good for a change," he responded. She didn't say what time, so he went early. Mom Myers greeted him and said, "We have a couple hours before Mary Ann gets home so why don't we go into the bedroom for a little extracurricular activity." They went into her bedroom and he banged her. She cleaned herself up and began cooking, and he asked, "What are we having?" "I went to the market today and bought some fresh caught fish; you will like it, if you like fish," she answered. "It will be a little while till it's done." He went out and sat on the front porch swing to wait for Mary Ann. She arrived about 10 minutes later, and she saw him sitting there, and got a mean look on her face. "How long you been here?" she asked. "You didn't say what time, and I didn't want to be late, so I came early," he responded, mildly. "Was Mom here when you got here?" she continued to ask. "Yeah, she's in there cooking," he replied. While they were eating, Mary Ann's eyes darted back and forth between her Mom and Wit. "Did you two do anything before I got home?" she asked, with jealousy building. Wit never thought much about it because Mary Ann had shared him with her Mom the first night, and he said, "Yeah, we did!" Mary Ann went into a rage; she jumped out of her chair and pointed her finger at her Mom and started screaming, "I shared him with you one time because I felt sorry for you and now you are trying to steal my boyfriend."

Her Mom never saw her react like this and just stared at her with big eyes. Wit, knowing he was in the middle of a lover's quarrel got up and said, calmly, "Ladies, it is time for me to go; I appreciate the supper, and Mary Ann, I think we need to find a new place to meet so I can continue working with ya."

Mom started showing up at Wit's apartment to get serviced, which he did, if she happened to catch him at home. She came one time, and he indicated he was on his way out, and she said, "I won't stay long; it will only take a few minutes." Just then a big burly Sergeant from the Special Forces, a neighbor from down the hall, came strolling toward them, and Wit said, "Mom Myers meet Big Johnny James. He will be more than glad to take care of ya." Without further ado, she took him by the arm, and they went down the hall to his apartment. A couple days later, while at the SF training camp working out with the troops, Wit ran into Big John, and asked, "How did you make out with that fine lady?" "She was great," he remarked. "She wants to see me again." "That's good!" Wit responded. "You can have her." "What?" Are you kidding?" Big John questioned. "No, I got her daughter!" Wit exclaimed. "Ha! Ha! Wit, you are the man!" the Sergeant laughed. Wit walked away and mumbled to himself, "That's another problem solved."

He didn't go to the camp for about 6 weeks, but he and Scott continued hitting the gym for regular workouts, and he continued working with Mary Ann, and visiting the hospitals. Big John informed him that their training was winding down, so he decided to make one more visit out there. He flew his chopper because he had planned to go to the hospital at Naha Military Port afterwards. Big John saw him fly in and went to meet him. Wit, trying to be funny, asked, "Who's running this dog and pony show now?" "That mean looking Colonel that's walking toward you. He looks like he could eat nails and spit rust," Big John commented. Wit looked at him and said, "Believe me, Sergeant, he can." "Major Shelton, or I should say Colonel Shelton, how long you been here?" Wit asked. "Wit, I thought you were still chasing Gooks through the jungle?" the Colonel responded. "I came several weeks ago, with hopes of getting these green troops ready. They are not taking it seriously and I am concerned about it. You have been there; would you be willing to address them and describe what it is like?" "I can try," Wit answered. "They made me leave, but I plan to go back as soon as I can. When do you plan to ship out?" "In ten days!" the Colonel responded.

The Colonel had the entire unit sit under a big tree and he introduced Wit, "Wit has spent considerable time in Vietnam; listen to what he has to say; it may save your life." Wit began, "I am Loren Whitson, assigned to the Chaplain's Service and, also a helicopter pilot. I went to Vietnam and spent over two years training with the Green Beret before the Marines landed in March 1965. I went to the beach and watched those fresh-faced young kids come ashore, and I commented, they have no idea what they are in for; they are energetic and ready to fight, but it is not a traditional war. An Army doesn't meet you on the battlefield, they are an unseen enemy running through the jungle wearing black pajamas, and only carrying an AK-47 and a knife, but believe me, they will see you. Their primary mission is to kill Americans. They are guerrilla fighters, assassins, barbarians, and you may see them working the rice paddies during the day like regular farmers, but they become your enemy at night. You may chase one and then he disappears, like a ghost. He may dive into a tunnel and wait till you give up and go on; then he comes out and shoots ya or sticks a knife in ya. They are clever fighters and, the French can attest to that, and they have spent decades digging an underground tunnel maze, with caverns large enough to hold a platoon or a field hospital." A couple of the troopers were not paying a lot of attention and were laughing, and that irritated Wit, "You two funny guys stand up. I want everybody to see what you look like now; you think this is all a joke, but I want to predict, and God knows, I hope I'm wrong. Two hours after you hit that jungle, you are going to be so scared, you will wet your pants, and two hours after that, they will carry you out wounded, or in a body bag. I have seen funny guys like you hanging from a tree by his feet and his testicles cut out and stuffed in their mouths. They weren't laughing any more. Your body will be sent home and your family will say he was always such a good boy; he always helped everybody; he always laughed and joked; he was a hero. Fact is, you are dead because you didn't pay attention to learn what to do to stay alive. Sit down and shut up! Colonel Shelton is trying hard to teach you about everything in that jungle is wanting to hurt you or kill you. Not only the Gooks, there are 5 poisonous snakes, rats, black and red ants that can hurt you bad if you are stupid enough to step on an ant hill; booby traps; over a hundred-degree heat and 100% humidity. Half the people you meet are the enemy, and you can't tell the difference, because they all look alike. There are no cute little honeys in the villages; they all went to the towns to sell their services to the Americans that have a lot of money. I might warn you, never go into a town alone; they might find your body in an alley somewhere; go with two or more to have each other's back. Always carry fresh water. You will see people with their water buffalo working a rice field, and then squat down and take a dump, and continue working; the rains come, and there are lots of rain, washes the dung into the creeks and rivers, and the fish live on it, and if you eat a fish or drink the water, you will end up with parasites and dysentery that will take the fight out of you. You are going to the most dangerous place in the world, and if you rely on your training, you may survive. I might mention that there are also man-eating tigers. I never saw one or heard one, but the ARVN boys said they heard them roar in the night. It was reported that one crept into a Marine camp and attacked a Marine and killed him in his bunk while he slept. Another place a unit guard spotted one and chased him away before he could attack. You know those young fresh-faced Marines I mentioned? I watched them, the ones that were left, prepare to leave at the end of their tour, and they looked 20 years older; sick with Malaria, swollen bellies from dysentery, swollen legs and arms that got infected and never healed; but they were tickled to death they survived and were getting out of that hell-hole." One guy jumped up and said, "You sound like we can't win that war." "In my opinion, we can't!" Wit answered. "A wise man once said, not too many years ago, that if a country should attack the United States, they could never win because they not only had to beat the military, but had to beat the people, and Americans are too strong to allow that. This is a politician's war! If they would allow the warriors to go fight because we have the most powerful military in the world, then we could win, but Washington is calling the shots, and they know nothing about it. I would rather fight the Commies on their ground than ours. Your unit is to support the Green Beret, and I am going to tell you the very first thing the GB impressed on me, and you cannot falter, or you will be dead.

Remember, **'FOCUS'**. You cannot stumble around in the jungle thinking about banging your honey at home; your hippy anti-war friends are taking care of that for ya. You must be conscious of everything and everybody around you and train your mind to think like that; nothing else. The next important thing is **'PRAYER'**. If you have never prayed before, you will now. You will be so scared you will promise the Lord anything to get you out of that mess. I suggest you start by going to church on Sunday." One guy jumped up and said, "If I ever went into church, the roof would fall in." "There's an old saying from the World Wars," Wit added. "You will never find an Atheist in a fox hole! I wish you all luck and good fortune; I will be praying for ya." Colonel Shelton said, "I don't know anybody that could have said any better; you could be an Ambassador." "Not me!" Wit responded. "That's politics, and I don't want any part of it." "When do you think they will allow you to go back?" the Colonel asked. "I'm hoping in a couple months," Wit replied, "I hope to go back to the Chapel in Da Nang. I have unfinished business to take care of. They slaughtered a couple villages of people that I thought a lot of, and I am going to make them pay." The Colonel saw the sternness in his eyes and the old warrior got a chill up his spine.

CHAPTER 49

The Special Forces Unit shipped out for Vietnam. Wit continued working with Scott, and it had been several months since they started; they did their regular workout at the gym and then sit at the beach and talk a while. "You should be proud of yourself, Scott, the way you have improved," Wit explained. "The Chaplain is pleased with your work; you have improved your appearance, walking tall and straight; you haven't mentioned any hang-ups lately. Have you given any thought to what your next move will be when your enlistment is up? I know you have been hearing the news about all the anti-war unrest at home. When you go home, all your Nerd buddies are going to hate you and spit on you and call you a baby-killer, and every other thing they can think of. They are scared to death they will be drafted, so they think the more noise they make, the more the politicians will decide to overlook them. The fact is, the reporters go over and spend a few days talking to a few people, take a few videos, and then go home and write, or get on television, and paint a bleak picture of what is going on; all it does is stir up the losers and make more news to further their careers. If you should go home, and wear your uniform, you will be an outcast among your friends and a lot of your family. It's a sad day because you put your life on the line and did what you were asked to do; help deter Communism."

Wit went to the hospital and ran into Uncle Roger, Scott's Uncle. "Colonel, have you noticed the improvement in Scott?" Wit questioned. "Yes, I have," he answered, "you have done a masterful job. I never thought Little Scottie would ever change, but he has considerably. He is even talking about re-enlisting, if he can stay as the Chaplain's Orderly; that is something I never thought possible." "Well, now you must do your part," Wit added. "It's not Little Scottie, or Nerd Scott, anymore; he is a man, a veteran combat soldier of the United States Army, and he should be spoken to and treated with all the respect he deserves, because he put his life on the line and earned it. You can pass that on to the rest of your family that thinks he is a nobody." "Are you chewing me out, Wit?" the Colonel asked. "Sir, I respect your position and I would never try to do that but, if the shoe fits, wear it," Wit replied. "I get it, Wit, and I owe you one," the Colonel remarked. "Well, I am ready to collect!" Wit said boldly. "You have a Nurse working with the casualties from the war, Mary Ann Myers, and she is suffering with nightmares from her traumatic experience of nine months in a field hospital, and she is now on a medical leave. I've been working with her, but I don't see much improvement, because I think whenever she goes to work in those wards, it seems to open old wounds in her mind. I would appreciate it if you would give some thought to moving her to a Pediatric Ward where she could work with kids, and maybe that change would give her some relief so she could respond to my efforts." "I don't know her," the Colonel added, "but I can ask around."

"She is very pretty and in her 20s; Scott met her the same day I did at the pool," Wit remarked. "Don't mention my name, just make up something like you have been noticing her work and there is an opening in Pediatrics that she might be better fitted for. I guarantee she is an excellent Nurse, so she won't have a problem adjusting to the change." The Colonel honored his debt and transferred Mary Ann to the kid's ward. After a week, Wit could see a change in her demeaner, so he asked her how things were going at the hospital, and she explained she had been promoted to Pediatrics, and it has eased her mind considerably.

Wit asked Major Storm if he would inquire as to when he could return to Vietnam. The Chaplain came back the next day and said they would cut orders in a couple more weeks. He informed Scott of the fact, and suggested Scott work with the returning vets like he had been doing. Scott was a little apprehensive until Wit explained that he was the most qualified to speak on their level, since he had experienced the same thing they went through and understood their problems. He asked Scott to accompany him to the hospital, and he would lead him through a couple of the casualties. After Scott worked with a few vets, he started feeling a lot better about himself, and was inspired to continue. Wit passed it on to the Chaplain, and he was pleased. Wit went regularly to Mary Ann's house to work with her, but he never mentioned he would be leaving because he wasn't sure how she would take it, and since she was progressing, he didn't want to set her back. Of course, the routine included making love. Two days before he was to leave, he made love to her, and she said, "Wit, I want to marry you!" He replied, "You will have to get in line for that." "What if I told you I was pregnant?" she continued. "Well, if you are, it's not mine, because I am sterile. Something happened in Korea that made me sterile, and I have been checked three times, and there are no active Spermatozoid, and being a Nurse, you know what they are," he commented, holding his crossed fingers behind his back because he was lying, and he was calling her bluff. "So, is there someone else?" he continued. "No!" she said, "I was only kidding. My Mom is pregnant!" "Is this more of your jokes?" he asked. "She is in her bedroom; go ask her," Mary Ann insisted. He went in and Mom was laying on the bed, not feeling too good, and Wit asked, bluntly, "Are you pregnant?" "Yes!" she answered. "Big John and I are in love and we talked about getting married when his tour is up, so the last time we did it, I didn't clean out." "Does he know?" Wit asked. "No, I haven't broken the news to him yet. We have been writing regularly, but I write about other things. I want to name him Loren because you are the one that got us together," "Ha, poor kid," Wit responded, "what if it is a girl?" "Well, we will call her Loreen." "Don't tell him!" Wit insisted. "He doesn't need anything to take his mind off his mission; it could cost him his life. Write only pleasant things, like how you are doing at work, or shopping, or anything, like how well Mary Ann is doing in her new job; how cool it has been." She agreed! The last day before his scheduled flight, he made a last visit to Mary Ann's house, and informed her he was leaving early the next morning, and he would, most likely, never see her again, and he wished her luck. She was shocked to hear it and asked to make love one more time. He said, "No, we are done. You tried to trick me and I didn't appreciate that, so I am saying goodbye now and I will say goodbye to your Mom."

He stopped at a bakery and bought an assortment of pastries which he presented to the mechanics at the air strip for their efforts and returned the chopper, since he would not have any more use for it. Scott drove him to Kadena Air Base early to catch his flight to Da Nang. He reminded Scott to continue working with Mary Ann, who was progressing well since Uncle Roger transferred her to Pediatrics. They shook hands and wished each other well, and he boarded the jet, and soon disappeared in the sky. Scott watched, sadly, because he just watched the best friend he ever had leave forever. Wit arrived at the Da Nang Airstrip and hitched a ride with one of the airmen to the Chapel. He was surprised to see his old chopper still sitting where he left it. He figured an insurgent would have blown it up but was pleased it wasn't. A new Chaplain had replaced Major Shoemaker, and he introduced himself as Captain Quinton Wilson. He explained, "The powers to be said Major Shoemaker had been here too long, so they transferred him back to the States. He said you would be back, and I kept everything just like you left it. Welcome back!" The Dinks and Mickey were excited to see him, and Mickey tried to hug him. He had grown considerably, for a Vietnamese, and he spoke excellent English, thanks to the efforts of Major Shoemaker. He and the Chaplain talked extensively about the grave situation there; describing it the best he could from his limited knowledge. Wit checked the chopper thoroughly for booby-traps or explosives, and finding none, he proceeded to the hospital.

 Doctor Susan saw him come in, and hurried to give him a hug, and asked, "Where have you been? You just disappeared without a word, and we had no idea what happened to ya, and we've been worried sick." "They said I had to go for a while, so I went to Okinawa until they allowed me to return," he explained. "I don't see Doc Ashby; is he still here? They replaced Major

Shoemaker." "Doc started having heart palpations, so they packed him up and moved him out; where to, I have no idea. Since I am senior officer, I have been running things, if, and when, they should replace Doc. It gets stressful at times and I could use an all-nighter with WT therapy," she commented. "You know WT! He is always ready to oblige a beautiful lady Doctor. Are you going to cook supper, like Grandma used to make?" he responded. "I can, but you will need to go buy a few ingredients I don't have," she answered. "You notice how cool it is in here? We now have air-conditioning; and window units in our apartments; beats trying to keep cool with a little fan." "You got that right!" he remarked. "I suppose you are still living in the same place," he surmised. "I'll pick up the stuff you need and meet you there when you finish your shift."

She arrived home, and right away, started to strip off, and said, "You mind if we eat later? I've had a stressful day and I can't wait for my WT therapy." After a couple hours, the stress was gone, and she was relaxed and mellow. They prepared the spaghetti and meatballs and garlic toast, like Grandma's recipe, and made small talk while they ate. He then asked, "How's Betty holding up? Any signs of weakening?" "She's doing fine; a great Doctor," Susan responded. "I explained to her what she did to you was wrong; what you were experiencing in the jungle was causing stress and took any opportunity to relax. That little Hussy meant nothing, but she threw herself in and made it so easy; any man would have done the same thing. She admitted that she fell in love with you at Fort Rucker, and regretted not expressing her feelings, and then meeting you again after all those wasted years, fired her up again. After your all-night encounter, she thought she had you at last. Then you broke the bubble with one instance, and she was so overcome with jealousy, it blew her mind, and she didn't know how to handle it after that. She feels humbly sorry and wants to make it up to ya." "How would she do that?" he asked. "She wants another chance for an all-nighter, and she wants to throw everything she has into making love." "I donno; I don't get over stuff like that very easily. We'll just see how it plays out," he responded. "It may be wiser to let it ride for now; I got enough on my plate and I don't need any more."

The next Sunday, at church, he recognized a Green Beret member, and approached him, "Where are you guys training these days? Same place?" "No, the insurgents lobbed a few shells on that camp, and we figured they were pretty well zeroed in, so it was wise to move. We joined another camp 20-Klicks to the northwest of where we were. As soon as I pick up a few provisions, I'll be returning, if you want to follow me out." He followed him out and found some of the old GB still with them along with a lot of fresh faces. The previous ARVN unit moved to areas where action was hot and active, so they had a new batch of green troops to train. He joined in with their PT routines, which he handled with ease after his workout regimen at Okinawa. He went through his regular target practice with the M-14 rifle, firing semi-automatic from the hip. They explained the faulty M-16 had been redesigned and modified to where it was a more effective weapon. He fired it in the same fashion until he became an expert like with the M-14. He agreed it made a better jungle weapon; being lighter and having less kick and being smaller. He spent a week at the camp regaining his confidence and learning new tactics, and then returned to the Chapel. He explained to Captain Wilson that he spent considerable time in the field assisting the casualties with evacuation and prayer, but he thought it not to be a good idea to try to explain about his other activities; at least, at which time he might understand better.

Rumors were spreading that the VC and NVA were forming larger units, like regiments and divisions, and the fighting was bitter and both sides losing large numbers of troops. Wit made up his mind he was going to try to make a difference and eliminate as many Gooks as he could, so he flew to the GB camp, donned his jungle outfit, and informed the GB Captain he was going scouting, and went into the jungle. Every PM(pajama monkey) he encountered, he killed with ease. Bodies were being found everywhere within a 10-mile radius, over a span of several weeks. He happened upon a village of friendlies, who were familiar with him, and went in for a cup of rice. Two of the older women argued which one was going to give him the rice, so they could get the hug he offered as thanks. He was sitting in front of a hut eating along with the Ancient of the village and the women. Children played as if he was no stranger. Then one of the women approached him and put a black sheet over him to make him look the same as the others. The old man said, "VC! VC!" in a whisper, so Wit got the message and never moved, except to continue eating. He watched from under the sheet, and a man dressed in a suit and two guards with him argued with the Ancient. The Ancient gave them a small bag, and one of the guards slapped him in the mouth, and each guard grabbed a boy, about 10-11 years old and left; the boys crying and fighting; the Mothers crying and wailing. Wit asked, "What happened? Who were they?" The old man said, "Tax Collector; not have enough rice or money, so they took boys to make them VC." Wit watched which trail they took when leaving, so he threw off the sheet, hugged both women quickly, hustled through the jungle, circling around to get in front of them, and let them come to him. The boys were still fighting and crying, leaving each guard occupied, trying to restrain the boys. When they reached the place where Wit was well concealed, he grabbed a guard and ripped out his throat, and by the time the other guard realized what happened, Wit had his throat ripped out. He took the money bag the Tax Collector was carrying, gave it to the boys, and motioned for them to run back to the village. The Tax Collector just stood and watched it all unfold when Wit grabbed him by his tie, close to his neck, pulled him up close, so he could look into Wit's eyes, and see the *Demon of Death*. He was frozen with fear and Wit held him long enough to take out his razor sharp knife, stuck into his abdomen on one side, cut horizontally to the other side, and then up vertically, (similar to a Jap committing Hari-Kari) and let his intestines fall out on the ground. He left him lying on the trail.

CHAPTER 50

The VC thought they were masters of terrorizing, but now they were being terrorized, and it seemed to make them nervous. Instead of dragging their bodies into the tall grass, like he formally did, Wit would sit them leaning against a tree. He wandered close to a village about daybreak, where he used to go, until they slaughtered all the villagers, and staying concealed, he observed the PMs were coming in from their night raids, and it appeared they had made the village into a headquarters; there were at least a 100 or more. He went back to the GB camp and reported it to the Captain, and suggested, "It would be a good idea if the Arty Boys (artillery) would lob a few pineapples in there and catch all the rats in their trap." He pointed out the village on a map, and further suggested, "Encircle the village with your ARVN Rangers; placed about one Klick out, at 0700; bombard the village for 15 minutes, no longer, then have your troops close the circle and kill any rats that try to escape or dive into their tunnels." The Captain suggested, "Maybe we could take a few prisoners." Wit demanded, "Kill them all!" The Captain

373

could read the bitterness on Wit's face, and replied, "Wit, you have been out there too long. You better go back to town and get yourself together." Wit said, "One last thing, and then I will go; do not let the Rangers know what the mission is. If it should leak out, it will fail." "You better stay out for a while," the Captain added, "they have doubled the reward for the Jungle Rat."

He walked to his chopper and changed into his 'Clark Kent' outfit, and then flew back to town. He thought as he flew, "The Captain is right; I feel like there is no more energy left in my body. Captain Wilson would never understand this, so the safest sanctuary I know is Doctor Susan's living quarters." He parked the chopper in the usual empty lot behind the living units and let himself in Susie's unit. He looked in the mirror, and realized, he didn't know that guy. He was hot, sweaty, stinking, and dirty, so he took a bath, and then turned the window air conditioner on low, and turned on the little tabletop Philco radio to soft music and lay down on the bed. As he was about to doze off, Hanoi Hannah came on and said, "Here is breaking news; the reward for The Jungle Rat has been doubled." "That's old news, Sweetie!" he responded, and went into a deep sleep. Susie came home and discovered him there dead to the world. She changed her clothes and began preparing supper; then went in and shook him awake, "You must have been dreaming; you kept saying 'Babs'." "Babs was the most beautiful and loving woman I ever knew, and I loved her deeply, and dream about her often," he responded. "What happened to her?" Susan questioned. He explained, "We were about to be overrun by thousands of Chinese; they were throwing everything at us; mortars and artillery and rockets, and we were shooting them down as fast as they charged, and then after it quieted down, I looked over at the treatment tent, and it had been blown to bits, and Babs too." He looked so sad telling about Babs that Susie felt sorrow for him and felt for him. He got up and put his arms around her, and squeezed her tight, kissed her on the cheek, and remarked, "You know, Susie, I love you, but it's not the same." She answered, "I know, but you have to stop squeezing me so tight, I can't breathe. Go in and wash up; supper is about ready."

While they were eating, he said, "In case you haven't heard, the reward for the Jungle Rat has doubled," and he smiled. "Why did they do that?" she asked. "What have you been up to? Haven't seen you for weeks." "I got 'em spooked!" he responded, with a gleam on his face. "I used to just kill them, but now I display their bodies in plain view so they can feel what it is like to be terrorized. I know you see gruesome stuff every day, but you don't see what I see; entire villages massacred; men, women, children bashed in the head, guts cut out and decapitated. Did I ever tell you about the baby I saved? I went into one of my friendly villages, and they had slaughtered everybody. I looked around, in case one may have survived, and I saw a pregnant woman with her guts cut out, and she was lying in a mess of intestines and afterbirth. I saw something move, and then an arm reached up, so I examined it and found the baby still alive. I pulled it out and tied the umbilical cord up near its navel with a piece of thong, and then cut off the rest of the cord. I took the baby outside and doused it in a tub of water to clean it off. Then I wrapped it in a cloth and ran as hard as I could to another village, which was about a mile away. I handed it to an old woman, and she ran out with it. I ask the old man where she took it, and he said she took it to a younger woman. I hope it survived. If I sound bitter, it's because I am. How would you feel if some barbarians slaughtered all your friends in a most brutal way, and leave them laying to rot? That's what they will do with me, or worse, if they ever catch me." She responded, "I can't imagine, and I hope I never have to see it. I don't want you to leave my unit for the next several days, at least. You have worn yourself down so bad, you can't even think straight. Lay in the bed and dream about 'Babs' and I'll prepare the meals, so all you will do is eat and sleep. That's the Doctor's orders. I will not mention to anyone that you are here; you can feel safe." "Thanks, Susie, you are a good friend," he replied.

He ate and slept for three days; the Doctor was right; he started to feel his own self again, but still had a way to go before he was strong enough to go back to the jungle. He was getting cabin fever, so he ventured to the hospital to see what was going on, Medevacs were coming and going, and he asked, "Why are the Medevacs coming here? I thought they dropped off casualties at the Naval Hospital?" "They do!" was the reply. "But they are full up and we have a little room, so they are dropping them off here, for now." He watched for a while, each 'copter unloading, and taking off again. A casualty was being unloaded that he recognized, and he said, "I know that guy; he's Big Johnnie James, how bad is he hurt?" The Nurse answered, "The report from the field hospital says he was in an explosion and he has a concussion and is in shock. They removed the large shrapnel, but he still has numerous smaller ones." "Can I talk to him?" Wit asked. "Do you think he is going to make it?" "We will do what we can," the Nurse responded. "He is incoherent, so you better give us a few days." He asked Susan to keep close tabs on him and keep him informed of Big John's progress. He prayed hard for John the next three days, and then Susan reported, "I think it's ok to talk to your friend. I think he will be alright, but his war is over."

Wit went to see John, pulled up a chair next to his bed, "Well, big guy, looks like you stuck your nose where it didn't belong." "Wit!" he remarked. "Gosh-darn, I never thought I would ever see you again." "What happened to ya?" Wit asked. "We were doing mop-up in a small town and I lifted a lid on a large metal container, and that's the last thing I remember. It must have been booby-trapped." "I never knew where you were from?" Wit asked. "I'm from Plano, Texas, born and raised," he answered. Wit got fidgety, wanting to tell him the good news, "I got nothing but good news for you, John. Your war is over, you are done. The best news is, you are going to be a daddy. Mama Myers is pregnant with your baby." "Wit is this another one of your jokes?" he responded. "I'm serious; she said you two were in love and planned to get married when your tour was over, so she didn't clean out the last time you made love. She even has a name picked out. Can you guess what it is?" Wit continued, more excited than John was. "I would guess it would be John," he answered. "No, Loren, because I was instrumental in getting you two together," Wit replied. "What if it is a girl?" John asked. "That was the first thing I asked, and she said Loreen," Wit explained. "I'm happy for you, John; now you two can go to Plano and raise a herd of little James'. I'm not going to tire you out, so I will be back tomorrow and write letters for ya, since your hands are all bandaged. We got good Doctors here, so do whatever they tell ya. The first chance you get, you might call your folks and Mama Myers and let them know you are going to be alright." He left John in good spirits and he was in good spirits himself.

He went back to see Big John the next day and he improved quite a bit and was more alert. Wit wrote letters for him to his folks in Plano and to Mama Myers. He asked, "What are your plans, John, when you get out?" "I hope I can ride and rope again," he responded. "That's all I know how to do." "You'll do that and more," Wit continued. "It'll take a few months, but you will be in good shape, and you can get out and pass ball with Little Loren, and if he gets as big as you, he might play football at University of Texas." "He won't be no dog soldier!" John exclaimed. "I'll see to that." "What ever happened to those two funny guys that were in your unit?" Wit asked. "I don't know; we got split up to support other units, and I never saw them again," John answered. "You better get some rest and I'll come back again," Wit promised. He mentioned to Susie that John seemed to be recovering pretty well. She said, "I think we can get him up tomorrow, and if doesn't have any problems, he might move to the hospital ship, and then on to the States."

Wit went back the next day and asked if they could try him in a wheelchair; he had no problem with that. Wit said, "They have a bank of telephones, so let's wheel over, and I'll put in a call to your folks; I'll hold the phone up to your ear." He wrote down the number John dictated, and he placed a person-to-person, collect call to John James, Sr in Plano, Texas. If John isn't available to take the call, Mrs. Lori James can take the call. "When they come on, tell them you are going to be fine," Wit advised. "I'm sure they are going to be excited to hear from you and have a lot to tell you. Then you can really get them excited when you tell them they are going to be Grandparents; make sure you tell them the Mother is an American, and you want her to come stay with them until you get home. Tell them she is a very smart and sweet lady, and they will love her; you are anxious to see them, and you love them." The big old tough guy teared up when he heard their voices, and naturally so, from all he had been through. They iterated that she would be welcome to come and stay and have his baby. "As soon as you can, write to Mama and tell her to pack up and go to Plano; she will be welcomed with open arms. You want her to start traveling as soon as she can because you don't want to take a chance of traveling that far being pregnant," Wit suggested. "They may be moving you to a hospital ship tomorrow, so I may not see you again, but I will continue praying for you. You and Mama start going to church and pray hard, and thank God for sparing you, so you can live a productive life." He shook John's bandaged hand, and walked out, a little choked up. He was feeling melancholy, and after supper, he told Susie all he wanted to do was hold her, and she agreed because she understood.

CHAPTER 51

Wit was lounging around, taking it easy, listening to the radio, when Hanoi Hannah stated, "Jungle Rat, they are closing in on you; why don't you give yourself up and we will treat you well." "In your dreams, Baby!" he exclaimed. He continued listening to her, and she was trying to get the Americans to stop fighting and go home to their families. She would ramble on about something that didn't make a lot of sense, but he detected she used the word, 'TET', four or five times. That must mean something, he thought, and flew out to the GB camp and asked the Captain if he knew anything about TET. "All I know it is some kind of holiday, like our Christmas," he replied. That didn't satisfy Wit, so he remembered Major Shoemaker studied Vietnamese history, and he had a small library of books, so he went to the Chapel, and started perusing the books about TET and found what he was looking for. He went to the Marine Compound and approached the Captain he was friendly with. "Do you ever listen to Hanoi Hannah?" Wit asked. "I don't pay any attention to that wind bag," the Captain replied. "Well do you know anything about TET?" Wit continued to ask.

"It's one of their holidays; that's all I know," the Captain replied. "I'm gonna tell you what it is," Wit explained. "It's the New Year in Vietnam, observed for three days after the first full moon, after January 20th. "So, who cares?" the Captain answered, unconcerned. "I'm gonna tell you what I think, Captain, and I think you better care," Wit scolded. "Hanoi Hannah is broadcasting signals about TET numerous times throughout the day, and I think something major is going to happen. I want you to radio General Westmoreland and relate what I'm telling ya; you can't risk being caught with your pants down." The Captain said, "Ok, if you are that serious about it." So, he radioed the General's Headquarters, and they waited for an answer. About a half hour later, they got the answer, and S-2 was aware of it, so the Captain said he couldn't do anything until orders came down from the top. Wit responded, "I'm going out to talk to some of the villagers and see if they heard any rumors. If I get anything solid, I'll let you know; that's only two weeks away."

He flew out to the GB camp and donned his jungle outfit, and worked his way to a friendly village, and questioned the ones that spoke the best English. In their broken English, they said there was a massive buildup of VC and NVA troops that were going to attack all the big cities and towns all at once on that specified day and wipe out the Americans. He returned to the GB camp and informed the Captain word for word and advised him to get his troops prepared. He then informed the Marine Captain word for word and advised him to alert all his units. He suggested he radio the General again and relate it to his staff word for word. He gathered up all the arms and ammunition he could lay his hands on and went to the Chapel and explained it all to the Chaplain, Captain Wilson. "We got two weeks to barricade the Chapel grounds, and prepare for an attack," he said. The Chaplain thought it didn't sound reasonable that the Communists would attack every city and large town in the entire country, all at once on the same day. He thought Wit was paranoid. The day came, and it was reported afterward that 100,000 Communist troops engaged in a bloody battle, for a mere few days, but were turned back in all locations, except the city of Hue, where they held out a couple more weeks. One of the main targets was the Da Nang Air Complex, and Wit killed his share when they approached the Chapel grounds in an effort to reach the air strip. The Communists lost 50,000 men, overall, but it was a strategic psychological accomplishment for them. U.S. forces knocked out the Communist forces decisively, though the American public was told the opposite by the media; it was one of the most dominating, one-sided victories in U.S. history. It was never mentioned if Wit's information was instrumental in the Allied success.

A year later there was an extremely bloody battle about 75 miles west of Da Nang, with many casualties, on Ap Bia Mountain, nicknamed 'Hamburger Hill', where the Air Force pounded the NVA with bombs and napalm, while artillery and helicopter gunships hammered them. It was finally taken after brutal bunker by bunker hand-to-hand combat. It was reported sometime later, after the bloody victory, they were ordered to walk away and leave it. The same thing at Khe Sanh, more than a year earlier, where a worthless mountain top defended for five months by the Marines, and finally linked up by the Army, survived a siege attempt by two NVA divisions. After it was over, they were ordered to walk off the mountain. *'A politician's war'*. The Air Force made routine bombings of the Ho-Chi-Minh-Trail, in an effort to slow down the movement of NVA equipment and arms, transporting from Hanoi, to resupply the Communist's fighting forces. When the scouting planes flew over at night, they could see torches along the trail, used but the people, repairing the damage so the movement could proceed again. Any person, men, women, or child, capable of using a shovel or any kind of digging tool were out there working all night to re-open the trail. Like the man said, "You can defeat the army, but you can't defeat the people."

Wit was sitting with Susie eating supper and listening to music on her little Philco radio, when Hanoi Hannah came on and said she had an announcement for the Jungle Rat, "Thanks for murdering the Tax Collector for us; he was a traitor and needed killing. We want to reward you! We will give you a small city and make you a king over it, and you can have all the beautiful girls you want, a different one each day." "Did you kill a Tax Collector?" Susie asked. "Yeah, I killed the no-good snake, and his two body-guards. The villagers didn't have enough money or rice, so they took two young boys for the payment. The boys were scared and crying, and the Mothers were crying, and when I rescued the boys, I gave them the money bag and sent them running back to the village. I was so incensed, I pulled him up close so he could see the *Demon of Death*, I then cut his guts out, and let them spill on the trail, and then let him fall into his own filth." Susie couldn't believe what she was hearing; this kind loving man seemed to kill for his own enjoyment; and was proud of himself. "Just giving them a dose of their own medicine," he added. "I bet you can't even imagine what they would do to you if they ever got their hands on ya; I can because I've seen it."

Hanoi Hannah said the trap was closing in on the Jungle Rat, but she was too stupid to know that she was telling him more fighters were moving into the area where he had been killing, and he had noticed it was becoming more congested with PMs, so he decided to let them have the area and he would move to a new area. He went to the Marine Compound to learn from the Captain where other LZs or FSBs were located. Something had changed; the smart mouth Lieutenant was gone and replaced by a BAM (broad assed marine-no disrespect intended), a lady Marine Lieutenant. The Captain introduced her as Lieutenant Robinson and him as Wit, in the Chaplain's Service. Wit, being the ever friendly Wit, "What do they call you, Robbie?" She looked very attractive in her camo-utilities and boots; hair tied in a bun. She never smiled and presented a mean demeaner, "You call me Lieutenant Robinson!" Wit thought, "Wow, excuse me!" He got to the point of his visit, and asked, "Will you show me where an LZ or FSB is located, if you have one, that is about 50-60 Klicks to the south. It is getting hot where I've been working, and I want to move into a new area." The Captain responded, "We have one that maybe you could help us out, LZ Eclipse. They have held off charge after charge, and have taken considerable casualties, and we had to replace them with green Marines. Lieutenant, show him on the map where the LZ is located." "Why should I help an Army Chaplain?" she replied, nastily. That irritated the Captain, because he knew of Wit's exploits and how he has helped them in the past. "Lieutenant, I said show him LZ Eclipse. That's an order!" the Captain demanded. Wow! She didn't like that a little bit, but she never hesitated, and pointed to the LZ location on the map.

He flew to the LZ and parked on the back side, as usual, and went to talk to the Platoon Sergeant, whom he had met previously. "Understand you got your hands full," Wit said. "We sure have," the Sergeant remarked, "they keep coming at us, but we've been able to hold them off; for how much longer, I don't know. They keep sending me green replacements, and they haven't gotten a handle on things yet." Just then four mortars came in and everybody scrambled for cover. "Here they come again," the Sergeant remarked, "they throw in a few shells, and then the shooting begins." Wit grabbed an M-14, set the selector on semi-automatic, and starting shooting from the hip, his standard procedure. He picked them off as fast as they showed themselves; emptied the magazine, reloaded and continued until they got the picture; they weren't making any progress, and faded back into the jungle. The Sergeant remarked, "I don't know where you learned to shoot like that; you made every shot count; they may not be back for a while." Wit said, "What I want to do is go into the jungle and kill them one at a time and give them something to worry about. That may discourage them enough to give you a break. I'll grab 'em and kill them while they are taking a dump." One of the Greenies commented, "That would be cruel and unusual punishment." Wit responded, "You'll think cruel when one of them sticks an AK-47 up your butt and gives you a lead enema." He went to the chopper and put on his jungle outfit. The Gooks in this area were not familiar with the Jungle Rat, and he had a field day slaying them one at a time, propping their bodies against a tree and disabling their rifles. Now they were getting spooked, like those in his former areas. He went back to his chopper and put on his 'Clark Kent' outfit; he noticed the shrapnel from the mortars had pierced holes in his chopper, but not where they were of any concern; and flew back to the Chapel. Word got back to the Compound how he saved the day. He went to the hospital, met Susie and she invited him to supper. He described the new Lady Marine to Susie, and said she had a hateful and nasty attitude.

Wit relaxed for a few days; ate good and napped; made his regular visits to the hospital; ran into Susie and she said she needed a massage and therapy, and she offered to reciprocate. Captain Wilson asked him to go the Commissary and pick up a few provisions and gave him a list. While he was cruising through, looking for the items on the list, he saw a young lady he wasn't sure he recognized. "Hi, Wit, finding everything you need?" she asked. She was the Marine Lieutenant, but she didn't look the same; she wore shorts and a blouse and tennis shoes, and her hair hung down on her shoulders; looked every bit like a true American girl. "Lieutenant Robinson, I didn't recognize you," he remarked. She was all smiles and pleasant, and said, "You can call me, Robbie, except when I am in uniform." Now she appeared charming and attractive, and for sure was well conditioned and built accordingly; not like the stiff necked Marine he met earlier. "I want to apologize for the manner in which I spoke to you the first time we met. Can I buy you a drink?" "I don't drink alcohol, but you can buy me a Coke," he responded. "Let's go to the diner and get something to eat." He finished shopping and loaded it all into his Jeep, hoping it wouldn't get stolen, and they drove to the diner, and selected a booth. "I hear their chili here is good and I like good chili," he remarked. So, he ordered a bowl of chili with beans and onions and cheese on top, with extra crackers, and a Coke. She ordered the same. To make conversation, he asked, "Where are you from, Robbie? Are you married or single or engaged?" She responded, "I am from Seattle, Washington and I am engaged to a Gunny Sergeant at Camp Pendleton,

California. We haven't seen each other in over six months; he's a ladies-man and probably got another woman by now," She spoke like it didn't matter, one way or the other.

While they waited to be served, two other ladies approached, Susie and Betty, "Hey, Wit, who's your new friend?" Susie asked, in a slightly jealous tone. "Come on and join us," Wit invited, so he and Robbie scooted over to make room. "This is Marine Lieutenant Robinson, and these two ladies are Doctors Susan McElroy and Betty West, from Da Nang General. They are not just good, but they are the best Doctors in Vietnam, and they are Army." He wanted to impress on Robbie you could be good and not be a Marine. The Doctors ordered their food. "Oh, is this the Marine Lieutenant you were telling me about?" Susie questioned. Wit had his fingers crossed that she wouldn't repeat anything that he said. Betty remarked, "Are you new here? Haven't seen you before." "Yeah, flew in a few weeks ago," she answered, "still learning where everything is. Ran into Wit in the Commissary and offered to apologize for being so nasty to him and buy him a Coke." Susie looked at her and concluded she was nothing like he described. "What will you be doing here?" Betty asked. "We don't have many women here except those that work in the medical field." "I'm a trained combat Marine and I hope to get my own Platoon," she explained. "I'm anxious to get out and show that women can do anything a man can do." Wit was listening and thought, "Ain't no way she will survive out there; she is greener than those kids he saw at LZ Eclipse. If they let her go out to fight, they have totally lost their minds; what has this war come to?"

After they ate, the Doctors excused themselves because they had an early shift the next morning. Robbie invited, "We have nice decent quarters; got everything we need. You want to check it out?" "Yeah, I can do that; is it close by?" he asked. They drove the Jeep and parked in a parking space in front of her unit; it was similar in every way to Susie's. "You mind if I have a drink?" she asked. "Would you like something?" "No, I'm good; you do what you want; it's your place," he replied. She mixed a drink and gulped it down, and then mixed another, and gulped it down. "I have a few records if you want to listen to some music. Do you like Elvis Presley?" she asked. "Some of his stuff I like alright, like 'Are You Lonesome Tonight', but I don't care for Hound Dog or Jailhouse Rock, and stuff like that; I like soft romantic music," he responded. "Do you mind if I put on my pajamas?" she asked. "Uh Oh," he thought, "is PJ-101 a required subject these days? She will put on her PJs and they will dance a little and end up in the sack; seems like a standard routine." He wanted to learn a little about her first, so he asked, "How did you happen to get into the Marine Corp?" She was feeling her drinks and started telling her personal secrets, "When I was 16, me and a bunch of my friends partied with the boys, and I got pregnant. I was in a car with them when we had a wreck and I lost my baby. It was quite a shock, so I settled down until I graduated from high school. I went to college under the Marine ROTC Program, and graduated a Lieutenant. I met my fiancé when I went through their boot camp afterwards but wanted something more exciting, so I signed up for duty here in Vietnam. I learned my lesson about getting pregnant, so now I am on the pill, and don't worry about it. What about you?"

He responded, "After Korea, I went home and met a girl that I thought I loved, and got married, and after six months I caught her with another man, and knew I was not cut out for civilian life anymore, so I re-enlisted for six years if they guaranteed me Helicopter Pilot Training. I gave her everything, and never looked back. I don't write or call or just don't care. I guess I'm still married; haven't heard anything otherwise." She mixed another drink and gulped it down, and said, "I drink to forget the bad things that have happened in my life, and hope to find something better. It seems to take off the edge. Would you like to dance?" She was feeling it now, and was doing a seductive dance that got WT excited, and she felt it, and asked, "Would you make love to me? I need it!" So, they hit the sack just like it is specified in PJ-101.

CHAPTER 52

A week later, Wit decided to go harass the Gooks, so he went to the Marine Compound to get directions to a new area. He entered and never saw Robbie, and asked the Captain, "Is Robbie still around?" "You better not let her hear you call her that," he remarked, "we had a Platoon Leader get injured, so she insisted on going out and taking over that Platoon." That incensed Wit, and he hit the ceiling, "What? Are you crazy? You sent a girl out to get killed?" "She's a trained Combat Marine," the Captain replied. "She's not trained for something like that! I can't believe you did something as stupid as that," Wit continued. "Watch your mouth, Whitson; you don't talk to me like that!" the Captain remarked, in his own defense. "Show me where she is; I got to go get her out of there before she gets killed, if she's not killed already!" Wit responded, ignoring the Captain's threats. "She is at the LZ about three miles south of Eclipse," The Captain responded. "If she is killed, it's on you Captain!" Wit exclaimed, as he stormed out the door. He flew at full throttle to get to the LZ, and landed at the back edge, like always. A fierce battle was going on, and Robbie was standing out shouting orders. He started running toward her, and she suddenly went down with a bullet in her upper chest and one in her hip. He grabbed an M-14 and emptied the magazine picking off the Gooks as they showed themselves. He checked Robbie and she was losing a lot of blood, so he yelled to one of the men to help him load her into his chopper. He took off and again went at full throttle to Da Nang General, where he landed at the entrance to the Emergency Room. Two Aids saw him come in and ran out with a gurney, and helped unload her, and wheeled her into the hospital. Betty happened to be close by, so she took the front of the gurney and wheeled it directly into the Operating Room. Susie, becoming aware of the commotion, came out and found Wit, fit to be tied. "I'm going over and really give that Captain a piece of my mind. That idiot let that girl go out and try to lead a Platoon in a battle for survival against those murdering Gooks." Susie grabbed him by his jump suit lapel, and yelled at him, "Get ahold of yourself; what's the matter with you, acting like this? You can't go do battle with the Marine Corp? Just sit down and shut up and think what you are doing. I'll call the Compound and tell them what happened, and she is here. You know we will do our best to save her." He respected Susie, and took a deep breath, and sat down to wait till they examined Robbie; and he prayed hard for her.

After a couple hours of constant prayer, Susie came out, and reported, "We got the bullet out of her chest and hip. She is still in shock and lost a lot of blood, so I think once she gets a transfusion, she will start to recover. You can't do anymore here today, so go to my place and try to relax and get some rest; I'll be home later and give you a massage to soothe your jangled nerves; you have had a trying day." Boy, did he! He never got worked up like that before, with the war being bad enough, some idiot pulls a stunt like that. Just like the black Nurse he rescued; some nincompoop sent her out to give shots; how stupid can they get? He stayed at Susie's all night and went in with her the next morning to check on Robbie to see if she progressed any overnight. She still was not awake, so he prayed some more, and then went to the Chapel to report his disgust with Captain Wilson. He went back the next day and she was awake, but still weak. She had asked how she got there, and they told her Wit went out and rescued her and rushed her in, otherwise she would have died. When she saw him, she got tears in her eyes, but managed to mutter, "Thank you!" He held her hand and prayed with her until she went back to sleep, and then he thanked God for saving her. The Nurses standing there got emotional and wiped tears from their own eyes.

They continued giving her fluids, and being young and healthy, she showed signs of a quick recovery. Susie said, "If she continues recovering at this rate, she will be transferred to the hospital ship in a couple days, and then on home." Wit went to see her one last time, and prayed with her, and said, "Well, Marine, you showed 'em! Now you have something to tell your Grandkids about; how you stood out there with the men and battled those Commie Gooks. Seattle should have a parade for ya, but they won't, because those anti-war draft dodgers will treat you like dirt; but we know, don't we? I told you we had the two best Doctors in Vietnam, and you should thank them because they made an extra effort to pull you through. Start going to church and thank God every day for giving you a new lease on life." He kissed her and wished her good luck for the rest of her life. Tears were running down her face when he walked off, never to see him again, but forever to remember him.

It took him a couple weeks to get over that episode, which in his opinion, should never have happened. Susie talked to him at every opportunity to get him back on track and listening and praying to the troubled vets at the hospital, added relief to his troubled mind. Eventually, he decided it was time to get back in the game, so he made a visit to the Marine Compound, but he thought it best not to mention anything to the Captain. There were new faces at the Compound, a Major and a fresh-faced Lieutenant. He introduced himself, "I am Chief Warrant Officer Loren Whitson, assigned to the Chaplain's Service," "I'm Lieutenant Gerald Coyle and this is Major Michael Alcorn," the Lieutenant responded. "Whitson! Whitson! Whitson! That name sounds familiar to me," the Major followed. "That's the name of the chopper pilot that rescued Lieutenant Robinson," the Lieutenant volunteered. "Yeah, yeah, was that you?" the Major asked. "That would be me!" Wit remarked. "In my opinion, that incident should have never happened, and if I might be so bold to say, with all due respect, it was totally stupid, with all due respect, sir." "The Marine Corp thought so, too; that's why the Captain was demoted to Lieutenant and transferred to a combat unit," the Major remarked. "What name do you go by?" "Mostly Wit, but also referred to as The Chopper Chaplain," Wit replied. The Major went to the filing cabinet and pulled Wit's file, leafed through it briefly, and remarked, "My gosh, Wit, you have been active, even back to the days of Korea. Says here that there is a highly classified document in Washington, sealed by the President. You want to tell me about that?" the Major questioned. "Sorry, sir, I took a vow never to reveal anything about that," Wit replied. "Well, I am going to put you in for an accommodation for the brave act rescuing Lieutenant Robinson," the Major added. "Please don't!" Wit begged. "Anything like that can get me killed. Hanoi Hannah would be in her glory if anything is revealed of what I do privately, and I expect it to remain confidential in this room, I am the #1 most wanted man in Vietnam, with a huge reward for my head or capture. Very few people know it, but I am known as the Jungle Rat; I roam the jungle annihilating Gooks, and I enjoy keeping them spooked and beat them at their own game. The areas where I have been operating is becoming congested because they have an all-out mission to get me, so I started moving to new areas, which is why I am here. I want you to show me an LZ or FSB where I can park my chopper, so I can go and do my work." "Your secret is safe here, Wit," Major Alcorn promised. "We have a Fire Base that is constantly under attack, trying to disable our artillery, and if you could do something to slow down those attacks, that would be most helpful giving our guys a chance to take a breather."

Wit flew out to the Fire Base, and found the men were truly exhausted from constant attacks from the Gooks. While he was talking with the Master Sergeant, who was trying to keep it all together, the Gooks lobbed in a few mortars, and then charged. Wit did his usual thing, grabbing an M-14 and picking them off as fast as he could pull the trigger, and then reloading a new magazine, continued knocking them down. The Marines were spraying bullets on automatic fire and machine guns. They beat the Gooks back and they retreated into the jungle. "Glad you showed up," the Sergeant remarked. "I think we killed enough of them this time it may be a while for them to return again. I've never seen shooting like that; where did you learn to do that?" "I practiced with the Green Beret before the war started," he answered. "I think we have enough time to break out a little chow and get a little rest; you want to join us?" the Sergeant asked. "Yeah, I'll break bread with ya," Wit accepted. The men welcomed the chance to eat their C-Rats in peace and drink some coffee and took turns getting a brief snooze. Wit said, "I'm going into the jungle and kill a few of the rats in their nests so that should give you a little more down time; be sure all your guns are reloaded and ready so you ain't caught with your pants down."

He went to his chopper and donned his jungle attire; warned them not to shoot him by mistake and entered the jungle. He thought from the number that attacked, he would see a lot of movement, but he never saw anything. He searched and finally found them; they were taking a *Gook Siesta*. Why not, they prowled all night and fought a battle all morning, and the little PMs were tired. He muttered to himself, "I'll help the little darlings sleep sound." He ripped the throat out of one, propped him against a tree; disabled his rifle, and said, "Sweet dreams, Gook baby." He ripped another and repeated propping him against a tree, and said, "Good night, don't let the lice bite." He repeated on another one, and said, "Lullaby and good night." He repeated on another one, and said, "Don't wet the bed, Mama will spank ya." He was enjoying himself killing a great number of them. Darkness was approaching, so he returned to the Fire Base and told the Sergeant he should have a restful night; he took the fight out of most of the Gooks. He went to his chopper and changed into his 'Clark Kent' outfit, wished them all luck, and flew back to the Chapel. A couple days later, while enjoying supper, and the air conditioning, with Susie, Hanoi Hannah came on the radio and announced,

Jungle Rat has hit below the belt this time, killing our innocent young men while they slept. He just smiled, and remarked, "I would like to get my hands on that pig; I would do with her the same as I did with the Tax Collector." Susie acted surprised to hear that, "You would kill a woman?" "When you going to wake up, Susie?" he responded, "That woman would slaughter you in a heartbeat, just like thousands of others wanting to kill Americans." [side note: the real name of *Hanoi Hannah* was Trinh Thi Ngo, and she was born in Hanoi in 1931. After the war, she moved to Ho Chi Minh City, formerly Saigon, with her husband, an Army officer. Her son escaped Vietnam in 1973 during the evacuation and ended up in San Francisco.]

Several weeks later, the Chaplain asked Wit to pick up a few things at the Commissary, so while he was sauntering up the aisles, he heard a familiar voice, "Hey, you Chopper Hillbilly!" He turned around to see who it was, "Hap and Dilly, did they run you two out of Bavaria?" he remarked. "Yeah, they started grabbing all the trained mechanics to come to this sauna, and here we are." Hap replied. "Where you stationed at?" Wit questioned. "We got it made; we're on a ship anchored about a mile off-shore," Dilly bragged. "A ship?" Wit asked. "I ain't never heard of no ship." "You ever hear of the USNS Corpus Christi Bay?" Hap explained, "We are a floating aircraft station with 350 of us keeping the aircraft flying. They don't have to send for parts or ship components back to the States because we are setup to make anything they need in our machine shop. They reported that we repaired 20,000 aircraft components last month and saved millions of dollars. We have machinists, aircraft mechanics, air-frame mechanics, great navy cooks, and air conditioning. Do you still have your own chopper?" "Yeah, and it is way overdue for maintenance, and got a bunch of holes in it. The Airmen mechanics are so overworked, they don't have time to mess with my little old chopper, "Wit complained. "First chance you get, fly over, and we can service it while you are eating a good Navy meal," Dilly offered, "and we got guys that'll patch those holes before you down the second cup of coffee." "I'm gonna take you up on that," Wit replied. "Come on and I'll treat you to a milk shake," "No thanks, we're heading to a bar," Hap added. "Take my advice and don't go anywhere alone, or you will end up in an alley with a knife in your back," Wit advised. "Every Vietnamese you see is not necessarily friendly, and you don't know the difference from the good guys and the bad guys. The girls are mostly teenagers that left their villages to sell their bodies to the Americans with all the money. Be careful with them, Dilly, they will give you a good case of a 'runny nose'. I want to stress the most important thing, do not, and I mean do not, mention that you have anything to do with helicopters; don't even use the terms pertaining to 'copters because there is a reward out for the head, or capture of pilots or gunners or anybody that works with 'em. If you have too much to drink and are blabbing, be aware that those little honeys will report it back to their Gook buddies; there are spies everywhere; and we don't have a Drunk Mobile here to take you back." "They have a fleet of four Drunk Mobiles back at Straubing, and they are marked 'Wit Drunk Mobile 1,2,3,4', so you left your mark for all to remember you started it all," Hap remarked. Wit later flew out to the ship, and they gave his little chopper a real work-over, holes and all, and he ate a great meal, and he thanked his friends who he always appreciated.

CHAPTER 53

After President Nixon took office in 1969, the long and tenuous discussions lasting up to four years to end the American presence in Vietnam, finally came to an end January 27, 1973 following 12 days of serious negotiations; known as **'THE PARIS PEACE ACCORDS'.** Wit heard about it and went to the Marine Compound to discuss with Major Alcorn his thoughts about what happens now. The Major's opinion was, "It was about time because the U.S. ground forces up to that point had been sidelined with deteriorating morale and gradually withdrew to coastal regions, not partaking in offensive operations or much direct combat for the preceding two-year period. Direct U.S. military intervention has ended. The treaty would, in effect, remove all remaining U.S. forces, including air and naval forces in exchange for the release of Hanoi's POWs. They say we got 60 days to get our military out; we will evacuate all the top-ranking officers first. Of course, it most likely will take a couple years to get everybody out, and we will assist that effort." "I want you to do me a favor," Wit requested, "I want you to get Chaplain Wilson on the very first plane leaving the country. I don't think he really understands the gravity of the situation, and I want to be certain he is safe." "What are you going to do, Wit?" the Major asked. "I'm going to help with the evacuation of the hospital, and then I am going to Saigon to lend a hand," he responded. "Drive him here early tomorrow morning, and I'll see that he gets out," the Major promised.

Wit went to the Chapel and informed Captain Wilson of how desperate things were going to become, and very quickly. "Major Alcorn, of the Marine Compound, said all ranking officers must evacuate, and he wants you to be at the Compound early tomorrow morning, and he will see that you get an early flight out," Wit explained. "Pack a small bag with all your personal things in it along with what clothing you will need, like your uniform; room will be tight, so you can't take everything. Say goodbye to the Dinks. I am staying to help with the evacuation of the hospital, and then I will go to Saigon to help out; I will try to get them out if I can, and don't forget your personnel file." He drove the Chaplain to the Compound, and they exchanged pleasantries, and a sorrowful goodbye, because chances were, they would never meet again. He drove to the hospital and found Susie a nervous wreck. "I'm scared, Wit," she stated, "I want you to hold me." "You can't be scared now," he assured her, "you got a big job ahead of you, evacuating all these patients; you got to stay focused. Has anyone said how to proceed?" "I don't think anybody really knows," she said. "One officer said the walking wounded would probably fly out somewhere, maybe to the Philippines. Hospital ships are arriving all along the coast, and the most critical patients will be transported to them, and where they sail to, I have no idea. The rest of them, along with the hospital personnel will likely be flown to the big carriers. They asked for volunteers to go to Saigon to help-out, and me and Betty volunteered. It will take a considerable amount of time, so I want you to come to my place and make love one more time, tonight." He agreed, and they did, and then she said, "I think it would be meaningful if you really gave Betty a good loving too, one last time."

He went to Betty's unit the next night, and they had a little something to eat. He said, "You know, Betty, we have known each other for a good 20 years, since Korea and up to now. Fate has a strange way of rearing its ugly head. I was messed up back then and working with you helped me somewhat. If I had known how you felt about me, things might have turned out different. We might have gotten serious and married and had a family, and who knows what all. But I went home, and all my friends had moved on to other interests, so I found new friends, met the girl I married, thinking I loved her till I found out she liked a variety of men. We were as poor as a church mouse, and we owed on everything, so I gave it all to her, enlisted for 6 years, and never looked back; no writing or phones calls or contact of any kind. You have always been very beautiful, and still are, with a good heart, and I thought some lucky guy would grab you and take you out of circulation. When I saw you here, it was almost a shock, because I never thought you would ever get back into this game. So now we are separating again, and this time maybe for good." "Wit, I cannot describe how miserable I feel for messing up and acting like a jealous fool." she remarked. "We have wasted a lot of valuable time when we could have been enjoying each other's company, like you and Susie, and I will regret it the rest of my life. I want you to make love to me and I want it all, and I don't want to stop till we can't go anymore. I have always been at the forefront helping other people, but now they can wait." So that's what they did, and it was monumental; most definitely something worth remembering.

After the evacuation of the hospital, Wit received a report that up to a million people, refugees and soldiers, were on their way to storm Da Nang to escape certain death, so he rushed back to the Chapel, knowing he better get out while the gettin' was good. He packed his bag and took his file from the cabinet and set them by the door. He started pulling all the files from the cabinet and piled them in the middle of the floor of the Chapel. Mickey came in crying, and Wit asked him, "Why are you crying? Where are your Mom and Dad?" He sobbed as he answered, "They killed them. Will you take care of me, Wit?" "We don't have time to cry now, Mickey, we got to get out of here. Go take the pillow out of the pillowcase on your bed and put your favorite clothes in it and bring it here. Run!" Wit directed. He found Mickey's file and when Mickey returned, he instructed him to take the files and bags by the door and put them into his chopper. He had stored extra cans of gasoline for an emergency, so he topped off the tank, loaded all he thought he needed to get to Saigon, took the rest into the Chapel and poured it on everything that would burn. He then set the Chapel on fire and he and Mickey jumped in the chopper and lifted off. He looked back and the Chapel was a ball of fire, and as he passed by the Naval Hospital, it was billowing smoke, and he told Mickey, "That's two buildings them Gooks ain't gonna make use of."

The Americans honored the treaty, but the Communists didn't; they got a 'get out of jail free card'. It was reported they had 30 divisions, up to 300,000 troops, well positioned in the south, with every intention of continuing the war, and only the South Vietnamese Army was left to try and stop them. They smelled victory, and they were determined that Vietnam was going to be one country, and it was going to be theirs. People were panic-stricken and tried to escape, but tens of thousands of refugees were slaughtered in Cambodia. Hundreds of thousands swarmed on Da Nang, trying to flee the onslaught, using every means possible. They overloaded every boat of every size and ended up drowning thousands of people. CBS News filmed the last airliner to leave Da Nang, and it was total chaos. As soon as it landed, the people stormed it on trucks, cars, motorcycles, bicycles and running to try and catch it to get on. The so-called top of the line good guys pushed their wives and kids and families out of the way and left them on the airstrip, while they crammed inside, 4-5 in a seat, some were hanging onto the landing gears and ladders, while in flight, and the cargo hold was jammed full. When it landed in Saigon, it was unbelievable how many unloaded from that plane.

The little chopper landed inside the Embassy Compound fence; with full intention of it not being damaged by desperate refugees. Wit asked the first MP he came to if any group was organizing orphans for evacuation to the States. The MP pointed and said, "See those two Nuns standing in front of that large tent?" "I don't see any Nuns!" Wit exclaimed. "Those two women standing down there are Nuns; the older one is the Mother Superior, and they really got their hands full," he responded. "They don't have Penguin Habits on like Nuns," Wit remarked. "Where you been, man? How long has it been since you were in the States?" the MP questioned. "They've changed all the rules; they even go to Mass on Saturday night."

I guess it's been about 18 years since I left," Wit answered, "I'll go down and talk to them; thanks for your help."

"I am Chief Warrant Officer Loren Whitson, more commonly called Wit, and this fine little gentleman is, Mickey," Wit introduced. The older lady said, "I am Mother Superior Margaret, and you can call me Peggy; this is Sister Cassandra, and you can call her Candy." Mickey stuck his hand out to Candy, and said, "Wassup, Candy?" That sparked a laugh from the Nuns. "Glory be!" Peggy remarked. "So now that we know each other, what can I do for ya? Are you volunteering to help?" "No, I understand you have your hands full, and I am going to do more than that; but first we have to make a deal," Wit began. "I am in the Chaplain's Service and I held the hand of this boy's Mother while he was being delivered, about 11 years ago. His parents worked in the Chapel, so he was raised there, pretty much being around adults most of his life. Our Chaplain, being a very studious man, taught Mickey from the time he was born to be an American. He speaks English better than I do, and being 100% Vietnamese, speaks that as well. His parents were killed before we left Da Nang. I can see you seem to be struggling with the language in trying to organize these Vietnamese orphans, and Mickey would be a perfect interpreter, and make your lives a whole lot easier. The deal I want you to agree to is, to guarantee that you will take him to America and find a good, and I mean good, family to adopt him and raise him in a loving home. Needless to say, he is special." Peggy responded, "I have prayed that the Lord help us, and it sounds like he heard my prayer. Of course, I will find him a good home in America. We are getting nowhere registering these orphans, and like you said, we don't understand the language fully, and that would be a Godsend if he could help us. We have been given 30 more days to get a maximum number of 200 orphans ready for evacuation, after the ship arrives. It breaks my heart, because as you can see, there are thousands and I can't take them all, so we had to think rationally, and decided to take ages 9-11, 100 girls and 100 boys. We don't have the personnel to take care of the smaller ones, and the older ones can most likely fend for themselves. There are people from the Embassy that come and lend a hand when they can, and that has been a tremendous help. The USO (United Service Organization) have been good about seeing we are fed, and our personal needs taken care of." "I have two Doctor friends here, if I can find them; it will be like finding a needle in a haystack, and maybe they could check the kids to make sure they don't carry diseases," Wit offered. "The first thing I would suggest, is you delouse them. Soon! If you carry disease or lice on that ship, the sailors would throw you all overboard. Do you know where the medical or hospital area is?" She described where he could find the area. He said, "I am going to leave Mickey here, so keep a close eye on him, and I'll explain to him how important his job is, and to do everything you ask." "Do you have a place to stay?" she asked. "No, I can sleep in my helicopter if I have too," he replied. "No, you come back here and share supper with us, and we can sleep in shifts; it's too hectic to sleep anyhow, so we only sleep in spurts," she offered.

He found Susie and Betty and they were hot, tired, and miserable, but working hard doing their job. They gave him a hug, and he explained about leaving Da Nang, burning down the Chapel, Mickey's parents getting killed, and bringing him here to get him into an orphanage, and Mickey's duties as an interpreter for the two Nuns, Mother Superior and Sister. He explained there were 200 kids that were destined for evacuation, should be checked out for diseases or any other abnormalities, and if they could find time, it would be very appreciated, and important. "Do you have places to stay?" he asked. "Yeah, we are in a large room separated by a curtain, and we share it with two lady Marines. It's hard to sleep sometimes because they are Lesbians, and ooh and ah all night, making love on their side of the curtain," Susie responded. "But I guess when you get tired enough, you can sleep through anything." He described to them the location of the Nuns' tent, and how they offered to share their supper and tent to sleep, so he bid them farewell and returned to the orphan area.

The USO provided pre-prepared meals; Mother Superior invited him to sit and eat. "I need to sit down for a while; my legs are giving out," she remarked. "I'm getting to old for this stuff." "You look like you are in good shape," Wit commented. "I'm going to be seventy," she replied, "and it's starting to tell on me. I think Mickey is going to be a great help; he is already communicating with the other kids, and that is what we needed. Thank you so much for bringing him to us." "I am giving you his file; it is a history of everything he ever did, so guard it closely; it is his only available identity," Wit offered. "It came to me, after you left that I have heard your name before. I know who you are, Wit," Peggy commented. "How could you know me; we have never met," Wit replied. "Do you know an old Chaplain by the name of Mike Malloy?" she asked. "Yes, he was one of the best friends I ever had; he was like a Father to me," Wit replied. "How do you know him?" "After they retired him, he lectured at different schools, and he came to our school. He talked about Loren Whitson in Korea who did things that any ordinary man never did, to his knowledge. He believed he had a *Demon* inside of him that possessed him and provided him protection. Reports from the battlefield stated that he seemed to have a shield around him that prevented him from being shot or wounded. He told how you prayed for the dying man until he took his last breath; how you put so much into your prayer, that it sapped all your strength and your knees buckled when you tried to stand." "Peggy, you know better than I do that there are a large number of people that don't know how to pray, or don't know God," Wit replied. "I never did anything for fame or glory, but if I could pray a man's soul into Heaven, then I was satisfied I did my job. You may not believe it, but a few times I prayed for a man and he closed his eyes and I thought he died, but he opened his eyes and started talking to me. I called the Medical Team and told them that the man wasn't dying but needed treatment. How long he lived, I don't know because I never saw him again; did the Lord give him a second chance? Father Mike said it would drive me crazy if I took each man's dying to heart; just do my best and be satisfied." "The Lord does things that man can never explain! He kept a running record of all your exploits," she explained. "I didn't know that!" he remarked. "What happened to the records?" Wit asked. "I wasn't aware of anything like that." "I understand they are sealed with other highly classified information in Washington," she answered. "He passed away about five years ago. He felt the same about you as you did him; a very fine man. He said in all his years he never got emotional over anyone, but he got all choked up when you left, and he continued to pray that the *Demon* would exit your body."

CHAPTER 54

Wit worked with the Nuns and the orphans until they were evacuated. He then helped Susie and Betty with the injured while they were being evacuated. Then the pressure was on; 36,000 crack NVA fanatics backed by a 100 Soviet made tanks rolled toward Saigon, which was ripe for the taking. 5000 ragtag South Vietnamese troops and a handful of Advisors tried to hold them off, but the effort was futile without the U.S. fire power to assist them. The final evacuation order, named Frequent Wind, was issued for April 29 & 30, 1975. The last two Marines were killed at Tan Son Nhut Air Base on the 29th in a rocket attack. The last helicopter, a Boeing Vertol CH-47 Chinook lifted off from the Embassy on the 30th, enrouted to the USS Hancock, anchored 17 Nautical miles from Saigon, with the last Americans aboard, and it was videoed and broadcast all over the world, marking the end of the Vietnam War, or America's War. But what they didn't mention was a little Bell UH-1H helicopter with 3 passengers aboard, with the markings painted on it 'CHOPPER CHAPLAIN', struggling to get to the Hancock. It sputtered and spit fluids and was full of bullet holes and the passengers prayed hard that it would make it to the carrier deck. It landed safely and two Army Doctors, Major Susan McElroy and Captain Betty West, threw their meager little bags out, and the pilot, CWO4 Loren Whitson, followed. The Seamen were pushing all the helicopters overboard to make room for the winged aircraft to land, and the little Bell was no exception. One Seaman said, "Mister, you got the last chug out of that old girl," as they pushed her over into the sea.

They walked across the deck where hundreds of Americans and refugees were lingering. Wit saw a smiling Marine Colonel approaching, and he said, "Well, Wit, we survived another war," and they shook hands while the ladies were observing. Wit introduced them and said, "These are the two finest Doctors in the entire US Army, bar none, Major Susan McElroy and Captain Betty West, and this is Colonel Chris Clark. We go back all the way to Korea. He was only a shave-tail Lieutenant back then. Have you had enough, Colonel?" "Yes!" he said. "I've put in over 25 years in the Marine Corp, and I am now finished." While they were standing and talking, Wit noticed a suspicious Vietnamese man among the refugees, working his way in a circle through the crowd. He watched him closely, with concern, and when he got closer, he noticed he was holding a knife along the side of his leg. Wit told the three he was talking to, to step back a few steps. The man lunged at him with his knife, and Wit spun him around and snapped his neck, killing him instantly, and the man dropped the knife on the deck. As Wit dragged him by his hair to the edge of the deck to throw him overboard, Susan smiled and remarked, "Jungle Rat!" The Colonel popped his eyes toward Susan, and she nodded toward Wit. He had heard many stories about the Jungle Rat, but never associated him with the Chopper Chaplain. Wit returned and remarked, "I guess my war ain't over yet; I can spot 'em a mile away." He picked up the knife and handed it to the Colonel, and said, "Take this home and frame it and hang it on your wall so it will be a conversation piece for all your anti-war friends. When you get home in Minnesota, you hug Evelyn and the kids every day; they have sacrificed plenty while you were away, and now it is time for you to pay them back. You two ladies team up and go to some small mid-western, quiet little town, and open your own practice. If you are lucky, you might find some old Doctor wanting to retire and you can take over his practice. Join the church and meet up with some of the prominent people of the town and your practice will take off. What do you think, Colonel?" "Works for me!" he replied. "What are you going to do, Wit?" Betty asked. "I'm gonna see if I can find some Navy Flyboy that is going to parts unknown and catch a ride, if I am lucky," he responded. "You guys better see about finding some decent quarters, or you are going to be sleeping on the deck. I'll touch base with ya later."

The next morning, Wit went on deck and met with his friends, and asked, "Did they give you guys a decent place to sleep?" "Yeah," the Colonel responded, "after they chased a bunch of refugees that had taken over and thought they had squatter's rights." "Good!" Wit replied. "Don't let em shove you around; you are the boss and they are the guests." "Where did you end up?" Susie asked. "You might say I was a little lucky," he remarked. "I met the ship's Executive Officer and we have mutual acquaintances, the Chaplain and the Flight Surgeon at Fort Rucker. He had done some flight training over there. I had a good supper with the ship's officers, and they found me a nice place to sleep; we had a good breakfast. Nice guys, them

PHILIPPINES

Squids. May be a flight out of here to Subic Bay Naval Base in the Philippines early tomorrow, and possibly later today; he thinks they will have space for me. I want to take a couple years to give my mind and body a chance to heal, and then I want to work my way to Japan and work the hospitals there. There are a lot of veterans there that are suffering with battle fatigue and injuries from the war, and I hope I can be of help. I'll get my own Geisha and let her give me baths and massages. In case I don't get a chance, I want to give you my final word: Every morning, when you awake and the sun comes up, thank the Lord for the opportunity to see it and praise him and thank him. There are over 58,000 that died in 'Nam, eight of which were Nurses, that will never see the sun again; their families will grieve and mourn, and their lives will be changed forever. Put all the horror on a shelf in the back of your minds; I know you cannot forget it, but do not dwell on it, or it will drive you nuts. Always look forward; never look back. Only God knows what the future holds; the Bible says, 'the Lord helps those who help themselves'; so, grasp it and run with it. It is unlikely that our paths will ever cross again, so I wish you all God-speed." They all teared up, even the hardened Marine Colonel, and they all embraced him with an endearing hug, as they bid farewell to their dear friend for the final time.

It was only about a 1000-miles trip to Subic Bay; being a smooth ride, he snoozed most of the way. He asked for directions to the Chapel and introduced himself to the Chaplain and conveyed his plan. The Chaplain suggested, since they had a lot of transients at Subic Bay, he would be better served to go to Clark Air Force Base, near Manila, where it was like a small city, and they had a huge hospital. He caught a hop to Clark AB, which was only about 60 miles, and introduced himself to one of the Chaplains there, because they had one of every faith. He found, and rented, a nice and clean mobile home in a Mobile Home Park, and settled in quickly, since he had very little luggage; the home was completely furnished, down to the last coffee cup. He then borrowed the Chaplain's Jeep and scouted around to find where everything he was interest in, was located. The neighboring residents were very obliging giving directions. He found the Commissary and purchase all the food stuffs and supplies he thought he would need for the ensuing week and stocked his cabinets and refrigerator. One of the young neighbor boys delivered to him a freshly baked cherry pie that his Mother had made as a welcoming gift, which he accepted graciously. He located a small diner and ate a delicious supper, and then went back to his home to settle in for the night. The next morning, he arose and cooked himself a good breakfast, showered and shaved, and then went to the Chapel to converse with the Chaplain about his plan of action for the next year or so. The Chaplain introduced himself as Air Force Major Mylan Gorby and briefed everything on which Wit would be concerned. He said the Hospital Administrator was Air Force Lieutenant Colonel James Bridges, a brilliant Doctor and a righteous man, who was easy to work with.

Wit introduced himself to Doctor Bridges and explained that he had better than average success over the last 20 years working with veterans who were suffering from battle fatigue or were generally confused and couldn't quite clear their minds. He explained he wasn't qualified to work with severe cases; he left those to the Doctors that specialized in those areas. He explained since he had personally experienced what they were going through, he could talk on their level and get them to open-up and reveal what was bothering them; they would then concentrate on those areas. His goal was to get them to the point of returning home. The Doctor stated that there was a section dedicated to those types of people and anything he could do to help would be greatly appreciated.

Wit went faithfully to the hospital every day for about six months and being he was trying to help himself through his own emotional problems, he would go to the gym and go through his routine workout to relieve his stress. He became well acquainted with a young Nurse, Jeanie Martin, and one Friday after work, she invited him to a beach party, "Everybody will be there, and they have a great time. They will have a live Heavy Metal Band." "It's been a long time since I left the States; what is a Heavy Metal Band?" he asked. "Electric guitars and drums and other instruments that are loud and lively," she answered. "That doesn't sound like my kind of music," he responded, "but I'll go, and if I don't like it, I'll leave." He picked her up and there was a huge crowd, but being a large beach area, she had no problem finding a place to spread a blanket. The girls wore skimpy little bikinis and the boys their usual swim trunks. The music started and was loud, but not too bad. It gradually started cranking up with the amplifiers turned up full blast, and the guitars started screeching and the drums banging, and it seemed to ignite a fire in their butts. They started dancing, or gyrating, in a wild array of individual performances. The thing that was strange to Wit was they never touched when they danced. He always liked the slow cheek to cheek, cuddling on the dance floor with the saxophone moaning and the bass drum thumping and the drummer raking the straws across the drum and the music slow and tantalizing. That was the 50s! The singers weren't singing; they were screaming at the top of their lungs and, the louder they got, the wilder the dance. They started passing bottles of alcohol and lit up their joints (weed cigarettes) and passed them around for everybody to get a deep drag. Jeanie tried to get Wit to join in, but from what he was witnessing, that wasn't gonna happen. Soon some started skinny dipping and some were pairing off and having sex on their blankets. About midnight, he had had enough, and he told Jeanie, "I'm leaving; this is not my kind of party. Can you get a ride home?" "You gonna be an old shtick in the mud?" she slurred. "I can get a way home." He drove home and his ears were ringing for about three hours afterward.

Sunday morning, while he was getting ready to go to church, there came a peck on his door. He opened the door and in stepped Jeanie; she wreaked of smoke and alcohol; from all appearances she looked like she had partied the whole weekend. She started to take off her clothes, and Wit said, "Stop! Don't do that! I'm leaving for church!" "She responded, "I promised you a good time; can we get together later?" "No, Jeanie, we're done," Wit replied. "We are too different; we can remain good friends, but no more than that. I'll see you at work Monday." He went back to his routine of working with the vets but keeping active in his down time. He had made a lot of friends but seemed to be more content being alone. He was too jittery to sit through a movie, so he tried bowling, but wasn't too good at it; he enjoyed swimming laps in the pool; he always fell back to his favorite, a vigorous workout in the gym. At night he tried catching the news on his little 12-inch Magnavox TV. It was aggravating to constantly have to get up and adjust the rabbit-ears antenna, but eventually falling asleep.

CHAPTER 55

Wit had been at Clark AFB for two years and, with steady workouts and working with the vets, he felt it was time to stick with his plan and go to Japan. He arranged a flight the following Monday. He went to the gym on Friday before his flight and put in a very vigorous workout. He was sitting, drenched with sweat, wiping his face with a towel, when he heard a ladies voice say, "Excuse me! I know you from somewhere, but I can't place it." He responded, "Hey, that's my line." He looked up and there stood a lady, drenched in sweat, the same as he was and she said, "My name is Becky." He responded, "I am Wit. I've been here about two years and I don't think I have ever seen you before; I work at the hospital with troubled vets." "Where were you before that?" she asked. "I spent 12-years in Vietnam; were you ever there?" "No, are you sure you weren't somewhere else?" she continued to ask. "I did take a break for 8 or 9 months and went to Okinawa," he replied. "That's it!" she remembered. "You worked in the hospital there. I spent a couple years there working with some seriously injured troops, and I knew I had seen you; you worked in a different area than

I did and that's why we never met. I was kept busy because we had so many casualties, and I worked 16-hour days, and by the time I went home, all I wanted to do was flop on the bed. Have you had supper?" "I haven't eaten since this morning, and believe me, I am famished," he replied. "Why don't we shower off and I'll treat you to a good supper; I know a little restaurant that has good food," she remarked. "I can't pass up an offer like that," he commented. "I'm game; I'll meet you out front." She looked a lot better after she cleaned up and straightened her hair. He drove them to the restaurant. and they found a suitable booth, and he commented, "Not a lot of people here tonight." She replied, "They are probably all at the big beach party. Ever been to one of them?" "Yeah, and I will never go to another; that was too much for me," he remarked. "Me neither," she responded. "They are insane." A man came up to their booth and said, "Nice to see you again, Becky; have you been busy?" "I sure have!" she answered. "Francois, I want you to meet my new friend, Wit. I've been bragging on how good your food is." "Nice to meet ya, Francois," you own this place?" Wit asked, being his usual self. "Oui, been here 20 years now. What can I get you folks to drink?" They both ordered lemonade, and Francois added, it was fresh squeezed.

Wit asked the age-old military question, "Where are you from, Becky?" "I was born and raised right here; well in Manila," she answered. "My Father was in the US Navy before the war, and his ship docked here, and he met my Mother. They fell in love and were married and had me. When I was seven, the Japs came, and they raped and murdered my Mother. While my Father was out to sea, they sank his ship, killing all aboard. I was raised in an orphanage by some American Missionaries. I don't have to tell you I can't stand the sight of a Jap; they destroyed my entire family. When I graduated from high school, I went to the University of Hawaii and studied medicine for eight years, courtesy of the US Government, since my Father was on active duty when he was killed. There were over 100,000 Japs in Hawaii but most of them were born and raised there, so they were not part of the war, nevertheless I did not associate with them, because a Jap is a Jap. My friends and I frequented a soda shop whenever we got a chance, while I was still in school, and that is where I met my Husband-to-be; he was in the Navy and stationed there after the war. He said he grew up in the hill country of West Virginia, wherever that is; he was handsome and happy-go-lucky and enjoyed life. We fell in love and got married and he taught me the art of lovemaking. You have probably heard the old saying 'a sailor has a girl in every port'? I studied hard and he went on cruises and it was wonderful when he got home, but then I got suspicious of his cheating on me. I am an extremely jealous person, and after he admitted it to me, I kicked him out. For about a year, he kept saying he was sorry and wanted me to take him back; I missed him and let him come back. Then I found out he was still cheating, and I kicked him out for good. I have remained unmarried and am wrapped up in my work, putting in long hours during the week, and try to relax on weekends; going to the gym is one way. How about you? What is your story?"

"Not much that you would be interested in," he responded. "I was drafted and trained as a combat soldier and went to Korea. When our ship docked, and we were waiting to be trucked to the front, I found injured men left to die having very little chance of survival, so I started praying with them until they took their last breath. The Chaplain observed for a bit and then ask me to be his Chaplain's Assistant; I had always been a quiet and decent young man, but that immediately changed my life. I was exposed to the most horrendous aspects of a brutal war; death, smoke, smell, fear, and noise, almost to the point of being unbearable. In the midst of it all, I met the love of my life, a Nurse Lieutenant; she was perfect in every way and we fell in love and made plans to raise a family and live happily ever after. Then the worst thing happened; hordes of Chinese were charging to over-run our camp, and they were throwing everything at us; artillery, mortars, shooting, screaming like maniacs. We shot back with everything we had, killing them by the thousands, and we repelled their attack. I looked over at the Medical Tent and it was gone; blown to bits and, Babs, the love of my life was blown to bits as well. When my tour was up, and was shipped back to the States, I had several months left, but I was an emotional mess, and elected to stay and work with other troubled vets, trying to get them prepared to go back to civilian life. I had considerable success, and the best part was, helping them helped me too. I went back home and found all my friends had moved on in their lives, and when I went to visit my old girlfriend, I found her married and seven months pregnant. So, I was introduced to a new girl and we dated and got engaged and after 10 months, we got married. I was having severe stomach pains; two Doctors couldn't figure what the problem was. I was working the evening shift and the pains were so bad I asked the Supervisor if I could go home, and he was sympathetic, and granted me the request. I slipped in as quietly as I could, so as not to disturb my wife, and there I found some dude humping the heck out of her, and she was really enjoying it. I almost killed him, and if it weren't for her screaming at me, I would have; I had visions of killing some Gook. That really scared me, and I paced the rest of the night, shaking and my stomach pains getting worse, but I decided I could never be a civilian again. I visited my Mother and said goodbye and re-enlisted for six years, providing I could get Helicopter Pilot Training. We were only married six months and owed on everything, so I gave her everything and never looked back; no calls or letters; no contact. The Doctor there solved my stomach problem, too much caffeine on an empty stomach; so, I ate a lot of cheese sandwich crackers and vegetable juice, and it was soon straightened out.

I then went to Germany and created a helicopter transport service and flew all over the area known as Bavaria; made a lot of friends all the way to Washington DC. All the while, I stayed in the Chaplain's Service. After about two years, I was informed that things were brewing in Southeast Asia, and they needed experienced helicopter pilots. They gave me four options, three of which were glamorous positions, but I took the worst option, Vietnam, because that was what I was trained for, and again staying in the Chaplain's Service. I was in that country 12-years, except for the time in Okinawa, from the start to the finish, and was likely the last to leave when it was over. I thought the Koreans were a bad lot, but nothing could compare to the Communist Vietnamese. The way they brutalized and maimed and slaughtered, even their own people, were barbaric and unmerciful. I feel exactly the same about the Gooks as you do about the Japs." They sat and talked to almost midnight, and Becky said, "Francois, I guess you want to close up; we just lost track of time." "No, stay as long as you like; I have work to do in the kitchen. I still have coffee left, so I will freshen yours," he replied. Then two other couples came in, and one said, "Francois, we saw your lights were still on and thought we might get a midnight snack." "No probleem! I feex whatever you like," he replied. Becky and Wit talked for about another hour and it was uncanny how similar they were; they were about the same age; their likes and dislikes; how they thought the same about a number of issues. "Would you give me a lift home?" she asked. "I don't like walking alone this late." "Certainly!" he answered. "Do you live far?" "No, I live walking distance from the hospital," she replied.

He drove her home and she asked, "Do you want to come in for a while? I never get the opportunity to just sit and talk and we have so much in common." "Yeah, I'm in no hurry," he remarked. They went in and she asked, "You want to hear some music? I have some of the latest tunes. Pick out what you like; I'm gonna put on my pajamas, if you don't mind." "Uh-oh!" he thought. "PJ-101; here we go again." He selected music that was slow and soothing, and they danced close; cheek to cheek; body to body. He slid his hand up the back of her shirt and stroked that hard body; a result of all that exercise in the gym. Without saying a word, she led him to the bedroom, and removed the PJs; there was no cellulite on those hips and the skin was tight. She had him undressed with strict precision and they proceeded to hit the sheets. A sex marathon took place all that night and most of the next day, except for a few bathroom breaks and a quick snack now and then. As Saturday was winding down, he said, "I need to leave and prepare for church in the morning. If you want to do something inspirational, you might come to one of our services; say 0930."

Wit was standing out front with Major Gorby when he noticed Becky walking toward them, dressed in a pink dress that accentuated her curves and dark hair. She was very attractive and caught the eye of a lot of the men around. Wit introduced her to the Chaplain and said, "This is Becky, my new friend I met at the gym late Friday; she works at the hospital. I never asked you where you worked in the hospital or even asked your last name." "I am a Surgeon in the OR (operating room) and you work in other areas; that is why we never met before; and my last name is Morgan," she responded. "Glad you could join us, Becky," the Chaplain replied. "Wit has done a lot for our Chapel since he has been here, and we are going to miss him when he leaves." After the service, Becky asked, "Have you had breakfast, Wit?" "No, I slept in and never had a chance," he responded. "Well, come on and I'll treat you to a brunch," she followed. "You treated me to supper last Friday, so I'll treat you today," Wit remarked. They went back to Francois' restaurant and ordered a big mid-day meal. While they were eating, she commented, "I didn't know you were leaving; where are you going?" "I am flying to Japan tomorrow," he answered, "just the next step in my plan." After they ate, she asked, "Do you mind if I smoke?" "Smoke?" he replied, kinda surprised. "Why do you need to smoke?" "I have a serious surgical procedure in the morning, and I get a little nervous and smoking seems to calm me down. I usually start getting nervous a couple days ahead, so that is why I do a strenuous workout. I will admit after our bedroom antics, I lost all my jitters," she explained. "Let's go back to my place and pick up where we left off last night." They went back and spent the rest of the day in the sack. Finally, she said, "I'm done! It'll take me a month to get over this." "Your West Virginia feller taught you well," Wit remarked. "I'll probably sleep all the way to Japan tomorrow." "You outperformed him by a long shot! If you were going anywhere else but Japan, I would resign my position and go with ya," she commented. "But you know how I feel about Japs!" After his flight left the ground, he thought, "Good thing I'm leaving; if I staid, we would likely kill each other in the bedroom. I guess there are worse ways to die."

It was about a five-hour flight and he landed at Tokyo Haneda Airport. He then caught a bus to the US Naval Hospital in Yokosuka, which was about 45-miles. He had never seen so many people all in one place at one time in his whole life, He concluded that he was going to need to find a place on the outskirts of town; it would be a madhouse living in this crowd. He checked in at the Chapel near the hospital and introduced himself. The Chaplain, Navy Commander Noble Conley, welcomed him and they had a sit-down and discussed what all transpired at the hospital, and also, they would lend a hand in case of emergencies, like floods or earthquakes or severe storms. He iterated they had branch clinics that they were responsible for. That gave Wit his opening, if possible, he would like his own helicopter because to try and drive anywhere in the vast crowds would be a nightmare. He mentioned he was supplied a helicopter at all his previous assigned locations. The Chaplain didn't think that was a problem. "Do you have any idea where you want to live?" the Chaplain asked. "I was hoping to get my own little house away from the crowds, and with enough room to park my chopper," Wit answered. "I am open for any suggestions you might have to offer." "We have a Realtor we deal with from time to time; I'll give him a call," the Chaplain offered. "Meanwhile you can sleep here in our spare room at the Chapel." The Realtor was a Japanese guy that spoke perfect English and he showed up with a thick book under his arm. He asked Wit what he had in mind and Wit explained he wanted a little house away from all the noise and with enough room to park his helicopter and he preferred it to be completely furnished. He leafed through his book of possibilities and then his eyes brightened, and he said, "I have exactly what you want. It belongs to an officer and after the last earthquake, it scared him so bad, he went back to America, and said 'sell it for whatever you can get out of it, I'm leaving', It is fully furnished, but there is one catch, there is a retired Geisha that he had that still lives there." "That sounds great," Wit remarked, "let's go look at it, and if it is everything you say it is, then we can work a deal." They checked it out and it was perfect for what he wanted. He met the Geisha, Suzuko, and she had the sweetest and kindest face, and Wit liked her from the very beginning; he had no idea of her age, but he guessed near 70. The Realtor explained that she had her own space in the house, but she was so quiet; he would hardly know she was around. She would do the laundry, cleaning, go to the market and prepare the meals and give him a bath and massage, when he wanted it; if she could live there free. They negotiated and he got it cheap, since the owner had already gone back to America. Moving in was easy since all he had was his bag. It had a little veranda on the back with a little table and several small chairs and pretty flowers blooming, which offered a sweet smell. The first evening he said, "Come on, Suzuko, let's go sit outside and get some fresh air." She wasn't sure what to make of that and offered, "You want tea?" "I don't drink tea; but do you have juice or coffee or water. You can get yourself some tea if you want it," he responded. She brought him some juice, looked like papaya, and it was delicious, and she had her little cups of tea. She spoke good broken English and he had no problem conversing with her. After a while, they retired and he slept like a baby, and dreamed about 'Babs'.

CHAPTER 56

Wit wasn't in any hurry to get up the next morning, and when he did arise, Suzuko was already up and piddling around. Wit said, "Suzuko, sit down at the table with me and I'll try to explain what I like to eat for breakfast." She sat down and he rattled off his southern style dishes that he liked for breakfast and she wrote it all down in Japanese, which looked like hen scratches to him. "Are those items available at the market?" he asked. She said, "Not sure but I try to find them." "Understand this," he added, "I don't want raw fish or raw meat or raw eggs; everything must be cooked done. I like vegetables about any way you can fix them; I will tell you if there are any I don't like, after you prepare them." "I understand," she replied, "I want to please you." "I know what I like may be strange to you, so I may need to teach you how to cook them," he remarked. She had toast with jam and juice and coffee, with cream. "I have dollars but no yen," he said. "Can you exchange them so you can buy what we need?" She said some places take dollars, but she can get them converted at the bank. He finally suggested that if she may not like what he likes, then she can buy what she likes to eat.

He called the Chaplain and asked him to have his Orderly pick him up so he could see about obtaining a helicopter. He was lucky to get one similar to his little Bell, but a newer model, and with low hours. He had the Navy mechanics service it, and like before, he drew a sketch of how he wanted the Chaplain's insignia and 'CHOPPER CHAPLAIN' painted on it. He then had the Orderly take him to the hospital so he could introduce himself to the Hospital Administrator, and subsequently get to work. The Hospital Administrator introduced himself as Navy Captain Austin Knight. They had a lengthy conversation about what he had done in the past and what he would like to continue doing at this hospital. The Captain explained that they had at one time a large number of patients with battle fatigue and bad memories of the war, but over time, most of them have recovered and returned to the States; however there are still some cases that have not recovered, and they also are still being treated for combat injuries. Wit then explained how effective his chopper transport service was in Germany, and with the difficulty of getting around, he could probably make use of it here; especially with the number of branch clinics. He explained, to eliminate joy riding, each transport was required to have an authorization form signed and delivered to Chaplain Conley, because he reports to the Chaplain, and since most authorizations would probably be generated at the hospital, some officer on the hospital staff might be assigned that task. "Sounds good," the Captain replied, "it is something we have needed, and I have the right man for the job, Ensign Thomas Allen." "They are still servicing the chopper and I must get forms made up, and then I want to talk to Ensign Allen and explain what we want to do," Wit responded. "And I need to explain it to the Chaplain yet to get his blessing; he may not like me adding more work to his busy schedule." When they finished, the Captain had a Charge Nurse, Kristi Kramer, give Wit a tour of all the areas of which might be of interest to him. The Chaplain had no problems with the transport idea because it was good for the Navy.

He had the forms made up and sat down with Ensign Allen and explained that in no uncertain terms would forged forms be signed to accommodate some of his drinking buddies. It would not set well for the Ensign; if an important transport was requested but couldn't be made because the chopper was on a pleasure run, or likewise in case of an emergency, it would not be acceptable. In the early stages, the passengers gave him directions to their destinations, and he gradually learned where places were located. And like Bavaria, the chopper transport became a very popular method of traveling short distances and saving time. Like in the past, he was meeting a lot of people and becoming well known. There were vets still recovering from their combat injuries and having trouble coping with life in general, and Wit would sit by their bed and talk endlessly, and always ended with saying a prayer. His days were long and tiresome and when he got to his *'chisanaka',* (little house in Japan), and ate what Suzuko had prepared for him, and then she gave him a bath and a massage, he was ready for a good night sleep. It became his routine for the next several months.

One late Friday afternoon, Wit had just finished a run and stopped in at the hospital. There seemed to be a lot of excitement among the Nurses, so he asked Kristi, "What's all the excitement about?" "Some rich Japanese businessmen are having a party and have invited some of our young Nurses to accompany them," she answered. "I guess it is like a status symbol to have a sweet young woman walk in with his arm around her. They lavish spending and affection all evening, and in most cases, end up in their hotel rooms." "What do their wives think of that?" Wit asked. "They don't have much to say about it," Kristi replied. "Did you ever notice when the man walks down the street, his wife follows behind him?" "No, never noticed because I never go out on the streets," he replied. "Are you going to the party?" "Oh, no, they don't want me; I'm too old and too tall. I'm 44 and they want 24, and I'm 5'9", and they want 5'1" to 5'4". The average man is 5'6" and he doesn't want a woman that looks down on him. If you don't have plans, how would you like to go to KFC and get something to eat?" she asked. "What's that?" he asked. "Kentucky Fried Chicken," she answered. "When was the last time you were in the States?" "It's been about 25-years, I guess," he replied.

They ordered their food at the counter and then sat a table to eat. "Where you from, Kristi?" he asked, like all military people ask. "I am from Tacoma, Washington, and I got my Nurse degree at University of Washington. Worked in a hospital, and then joined the Navy after the Vietnam War, and came here to make myself useful taking care of the wounded," she answered. "Have you ever been married?" Wit asked. "I was engaged twice. My first fiancé was from a very rich family and his Mother decided that I didn't meet the standards of their uppity relation, so she convinced him to cut it off, which we did. I lived with my second fiancé for 3 months to see if we could get along well enough to get married, but we discovered we didn't love each other, and that ended that," she explained. "How about you?" "While in Korea, I met the love of my life, a Nurse Lieutenant, and we made plans to go home and raise a family and live happily ever after," he commented. "Then the worst thing that could happen did happen, an artillery shell hit her treatment tent and blew her to bits. I will never love another like I did her. I went home after the war and met a girl and we got married, and then six months later, I caught some big dude humping her, so I reenlisted for 6 years, gave her everything, and never looked back; don't call and don't write, and don't care. She never got a divorce, so I guess I am still married." They finished their chicken and he took her home to her place and she invited him in. He started kissing her and she kissed him back, and then he started feeling around, and suddenly she surprised him and said, "You better leave before I do something I may regret!" She walked him to the door, and he kissed her on the cheek, said goodnight, and left.

The following Monday, he entered the hospital and Kristi approached him and said, "I want to apologize for leading you on; it was not my intention, and I am deeply sorry." "Not a problem; didn't bother me at all," he responded. "I went home, and my Geisha gave me a bath and a massage, and I slept like a baby. We are friends and will always remain friends. What I went through in Korea, I vowed that if I got out of there with all my skin, I would never let anything bother me again, so you can relax; we're good. I see the little honeys survived their Japanese adventure." "Yeah, that's all they have been talking about," Kristi replied. "They think it was funny that the men wanted them to perform on top." Wit spent the week transporting and praying with the vets, and Friday evening, Kristi asked, "If you haven't eaten yet, I thought we might go to the new McDonalds." "What's a McDonalds?" he questioned. "That is what they call a 'fast food joint'," she answered. "They sell hamburgers and fries and stuff like that; you place your order at the counter and pay for it, and by that time, they hand you a tray with your order on it; ala fast food. Their specialty is the big Mac, a double decker hamburger. You can eat it there or take it with ya."

For the next several months, Kristi and Wit spent a lot of Friday evenings together, not all of them, but most of them. Then one Friday she informed him that one of the patients, Larry Browning, that she had been caring for, had reached a level where he was able to go back to the States to the Walter Reed Hospital in Maryland; they had developed new procedures that could enhance his condition in a short time to where he could go home. She commented, "I have been nursing him for the last two years, writing his letters, reading his mail and have gotten acquainted with his family where they say they are anxious to meet me someday and appreciate all I have done for him. There is nothing more for me here, so I thought I would go with him and continue nursing him back to health. You have done a good job working and praying with him and I think he is emotionally ready." "I'm proud of you, Kristi," Wit remarked, "that is a huge sacrifice and I hope something good comes of it." "Me too," she replied. "I am quite a bit older than him, but I suppose when you have feelings for someone, age doesn't matter. Looks like we are scheduled to leave on Monday, so I guess we better say goodbye now." "You have been a good friend and I will be praying for ya," he replied. He was on a transport run on Monday and never got to say goodbye before she left.

About a month later, he went into the hospital and an elderly lady was sitting on bench; he looked at her curiously and then recognized her and said, "Mother Superior, what are you doing here? I thought you would be retired and living in a Retired Nun's Home." She laughed and remarked, "No, Honey, I will retire when they carry me out; I couldn't stand to live with those old women. I'm surprised to see you here. Don't you ever stay in any one place at a time?" Then one of the Nurses said to the elderly Nun," Do you know Chopper? Everyone loves Chopper." "Yes, I know him; if he had been Catholic, he would have been a Cardinal," she responded. "Ha, now that's a stretch, Peggy," he remarked. "Whatever happened to that Vietnamese boy, Mickey, I brought to you to find a good home to adopt him?" "I did what I promised," she answered. "I found him a good family in Syracuse, NY and he grew up and attended Syracuse University and rates near the top in his class. He has been offered positions in the State Department as an interpreter when he graduates. He is loaded with personality and his favorite say is 'it doesn't cost anything to be friendly'; wonder where he got that from." "That really pleases me, Peggy," he replied. "Where are you staying?" "Nowhere yet," she answered, "I just got here, and my bags are next to the door." "Good!" he exclaimed. "You shared your tent with me and now I am going to share my house with you," "That's mighty kind of you, Wit," she said. "That's settled," he responded. "I'll have my Geisha give you a bath and a massage and you can get a good night sleep." "My old bones could use a good massage. How old is this Geisha?" she continued. "She is about your age and you will love her. Have you eaten anything?" he asked. "Yes, I ate right after I got here." She answered. "She can fix you something to eat later, if you ask her," he offered. He took Peggy home and introduced her to Suzuko and explained that Peggy was a Holy Woman and he wanted her to have a bath and a massage and fix something to eat later. He asked Suzuko to take her out on the veranda and have tea and enjoy the flower garden. He then said, "I hate to do this to ya, Peggy, but there is a meeting at the hospital, that

I must attend, and they always run late because they all agree to disagree and argue. I don't know why they insist I be there because I don't have much to offer. Suzuko will take good care of you and you will most likely be asleep when I get home, so I will see you in the morning."

Suzuko and Peggy were asleep when he quietly slipped in at a late hour. The next morning, Suzuko prepared breakfast and Wit asked Suzuko to sit with them and eat. Normally a housemaid doesn't, but Wit always includes her as part of his family. "Well, Peggy, did you get rested? Did Suzuko take care of ya?" Wit asked. "Yes, she did," Peggy replied. "She is the sweetest thing; we sat outside and drank tea and she gave me a bath and the best massage I have ever had. You have a wonderful place here and you are lucky to have her." "I know," he responded, "she came with the house and we take care of each other. How long are you staying?" "They are picking me up this afternoon and will next go to Yokohama; I am checking all the orphanages, so I don't have time to stay at any one place very long. It has been a blessing that I ran into you and shared your little estate." "Like I said, you shared your tent with me in a lot worse conditions, and I appreciated that," he remarked. He took her back to the hospital, and they embraced, and he bid her farewell and had some runs to make.

Several weeks later, Wit stopped in at the hospital, and Captain Knight said, "We got in some new Nurses; let me introduce you to the new Charge Nurse." "Which one is she?" he asked, while he was looking around the room. "She is that cute one at the end of the room," the Captain remarked. Wit said, "Never mind, I already know her." He walked up behind her and said, "Did anybody ever tell you that you were gorgeous?" Mimi snapped her head around and, seeing him, she started hugging and kissing him. A Nurse said, "Everybody loves Chopper!" Mimi said, all excited, "Nobody loves him like I do." Another Nurse asked, "Miss Monroe, what do you want to do with the patient in B-34?" Mimi responded, "You girls do whatever you think best because I am going to be tied up for the next couple days." They all went, "Oooh!" She took Wit by the hand and said, "Come on, we are going to my place. You are never going to get away from me again!" She latched the door and led him to the bedroom and started peeling off her clothes. He always thought she had a strong resemblance of Babs, and now she was looking better than ever. He couldn't resist and started peeling off his, and remarked, "WT is ready!" "WT?" she asked. "Yeah, Wit's Torpedo." he answered. She laughed, and said, "Tell him MS is ready to be torpedoed." MS?" he questioned. "Yeah, Mimi's Ship; tell him to up periscope and fire tube #1 into the hull," she ordered. "Where did you learn all this Navy talk?" he asked. "I watch all the old World War 2 movies," she responded, and laughed. She was right, she was tied up for the next couple days, and they wore themselves out. When they were relaxing, she commented, "I have thought of you every day for the last 25-years and dreamed about you every night, and now I am keeping you forever." "What happened to the big Olympian," he asked. "You know all the scenarios we went through that last night?" she explained. "When he came home, I looked him in the eye and asked him straight out 'are you having an affair?', and his answered was none of those we guessed it would be. He said, 'yes and I am in love with her and want a divorce'. Didn't bother me a bit; I felt relieved; no more guessing or worrying; it was like a weight was lifted from my shoulders. We divorced and when his enlistment was up, he went back to the States. Haven't heard from him since. I went home a couple years later, and then reenlisted. What about you?" "I spent 12-years in the jungle in Vietnam. Some of the things I did, or had seen, would make you sick; or any average person sick. Them Commies terrorized everybody, even their own people, and I made it a mission to give it back, in kind. I became Enemy #1 on their most wanted list and there was a huge reward out for my head, dead or alive. I lost focus once and was captured, but there isn't a Gook smart enough to hold me; believe me, I never lost focus again. It was a Politician's War, but they never had to fight; over 58,000 young Americans died fighting a war they were not allowed to win; leaves a bitter taste in my mouth. Took several years to get my mind and body back to normal," he explained. "You are safe now," she remarked, "and I am going to see to it." She moved in with Wit and Suzuko, and they lived happily together, all taking care of each other.

CHAPTER 57

They were sitting on the veranda, as they routinely did, and Mimi asked Suzuko, "Suzuko, do you have a family?" She responded, "Yes, I have a son, and he lives in Yokohama." "Does he have a family?" Mimi continued to ask. "His wife died, and his two children moved out to have their own families," she answered. "Does he ever come and visit?" Wit asked. "Two times," she answered. "You mean he comes two times a year?" Wit continued to ask. "Yes, two times," she confirmed. "How would you like to go see him?" Wit asked. "You can catch a train and it should only take about an hour. Write to him, or call him, and have him meet you at the train station. I will pay for it. You call the train station tomorrow and get a ticket, and I will get you to the station." "Oh, no!" she exclaimed. "My work is here." Mimi said, "We will take care of things here till you get back; you go visit your son. We will be alright, and your work will still be here." So Suzuko took a holiday and went to Yokohama for a week.

While they were sitting on the veranda, Wit asked, "What ever happened to the old gang after I left?" "Well, Colonel Joe started having heart palpations about ten years ago, so they retired him, and he and Priscilla went back to the States. I heard he had died 5-years ago. Priscilla's sister Lisa got married and had a couple kids, and Priscilla moved in with them. She clung to Joe like glue, and if anybody would make a suggestion, she would simply say, 'no, Wit said ….', and that was gospel. After Captain Weikart's girlfriend hooked up with my ex, we went to the movies a few times, and then he transferred back to the States. I heard the Provost Captain committed suicide. Bradley and Virginia got married and she moved to Straubing. You must have made an impression on him because they never missed church on Sunday. I guess you heard about Helga and Major Ray; he transferred to another Chapel in another town, and I heard he tried to kill himself. They gave Russ a commission and put him in charge of the Helicopter Rescue and his wife came over and they got a little place in town and had a couple little girls. I assisted Virginia in delivering them; they sure were cute. About the time I left he made Captain. They built a large hangar and named it 'LOREN WHITSON HANGAR'. They increased the Drunk Mobiles to four and named them Wit's Drunk Mobile #1, 2, 3, and 4. Smokie, the cook, retired. Colonel Rankin retired. Everybody talked about you for a long time after you left, but after they transferred in all new people, they didn't know anything about ya, except me. When I would start feeling sorry for myself, I would think of you and have crying jags. We are a lot older now and I hope we can have a long life together in our remaining years," she offered.

They settled in and did their jobs and volunteered when there was an emergency; like a minor earthquake or damaging storm, and the years started passing by. The Chaplain called Wit in, and said, "I got some news for ya. You have been promoted to CWO5; that ought to give you a nice raise." "You mean give my wife a nice raise," he responded. "I didn't know you were married," the Chaplain commented, a little surprised. "Yeah, when I returned from Korea, I got married and it didn't work out, so I reenlisted and now I am a career soldier, married to the Army," Wit added, not going into any details. "The other news is, America is going to war again," the Chaplain offered. "Iraq has invaded Kuwait to get control of their oil fields, and America, along with about 50 other countries is going to push them back across the border. It is going to be a new kind of war; missiles and rockets and huge tanks; the latest in warfare." "Is this going to be another Politician's War that we are not allowed to win?" Wit questioned. "No, this President was in World War 2; he was a fighter pilot and was shot down and fished out of the sea. He knows about war and is building up to throw the works at 'em. We are going into the 90s and everything is going to be high tech, the latest in smart weapons and armament. The buildup is called 'Operation Desert Shield'," he noted. "I never heard of Kuwait; where is it?" Wit asked. "It's in the middle-east, desert country, near the Persian Gulf," the Chaplain replied. "So, we are going from swamps to sand dunes; that should be a switch," Wit added. "Doesn't matter, I got to go, that is my job." "I understand everything is in disarray right now," the Chaplain said. "They are moving in ordinance of all kinds, by ships and big cargo planes, and they put a General in charge that has been trained and geared for this type of war, General Norman Schwarzkopf, and unlike Vietnam, he is in charge. The best I could do for you would be to put you on an aircraft carrier, and then, when they get the land bases established, you could move off the ship onto land. Probably be over by the time you get there. I understand the Iraqis only have about 300,000 soldiers, but they have been training to fight in desert conditions for the last 1000-years."

Wit went home excited, and Mimi noticed it, and asked, "Ok, let's have it!" "I am going to leave you again," he responded. "America is going to war again, and I have to be there." "What are you talking about?" she remarked. "You're too old to go to war; you are almost 60-years old." "I'm not too old to pray," he stated. "As soon as they can get everything arranged, I am out of here." "Where is this wonderful war?" she asked, slightly aggravated. "It's in the middle-east; Iraq has invaded Kuwait, which I never heard of before; it's about 6000-miles from here in the desert; they want their oil wells and the United Nations said, 'ain't gonna happen'," he answered. "What are you going to do about this house?" she asked, frustrated. "I'll give it to Suzuko; I won't be coming back here again," he explained. "Well, I'm going with ya; I don't want to be here without you, and I said you were not ever going to be out of my sight again," she replied. She moved back into her old place and he stayed busy the next couple weeks preparing to leave. He contacted the Realtor and had him transfer the house and property into Suzuko's name. The Realtor wanted to put it up for sale, but Wit didn't want to chance her being put out and made homeless after she had been good to him the years he was there. He had never seen any emotion in her eyes before, but now she had tears running down her cheeks as she squeezed him with an endearing hug and kept saying thank you over, and over again. He got the word his trek was set up and the Navy was flying him, making several stops on the way, and then eventually landing on the USS John F. Kennedy aircraft carrier moored in the Persian Gulf.

KUWAIT

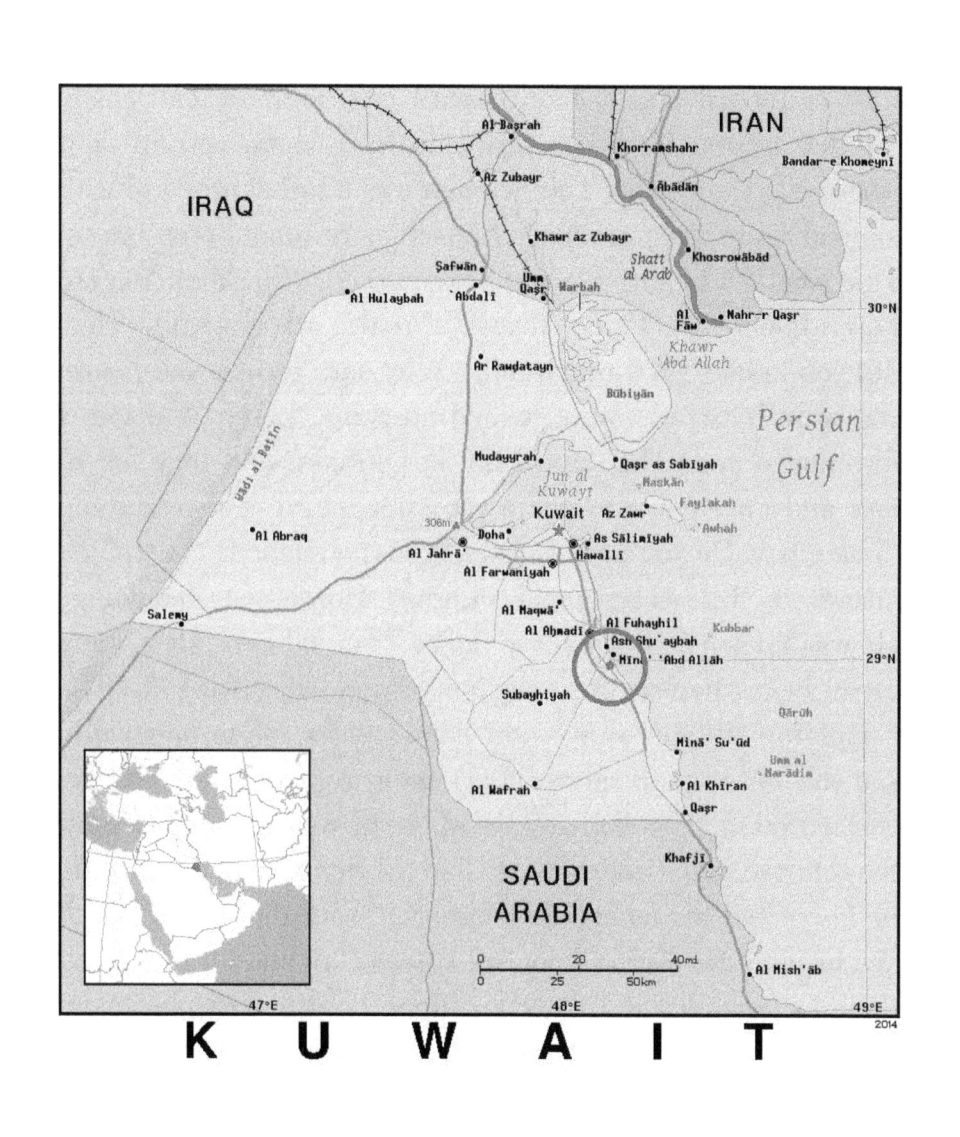

A snappy young officer approached him and welcomed him to the JFK and introduced himself as Ensign Dean Winton. I'll have a Seaman show you your quarters and give you directions, so you don't get lost. This ship has roughly 5000 men and women aboard and is like a small city, and you can easily wander around for hours trying to find where you are and where you want to go. The Seaman was a tall skinny kid with a broad smile and introduced himself as Seaman Loren James. That took Wit by surprise and he remarked, "Eh, what! You are Loren James from Plano, Texas?" "Yeah!" the boy said. "How did you know?" Wit remarked, "Why son, I knew you before you were born; you were named after me, Loren Whitson. I introduced your Mom and Dad on Okinawa and they fell in love and were going to name you after me, if you were going to be a boy. Do you have a sister?" he questioned. "Yeah!" he answered. "I'll bet her name is Loreen. How is your dad doing? He was known as Big Johnny James," Wit added. "He's doing great; I can't believe this," the boy responded, surprised. "The Chaplain said you were a war hero and for me to personally see you were taken care of. Let's go to your quarters and get you settled in." Wit had no idea where he was 10-minutes after they started to his quarters. He had the Seaman sit down while he unpacked his meager belongings. "Your dad was a hero," Wit began. "He was in a Special Forces Unit and I trained with them for a while, and then he shipped out to Vietnam about 6-weeks before I left. After he left, your Mom invited me to dinner; she could cook the best fish I ever ate; she then told me she and Big John were planning to get married when all the war mess was over. I was at the hospital when the Medevac came in with him on a stretcher. The two best lady Doctors in all of Vietnam were personal friends of mine and I asked them to do whatever it took to save him. His unit was doing mop-up in a town and he opened a huge metal container thinking it was big enough to hide a couple Gooks. It was booby-trapped and exploded in his face. He had a concussion and was in shock and his body was riddled with shrapnel. I sat by his bed and prayed harder than I ever prayed before and the Lord heard my prayer. He had both hands bandaged, so I wrote his letters and read his mail. After a few days, he was able to sit up and talk. Then they said they needed the space and were transferring him to a hospital ship. I suggested that one thing we had to do was call his Mom and Dad and let them know that he was alright and would come home as soon as he was released. I wheeled him to a bank of phones and made a person to person call to your Grandparents, and then held the phone up so he could talk to them. He told them he was alright, and he fell in love and wanted to bring her home and assured them she was an American. He said he was going to have her pack up and head for Plano and asked them to take her in until he got home. They were excited and pleased he had found someone. I'll tell you, Loren, she was very beautiful.

I met her when I worked with your half-sister, Mary Ann. Mary Ann was a Nurse in the hospital and was on medical leave. She had spent 9-months in a field hospital, the first stop for a freshly wounded soldier, prior to being transported to a big hospital. She had seen the most grotesque and horrible and traumatic sights until she couldn't take it anymore. I worked and prayed with her but wasn't making much progress, and then I got the idea that she was reliving all the bad stuff whenever she went into the wards to treat the injured soldiers, so I ask the Hospital Administrator to transfer her into the Pediatrics Ward. She was having nightmares and couldn't sleep and was tired all the time, but after that, she started responding. Did you see her very often?" "Yeah, she would come a few times a year with her husband and two kids," he replied. "She married a guy named Scott Ivey and they live in his hometown near his parents." "I worked with Scott too; in fact, we met Mary Ann at the swimming pool when she came by looking for a place to sit because it was pretty crowded, and all the tables were taken. Scott was having real problems; His combat unit was in one of the largest operations in the Vietnam War, Operation Junction City. He and his buddies made a pact that, if they should all get killed but one, that one that survived would go home and visit their families. He watched them all get killed and he felt guilty that he was lucky, and there was no way he could go visit their families. His Uncle was the Hospital Administrator and he asked me to work with Scott. That was a real challenge because I had to convince him it was not luck, but that the Lord had spared him for a reason, and we prayed and talked at length, and I started reaching him and got him a job as the Chaplain's Orderly. He liked the job because he felt it was rewarding and the Chaplain liked his work and attitude. He started going with me to the hospitals and working with the injured and troubled vets. When I left, I ask him to continue working with Mary Ann to continue her progress. I am glad to hear they are together; makes me feel like my work was of great value and not in vain," Wit summarized. "When we all get together, your name always comes up, and they all get emotional," Loren said, "and they never miss church on Sundays." "What is your job on this big tub, Seaman James?" Wit asked. "My Dad said I was never going to be a dog soldier, but a Sailor or an Airman, and I was to ask to get a high-tech school and a very important position, so my goal was laid out for me. I am in Satellite Communications.

I know you are old-school, so the best way to explain it is to demonstrate it," he explained. "You get settled in and get some chow and tomorrow I will take you up to my station; I still find it fascinating and I know you will too."

Wit had a good night's sleep and, early the next morning, Seaman James showed up and said, "Let's get some breakfast and then I will show you what I do." They walked into the large room that was filled with computers and equipment and screens and control panels and a large group of Seamen busy at their stations. Seaman James explained, "The satellite circles the earth in an orbit and, as it passes our area, it takes photographs, but only for a certain amount of time, and then we wait for the next orbit. Let me show you some photos it took yesterday. See that disabled tank; most likely hit a land mine; the tank crew is getting out and the enemy soldiers are picking them up in their stake bed truck and hauling them away to the north, probably on their way to Bagdad. Now I will show you what they did to some they captured last week; they drag them through the town by their feet and people beat them with sticks and throw rocks at their bodies. I can get the finest detailed photos; even read a license plate. The Navy Seal Teams will go out and try to rescue the live ones and retrieve the bodies of the tortured ones." The brutal scenes were causing anger to build up inside Wit, and he remarked, "I would like to go out and make them pay."

Unlike the old Army, only the top-ranking officers shaved daily and the Seamen were permitted to be bearded, if they so choose. The female sailors kept their hair short or tied up, mainly for safety reasons. Wit spent his time roaming around the decks and watching the aircraft fly in and fly out, and it was mind-boggling at how many different types there were.

The fun part was when the Iraqis fired a Scud Missile toward Kuwait, the US made Patriot Missile intercepted it and blew it out of the sky. It had to be frustrating to continue shooting and never reaching the target. A few days later, there was some excitement on the flight deck, and Wit inquired what was going on. He was told two of the Seamen, that launched the jets, went ashore to ride camels, and never returned. That concerned Wit after watching the photos of how Americans were treated if captured. He contacted Seaman James and asked to see if photos were taken of the incident. Only the tail end of the photo period was showing some possibility that the image was, in fact, the two Seaman, and they were being led away toward some buildings. At the next orbit, they zeroed in on that area, and it looked like there was an alleyway between the buildings. "My gut tells me that is where they are being held and I got to get over there," Wit insisted. "What are their names?" Someone answered, "Mark Combs and Keith Mahaffey." They flew him by helicopter to the US Army Camp Arifjan, which was still under construction, but had a Command Center up and running and directing operations. He went in and was intercepted by a Master Sergeant and was asked to state his business. He introduced himself and said he wanted to set up a rescue operation to get two Seamen out of the hands of the Iraqis. The Master Sergeant relayed the information to a One-Star-General, who spoke gruffly, "What makes you think you can rescue anybody in hostile territory, you being a Chaplain?" Wit responded, "General, I've been in this man's Army for over 35 years and spent a tour in Korea and 12-years in Vietnam and I trained over two years with the Green Beret. I trained with the 101st Airborne Infantry and I am a trained killer. I have killed more Communists and rescued more people than you can count." "I spent time in 'Nam; where did you serve?" the General continued to ask. "I spent my time in Da Nang and the surrounding areas," Wit answered. "That's funny; I spent 5 years there and I never heard of you," the General replied, doubtfully. Then Wit hit him with the big one, "Did you ever hear of the Jungle Rat?" "My God yes!" he exclaimed. "And that is you? Sergeant meet the most feared man the Commies ever knew and never could find him. He was number one on the most wanted list, and whoever brought him in, dead or alive, was promised to be made King over a city and blessed with more gold than they could carry. Do you have a plan?" "Yes, I have a plan and I am going to need your help," Wit stated. "I need to look like an Iraqi local, so I will need a common outfit. I haven't shaved in weeks, so I should look somewhat like one of them. If you have an English-speaking local that you work with, I will need him to guide me; I think I know where they are; I studied satellite photos from aboard the carrier." "We got just the man," the General replied. "Sergeant, radio Abdul Hassan and tell him to get his ass in here forthwith. Abdul was born and raised here and graduated from Harvard; he is a CIA Agent and knows every nook and cranny within 50-miles."

CHAPTER 58

Abdul showed up, and when he walked in, he asked, "Wassup?" He sounded as American as you could find anywhere. The General introduced, "This is Wit Whitson and he needs you to go on a covert operation with him to rescue two Sailors taken hostage." "Sounds like my cup of tea," Abdul responded. "When do we start?" "Right now!" Wit replied. "I need some maps, and I think from the satellite photos, I know where they are, and I can show you on the map. I need some clothes to dress like they do, and if we could get a panel truck, like what is popular, we could cruise right in close. A pickup truck would be too open and if we had to shoot our way out, somebody may get hurt. I will need a .45-automatic and a K-Bar knife to carry under my cloak." He pointed out the location on the map and asked, "How far is that and how long will it take us to get there?" Abdul answered, "We will be traveling in open country most of the way, after we leave the camp, but I would say we should reach that town in a half-hour." Wit continued, "The photos showed an alleyway between large buildings that are too narrow to drive through, so if we park at the head of the alley, I can walk down to the other end, and you wait for us and be ready to move out." "If we get there real early," Abdul explained, "there shouldn't be many out on the street, and if they are holding them inside, you might be able to get in without too much notice. It starts getting daylight about 0600, so I think we should leave about 0515. Hopefully the wind doesn't pick up and start blowing sand. I'll take a few extra guns and ammo; do those Sailors know how to shoot?" "Beats me," Wit remarked, "the only thing I know about Sailors is they cook fine meals."

They climbed into an old white panel truck with rust around the wheel wells and covered with dust. Wit put on clothes to look like all the towelheads, and with his scruffy beard and long hair, you would think he was one of them. He took a stick to walk like he had a limp. Abdul parked at the end and across the street of the alley, so he could watch and not be noticed. A few kids came out and started kicking a soccer ball, and Abdul talked with them and found out the Sailors were in the last building on the left at the far end of the alley going into the main street. Wit limped the entire length of the alley, looked back, and a guy was coming up behind him leading a donkey. Wit sat down in the doorway and held out a cup for a donation, and when the donkey man approached, he kicked Wit and said something Wit didn't understand. Wit grunted and pointed to his mouth and ears indicating he couldn't speak or hear. He tied the donkey and went inside, and then the donkey dropped a big pile of donkey biscuits right beside Wit. Wit thought to himself, "Thanks a lot, jerk. If I get a chance, I will make you eat a couple of 'em." He began hearing screaming and yelling and concluded that the donkey man must be slapping the boys around. There still wasn't a lot of activity on the streets.

Wit got up, picked up a couple biscuits, and crept inside and saw the donkey man beating on one of the Sailors. There were several AK-47s leaning in the corner of the room, He grabbed the donkey man by the hair with his knee in his back and tore out his throat. The boys were tied in a chair and he cut loose their ties. There were two women in camo-fatigues laying crumpled on one side of the room. "I'm an American; who are those women laying over there?" One boy replied, "They were driving a supply truck and got lost and hit a roadside bomb that knocked them unconscious. They dragged them in here and have been beating on them for sport." "Did they teach you how to do the firemen's carry in boot camp?" Wit asked, trying to hurry. "Yes!" they both answered. "Do not utter a sound till I tell you," Wit commanded. "Each one of you throw a woman over your shoulder; grab one of those rifles. Go to your right out the door and run to the end of the alley and there is a white panel truck waiting for you." He jammed the donkey biscuits in the donkey man's mouth, when a woman ran in shrieking, and one of the boys laid a haymaker square in her face, knocking her limp against the far wall, and then it got quiet. He told the boys to get going and he would follow, so they started running, carrying a female soldier and a rifle. Another man came in and Wit gave him a powerful 'vertical butt stroke' under his chin with the rifle butt that made a loud crack, knocking him cold, or possibly killing him. He hurried out and untied the donkey and said, "Come on, Jack (jackass), you have to be my shield if they start shooting." The old jack wasn't in a hurrying mood, but when bullets started flying behind them, ricocheting off the walls and bouncing off the ground, apparently stinging the old jack with every hit, he started braying and bucking and kicking and running, and Wit tried to stay ahead of him so he wouldn't get trampled. The boys reached the truck, put the women inside, and were laughing, and their white teeth showed through their blood covered faces. The old jack got the fatal shot and went down. Wit kept running and getting about 10-15 feet from the truck, he caught a slug in the back of his knee and went down. The boys ran out and grabbed him, one with each arm, and dragged him to the truck. He was mad now and grabbed one of the rifles and started shooting from the hip on semi-automatic, hitting all of them that was running after him, therefore buying them some time. Abdul had the motor running and when the boys got him into the truck, he started driving slowly away so as not to attract attention. He drove around, as if in a maze, working his way to the road to the camp, and then hit the gas and made their escape. Wit was in pain but managed to ask, "Are you boys Combs and Mahaffey?" One said, "I'm Combs!" "You have an Aunt Maggie?" Wit asked. "Yeah, that's right," Combs answered. "Well, I am your Uncle Loren," Wit remarked, and then he went faint from the pain.

The next thing he knew was he was in the Infirmary laying in a bed. "Did the boys get back alright? Are the two female soldiers gonna make it?" he asked. "Yeah!" the Doctor said. "They were bruised and cut up a little, but we cleaned them up and sent them back to their ship. It's going to take a while for the two women to recover; they are pretty well battered, but should survive, in time. Your Army days are over for you, old war horse; your knee is destroyed." "Does that mean you are going to cut off my leg?" Wit asked, concerned. "Nah, that's what they did in the Civil War," the Doctor remarked. "This is the 90s; you will get a total knee replacement with stainless steel and plastic, and they will have you up and walking the next day. Unfortunately, we are not equipped to do that here, so we will fly you to Ramstein Air Base in Germany and then shuttled to Landstuhl Regional Medical Center. The General came to see him before he was scheduled to leave, and commented, "Well, Wit, you pulled off the impossible. I'm sorry you are wounded; we could have used you around here. Abdul wrote an astounding report and the two young Sailors' accounting concurred with all he said, and you saved those two supply truck drivers from certain death; the report was sent to the Pentagon. I'm putting you in for a medal." "No, thanks, General, I was just doing my job," Wit replied. "I don't need any medals; the Lord will reward me in his own way, but thanks for coming."

He was prepped for surgery and they demonstrated with a mock-up his new knee. He woke up in the Recovery Room and a pretty set of eyes were down in his face and he asked, "Am I in Heaven?" It was Mimi and she said, "No, you Dingleberry, that's what you asked me over 30 years ago when you woke up in Bavaria. I told you I was never going to let you out of my sight again, so now you are stuck with me for the duration." He was pleased she was there, and forcing a sheepish grin, he asked, "Did anybody ever tell you that you were gorgeous?" "Not since the last time you told me and I don't want you to ever stop saying it," she replied. They moved him to a room and put a mechanical device on his leg, activating his knee. The Surgeon and a Nurse came in to check on him, and the Surgeon said, "Your Army days are over, and after about a month of therapy when you can navigate on your own, we will ship you back to the States," Wit replied, "Then what would I do? I don't know how to do anything else." The Doctor responded, "I know what I would do; I would buy a nice little beach front house in Florida and sit and watch the pelicans dive for fish; and maybe throw in a line from the surf." Mimi said, "I would love that; then I could work on my tan." The Nurse added, "I know the perfect place, Siesta Key; we vacationed there a lot when I was a kid." Because of his excellent condition, his recovery went well.

After a grueling 6000+ miles of puddle jumping, Mimi and Wit landed in Jacksonville, Florida. They stopped at the Information Desk and said they were destined to go to Siesta Key but were strange to Florida. The lady said that it was on the Gulf Coast about 300 miles away. If you don't want to drive it, we have commuter planes that travel to Sarasota several times a day. There is a desk at the end of this concourse, and they can give you all the information. The lady at the commuter desk ask where their destination was, and Mimi said, "We are trying to get to Siesta Key, and hope to buy a beach house there." "Oh, my Lord, Honey, lucky you, that is the prettiest place in all of Florida. I have been there, and I can say you will fall in love with it. We have a plane leaving in an hour, if you want to catch it." Wit told Mimi, "I have to get down; my leg is killing me, and I need to do my leg-lifts, so we better get a room for tonight and travel tomorrow." The lady said, "I thoroughly understand, and we have a flight tomorrow at 11:30, and that should get you there by 1:30 or 2:00, depending on the weather; rain pops up from time to time in Florida. Stop at our agency desk when you get there and tell them your plans and they will recommend a Realtor that has a thorough understanding of the area." They booked the flight and found a room at one of the numerous hotels and Wit asked Mimi to call for room service and order in supper. He felt relieved to lay down and elevate his leg. Mimi asked,

"Have you taken your pain pills?" "Nah, them things make me feel crazy; I'll take one before I go to bed for the night," he responded.

They landed at Sarasota and went to their Information Desk, just like the lady recommended, and explained their intentions. She called the Realtor and said, "She will be here in 15 minutes. Her name is Tammy Finch and we rely on her because she puts satisfying the client over making the sale. That's why she is the leading salesperson in her office." Tammy arrived and she was dressed casually wearing flip-flops and her hair died a bright yellow and wearing too much lipstick and mascara and eye shadow; displayed an infectious smile and well-built for someone that looked to be in her 50s. Introductions were made, and she suggested they sit at one of the tables in the waiting area so she could get an understanding of exactly what kind of property they were looking for. When they mentioned a beach-front house, Tammy asked them to wait a minute and went to her car and brought back a huge binder containing available property on the beach. When they described what they wanted, and in Siesta Key, it sounded like something that came out of travel catalog. Tammy got a far-away look, and then said, as if a light bulb lit up in her head, "No sense looking in the book. I have exactly what you want, and I know you will fall in love with it and write an offer on the spot. It is a 3-bedroom, with a bath in each bedroom; a large kitchen with a lot of cabinets, with no steps in a serene setting in a private little cove, shaded by beautiful trees. It has a gazebo between the house and the beach with built-in benches all around, and a large tool shed. The owners are getting a divorce and the court has ordered them to sell everything for the settlement. They had a boat but sold it, and it was a steal. It is completely furnished, and everything there, stays there. It's not ethical to tell you this stuff, but the owners have been fighting for over two years, and they are tired of the mess, and they both said to get what you can out of it. It's about 20-miles from here, so let's jump into my car and check it out." As they rode to the house, she wanted to know a little about them, so they explained that they were both retiring from the military and wanted to settle down in a nice clean and quiet community.

It was everything Tammy described, and their first impression was, it was perfect. Mimi checked out the inside and was excited to see the roomy kitchen and nice size laundry room, and everything that a woman looks closely at because that is where she spends most of her time. Wit walked around the outside checking for anything that needed repairs, especially the roof and around the windowsills. He looked in the tool shed and saw the various fishing poles and tackle, and lawn care tools, and the huge plywood panels laying across the rafters, marked left front; right rear; and so on. Tammy explained those were to cover the windows when there was a threat of a hurricane or severe storm. He limped out and sat on a bench in the gazebo and watched the waves gently lapping up on the sand, and sure enough, the pelicans were diving into the water for a fish, just like the Surgeon said. They had their minds made up, but never showed any emotion, but they were going to own this house. Tammy told them the list price, and then said, "They were open for an offer." Mimi and Wit huddled in the gazebo and talked about the offer, and they decided to make a ridiculous low offer, and Wit said, "We can always go up, but we can't go down when we negotiate." Then he said, "Ok, Tammy, here is our offer," and then he said, "I'll make a $50,000 deposit, and cash when we close." That lit the old Realtor up. She started to perspire, and her mascara began to run, and she ran to the car and got the forms to fill out, and she didn't waste any time filling in the blanks, and Wit signed them and initialed them, where appropriate. She ran back to the car and got on her car phone, had a conversation with someone, and returned, and said, "They accept your offer, congratulations!" Then Wit asked, "Did they agree to all the contingencies I noted; smells like they were smokers so I want the house fumigated; I want a whole house and termite inspection; I want a title search and property insurance to guarantee they are the lawful owners; I want all the mattresses replaced with new ones because I don't know who or what has been sleeping on them. We need to get to a bank so I can give you a cashier's check for the deposit. We don't have anywhere to stay, and we don't have a car, got any suggestions?" She said, "I'll take you to the local bank and there is a motel on the main street through town. I'll get the sellers to sign off as quick as I can and set up the closing. I'll ask them if they will agree to let you move in right away, since you need a place to stay. Give me a couple days." They settled into the motel and Wit couldn't wait to lay down and get off his leg. He got a laugh out of Mimi hotfooting around trying to avoid the little geckos running on the sidewalk, and remarked, "I got a feeling those things are all over Florida, so you better get used to them being around."

It all worked out and they moved into their dream home; wasn't much moving done since all they had were their bags. Then Wit asked, "Mimi, do you know how to drive?" "Yeah, I got my license when I turned 16," she replied. "Why?" "We have to buy a car, and I imagine we will need to take a test to get a Florida license," he answered. "Back in my day, all you had to do was have someone take you out in the country and teach ya, and then you took a written test, and a guy went out with ya to make sure you could drive, and the worst thing was to park." "Are you saying we may have to take classes and pay some company to teach us, so it will be legal?" she asked. "Yeah, but you know the tricky part?" he continued. "You have to take your own car, and how do you do that when you don't have a license so you can buy one?" "Maybe we can borrow one," she suggested. "But I don't know from whom, since we don't know anybody." "I got an idea," he said, "Why don't we go to car lot and promise them we will buy a car from them if they will lend us one to get a license." They walked to the main street and saw 'Uncle Louie's Auto Mart'. Wit explained to the salesman his problem, and he readily agreed to go along with the idea, providing Wit promised to buy a car from him. "Are you Uncle Louie?" Wit asked. "No, I'm Little Louie. Uncle Louie is recovering from a hangover. He partied hard all night and had too much alcohol and marijuana and women," Little Louie explained. "He sure knows how to party." "I'll bet he was an anti-war demonstrating hippy with long hair and beard," Wit guessed. "Then after the war he cleaned himself up and went into business. Did you do that stuff?" "You are right," Little Louie replied. "But no, I don't do that stuff; I'm married with two mean little kids, and we go to church every Sunday. But let's find you something easy to drive; medium size car with power steering and automatic transmission." Wit didn't need any practice because he drove military vehicles continuously, but Mimi needed a lot of practice and she made him a nervous wreck, and he had his fingers crossed when she took her test. It worked out just as planned, and Wit informed

Little Louie that the car they used destroyed his knees getting in and out, and he preferred a car that he could slide into easily. Little Louie had just the thing, a minivan with low mileage and guaranteed they would fix anything that went wrong within 90 days. He offered a payment plan where you buy here, you pay here. Wit said, "No, I will pay half now and the other half in 90 days, like 90 days is the same as cash." "But we make our money financing the cars," Little Louie replied. "I don't want any debt," Wit remarked, "that's the deal." Little Louie agreed and said, "You should have been a car salesman." "When I was a teenager, we visited used car lots and drove their cars and burned up their gas, but never had money to buy anything," Wit grinned.

They went to the local supermarket and bought everything they needed to stock the shelves and the refrigerator and freezer. They loved their little *'Precious Place'* and for the next several years they couldn't have been happier. She walked the beach looking for shells while he tried desperately to catch a fish, standing in knee deep water and casting as far as he could. One day he was sitting in a beach chair waiting for a big fish to take his bait, when an old dog came up and nuzzled him and wagged his tail, like he needed a friend. "What do you say, old buddy?" Wit greeted. He petted him and looked for a collar to see if he had any identification but found none. Mimi approached and remarked, "I see you have found a friend." "He must be lost; I don't find a collar, and I don't see anybody around that he is with," Wit responded. "What kind of dog is he?" Mimi continued to question. "He looks like a pure-bred German Shepherd, and he appears to be old, so maybe somebody decided they didn't want him anymore," Wit concluded. They walked up the boarded walk toward the house, stopping at the shower to wash off the sand, and Wit said, "Come on, Hund, you need to wash off the sand or Mimi will be mad at both of us." The dog seemed to enjoy the shower and drank from the little hose used to spray off the legs. "He seems to be well trained and responsive," Wit stated. "What did you call him?" Mimi asked. "Hund!" he answered, "That's German for dog." They fed him table scraps and gave him steak bones, and he gnawed them for hours, and then buried them. The next time they went to the store, they bought a bag of dried dog food and a bag of milk-bones for a treat, and a feed bowl and a water bowl. So now they have adopted a dog, and he adopted them. He would lay by the door waiting for them to come out and lay in the gazebo while they were in there enjoying the view over the water.

CHAPTER 59

Their favorite place was the gazebo where they talked and enjoyed each other's company, looking out over the sea at the sunsets and watching the birds forage for food. Mimi started complaining about cramps and pelvic pain and being tired and wanting to take frequent naps, and Wit said it wasn't normal for her to be that tired all the time. Taped on the refrigerator was a list of all the phone numbers of people and places that was familiar with this property, and at the top of the list was, 'Dr. Edith Slattery, Family Practice'. "Call that Dr. Edith, whose name is on the refrigerator and get checked out. You may only need some antibiotics, or something," he suggested. After she returned from the Doctor, she explained, "She isn't sure what the problem is, so she took a blood sample and said it would tell more about it, and she would call in a couple days with the results." Dr. Edith called and reported that her white blood cell count was off and the needed more tests, and she would set it up. Wit drove her to a clinic, and he sat in the waiting room for over two hours while they ran the tests. The next day, Dr. Edith called and reported they were 90% sure she had cancer and she was turning her over to a Dr. Woodhouse, an Oncologist, for further evaluation. They went to a cancer center and Dr. Woodhouse ran more tests and asked Mimi and Wit to wait in his office until he got the readings of the test. He made the disturbing report, "She has Cervical Cancer!" Wit asked, "They can treat that, can't they?" The Doctor answered, "Normally, yes, but it has gone into her Lymph Nodes, and it is too late." Mimi shakenly asked, "How long do I have?" The Doctor responded, "It's hard to predict these things, but my guess is about three months. I am so sorry!" That knocked Wit for a loop, but strangely, Mimi was a lot calmer than he was. He had a lump in his throat and couldn't speak all the way home, and she said, "Well, Wit, I just got a death sentence."

They couldn't eat or sleep and just held each other for most of the night, until she finally went to sleep toward dawn. He got up and went to the gazebo to think and Hund followed him and kept him company. After a few hours, Mimi came out, and Wit said, "I know you are not going to like what I am going to say, but I think its best that you go back to Pittsburgh and get reacquainted with your brothers and their families and spend the rest of your time there. There is really nothing here, and they will see that you are taken care of." She started to sob, and said, "We have finally found our little paradise, and now, suddenly, it's over. I don't want to leave you." "Don't worry about me," he commented. "Me and Old Hund will be alright. Pack everything you want to keep and take all your important papers. When you get there, have one of your Brothers take you to a Lawyer and write your will. Leave everything to them, or whoever you want, but don't leave anything to me. I certainly don't need money; for four decades my Army pay, and all my re-enlisting bonuses went into the bank because I had nothing to spend it on, except that little house in Japan, and that wasn't much by American standards. The Army provided me with everything I needed, and can you imagine how much interest it accrued over all that time? No, leave it all to them. I'll call for a straight through flight to Pittsburgh, so you won't have the drudgery of changing planes." He reserved her a first class, straight through, flight but it had to be out of Tampa, which was about a 70-mile drive. She was understandably upset and nervous and kept talking, like don't forget to do this, or don't forget to do that. They called her flight number and they embraced for the last time. There is an old saying that it is bad luck to watch a plane disappear when it takes off, but he watched it nevertheless.

Driving home, he realized he was alone for the first time in his life; he was born and raised in a big family and then, for more than 40 years, he was always surrounded by the military, and then he had Mimi, and now it was him and Old Hund. He kept himself slightly busy doing the necessary things but had no desire to do anything other than that. He and the old dog would go to the gazebo and stare out over the water and listen to soft and pleasant music on his favorite radio station. The lady commentator would sign off by saying, "God bless you, Chopper Chaplain; I wish you well." And then she would play an old Frank Sinatra tune, 'Softly as I leave you'. It plagued him slightly wondering who that woman was that knew 'Chopper Chaplain'. About 6-weeks later he received a call from Mimi's Brother, Bob, and he said she was fading fast, and they put her in a Hospice so she would pass peaceably. Then he got a call early in the morning about 2-days later, and Bob informed him that she passed during the night. Wit said, "She's in the Lord's hands now; she was a grand lady and a great American. Your family should be proud of her." "We are, and thank you, Wit." Bob followed, and they hung up. He was very saddened and went out to sit in the gazebo. Hund wasn't at the door, like always. When he reached the gazebo, he found Old Hund had passed during the night also. "That is a double whammy!" he remarked, sadly.

For the next couple months, he began to become more adjusted to being alone. He was listening to the radio and they began warning people of a massive hurricane heading in the direction of Florida. He continued listening to the prediction and they said, if it enters the Gulf, it could strengthen and cause unbelievable damage. He called the number on the phone list on the refrigerator for Storm Prep. The lady said, "We have been taking care of your property since it was built, and we know what to do and where everything is stored. Take my advice and when they come around for you to evacuate, don't act brave and think you can ride it out. We have buried a lot of those idiots or plucked them off the rooftops. Go right now with all your important papers and put them in a safety deposit box at the bank, and then go to your local Fire Department and ask where the storm shelter is when you evacuate. Then go to the supermarket and stock up on bottled water and batteries and candles and enough canned goods to last you for a couple weeks. People wait till the last minute and clean off the shelves to where there is nothing left. If there is a power outage, you don't want to be stumbling around in the dark and, when you can return, you want to have enough food to keep you until everything gets back to normal. I was born and raised here, and I don't want to get your hopes up, but I have seen these things veer off to the right toward the Carolinas or to the left toward Louisiana and Texas, and all we would get was high seas and a lot of rain. Don't chance it; we can replace material things, but we can't replace you. Go, Now! We will watch it closely and if it looks like it will hit here, you can be assured we will prep your property." "Thanks Ma'am!" Wit said. "That's good advice. I have seen the damage Typhoons did in the Philippines and Japan, and it ain't pretty."

He went to the bank and the Fire Department and then proceeded to the supermarket and loaded the cart, top and bottom, with everything he thought he would need. He had been on his feet all day and his knee was telling him there was going to be a weather change and when he got into the checkout lane, of all things, there was a customer in front of him that was having a serious discussion about what she was buying. The Cashier was saying, "You can't buy all the items you want if you don't have enough money to pay for them." The customer was a black lady, looked to be in her 40s, and she was pleading. Wit interrupted and said, "What's the problem?" The Cashier explained the problem and Wit said, "Give her everything she wants and put them on my receipt." The black lady waited for him to come out, and she said, "Thank you sir, that was very kind of you." He responded, "No problem, but you could do me a favor, if you are not in a hurry. I would appreciate if you would go with me to my van and help me unload all this stuff." She replied, "Certainly!" They walked to the van and she had it unloaded in no time, and then she asked, "Are you going to be able to unload it when you get home?" "I think I can manage, carrying a few items at a time," he answered. Then she said, "You have been kind to me, and I am not in a hurry, I can go with you and unload it for you, if you will drive me home, because I don't have a car." "How did you get to the store? Do you live nearby?" he asked. "I walked," she answered. "I only live about a half mile from here." "You got a deal," Wit said, "they call me Wit." She said, "My name is Caledonia, but they call me Callie."

They drove to Wit's house, and he asked Callie to pile everything in the middle of the house because he thought that might be the safest place when the storm hit. He noticed her admiring the house and he asked, "What do you think of the house?" She responded, "It's the most beautiful place I have ever seen." He said, "Let's get something to drink and go out and sit in the gazebo. You think this is nice, wait till you look out over the beach. It's my favorite spot and I pray that the storm doesn't destroy it." They sat for a while and he rested his knee. "Mr. Wit," Callie remarked, "They have predicted more hurricanes that was going to blow us away, and they most always turn and go somewhere else. I wouldn't fret just yet." "I appreciate your help, Callie, but I better get you home, but you will need to give me directions because I am rather new around here," Wit offered. "That's easy," Callie replied, "I live in my Cousin, Big Jimmie's Junk Yard. I have a nice setup in a van that sits next to his office, and I use the bathroom in there. He lives in a room in the back of his office." On their way to the junk yard, Wit asked, "Callie, how would you like a job? I need a live-in housekeeper. You can select your own bedroom with your own bathroom, and your job would be to cook, clean, do the laundry, and help me whenever I need help. I have a few strict rules: no smoking in the house or drugs or drinking or bringing in men. I am extremely strict about lying and stealing." "I don't do none of that stuff. I lied to my Mama when I was a little girl, and she thrashed me good, and I never lied again. I would be thrilled to death to work for you, Mr. Wit. When do I start?" she questioned. "You already started,"

Wit answered. "You can pack up your belongings and we can go back to the house."

The sign said 'Big Jimmie's Auto Parts', and it was a huge operation with men moving junk cars with a backhoe, and people, probably mechanics needing parts, were removing parts from the wrecked cars and vans and pickup trucks. There was about a 10 or 12-foot high fence around the junk yard and they drove through a wide double gate. Big Jimmie came out wearing just bibbed overalls and no shirt, and he was exactly like his name, about 6'6" and weighing about 400-pounds. His arms were like clubs and when he stuck his massive hand out to shake, it swallowed up Wit's hand. Callie introduced them, and a teenage boy came by and Callie asked, "Goat, will you give some feed and water to the dogs?" "Yeah, Callie, I can do that," Goat answered. The dogs were 4 big Rottweilers weighing about 150 pounds each, chained with log chains to large dog houses. Callie said Big Jimmie turns the dogs loose at night after he locks the gate. She noted that Goat's parents were sitting on their front porch one night when some boys from the 'hood drove by and shot 'em dead. Goat was only 12 and he was in bed, so then he became homeless. Big Jimmie took him in and gave him a job and he sleeps in that Cadillac on the other side of the office. He said he would send him to college if he kept his grades up.

Callie didn't have much to pack; she had everything in three paper shopping bags. When they got back to the house, Wit suggested that she do the laundry first thing because if they must evacuate, they would want to take clean clothes. He found a couple items that needed washing, so he took them to the laundry room. Callie was standing at the washer with not a stitch on, and Wit acted like he didn't notice. She said,

"I'm sorry, Mr. Wit, but I put everything I own in the wash." "No problem, Callie, after the storms settles down, we will go buy you some clothes and take you to get your hair done," he replied. He had a couple bath robes and took one in for Callie, and said, "Put this on; it should fit. Then while the wash machines are running, fix us something to drink and come out to the gazebo and relax. We may not have it much longer." While they were sitting in the gazebo, Wit said, "You said you had a pretty nice setup in your van; you can do whatever you want in your bedroom to make it the way you want it. I want you to feel at home." The storm did veer off toward Texas but produced high waves and winds and blew things around a bit, but no damage to speak of. Callie being there helped Wit adjust to losing Mimi, and they had great rapport. She was an excellent cook and was willing to prepare his food exactly the way he liked it; she kept the house spotless and the laundry done up and the food well stocked in case of another storm.

About a year later, Wit was sitting in the gazebo and Callie was in the house taking care of business when he heard a voice yell out, "I'm looking for Loren Whitson; do I have the right place?" "Yeah, I'm out here! Come in Old Hammerhead, if your nose is clean." The man stepped into the gazebo and he was a smartly dressed black Captain in his summer khakis. "I'm Captain Dominic Thompson; you are a hard man to find." "I knew where I was all the time," Wit joked. "Now I know why they call you Wit," the Captain replied. "Roughly 80 years ago, a Preacher came to my Grandmother's house in the hills of Kentucky and banged on the screen door. She had no idea who it was and just yelled out, 'come in Old Hammerhead, if your nose is clean'. That has been a little family humor ever since," Wit added. "You look thirsty; could you use a nice cold drink if lemonade?" "That sounds good," the Captain responded, "it's been a hot afternoon." Wit pushed the button on the intercom and whistled into it. A voice came back in the speaker, "What cha need, Mr. Wit?" "We have a thirsty guest out here; why don't you bring out three frosty mugs of lemonade?" Wit requested. Callie had her hair done earlier and just took a shower, and put on some new clothes she bought, and was looking good. She came out carrying a tray with the frosty mugs, and the Captain remarked, "Callie Jefferson! I often wondered what happened to you." "Well, Dominic Thompson, you are looking rather spiffy in your Army threads. I've been working for Mr. Wit for about a year now," she answered. "You two know each other?" Wit asked. "Oh, yeah," the Captain replied. "We are from the same old neighborhood, and I went to elementary school with her two boys, Tom and Jerry. What are they doing now? Is Old Jeff still around?" Wit looked kind of puzzled; he knew nothing about her former life, and never asked because he figured, if she wanted him to know anything, she would have told him.

Callie explained, "Jeff got a job in a big factory and he met a girl there and they had an affair. He came home one day and told me about it and told me to hit the bricks; he didn't need me anymore. In our divorce, he had money for fancy talking lawyers, and I had no money. He left me with only the clothes on my back and no place to live, so Big Jimmie allowed me to stay in one of his cars in the Junk Yard. He convinced the Judge that I could not possibly support the boys, so the Judge granted him full custody and I have not seen or heard from any of them since. I thank the Lord every day and ask him to bless Mr. Wit for finding me and giving me this wonderful job in this wonderful place. I want nothing and I need nothing because he provides me with everything, and I have my own space, and I will serve him with all my ability." Wit had the radio playing and the Lady Commentator said, "God bless you, Chopper Chaplain, I wish you well." Wit interrupted and asked, "Listen to that Lady; do you know who she is?" Callie and the Captain said at the same time, "I do!" "How does she now about Chopper Chaplain?" Wit asked, hoping for answers. "Do you remember rescuing a black Nurse from the Viet Cong?" the Captain responded. Callie was listening with great intensity because she had not heard anything about that incident. "I can tell you every detail and every word you spoke to her, verbatim, because I heard it over a 100-times while I was growing up," the Captain continued. "She is my Mother, Bertha Thompson." "Well, blow me down!" Wit exclaimed. "I didn't ask her name; I was too focused to get her out of there. I will tell you the front part of the story that you don't know. I just returned from R & R in Saigon and the Chaplain said that I was requested for assistance at LZ-Carol. I never heard of a place by that name. When he showed it to me on the map, I recognized it as the old Green Beret camp where I trained before the war ever started, and I knew that jungle like the back of my hand. I took my old Vietnamese friend, because he could speak French and English, and we flew out there in my little chopper. An old friend from Korea, Marine Major Chris Clark, said they were overrun, and they took hostage a black Nurse. The ground was littered with injured and dead troops; I was ticked off because some idiot sent her out there in the first place. It was soon to be dark and all the young Marines were keyed up to go into the jungle after her. I told him that they were so excited they would probably shoot each other, but let me go in alone, and if I wasn't back by morning, they could proceed. I told my friend, Whiny, who was a very old man, to gather up some weapons and grenades and ammunition, and we would stash them, in case we had to fight our way out. I had a good idea where they might be, if they hadn't moved her to the north, but time was on my side because it all happened just hours before, and they camped in a small vacant village. You know the story from there, and as soon as we entered the LZ, they whisked her into a Medevac, and I never saw or heard of her since. I told her I was an American Chaplain, but how did she relate that to Chopper Chaplain?" "When the Medevac took off, she looked down and saw the little helicopter with 'CHOPPER CHAPLAIN' painted on it, and she put two and two together, and knew that had to be you," the Captain answered. "She sure was scared, and I was concerned she might faint or something, and I couldn't carry her out, because she weighed about as much as I did," Wit added. "Sure is a small world!" "Do you want to meet her?" the Captain asked. "Oh, no!" Wit replied. "That was a Politician's War and I get mad when I think of how many lives were lost because of their stupidity. I put in 12-years there and I try to think of more pleasant things, like Callie's fried chicken, and watching the clouds go by."

CHAPTER 60

"The reason I came here," Captain Dom began, "was to talk to you about your medals and classified information in Washington. I do a variety of jobs in the Pentagon, and it came to my attention that the classified information of your activities in Korea, that was sealed by the President for a duration of 40-years, was now eligible to be de-classified. There is still a problem, however. Because of the continued unrest with North Korea, and since there was only a cease fire and not a treaty, even though most of the leaders from that time are dead and gone, the thinking is that it might not be a bad idea to keep it sealed for at least another ten years. They want you to agree and sign off on it." "Are you kiddin' me?" Wit answered, frustrated. "It wasn't my idea; I never signed it in the first place. That's water over the dam, and I couldn't care less; what will happen to it when I'm gone? They can do whatever they want to with it, but I'm not signing anything. Those Politicians will irk me to no end."

Captain Dom then said, "The next thing I have for you is two boxes of medals." "Medals?" Wit remarked. "I don't want any medals. I told them that I didn't do things for medals; I was just doing my job." The Captain opened a box and said, "With all the years of fighting in three wars, you never got a Purple Heart until your last mission in Kuwait. There is a little description attached to each medal and it said you were wounded trying to outrun a donkey." The Captain smiled and Callie laughed, and remarked, "He got a medal for trying to outrun a donkey; never heard of such a thing." "I wasn't trying to outrun him; I was trying to stay in front of him so I wouldn't be trampled," Wit responded. "I should try and explain it. Two Sailor boys left the carrier to take a camel ride, a stupid thing in hostile country, and they must have gotten lost, and they ended up being taken captive by enemy infiltrators. I had a friend that was a Satellite Technician on the carrier, and we viewed the recorded photos of that area, and I concluded where they most likely were being held, and I convinced them that I could rescue them, hopefully unharmed. I needed someone that knew the area and could speak the language, so they assigned a CIA operative, Abdul Hassan, that was born and raised there, and a graduate of Harvard. I guessed they were being held at the end of a long alley, so I dressed like one of them and acted like I was a beggar that couldn't speak or hear and limped to the end of the alley. Abdul stayed back with the old panel truck we used to make our getaway and waited. A guy I called 'donkey-man' followed me through the alley with his donkey. I sat down at the doorstep of the building and held out my cup for a donation. The donkey-man tied his donkey next to me and kicked me when I shook my cup and went inside. The donkey took a dump right beside me, leaving a pile of donkey biscuits. It was only minutes when I heard slapping and yelling and moaning from pain. I took a handful of biscuits and went inside and killed the donkey-man, who was slapping and screaming at the boys, and shoved the biscuits down his throat. There were two women that drove an Army supply truck and got lost and were captured and beaten within an inch of their lives. I cut the Sailors loose and told them each to throw a beaten woman over their shoulder, grab a rifle and run down the alley, when I gave them the clear sign. A woman came in and started screaming and screeching and one of the boys hit her in the face to shut her up and she flew limp against the wall. Another man came in and I hit him so hard with the rifle butt, that I probably killed him. I went out and untied the donkey and started leading him down the alley. About four or five of them came out and started shooting at us; I might say they were poor shots, because the bullets were ricocheting off the walls and the ground. The donkey was shielding me, and he started feeling stings from the shots and started bucking and kicking and braying and running behind me until he was hit by a fatal bullet and went down. I kept running until I got hit in the knee about 15-feet from the truck. The boys were laughing until I went down, and they grabbed me and pulled me to the truck. I was mad now, so I took one of the rifles and started shooting from the hip like I learned with the Green Beret and, standing on one leg, I killed all my pursuers, but they ended my career. I suppose when you think about it, it was a funny sight. The women were treated and thought to be able to recover, but were to return to the States. The boys were ok, bruised and battered, but transported back to their ship."

"That is a great story," Captain Dom remarked, "I'll bet there is a great story behind every one of these medals." He removed another one from the box, and remarked, "Here's one you got, but not from fighting, and it says you rescued the Colonel's wife in Germany." "That was one of my greatest achievements," Wit said, "Callie, you better refresh our drinks because it is a long story, and I will need to tell you what led up to that." She raced to the house and returned with new frosty mugs of lemonade. "I just graduated from flight training and I was assigned to an Army post in Bavaria, which is like the foothills of the Alps, in Germany. I was issued a helicopter and setup a transport service hauling personnel to various places, which saved a lot of time over traveling by roads. It became so popular that they allowed me to get a second helicopter and a pilot. He was making a run, transporting a young Lieutenant, when his chopper developed a mechanical problem and he had to make a forced landing. They weren't hurt but the chopper had seen better days. I flew out to survey the situation and decided the two needed to get checked out at the Infirmary, which was about 40 miles away, because they were both badly shaken up, and rightly so, because not many people walk away from a helicopter crash. It was the first ride for the Lieutenant, and he flat out refused to get into my chopper; he preferred to walk back. I was in no mood for some pampered shave-tail Lieutenant to start giving me problems, so I got up in his face and ordered him to get into the helicopter. I was wrong to a point because he outranked me. We arrived at the Emergency Room at the Infirmary in about 20 minutes, so while they were being checked out, I returned my chopper to the motor pool for service and refueling, and they drove me back to the Infirmary. Doctor Bradley's Nurse said their blood pressure was sky high but they would be alright, and she would release them, and I said no, they need to stay here overnight for observation. He said they weren't staffed for that, and I said I will stay with them. He gave them a sedative and they went to sleep. The Regimental Commander, Colonel Krause, was a mighty warrior in the big war, and he was noted for caring for his men. His wife, Priscilla, considered us all her boys and especially me; she made sure I was well fed and cared for, and we became close; even the Colonel would ask me to be sure she got home safely at times. They lived in town, which was 3-miles from the Post. They were old enough to have been my parents; she only saw the good in people; never the bad. After I met the Captain of the Provost Marshal's Office, I got an eerie feeling that he was an evil and dangerous man, and I warned Priscilla to steer clear of him.

I called the Colonel's home and he wasn't there so she said she was coming to the Post to help out. I told her it wasn't necessary because they were ok but were staying overnight for observation; she insisted she was coming. I sat up with the two guys as long as I could stand it, and then I crawled into one of the other beds and went to sleep. The next thing I knew, a Nurse was shaking me and telling me the Colonel wanted to see me in his office. My day normally started at five in the morning, and I hadn't eaten and had been in my flight suit since the day before. I splashed water on my face to try and wake up, and then went to the Colonel's office. He had never chewed me out for anything before, but he was giving me down the road for the way I spoke to the young Lieutenant. When he finished, he asked if Priscilla had stayed at the Infirmary all night and I said I never saw her, but told her that it wasn't necessary for her to come. He said she left him a note saying she was coming if she could catch a ride. He checked with the gate guards that were on duty all night and they hadn't seen her, so we got concerned she may have been in an accident. I told the Colonel the best way to search was from the helicopter, so we flew along the road and over the streets in town, and then I asked the Colonel if he knew where the Provost Captain lived, and when we flew over his house, his car was still in the driveway, and I asked the Colonel if he normally was in his office at that hour. He said yes, and I said that is where she is. I landed down the street and we ran to the house; he went in the front door and I went in the back door. When I entered, the Captain was covered in blood, and I grabbed him by the throat and made him tell me where she was, and he said she was in the bedroom. I was about to rip his throat out when he looked me in the eyes, and became paralyzed with fear, and froze stiff as a board. The Colonel entered and I said she is in the bedroom, and I wasn't sure at that point if she was still alive. I said call the local police and have them lock up the Captain and I was going to get the chopper. The streets were narrow, but the house was on a little intersection, like a T. I landed the chopper in the intersection praying I didn't hit any wires or tree limbs. The Colonel suggested we call for an ambulance, but I said by the time the ambulance got there and back to the Infirmary, she would be dead. I said wrap a blanket around her and let's get her in the chopper. I lifted straight up to get clear and then made a bee-line to the Infirmary. I radioed for them to get ready, and they ran out as soon as I landed at the Emergency Room door. Doctor Bradley and the Nurses wasted no time. I sat with the Colonel waiting for some news, and the Doctor came out and said her condition was bad and she may not make it till morning. I said I got to see her, and he said no, she needs her rest. I shoved him aside and went in and sat on the side of her bed and held her hand and I prayed harder than I had ever prayed before. I could feel a weak pulse and she wasn't conscious, but I continued to pray till beads of sweat ran down my face. Everybody was concerned and were standing and watching, and then she opened her eyes and faintly asked, 'Am I going to die, Wit', and I said no you are not going to die because the Lord told me you were going to live. You are in bad shape and it will take time, so go to sleep now and I will come back in the morning. I tried to stand, and my knees buckled, and they helped me to a chair, and I sat till I got my strength back. I walked out to where the Doctor was and he asked, 'how can you in good conscience tell someone they are going to live', and I said Bradley, don't you believe in prayer? He said I don't believe in that mumbo-jumbo and I said, Bradley, the Bible says that faith can move mountains, and tonight we moved a mountain. He said get out of here so I can do my work and I asked him, joyfully, if he liked to sing and he said he liked to belt out a tune or two, and I said come to church on Sunday, and belt out a few tunes to the Lord. Funny thing was he showed up at church and from what I heard later he never missed a Sunday. He married a lady Doctor and they both attend regularly.

Priscilla did recover in time. I visited her every morning, first thing, and we prayed. I was in the Chaplain's Service for over 40-years, and I have prayed dying troops into Heaven with their last breath; even some that admitted to being Atheists. That was my job and I don't need medals for that. As for Priscilla, that medal should go to the Lord, not me. The Provost Captain was sent to Leavenworth Prison and they said he was insane and kept repeating the *Devil* was going to get him. Years later I heard he committed suicide. They said they needed experienced chopper pilots in Indo-China, so I had to leave. I was offered positions in four places; a General in Washington offered me a commission to be on his staff; the General of Vll Corps offered me a position on his staff but I had to take a commission; they wanted me to be a training officer but I had to take a commission along with it; so I said I was a trained combat soldier and a trained killer and I was going to stay in the Chaplain's Service where I belonged. I spent 12-years in Vietnam." Callie was sobbing, "That's the greatest story I have ever heard." "There is a story behind every one of those medals, but that has to be my greatest of all time," Wit remarked. Then the Captain said, "I've got to go!" Wit said, "You are welcome to spend the night; we have plenty of room." The Captain responded, "I appreciate it, but I promised my Mother I would be back for dinner. I'll stop back tomorrow."

The Captain returned early the next morning, and asked, "Getting back to the medals, what do you want me to do with them? I have two boxes and there is a description attached to each one spelling out briefly what action was taken to earn the medals." "I have no use for the medals," Wit replied. "I told 'em, at the time, I didn't want 'em. Why don't you send them to my wife in Ohio so she can entertain herself sorting through them? I don't know the address but I'm sure you have it on file, since you send her a check each month." Captain Dom added, "Also, I really enjoyed your stories yesterday, especially filling in the blanks about my Mother, and I know Callie did too. If I might suggest, we have several VA hospitals not far from here, and you could continue your service, not officially of course, by visiting them and sharing your stories with those patients. They most likely have stories of their own they might like to share. It may give them a break from their boredom, and you could continue making use of your talents. I'll take care of the medals, but now I got a plane to catch, and I'll stop in the next time I come back."

CHAPTER 61

Mrs. Maggie Whitson unexpectedly received a box from the US Army at her home in Southwest Ohio. She had no idea what was in it and it made her nervous, so she called her Brother, Lonnie Combs, and her Nephew, Mark Combs, to come as soon as they could. Since she had no closer relation or friends, she built her life around them after Wit left, many years ago. There were two smaller boxes in a larger box, and Mark wasted no time ripping open the boxes, and he remarked, "Wow! Look at all these medals." He started reading the descriptions attached to each one, and being surprised, he commented, "Uncle Loren must have been the most decorated soldier in the whole damned Army. Here's two I recognize because he got them rescuing me and Keith Mahaffey and two Army women truck drivers. That was so funny watching him trying to outrun an old donkey, but then he got shot in the knee, and it wasn't funny anymore. When he reached the truck, he grabbed a rifle, set the selector on semi-automatic, and holding it on his hip, shot every one of them damned towelheads that was chasing him down that alley. I've never seen anybody shoot like that. This Purple Heart was from getting shot, and it's the only Purple Heart in the boxes. There was a bastard beating me and Keith, and when he came in, he ripped the guy's throat out slicker than snot, and then jammed donkey turds in the bastard's mouth, like he had been practicing it for years. After he untied us, an old woman came in screaming, and Keith hit her so hard, she flew against the wall across the room. He told us each to carry a woman driver, take a rifle and run down that alley to a truck that was waiting, and he would follow. The driver was a CIA agent; it gave us time to escape; he sure saved our asses."

Lonnie explained, "We were ambushed by the NVA and they killed all but four of us. It looked like we were headed toward Hanoi, and when they stopped and made camp, they put us in cages, like animals in a zoo. One guy tried to escape, and they shot him running, but only wounded him and he hid in some tall grass. Loren snuck up behind our cages and unlatched them, and told us he was an American Chaplain, and not to make a sound until he gave us the word. Our guards got drunk on some kind of alcohol and smoked weed, and when they went to sleep, he gave us the word, and we got out and bashed their heads in and took their rifles. Another Gook happened in and Loren spun him around and ripped out his throat, and he ordered us to follow him because he knew the way back to our lines. We found the wounded guy and half-carried him. When we got back, there was a Medevac waiting for us, and there was a little chopper there that had painted on it, 'CHOPPER CHAPLAIN'. The Medevac gunner told us we were lucky because we had just met the 'Jungle Rat'. He wasn't dressed like an ordinary soldier; he was dressed like a guerrilla fighter, and I hardly recognized him. He said he got word from my Sister that I was missing. The wounded guy went home, and the other two guys were later killed, but I survived, and I will always be grateful for that. Here's a document that says the highly classified document concerning Sgt. Loren Whitson's activities in Korea, sealed by the President was to be declassified, but due to the present circumstances, it will remain sealed for at least 10 more years. Sounds like he was a pretty important guy; and busy too, getting all these medals."

Mark questioned, "Aunt Maggie, whatever happened between you two? I was always afraid to ask." "I screwed up royally, and it was all my fault, and I have regretted it ever since," she explained. "I dated a lot of guys, most of them were jerks or assholes, but when I met him, right after he returned from Korea, he was the kindest and sweetest guy I had ever known. He had a little rubber ball he squeezed all the time, and he said he needed to strengthen his hands. He was suffering from severe stomach pains, and just the thought of food, made him gag and dry heave. I took him to a couple Doctors, but they couldn't find his problem; they treated him for peptic ulcers, but they admitted he never had anything like that. We dated for about 10 months, and then ran off and got married. He said he was extremely jealous and if I ever cheated on him, it would not go very well. I convinced him he had to trust me. He came home early from work one night, suffering with stomach pains, and caught me in the bed with a lover; we were only married 6 months. He went into a rage, jumped like a cat on my lover, who was 60 or more pounds heavier than Loren, and he was about to rip out his throat. I was screaming at him and trying to pry his hands loose, but he was extremely strong, and then I saw his eyes. They were crimson red, like a blazing fire, and I could tell he wasn't in there, but possessed by a *Demon*, and

I knew I was looking at the *Devil* that night. He seemed to come to his senses and got up and went into the living room, nervous and shaking, and grimacing from the pain. My lover gathered his clothes and shoes under his arm and went for the door cussing and threatening Loren. Our apartment was on the second floor and he always kept a ball bat behind the door. He swung the bat and hit the guy as hard as he could, and knocked him down the steps, head-first. The guy lay at the bottom of the steps on the landing, dazed for a while, and then gathered his stuff and ran out the door, continuing to cuss and threaten. Loren told me I better leave, so I went to some friends' apartment across the street, and I could see him pacing in front of the picture window, and he paced all night, and at dawn he went to visit his Mother across town, and told her he was re-enlisting because he couldn't adjust to civilian life. We owed on everything, so he said with his signing bonus and Army allotment, and what I made as a Nurse, I should be able to pay everything off. He said we were done; no writing; no phone calls, no contact of any kind, and that is the way it has been for over 40 years. Having met the *Devil* that night, it put the fear in me that I haven't been able to shake, and that is why I don't have any desire to date or associate with other people. He became a helicopter pilot, and a Congresswoman from Utah came to visit, and we drank tea and she said she met him in Germany, and he transported her to all the military bases in the Bavaria area. She said an Army Doctor solved his stomach problem and he was doing just fine; he was the most loved man in all of Bavaria and respected by all ranks all the way to Washington. Whenever he gets a promotion, I get a raise. I take full blame for my actions and for ruining my life, but I think he went on to succeed, and like you boys said, he must have been a mighty hero." Lonnie said, "There are medals and ribbons here from Korea, Germany, Vietnam, and the Gulf War, but if he got his knee shot out, they probably retired him. He's got to be in his 60s; I wondered where he ended up?" Mark said, "I saw those eyes when he ripped the throat out of that camel-jockey. I get chills just thinking about it." "I saw 'em, too," Lonnie said. "I never thought much about it, being so glad to get the hell out of there, but for him to be in all those wars and not get scratch, he had to have been protected by some spiritual force, and it had to somehow been connected to those mysterious eyes. Scary, ain't it?"

Wit told Callie he was going to visit one of the VA hospitals around Sarasota and ask her if she wanted to go along. He said it would give her a break and a chance to shop in some different stores. She said she didn't need anything, and she wanted to do the laundry. He walked in, using his cane, and there was a Nurse sitting inside a glass enclosed office and had her name on the door, Lori Foster, RN. He went in and remarked, "I guess you are the Big Mama that runs this dog and pony show?" She looked up surprised and answered, "Glory be, Wit Whitson!" He replied, "How do you know me? I don't recall seeing you before." "No, but I've seen you at Clark AF Hospital," she responded. "Gosh, that must have been 15-years ago. What's with the cane?" "Some camel-jockey in Kuwait was using me for target practice, and got a lucky shot, and blew out my knee," he answered. Two young Nurses walked in and one said, "Miss Foster, we are going to take off." "Girls, I want you to meet Wit Whitson, more commonly known as 'Chopper Chaplain'," Nurse Lori introduced, "When he walked into the hospital in the Philippines wearing his sharply pressed flight suit, all us girls swooned. That was about 15-years ago; I'm not that hot little Nurse now; I look into the mirror and see a graying old woman." "I don't agree with that," Wit remarked, "you look plenty attractive to me, and back then, you must have been a knock-out. I'm sorry if I never noticed you; I spent 12-years roaming the jungle and I was there for two years trying to recapture my sanity and become a human again." "Is everything alright out there, girls?" Lori asked, before they signed out. "Yes," one said, "Old Harry Weed is his obnoxious self, but everything else is quiet. We're going to the beach while there is still some sun and before it rains again," and they gave Wit a smile and left. "There's a perfect patient for you to work with," Lori noted, "he lost his leg in Vietnam and hates the world; the girls tolerate him but don't like his attitude." She gave him a visitor's pass and escorted Wit to the large spacious lounging room where vets were playing cards and checkers and watching television, and she pointed out Harry sitting in a wheel-chair next to a window, just staring out. Wit walked over to Harry and thought he would break the ice, when he said, "Listen up, Private, I'm putting you on guard duty." Harry looked at him with scorn and replied, "Who the hell are you?" "I'm Wit Whitson and I came to visit with you and pray," Wit replied. "Pray!" Harry remarked. "I ain't prayed since my dear old Mama made us go to Sunday School." "You must have had the same Mama that I did," Wit responded. "She said if you can play ball and run around with them other heathens, then you can go to Sunday School, and we never missed a Sunday. Sound about right?" "Sounds exactly right," Harry answered, a little more relaxed. "I was raised in a big family and we were as poor as dirt. Did you have a big family?" Wit asked. "Only my kid Brother and my Dear Old Mom, God rest her soul," Harry answered, solemnly. "My kid Brother was one of them protesters and ran off to Canada to avoid the draft, and stayed there till the war was over. He came to visit me one time and I told him to never come back, I didn't want to associate myself with a traitor." "I hate to say it, Harry, but I feel as strongly about it as you do," Wit followed. Then he cut to the chase, "So how did you lose your leg?" Harry explained, "In July 1970, in western Thua Tien Province, in a place named Fire Base Ripcord, we were surrounded by 10,000 NVA troops and we weren't doing so good. When there was about 300 of us left, we were ordered to get the hell out of there and let the Flyboys destroy them. I never could run fast, but I ran faster than I ever ran in my life, and when I thought I was safe, I stepped on a land mine and blew my leg off. I didn't know what happened; I couldn't feel my leg and I was numb, and I couldn't think straight, and I guess I went into shock. The next thing I remember I was in a field hospital and the Doctor said my war was over. They are doing a lot of things with prosthesis these days, but since I don't have a lot of leg to work with, they haven't been able to come up with anything. Maybe someday they can get it all figured out." Just then a lady came in with a food cart with full shelves spaced from top to bottom, and said, "Mr. Weed, are you ready to eat?"

The food lady read Wit's name on his visitor's pass and ask him, "Mr. Whitson, would you like a tray? We are having lasagna and garlic toast." "That sounds good," Wit said, "yes, if you please. I am enjoying my visit with Harry and I haven't eaten." She offered water, lemonade, and Coke and he selected the Coke. "Harry, they are feeding you pretty good here. The place is nice and clean and everybody I have talked to is friendly, so why are you so mean to them?" Wit asked. "These people never caused your problem; in fact, they weren't even born yet. They seem to be going out of their way to make you as comfortable as possible." Harry didn't know how to answer that, so he silently continued to eat, and then he asked, "Were you in 'Nam?" Wit commented, "I spent 12-years there; two years before the first Marines landed, and I was the last to leave. The news made a big ta-do about the last Helicopter that took the last Americans from the Embassy, but I'm here to tell you, Harry, there was a little Bell UH-1H that followed it, and I was the pilot and had two lady Army Doctors aboard. That little chopper was riddled with so many bullet holes and we were leaking oil and it spit and sputtered and we prayed we would make it, and the Lord answered our prayer and we landed on the deck of that big carrier, and they pushed it over the side into the sea. I have seen it all and done it all, and I have prayed beautiful young men, no more than 20-years old, into Heaven with their last breath. I held some in my arms and some by the hand, those who had hands, and some had faces missing and their intestines showing, and more sickening things you can ever imagine. You think that was tough? There were times I didn't think I could continue, but the Chaplain told me in Korea, if you take each one to heart, it will drive you crazy; just do your best and be satisfied and move on to the next one. I put in over 40-years, Korea and Vietnam, and never got a scratch, but then in the Gulf War, I took a round in the knee that ended my career. You need to rethink your situation, Harry, and start doing what your Mama taught you, pray and pray hard. You could have been one of those 58,000 that never returned; never had a chance for a family or a life of any kind, but you were given a second chance, tough I know, but still a chance, so pray that you can be a model patient, and thankful for what you have. I want to say a little prayer with you and then I got to go." He and Harry bowed their heads and Wit said a prayer, and all those in the room were listening to the conversation and they all bowed their heads. As he got up to leave, Harry asked, "Will you be coming back?" "I plan to come twice a week, so I'll be checking with ya," Wit answered, and they shook hands, and Harry cupped Wit's hand in both of his.

As he was leaving, he reported to Lori, "I think he is going to be alright; I just had to meet him on his own level and let him know he wasn't the only one injured in combat. I plan to visit the hospitals in the area twice a week, so I'll be back next week." "Just so you know," Lori said, "I plan to retire at the end of next month; I've put in a lot of years and I have had enough." "What do you plan to do when you hang up your stethoscope?" Wit asked. Lori explained, "I have family in this area and my fiancé is a Filipino, and he came with me five years ago to be near my family. Since we have been here, they never call or visit or include me in any of their functions, so we decided to go back to Manila; buy a little place and raise a little garden and live the good life. I have been invited to teach Nursing, but I said I might teach a class part time, but no more than that. The girls will probably be having a little going away party, so why don't you join us?" Wit went into a couple other hospitals the following week and then came back to check on Harry. "You really worked your magic on Harry," Lori remarked. "He came out of his shell and started telling old stale jokes, and then the other old guys starting telling their old stale jokes, and that room went from a quiet and solemn place to a happy and joyous place with a lot of laughing and joking; everybody's spirits were uplifted and the girls are much happier." Wit made regular visits and prayed with Harry and all his fellow patients. Lori's last day arrived, and Wit asked Callie to join him, and she gladly accepted. The place was decorated with streamers and balloons, and a nice colorful cake sat on a table; a lot of talking and laughing filled the room. Wit told Lori, "I think I am quitting, too. When I was younger, what I did, didn't bother me, but now it's bringing back memories that I am trying to forget." When he had partied enough, he said, "I want to wish you all the luck in the world, Lori. I am going to see Harry and then we will take off." "Wit," she responded. "You hadn't heard? Harry passed away last Saturday night. He had a bad heart, and it finally gave out. They took his body away and said they were going to have a small graveside military service with taps and 21-gun salute." Wit never spoke all the way home and Callie knew he was grieving for his friend.

CHAPTER 62

With death being so close, Wit started thinking that it was time for him to write his will. He leafed through the yellow pages of the phone book for an Attorney that specialized in wills and trusts. He found one with a name he could remember so he wrote down the name and address and phone number. He said to Callie, "I have some business to take care of so I will be out for several hours." He went to the bank and retrieved some papers from the safety deposit box and drove to the Attorney's office. The name on the door was Brinkman and Brinkman, Attorneys at Law; Wills, Trusts; Investments. He walked in and a pretty young black girl was sitting at the desk, and asked pleasantly, "Can I help you, sir?" He replied, "My name is Loren Whitson and I have come to see about making a will, so if you will call Mr. Brinkman, I would appreciate it." "Do you want the older one or the younger one?" she asked. "I'll take the older one," he answered. She pushed the button on the intercom and said, "There is a gentleman here to see about making a will." "Does he have an appointment?" came the reply. "No, he just walked in," she said. "Bring him in and

I'll take care of him," was the answer. She led him through the door and introduced him, and the Attorney stood to greet him. He was a distinguished looking black man with graying around the temples and wore an expensive looking suit; best guess was he was likely in the low 50s. "My name is Jay Brinkman; what made you select this firm?" he asked. "I looked through the yellow pages and saw Brinkman and I remembered a kid I went all through school with that had the name of Brinkman, so it was a name I could remember. He was as white as a ghost and from a well-to-do family, and because of that, he was one of the Teacher's pets. He wore good clothes and I wore hand-me-downs because I was from a poor family, but he was a good kid and we got along fine. He went to college and I was drafted into the Army." "Do you have a problem dealing with a black firm?" Jay asked. "Not a bit," Wit replied, "I spent over 40-years in the Army, and I have friends all over the world; black, white, and yellow, and any other color you can think of. I am color blind when it comes to that, and I only see what is in their heart." "How can we help you today?" Jay asked. "I had some friends die recently and I figured it was time to make out my will," Wit responded. Jay pushed the button on the intercom and said, "Makil, you may want to sit in on this."

A younger black man, around 30, came in and Jay introduced him as his son and partner. Jay had the necessary forms and a note pad, and they proceeded to write all the pertinent information. A young lady and two young girls, about eight or ten years old, came in and Makil introduced them as his wife Caitlan, and the girls, Lura and Rachel, and this is Mr. Whitson, a new client. "My friends call me Wit," he replied. She said, "My friends and family call me Cate." "What are you doing here?" Makil asked Cate. "These girls have all this energy and are driving me nuts," she remarked. "I had to get them out of the house." "If they like the beach and like to swim, I have a house on the beach, and you all can come and spend the day," Wit remarked. Makil asked, "You girls want to go to the beach and swim?" "Yeaaah!" they answered, all excited. "Get your swim-suits and beach towel and come back and follow Wit home. We should be finished here by the time you get back." They went out the door jumping and yipping, and Jay said, "They are my pride and joy." Cate and the girls followed Wit home, and Callie came out, and Wit said, "Callie, we have some new friends; Cate, Lura, and Rachel Brinkman. They want to go to the beach. I think there are some beach toys in the shed, if you wish to look." "Glad to meet ya, Callie," Cate said, "hope we are not imposing?" "Not at all," Callie answered, "glad to have ya." "You have a beautiful place here," Cate commented. "We call it our *'Precious Place'*," Callie responded, proudly. They spent the rest of the day and the girls were worn out when they left, and Wit said, "You are welcome to come anytime." They liked Callie and Wit and, the feeling was mutual, and they came back often.

Callie and Wit were sitting in the gazebo and they heard coming down the street an old rattle trap with a blown muffler. "Sounds like that thing should go to Big Jimmie's," Callie commented. It pulled into their driveway and a young black man and his white squeeze got out and started walking toward the gazebo, and he said, "Hello, Mama, I'm your baby boy, Jerry, and I come to see ya." His girl was a sight to behold; she wore a miniskirt that was two sizes too small and she was rather beefy, and she had a ring in her eyebrow and nose and lip, and a low-cut top with her huge jugs about to plop out. Callie minced very few words with him and said, "You ain't coming to see me. Turn your black-ass around and ride on out of here and take your white slut with ya." "But Mama, I told Millie that you would cook us some supper. You are the only family I got; Tom is in prison for armed robbery and assault; Daddy was killed in a bar fight in Orlando, and now it's just me and you," he begged. "I said git, you worthless trash," she ordered. He got back into the car and the slut had a hard time raising her leg with the tight skirt, so she pulled it up over her huge bare cheeks, showing she had no underwear on and a tattoo of a dagger dripping with blood, slid in, and they drove off. Wit commented, "Wonder what dumpster he found her in?" "Probably the same one he lives in," Callie replied. "You were rather rough on him, weren't ya?" Wit remarked. "Mr. Wit, I've been beaten, kicked, mistreated, thrown out like garbage with only the clothes on my back; not a nickel to my name, and nowhere to sleep and no hope of ever getting enough to eat, and they have had 20-years to come and visit and act like a family; and then come and want me to cook for 'em and be a loving Mama; not going to happen," she explained. Wit said, wanting to soothe her jangled nerves, "Callie, you are my family! Go put on a nice dress, and me and you are going to a fine restaurant and get us a big steak dinner and give you a night off. How does that sound?" "Mr. Wit, I don't know what to say," Callie answered. "Where is there a fine restaurant around here?" "I noticed a place next to the Firehouse that is called 'Firehouse Eatery', and I've seen fine folks go in, so we can give it a try," he replied.

They went in and a hostess seated them and handed them a menu and said the waitress would be there shortly. A pretty black waitress approached and said, "Callie!" and Callie said, "Carmen! It's been a long time. How long you been working here?" "About five years now," Carmen answered. "We get a good class of people that come in and they tip well. What can I get you to drink?" "Me and Carmen went to the same church together when we were young," Callie explained to Wit. "I haven't seen her in ages. Mr. Wit, did you see the prices in that menu? Yikes! $30 for a steak?" Carmen returned with their lemonade and Callie said, "I want to introduce you to my best friend, Mr. Wit." They exchanged greetings and Carmen asked, "Have you decided what you want to order?" Wit responded, "I want the filet-mignon, well done; the cook can even butterfly it; garden salad with ranch dressing; baked potato with butter and sour cream; hot rolls with plenty of butter; bring me coffee when you bring the meal." Callie just looked at him not knowing what to say, and he noticed it and said, "Callie wants the prime rib and the same sides as I'm getting. How do you want your meat cooked, Callie? Medium rare? Or with just a touch of pink?" "Just barely pink!", she responded. After Carmen walked away, Callie said, "Mr. Wit, that's $20." After they finished eating, Carmen asked if everything was alright and they said yes but would like another cup of coffee. Carmen got a little antsy and said, "See all those people standing at the door? They have reservations and your table is reserved." Wit said, "You mean we have to leave?" She responded, "I'm sorry, but it's not me; it's the rules, so they can serve as many people as they can." She handed Wit the bill inside a black leather folder. He looked at it and it totaled $80, so he put a $100-dollar bill inside, and handed it back to her, and said, "Nice meeting you, Carmen. You can tell the management we are going to stop at the little diner up the street and get a cup of coffee."

When they returned home, they found it had been broken into and vandalized and was trashed; everything thrown around and food scraps on the table and the refrigerator door standing slightly open. Wit told Callie to call the Police and don't touch anything, and he disappeared momentarily and came back with his Army .45 Semi-Automatic handgun. "I'm glad I had this well-hidden, or they were too stupid to know where to look," he remarked. It was only a matter of minutes when two uniformed Policeman knocked on the door, and they introduced themselves as Sergeant George Stang and Patrolman Rick Meinhardt. As soon as they went in and saw the mess, they radioed for two people to come and get fingerprints and photographs. After they checked the table, Callie cleaned it off so they could sit and write their report, and Sgt. George asked, "Do you have any idea who would have done this?" Callie answered, without hesitation, because she was really pissed and because her *Precious Place* had been violated, "Jerry Jefferson, a black guy about 26-years old, and you will probably find him on some bar stool with a white slut sitting with him. He's driving an old beat up car with a blown muffler. Can I close the refrigerator door now?" "Yes, of course," the Sergeant said. "We have the prints from the door handle." Big Jimmie walked in and said, "I guess I'm too late. I came to warn ya that Jerry was in town and wanted to know where you lived. He needed money so I gave him a $100. I'm sorry, Callie, I didn't know they would do anything like this. George? Looks like you are on the job. Jerry is Callie's boy, but he's no good; Hope you catch him and throw away the key." Then he related to Wit and Callie, so they understood he was well acquainted with the Police Department, "George drags in wrecked cars to my place and keeps me in business." Sgt.

George finished the report and they got all the photos and fingerprints they needed, and he said they could go ahead and straighten up the place.

The next morning Callie and Wit had their breakfast and were relaxing in the gazebo enjoying their coffee when Sgt. Stang appeared and strolled out to the gazebo, "Well, we got 'em; it was easy from your descriptions. We have had a rash of break-ins in the area and their fingerprints matched most of them, so they will be doing some time in the lockup." He began looking around and said, "I pass this place often but never saw it up close. This is the most beautiful place on the entire strip; it's like you have your own little park." "That is why we call it our *Precious Place*," Callie said, proudly, like she claimed a share in it. "That is a magnificent grill," George remarked, "Whoever built that knew what he was doing." "I wouldn't know," Wit replied, "we never use it. I was out of the country for 40 years and never had a need for one." "I know how to use it," George remarked. "I'm the Grill Meister." "Do you have a family, George?" Wit asked. "Yeah, I have a lovely wife and three beautiful kids," he answered. Then Wit said, "On your next day off, bring your family and spend it with us and Callie can buy some steaks and hotdogs and hamburgers, and we will see how good you really are. Come early enough so the kids can enjoy the beach and your Wife can go with Callie and buy up everything we need, and we will have a picnic, in our little park. Do you know Makil Brinkman? His Wife and kids spend time here and have a grand time. If you have no objections, we can invite them and have a real picnic, and the kids can wear themselves out on the beach." "Yeah, I know Makil," George answered. "We graduated from high school together; he went to college and I joined the Police Force. I think my Wife and kids would really enjoy that. What do you want us to bring?" "Nothing," Wit answered, "Callie can get everything we need at the market. Sound ok with you, Callie?" "Sounds exciting to me," Callie responded, "I haven't been on a picnic since our Sunday School had one when I was a kid. What day we having it? I'll call Cate and invite them." "I might warn you," Wit said. "There won't be any alcohol served here; just good clean fun."

They all arrived around 10:00 am on a Saturday morning to make the best use of the beach, and also, to allow Callie time to go to the supermarket. George introduced his wife, Mary, and their kids, Michael, Ricky, and Valerie, and then Cate, and Mary went with Callie to buy everything they needed. Callie ran into Big Jimmie at the store and invited him also, and he accepted. The kids took all the beach toys from the shed and headed, yelling and screaming, to the beach. George found enough charcoal and lighter fluid in the shed, and started dusting off the grill and scraping the grate. When Big Jimmie showed up, Wit told him of all the fishing poles and tackle in the shed, so he went to the beach to fish from the surf. Makil went to the beach with the kids and joined in playing with them; beach paddle ball, frisbee, building sandcastles, and just general running into the water. The ladies returned carrying in all their morsels along with a couple large bags of ice for the soft drinks and loaded the large cooler that was in the shed. They bought strip steaks for the adults and hotdogs and hamburgers for the kids and all the necessary condiments. Callie bought 3 steaks for Big Jimmie, knowing how he eats. They bought small tubs of potato salad, coleslaw, macaroni salad, and chips. They bought marshmallows to roast later. George didn't lie; he grilled everything to perfection, and everybody had their fill. Big Jimmie caught several nice sized bluefish but then released them. The weather cooperated and it was a very enjoyable day. Fact was, this became their little tight knit group of close friends. When it was time to leave, the Mothers told the kids to give Callie and Wit a hug and tell them they loved them and thank them for the perfect day. Callie teared up and Wit kinda choked up because they knew it was sincere and they would always be their friends.

CHAPTER 63

A week later, Jay Brinkman, the Lawyer, called and wanted to stop by and have Wit look over some papers and sign them, if they looked alright. For no special reason, Callie had cleaned up and was looking good. When Jay walked in, Wit noticed the gaze between Callie and the Lawyer, and the sparks that were flying. He sat at the kitchen table to look over the papers, and mumbled to himself, "I'll take it from here, Callie." He introduced them and asked, "Are you married, Jay?" "I was," he responded. "My wife, who was Makil's Mother, was diagnosed with Lymphoma and they treated her for years and they thought she was going into remission and we had hopes she was going to be alright, but then things went sour and she passed away 8 years ago. The Grandkids are my life now. I've been hearing glowing reports about your little park here and how much fun they have and how they learned to love you two." "The feeling is mutual," Wit replied, "and Callie is a natural with kids. You are welcomed to join us whenever they all come. If you should get lonely and want a night out, I think I can spare Callie for an evening." "Mr. Wit!" she exclaimed. "I can't believe you said that." Jay remarked, grinning, "I was thinking the same thing. I'll pick you up next Friday evening, if you are available?" "She will be ready; what time," Wit offered. Callie was speechless and stood with her mouth open. "These papers look good," Wit remarked. "Do I sign at the X at the bottom of each page?" "Yes," Jay answered. He gathered up his papers and as he left, he said, "The office closes at 5:00 on Friday and I will come pick you up, Callie. We can go out and eat and maybe dance a little. It's been a while since I've danced, so I might be a little rusty." After he left, Callie remarked, "Me, going out with a Lawyer. I don't know what to wear or how to act; I'm nervous." Wit responded, "Callie, you are a good person and have a good heart; just act yourself and I think you will be fine. If you need a nice dress, go buy one; get some shoes to match and get your hair done."

Jay took her to the same restaurant where she and Wit went. They were seated and Jay excused himself to go to the men's room. Carmen came up and said, "Girl, look at you; running in high society; sporting new threads (dress) and wheels (shoes); you are going to be the talk of the town." Jay returned, and remarked, "What are you two talking about?" Carmen responded, "Me and Callie have known each other way back when we were in the same Sunday School Class, and as much as I hate to admit it, that was many years ago." While they ate, Jay asked Callie, "How did you get hooked up with Wit?" She explained how he came up behind her in the Supermarket and offered to pay for little hand basket of items; how he asked her to ride home with him to help unload his car with a large stock of items he bought in case the storm hit; then offered me a job to care for the *'Precious Place'*, and she knew the Lord had answered her prayers. "I can tell you he has a lot of respect and admiration for you," Jay remarked. "I can tell you I feel the same way; the things he says and does is like he is some kind of prophet," Callie responded. "He tells me if there is anything I want or need, get it. All the troubles and despair I have been through in my life, I never dreamed I would be in the position I am in right now."

Wit was sitting up and waiting for her, like a Father waits for his teen-age daughter on her first date. She came in around midnight and went straight to the bathroom. When she came out, he asked, "Did you have a good time?" "Oh, yeah," she answered, "we went to the same restaurant you and I went too, but they never asked us to leave like before. I guess it was because he is a Big Shot Lawyer, and Carmen says he comes in often. Then we went to his big mansion and listened to music and danced a little." "Did he treat you right?" Wit asked. "Yeah, he was gentle and respectful," she replied. She knew what Wit was referring too, and she commented, "How did you know?" "You didn't get your dress buttoned back properly," he answered, and grinned. "Oh, Mr. Wit, I haven't done anything like that in 20-years. If I have upset you, I will never get over it," she responded. "Relax, Callie, you didn't upset me," he remarked. "It's a natural thing for two people that are craving companionship. The only thing that would upset me would be if you decided to leave; you have become a part of our *Precious Place*, and it would never be the same." She teared up a little and said, "A herd of wild horses couldn't run me away from you and our *Precious Place*." "Go get a good night's sleep because I got a big surprise for you in the morning," Wit said, with his usual grin. "Tell me now!" she exclaimed, "I won't be able to sleep a wink." "No, no, it has to be tomorrow," he taunted. "I'll tell you after we eat breakfast."

The next morning, she was as excited as a kid on Christmas morning; she choked down her breakfast, and asked, "Now what is the surprise?" He said, "Callie, I am now a senior citizen; I am 65-years old today." "Mr. Wit, I'll bake you the prettiest cake you ever saw, and we can have a party." "I don't need a party; just me and you," he replied. Now she was extremely excited, and stated, "You can't have a Birthday Party without kids. I'll call Mary and Cate, and we will go buy everything and decorate the house and the gazebo, and I'll even invite Big Jimmie. He's like a big kid when it comes to parties." "Well tell them absolutely no presents. I got everything I need," Wit responded. Callie called Mary and Cate, and when she mentioned there was going to be a Birthday Party for Wit, the kids could be heard, over the phone, screaming with excitement. The ladies bought up all the food and decorations and the kids helped decorate and it was an exciting day with their little group of friends. George did his usual fine grilling and they all stuffed themselves and then Callie brought out the cake with the candles burning, and they all sang as Wit blew out the candles. The cake could have taken first prize in any contest and decorated to perfection. Then George said, "You said no presents, but we had to buy you a little something." Wit opened the small package and pulled out a bright shiny gold colored fishing plug. Big Jimmie got excited, and remarked, "That's an artificial Mackerel bait; I love baked Mackerel. Maybe George could bake one on that nice grill; they slice them down the back and spread them open and bake them with the head still on." The kids went, "Ugh!" Lura handed him their offering and he opened it with anticipation. Makil remarked, "It's a floppy brim sun hat to protect your head while you are on the beach." "I sometimes wore one of these in the jungle. The nice thing about these is you can roll them up and put them in your pocket. Thank you all; I appreciate your gifts and will treasure them always." Callie said, sadly, "You said no presents, so I didn't get you anything." Wit commented, "Callie, you are all the gift I need; look at this beautiful cake and the fine decorations; what more could a man ask for; and I have you looking after me." She teared up because he always knew the right things to say to her. They were all aware of the great admiration he had for Callie. "Big Jimmie, take that plug out to the beach and see if you have any luck," Wit offered. Big Jimmie caught three nice size fish, but then released them, "I'm coming back to catch a stringer full and we can have a real fish dinner." The sun started to set and that brought out the insects and the bug zapper in the gazebo started working overtime. That was the signal it was time for all to go home, and they left full of good food and joyous.

There were more little beach parties the ensuing year. It became the place to go for the beach and fun and friendly companionship, and most especially for the kids. They acquired deep feelings and admiration for Callie and Wit, and they openly expressed it often. Even Big Jimmie came more often and created a lot of fun for the kids, because he was like a big kid himself. The *'Precious Place'* for Callie and Wit became the *'Precious Place'* for their little group of friends.

Callie had gone to the market and Wit was watching a program on the television, and when she walked in, he said, "Come 'ere Callie, you have to watch this." "Wait till I put the groceries away," she replied. "No, no, you'll miss it!" he exclaimed. "That lady Doctor, Susan McElroy, wrote a book called, *'It Happened One Night'*, and it's a best seller. I know her from over 25-years ago, and the book is about something

I did, and she is a guest on the show, and being interviewed about the book."

Interviewer: "Why did you write the book?"

Susan: "I wanted to write it sooner, but now that I am retired, I have more time. It's a true story about what happened to me during the Vietnam War and how one of the finest friends I ever had, known as 'Chopper Chaplain' saved me from certain disaster. He was a Warrant Officer in the Chaplain Service and he literally prayed with thousands of sick and wounded troops and those that were about to take their final breath. He also worked with those suffering with battle fatigue and emotional problems. I had been working non-stop for about two days, not eating or sleeping properly and I had become a real basket-case, not functioning as a real Doctor should, and not being a benefit to anybody. He observed my condition and said 'Come on, Doctor, I am taking you home'. I was not aware of how bad I I had become, so I fought him and cussed him and threatened him, but he insisted, and took me to my living unit. He said, 'Your skin is like parchment paper and your mind is not functioning, and you are on the verge of collapse, or possibly a stroke. I have some ideas of therapy that might save you but it will take days, if it works, and a lot of prayer'. I continued to resist and refused his treatment, and then I looked in the mirror, and I didn't recognize the person I was seeing, and then I started sobbing uncontrollably. He said, 'If we don't do this now, when I come back in about three weeks, I will watch them load a box into the cargo plane with the other bodies, and there will be a flag draped across your box and a label with your name on it'. He put his fingers under my chin and raised my face up and kissed me on the forehead, and said very softly and tenderly, 'We have to do this, and I will help you'. There was something about his voice and touch that made me relax and adhere to his wishes. I won't go into all the details now, because it is in the book. I relaxed and fell into a deep sleep, and when I awoke the next morning, he was cooking a big breakfast. 'I looked for something to eat and all I found was some moldy bread and sour milk, so I made a quick run to the Commissary,' he commented. 'Go to the bathroom and it will be ready by the time you get back'. For the next several days I did a lot of sleeping eating, and he did a lot of praying, and when I looked in the mirror, I saw my color coming back, and I felt stronger, and I told him I felt good enough to go back to work. He said, 'No, I had a vision last night. We got your body in better shape, but now I want to clean up your mind. The Lord instructed me on what to do, and if it works, you can write it up for Medical Journals and become world famous. I have never done it before or even heard of it, so I am anxious to see if we get good results.' That is what the book is about. I can tell you it worked. I was a totally different person, going from a despised person to a well loved and respected person. I believe he had divine powers; he spent 12-years in that horrible place and came out without a scratch. It was reported he would show up and take part in firefights preventing groups from being annihilated, rescued people taken captive and loved by friendly villagers. The village women would fight over which one would give him a cup of rice because he would give her an affectionate hug. They knew him as a Holy Man. He told me how he saved a newborn baby. He stopped for a visit and found the Viet Cong had slaughtered everyone in the entire friendly village; they cut open the bellies of all the pregnant women. He looked around for some sign of life and saw a little arm reach up out of the afterbirth so he lifted the baby up and it was near full term, and tied a thong around the umbilical cord up close to the baby, and then cut the remaining cord. He took the baby out and doused it in a tub of water to clean it off and then wrapped a scarf around it, and carrying it like a football, he ran to another village, praying all the way the Lord would let him make it in time; that was about a mile through the jungle. He handed it to an old woman, and she ran out and gave it to a younger woman. It angered him greatly to see his village friends slaughtered uselessly, but I only saw him extremely mad one time. The Marines sent a lady Marine Lieutenant out to command a Platoon of combat troops at a Firebase. When he found out about that, he raced his chopper out to get her and got there in time to see her shot in the chest and hip. He loaded her in his chopper and raced back to our hospital and landed it at our Emergency Room door. We ran out and wheeled her into the OR and started working on her; she had lost a lot of blood. He prayed so hard for her that it mesmerized us all, and we all had choked up at the sight of it. She woke up a couple days later and wondered how she got there, and we told her Chopper rescued her. He came in later and said, 'Well, Marine, you showed 'em. You can tell your Grandkids how you stood up to the Commies and fought like a man'. She was tough but she melted at the sight of him, and had tears running down her cheeks when he said goodbye to her. I always said he was a Prophet sent by God, because he was a Savior to so many people."

Interviewer: "What ever happened to the Chopper Chaplain?"

Susan: "After the Peace Accords, we had 60-days to evacuate the hospitals; they released all the POWs. Approximately 2-million North Vietnamese were storming southward to escape; overrunning everything in their path. Chopper arranged with the Marines to get the Chaplain out of there to safety. He stayed back and burned all the files and then set fire to the Chapel so they would not be able to use any of it. The Naval Hospital went up in smoke. Dr. West and I volunteered to go to Saigon to help evacuate the sick and wounded, and Chopper showed up later. He had a Vietnamese boy, that they raised in the Chapel since birth, and raised as an American, with him. He made a deal with the Mother Superior, who was organizing 200-kids to evacuate to an orphanage in the States, that he would let her have the boy to serve as an interpreter, if she would find a good family to adopt him and raise him. The NV were smelling victory and were at the gate of the Embassy while the Marine helicopters were moving the last of the personnel to an aircraft carrier. It was being blasted around the world the last huge helicopter leaving the Embassy was a sign the war had ended. What they didn't show was a little helicopter with 3-passengers aboard, Dr. Betty West, and me, and the pilot, Chopper Chaplain, hot on the heels of the Marine helicopter, trying to reach the carrier. We were praying hard because that little chopper was shot full of holes and fluids were spilling out and smoke was pouring from it, and when we landed on that carrier, one seaman said, 'you got the last gulp from that old girl', and they shoved it over the side off the deck. Chopper went to find where that 'old tub' was sailing too. The next morning, he appeared on deck to say goodbye; he had a ride with one of the Navy Airmen somewhere; he knew not where, but it didn't matter. He spent 12-years in that hellhole and had to go somewhere to heal his body and mind. The last words he spoke to us was, 'When you get up each morning and see the sunshine, thank God for the opportunity, and be thankful you are not one of the 58,000 that gave their lives and will never get that opportunity. He saved me from total destruction, like I spell out in the book, and like I have said many times, he had to be some sort of a Prophet because no earthly human could do what he did, and I hope, still does. I never saw or heard from him again."

Interviewer: "That's a great story, Doctor, and we thank you for coming and sharing it with us, but we are out of time. Buy the book and you will truly be inspired, 'IT HAPPENED ONE NIGHT'."

"Is that true?" Callie asked, after the program ended. "Every bit of it," Wit said. "She's got to be 75-years old. She looks good; a little grayer but looks good."

CHAPTER 64

About six months later, Wit was sitting in the gazebo when Callie came out and asked, "What would you like for me to fix for you for supper? You haven't eaten a bite all day." "I know, but I just don't have a taste for food right now," he answered. "Callie, did you ever watch the clouds? They move around and sometimes form a shape like some animal or place you recognize, or even a person you know." She responded, "No, I never did! Mr. Wit, you are scaring me. I'm going in the house; I got work to do. If you decide to eat something, let me know." It was a perfect cloud day; the sky was clear and blue, and the clouds were a brilliant white and puffy. He watched two clouds move together into one big cloud and it started forming into a shape. He watched it with interest because it started forming into a shape of a person. The radio was playing, and the lady Commentator said,

"That's the end of our show for today, and I would like to end by saying,

'God bless you, Chopper Chaplain; I wish you well'."

Radio music: "Softly, as I leave you," [Ref: Frank Sinatra Lyrics]

The clouds continued to come together; his heart started beating faster; faster.

Radio: "I will leave you softly, for my heart would break."

A lightning bolt flashed in the distant sky. The cloud kept forming; heartbeat increasing.

Wit: "I can't believe this; Lord help me to understand it."

Radio: "My heart would break if you should wake and see me go. So, I leave you softly long before you miss me."

Wit: "This is crazy; it can't be real."

His heart was pounding like a drum roll for the grand finale; increasing, harder and faster.

Radio: "For one more hour or one more day; After all the years."

Then finally the image formed, in vivid color and detail, and Wit spread out his arms toward the sky, and yelled, **"BABS"**.

A lightning bolt struck, a gust of wind whooshed through, and with a loud deafening screech, the **Demon** was extracted and lay fried on the deck, like a black rock. Another gust of wind blew it out into the sea, gone forever more.

Radio: "As I leave you there; as I leave you there!"

The next day, the radio Commentator reported on her show, "You have heard me wish 'Chopper Chaplain' well every day on my show, but I sadly report he passed away yesterday and I dedicate today's show to him. I know you have wondered why I blessed him daily, and to say it simply, he rescued me when I was taken captive by the Viet Cong when I was an Army Nurse serving in the Vietnam War. If it were not for his brave and unselfish courage, I would not be here and broadcasting to you today. Please say a little prayer for his soul, which I know is in Heaven."

A couple days later, Captain Dom brought his Mother, Bertha Thompson to see Callie. As soon as they met at the door, they embraced and started sobbing. Bertha remarked, "We both lost the one person that was dear to us and I felt I had to come and share your grief." They sat down and Callie offered them something to drink. Captain Dom reported, "His last wishes were to have only a small service and then be cremated and his ashes to be flown high over Fort Rucker, Alabama, in a helicopter and released. I can take care of that! Callie, I can pick you up and take you to the service." "Oh, no!" she replied, emotionally. "I want to remember him like he was. I could never look at his lifeless body." The two women started sobbing again and Captain Dom said, "You two are killing me; I got things to do so I'm getting out of here."

Three weeks later, Lawyer Jay called Callie and said he was coming out to go over some things with her. First thing she said was when he entered, "When do I have to get out?" He said, smiling, "Don't start packing yet! Wit told me how much he admired you and appreciated your loyalty, but I didn't know how deeply he felt, until we made out his will. He had banked all his military pay and re-signing bonuses and over the forty some-odd years, it accumulated into quite a sum. Brace yourself: he is leaving you the *Precious Place* with all the contents, from every blade of grass to every grain of sand on the beach. He is also leaving you the car." Her jaw dropped and her eyes got big, and she felt like she was going to faint. "Are you joking, or are you for real?" she asked, almost in shock. "Here's the best part," he continued. "He set up a trust fund with investments that should give you an income for the rest of your life." Now she was speechless, and just stared at him. Finally, she asked, "What about his wife in Ohio?" "She gets nothing! He said she has already gotten more than she deserved. She must have done something awfully bad for him to feel that way," Jay remarked. "The remaining amount is to be divided among his siblings, if I can find them."

The Stangs and the Brinkmans continued visiting, and the kids grew and went off to college. Goat, the orphaned kid Big Jimmie took in, graduated from college, and Big Jimmie arranged for him to buy the junk yard on installments, which allowed him to have a steady income in his retirement. Callie's son, Jerry, was shot dead trying to rob a convenience store the day after his release from prison. So big Jimmie moved in with Callie, being her only remaining relative, and he didn't want to leave her living alone, and he enjoyed sharing the beach and fishing. Bertha Thompson retired from broadcasting and became almost like a sister to Callie. Captain Dom never failed to stop in when he came to town. Lawyer Jay took her out on occasion, but her heart wasn't in it, so nothing became of that. Callie would sit for hours in the gazebo and watch the clouds, and with a broken heart, hoping she might see a cloud form to look like Mr. Wit.

So, the little kid, that went to school wearing hand-me-down clothes, became known throughout many parts of the world as, **CHOPPER CHAPLAIN**, who prayed to the Lord for countless thousands, and he was most loved by everybody; everywhere! What a legacy and pious example of love and dedication to your fellow man! ***The Lord works in mysterious ways!***

FINIS

THANK YOU,
WHIP WILSON

Lightning Source UK Ltd.
Milton Keynes UK
UKHW011846190721
387436UK00005B/496/J